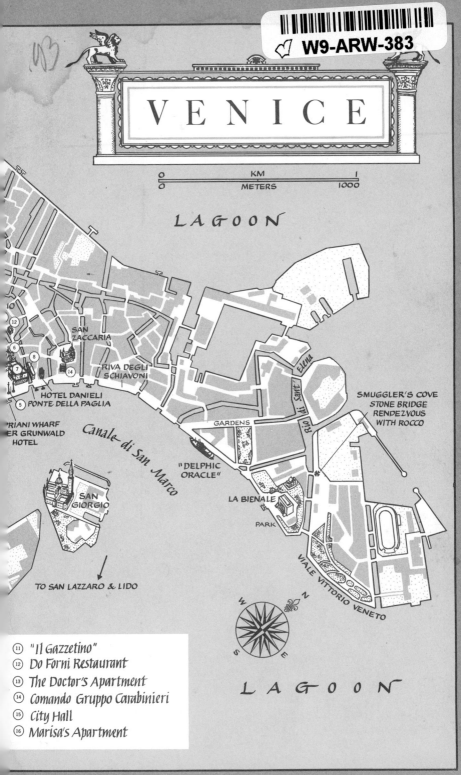

VENICE

KM
0 ——————————— 1
0 ——————————— 1000
METERS

LAGOON

SAN ZACCARIA

RIVA DEGLI SCHIAVONI

HOTEL DANIELI
PONTE DELLA PAGLIA

...RIANI WHARF
...ER GRUNWALD HOTEL

Canale di San Marco

SAN GIORGIO

TO SAN LAZZARO & LIDO

Rio di Sant' Elena

SMUGGLER'S COVE
STONE BRIDGE
RENDEZVOUS
WITH ROCCO

GARDENS

"DELPHIC ORACLE"

LA BIENALE

PARK

VIALE VITTORIO VENETO

LAGOON

palacios

BY IRVING WALLACE

FICTION
THE PIGEON PROJECT
THE R DOCUMENT
THE FAN CLUB
THE WORD
THE SEVEN MINUTES
THE PLOT
THE MAN
THE THREE SIRENS
THE PRIZE
THE CHAPMAN REPORT
THE SINS OF PHILIP FLEMING

NONFICTION
THE TWO
(with Amy Wallace)
THE BOOK OF LISTS
(with David Wallechinsky and Amy Wallace)
THE PEOPLE'S ALMANAC 1 and 2
(with David Wallechinsky)
THE NYMPHO AND OTHER MANIACS
THE WRITING OF ONE NOVEL
THE SUNDAY GENTLEMAN
THE TWENTY-SEVENTH WIFE
THE FABULOUS SHOWMAN
THE SQUARE PEGS
THE FABULOUS ORIGINALS

IRVING WALLACE

The Pigeon Project

▶ ▶ ▶ ▶ ▶ ▶ ▶

SIMON AND SCHUSTER

NEW YORK

Published by Simon and Schuster
A Division of Gulf & Western Corporation
Simon & Schuster Building
Rockefeller Center
1230 Avenue of the Americas
New York, New York 10020

Designed by Helen Barrow
Manufactured in the United States of America
Printed and bound by Fairfield Graphics, Inc.

1 2 3 4 5 6 7 8 9 10

Library of Congress Cataloging in Publication Data

Wallace, Irving, date.
The pigeon project.

I. Title.
PZ4.W1875Pi   [PS3573.A426]   813'.5'4   78-24352
ISBN   0-671-22622-3

"The last enemy that shall be destroyed is death."
I Corinthians 15:26

For My Three Favorite Venetians
SYLVIA, DAVID, AMY
With Love
IRVING

I

▶ ▶ ▶ ▶ ▶ ▶ ▶

As he took up his pen, momentarily holding it poised over the blank page of his daily journal dated August 15, he stared down at his veined hand crisscrossed with the delicate lines of age and he was surprised at its steadiness. He should have been trembling with excitement. After all, hadn't the Greek mathematician Archimedes, upon sitting down in a bathtub and watching the water rise and thus discovering the principle of displacement, leaped out of his tub in joy and run naked through the streets of Syracuse shouting "Eureka"? But unlike Archimedes, he had seen his own discovery coming closer with every passing month. At first with disbelief, and then with steadily diminishing doubt, he had seen it happening, and finally, fifteen minutes ago, it had happened. Absolute certainty. Confirmation.

Eureka.

His firm hand touched pen to paper, and quickly he began to record the momentous event, perhaps the greatest find in the saga of the human race. He wrote:

What Ponce de León so desperately sought in the land of Bimini, I have found in the Caucasus. After twelve years of ceaseless search and experimentation, in my native London, in my adopted New York, in places as far away as Vilcabamba in Peru and Hunza in Pakistan, I have found it in my laboratory outside Sukhumi, in the region of Abkhazia in Soviet Georgia. At 5:15 this afternoon, I was certain. It was as if I found the key, turned it, and the door to the prolongation of life had opened. From this day on, my formula, C-98, will extend the longevity of every human being on earth from an average age of seventy-two to an average age of 150. Perhaps the first step on the road to immortality. But for now, enough. To have more than doubled the life-span of every man, woman, and child on earth—surely the most meaningful, the most desired, perhaps the greatest discovery in the history of science.

An afterthought: I am awed and humbled by the immensity of what has just happened. It is beginning to strike me. I must contemplate no more. A time for a small celebration, certainly. I will have Vasily bring out the champagne I have so long hoarded against this day. I will inform Leonid and have him join me in a toast. And next week—before the International Congress of Gerontology in Paris—I will make the announcement to the world.

His hand was trembling now, and he laid down his pen.

For a man of seventy-four years, suffering slightly from arthritis in each knee, he came up out of the desk chair quickly and vigorously. The blood coursed through his head. He felt exhilarated as never before.

"Leonid!" he suddenly shouted across the living room. "Leonid, I have found it!"

▶ ▶ ▶ ▶

Professor Davis MacDonald sat deep in the drab brown sofa, holding his empty wineglass and trying to bring into focus the two Leonids in the armchair across the coffee table from him.

He had not been this intoxicated in a half century, not since that night of his youth when he had left Oxford for London. It was a good feeling to be so light-headed, to let go of the thousand thoughts that until now had teemed in his mind and had now evaporated in the mist of champagne.

"Leonid," he said to his laboratory assistant.

"Yes, Professor."

MacDonald squinted and at last found one Leonid, also holding a wineglass, waiting attentively. He looked at his assistant fondly. The thirty-two-year-old Russian Jew, with his high forehead and bushy eyebrows and sensitive mouth, was one of the few persons in the U.S.S.R., in this remote corner of the Soviet Union on the Black Sea, whom he could trust and with whom he could relax. Six years ago, having been invited to lecture at the Institute of Gerontology in Kiev, MacDonald had requested permission to do research in the Abkhazian Republic, where, so he had read, a population of 500,000 contained a remarkable 5,000 healthy centenarians. Permission had been granted, as it had to other foreign gerontologists, who agreed to share their findings with the Soviet Union and scientists of all nations. MacDonald had traveled down to Sukhumi, the capital of Abkhazia, a quiet port city of 100,000, where he had rented a large cottage on the outskirts of the city, converting half of it into a laboratory. During his first week, he had visited Sukhumi's Gerontology Institute, and there he had found Leonid and liked him and had received permission to hire him. Shortly after, some government official had insisted that he must have a housekeeper and had brought him Vasily, a tall, silent native Georgian in his late twenties with the face of an Egyptian mummy. Like Leonid, Vasily spoke English. But unlike Vasily, who had been selected for him, MacDonald had himself selected Leonid, and therefore he had trusted him from the start.

"Yes, Professor?" he heard Leonid repeat.

He tried to remember what he had wanted of his assistant, and then he remembered. "The champagne, Leonid. Is there any left?"

Leonid stood up and lifted the bottle from the table. "More than enough for another round."

MacDonald held out his empty glass, and Leonid filled it. MacDonald's gaze followed the bottle down to the table. "G. H. Mumm and Company," MacDonald said. "Good champagne."

"Very good," said Leonid.

Sipping his drink, MacDonald blearily made out the time on his watch. Over two hours had passed. They had been sitting, drinking, celebrating for over two hours. He tried to recreate what had taken place earlier. He had been in the laboratory with the test animals. The first of the mice and guinea pigs, injected with C-98 four years ago, had died in the afternoon. The average life-span for a mouse was less than two years, for a guinea pig two years. Yet both sets of laboratory animals had lived healthily for double their life-spans after receiving shots of his formula. Even the special cages of animals with artificially induced terminal ailments, from various forms of cancer to heart deterioration, had survived to twice their normal life-spans. In every instance, the cancers had gone into remission, the heart diseases had been arrested, other sicknesses had been curbed, and the animals had thrived. New tests had finally confirmed the incredible. Given the same shots, human beings who might expect to live to seventy or seventy-two would now, barring accident, be certain to live to 150.

The magnitude of his discovery had not fully overwhelmed him until he had entered it in his daily journal. Only then had he been shaken and aroused. He remembered calling for Leonid, finding him, blurting out the news. He had wanted a private celebration, a marking of the historic moment, before all mankind would celebrate him.

He had gone into the kitchen to ask Vasily to open the magnum of champagne he had once bought in Paris, and carried with him ever since for this very occasion which for so long had seemed beyond the hope of any scientist. Although, truly, he had always believed it might come about in his lifetime. Once he had understood the DNA—deoxyribonucleic acid—molecules that inhabit every cell, once he had realized humans were programmed for death by aging genes, he had got himself into genetic engineering. He had sought to create synthetic genes that could be transplanted to replace aging genes. Here in Abkhazia, between the Black Sea and the dark range of the Caucasus Mountains, researching to learn what its 100- to 135-year-old citizens all had in common, he had stumbled on the secret. For his experiment labeled C-98 he had isolated the unique ingredients in the Caucasus drinking water. He had added these to his formula four years ago, and waited and watched and hoped. And today it had been confirmed. Of all the formulas, the unceasing trial and error, this one had worked. He had discovered the Fountain of Youth.

And it had been mini-celebration time, before all the world learned and sent off skyrockets. He had got the bottle of champagne from Vasily, whose phlegmatic countenance bore a rare question mark. He had not answered the unspoken question or explained the reason for celebration. Not to Vasily. He had not forgotten that Vasily had been sent to him, not selected by him.

MacDonald had returned to the living room and allowed Leonid to open the bottle.

Leonid had toasted him, and the luck of all the living who would now continue to live on and on, and they had begun to drink together. He had meant to have one glass, possibly two. But now the bottle was almost finished. And throughout it all, in a slurred drawl, MacDonald had talked, perhaps talked more than he ever had before to another human being in his life. Leonid, as always, but more so now, had proved a hungry and worshipful listener.

MacDonald had confided much to Leonid, but not his secret. He had never discussed his formulas with his assistant or anyone else. Leonid had been allowed to know the end, but not the means to the end. MacDonald had not even put the successful formula on paper. He had kept it in his head. Only next week, after he had stunned and thrilled the world with his electrifying announcement at the International Gerontology Congress in Paris, would he put it to paper for all humanity, who would start not a gold rush but a life rush—a rush by everyone on earth for the prolongation of life.

Instead, through the waning afternoon and early evening, MacDonald had reminisced about his early years, about his interest in geriatrics before his mother's last illness, about his decision to specialize in gerontology after his mother's death.

"They are quite different, you know," he had explained to Leonid unnecessarily. "Geriatrics is the study of old people's diseases. Gerontology is the study of means to prevent people from becoming old."

For almost fifty years he had been immersed in every aspect of gerontology. He had left his laboratory here in the Caucasus only three times in the last six years, and the last time over twenty-five months ago. He had enjoyed and admired the hearty and long-lived Abkhazians. They lived by the toil of their hands in the fields. Each of their homes had a vineyard, and they daily drank wine and grape vodka. They ate goat cheese and highly spiced boiled cornmeal patties, buttermilk diluted with water, and loaves of bread two feet long. They dwelt placidly, without tension, in close family units, with no words in their language for "retirement" or "old people." And there were five times as many elderly in this tiny place who lived to be over 100 as there were in the entire United States.

Through them he had found the formula that would give their gift of long life to people everywhere.

"I've been talking too much," he said suddenly. As he swallowed the last of his champagne, he caught a reflection of himself in the glass of the bookcase that protected his science textbooks. Usually, he did not mind seeing himself. Considering his seventy-four years, he was still well put together. His round face, crowned by short white hair with bald spots visible, was still relatively smooth. The bridge of his pug nose held ridiculous wire-framed spectacles. His short but full white moustache was distinguished. He carried his five-foot-nine-inch frame—only 158 pounds, with a small belly—erectly. But now, in the glass panel of the bookcase, he appeared a casualty of overwork and G. H. Mumm. His blue eyes were watery and baggy. His moustache was partially wet and partially dry and looked askew. His perpetual bow tie sat at an angle.

He turned back to Leonid. "It'll take us a week to get ready, but next week we will go to Paris with our secret. I'm taking you along, Leonid."

Leonid shook his head mournfully. "You forget, Professor. I am a Jew. They will not let me go."

MacDonald puckered his lips. "You forget, Leonid, I am the new savior of mankind. They will do anything for me."

"I hope so, Professor."

"Yes, next week to Paris." He set down his glass and rose unsteadily. "But right now, to bed. I must take a nap, sleep this off. Tell Vasily I won't have dinner. I'll make a sandwich for myself later."

As he started for the bedroom, he added, "This is a great day for mankind, my friend."

"My congratulations from the heart, Professor."

"Congratulations to all of us."

He had reached the bedroom door, begun to push it open, when unaccountably something he had read in the *Bulletin of the Atomic Scientists*—a statement by Kenneth Boulding, which had annoyed him at the time— came to his mind again: "Perhaps the biggest threat to the human race at the moment is not so much the nuclear weapon as the possibility of eliminating the aging process."

It annoyed him once more.

He was too tired to examine it, too tired to explore implications. To give people the supreme gift of living twice as long. That was good enough. What could be better?

Right now, only sleep.

He removed his crumpled lightweight beige jacket, dropped down onto the narrow soft bed, stretched out, and closed his eyes and mind to the miracle and the glory.

▶ ▶ ▶ ▶

The pressure on his shoulder awakened him from his dream. He had been dreaming he was in some detached place between heaven and earth, kneeling before a wide golden throne on which sat Einstein, Pasteur, Newton; and a disembodied hand had placed a jeweled crown on his head, but abruptly the crown slipped off his head and went tumbling into space and he leaped up trying to retrieve it, and then—and then he felt the pressure on his shoulder and the dream evaporated and he was awake behind his closed eyes.

The something on his shoulder—it was a hand—shook him, and a voice close to his ear whispered, "Professor, wake up. Please wake up."

He opened his heavy eyelids and made out that it was Leonid's head bent close to his own.

When he started to move his lips, Leonid's hand moved quickly from his shoulder to cover his mouth.

"Don't speak," said Leonid at his ear. "I don't want him to hear you. Are you fully awake?"

MacDonald nodded.

"Then listen," said Leonid, removing his hand. "Vasily has told them. He has found out about your discovery and told the KGB."

KGB. Committee of State Security. MacDonald was not only fully awake, he was alert.

"I suspected Vasily was a planted informer from the start," Leonid went on. "Remember, I cautioned you. Anyway, he must have been suspicious of our celebration. When you went to the bedroom and I went to the laboratory, he must have come into the living room, found your journal, and read the last entry you made on C-98, on your discovery. I happened to go into the kitchen, and I heard him on the telephone in his quarters. I went closer to his door and listened. He was calling KGB headquarters in Odessa. He spoke to someone there—I think the chief—someone named Boris Kedrov. He reported the news of your discovery. Apparently Kedrov asked where you were. Vasily said you were sound asleep in bed. Then Kedrov told him they would come at once and Vasily said he would be waiting for them and would keep an eye on you until they arrived. I immediately slipped out of the kitchen and came to wake you."

"Why are they coming here? What do they want from me?"

"Your discovery. They want it for themselves alone."

"No," said MacDonald, frightened. "No, that must never happen."

"It won't, if you do what I tell you," Leonid said. "I have made arrangements for your escape." He glanced at his wristwatch. "We must be quick. I checked with the Sukhumi Airport, the military airport not far from here. I learned there are three flights tonight. Two inside the country, one to the outside. The outside one is a special Tu-154—a Tupolev—carrying a cultural delegation to Venice—to Italy—where the members are to meet with their newly elected Italian Communist comrades. There is room for you on the flight, as long as your papers are in order."

"My papers are in order. Because of my research travels, I have a special visa to come and go as I wish."

"The plane leaves in forty-five minutes. We must hurry."

MacDonald pushed himself off the bed and stood a moment, wavering, briefly bewildered.

"My things," he said, starting for the door.

Leonid grabbed his arm. "Please, no—"

"But my journal, the animal test charts, the—"

"You don't need them," said Leonid urgently. "All you need is your head. You can't risk being seen. If Vasily suspected you were leaving, he might hold you here with a gun—or at the least, he would alert the airport and you would not be allowed to board the plane. Believe me, Professor."

MacDonald nodded. He picked up his jacket and began to pull it on.

"Your travel papers—are they in this room?"

MacDonald nodded again. He stepped to the dark brown bureau, opened the top drawer, found his passport, his Intourist VIP travel permit, and two books of traveler's checks.

Leonid was at his elbow. "I'll lift the rear window and go out first. It is a short drop. I'll help you down. The car is parked on the other side of the orchard, just off the highway. Vasily will never know. He will think you are still safely asleep."

At the window, MacDonald paused. "Leonid, what will happen to you?"

"Never mind. I'll manage. I'll make up some story. The important thing is to get you out of here, before they come for you. Soon, tonight, you will be in Venice, free. Tomorrow you will be in Paris. After that, your discovery will belong to the world."

MacDonald smiled grimly. "When I was young, I used to pray to God. I hope He remembers now."

"Come," said Leonid, slowly, silently lifting the window. "There is not a second to lose."

▶ ▶ ▶ ▶

Three hours had passed when Vasily answered the doorbell. He held the front door wide, admitting the five men.

The one who was obviously the leader, a stocky, uniformed older man of middle height, hatless, black crew-cut hair, close-set eyes, broad nose, thick lips—almost Mongolian features—glanced about the living room and rested his gaze on Vasily.

"You are Vasily?"

"I am," said Vasily almost inaudibly, offering a half bow.

"Good work. I am Major Boris Kedrov. I have brought along two of our foremost scientists, Grigori Kapitin and Vladimir Petrovsky, of the Sukhumi Gerontology Institute, to ascertain whether this is a legitimate find or some kind of hoax. With us are two of my KGB agents, Yagoda and Shvernik. The professor—he is still asleep?"

"Yes, sir." Vasily pointed to the bedroom door.

"Excellent. Let's waste no time. Before we rouse Professor MacDonald and confront him, let us be certain that this discovery of his is genuine. What do we have, beyond your suspicions, to prove that the professor has found the secret to the prolongation of life?"

"His private journal, Major. I spoke of it on the telephone—"

"Yes, his journal."

"It is there on the desk," said Vasily, "still open to the last entry this afternoon."

Major Kedrov sniffed. "Is there anything more—any other evidence?"

Vasily gestured toward a corridor off the dining area of the living room. "There is his laboratory. There are test animals, mice and guinea pigs. Leonid kept records—"

"Leonid?" said Major Kedrov sharply. "Who is Leonid?"

"His laboratory assistant. A young Jew."

"Is he on the premises?"

"Yes, sir."

"Where?"

"Probably in his room, near my own, just past the kitchen." He raised his arm, pointing off. "On the other side."

Major Kedrov signaled to his men. "Yagoda—Shvernik—find him." As they hastened toward the kitchen, Kedrov turned to the others. "Dr. Kapitin, you read English, I believe. Have a look at the professor's journal. Tell me what you think. As for you, Dr. Petrovsky—Vasily will show you the laboratory. See if there is any corroborating evidence."

Major Kedrov watched Kapitin go to the desk and take up the journal, and then watched Petrovsky follow the servant into the corridor. For a while he remained immobile, staring at MacDonald's bedroom door. After three or four minutes, he began to pace in a small circle, waiting.

It was Dr. Kapitin who intercepted him, brought him to a halt. The scientist held up MacDonald's journal. "It is here," Dr. Kapitin said cautiously. "The professor claims to have found it. He is very explicit." He opened the journal and located the passage. He read it aloud. " 'At 5:15 this afternoon . . . From this day on, my formula, C-98, will extend the longevity of every human being on earth from an average age of seventy-two to an average age of 150.' "

"Can that really be?" said Major Kedrov with wonder in his voice.

Dr. Kapitin's brow wrinkled. "I do not know. Great progress had been made in the field, but even the most optimistic did not expect the discovery to come for another forty or fifty years." He tapped the journal. "Of course, this could be an elderly man's delusions or plain romantic nonsense—more wish and hope than reality—leaping prematurely at conclusions." He hesitated. "Still, Professor MacDonald's work is not unknown to me. While I am acquainted with him only slightly from his many visits here, I have read his papers. He is greatly respected internationally, has high standing in the field. But this . . ." He closed the journal and rubbed the cover thoughtfully. "It is impossible to say. We would have to know more."

"We do know more," a voice interrupted. The speaker was Dr. Petrovsky, approaching with a sheaf of charts attached to a board. Vasily followed closely after him. "These meticulous records of MacDonald's tests on his laboratory animals are conclusive. The segregated group he injected with some kind of formula he calls C-98 has lived twice its normal life-span. There can be no question in my mind. Professor MacDonald has made some landmark discovery, perhaps one of the most important of all time—one of such meaning and magnitude as to be almost incomprehensible in the effects it will have on the human race."

"I am not interested in the human race," said Major Kedrov flatly. "I am only interested, first and last, in the welfare of the Soviet Union, our beloved Motherland."

"Of course, of course," agreed Dr. Kapitin.

"So now we deal with reality." Major Kedrov stared once more at the bedroom door. "It is time we congratulate Professor MacDonald."

As the three started toward the bedroom door, Vasily darted ahead of them. He wrenched at the doorknob and flung the door open, stepping back to allow his superiors to pass him.

Major Kedrov reached inside, snapped on the light, and entered. He stopped in his tracks, eyes widening at the empty bed. He glanced about the room, walked slowly to the closet, opened and closed the door. He moved to another door beside it, opened it, and peered into the bathroom. He backed away, once more studied the room, and then he observed the open window.

"Well, now," he said. He half-turned, narrowed eyes fixed on Vasily. "You are sure he went to sleep?"

"Leonid told me he was going to take a nap," said Vasily nervously.

"Could he be anywhere else in the house?"

"No, sir. I kept an eye on the room here."

"The window. Did he always keep the window open when he slept?"

"I-I don't remember. I don't think so."

Shvernik reappeared in the bedroom doorway. "Major—"

"Yes?"

"We have found the assistant, Leonid, in his room. He was undressing for bed. We questioned him about the discovery. He claims to know nothing about it. He says his duties were limited to keeping the laboratory in order and watching over the test animals."

"He lies," Vasily interrupted. "He and the professor were in the living room for two or three hours drinking, celebrating. He must know what happened to the professor."

Major Kedrov nodded. "Yes, I think our Leonid can tell us more." He addressed one of his agents. "Shvernik, Professor MacDonald is missing. We must know as quickly as possible where he has gone. I suggest you and Yagoda question this man more persistently. Go as far as is necessary. I want an answer, the truth, in the next five minutes."

After the agent had gone, Major Kedrov surveyed the bedroom once more, then went to the bureau. He began pulling out the drawers, one after another, looking inside each, examining the clothes inside. Finished, he crossed to the bed, opened the drawer of the bedside stand, closed it.

"I wonder where he keeps his passport," Major Kedrov said. "It is not in this room."

Lost in thought, he left the bedroom and returned to the living room. The other three followed him. At the coffee table, Kedrov stopped, dug a pack of cigarettes out of a pocket, extracted a cigarette. Dr. Petrovsky hastened to light it for him.

From behind a stream of exhaled smoke, Major Kedrov spoke quietly. "Perhaps I am unduly alarmed. Perhaps our guest merely went for a stroll and will return any minute. Possibly there is some other innocent explanation. I would hate to contemplate any other reason for his disappearance. You see—"

He was momentarily distracted by a shrill, prolonged scream from beyond the kitchen. He looked in that direction, listened, and heard moaning, indistinct sounds of protestation, and suddenly another scream.

Major Kedrov gave a short shrug and devoted his attention once more to the two troubled scientists opposite him. "You see, gentlemen, I consider this the most important assignment of my career. There would be no explanation acceptable to the Kremlin if we failed to deliver Professor MacDonald and his C-98. Exclusive possession of the formula by the Soviet Union would change future history. For one thing, the premier himself is seventy-five and not in the best of health. To possess a potion that would give him another seventy-five years—you can see how vital this would be to him personally." Major Kedrov puffed on his cigarette, then resumed. "But even more, think what this discovery, in our hands alone, could mean to the Soviet Union. It would mean that our leaders—members of the Politburo, our wisest inventors, generals, economists, artists—could live on and on, while their counterparts in America and other nations, limited to normal lifespans, would die off and those countries would have to start afresh with new people in every field. Our advantage would give us dominance of the world in every area imaginable. This would be the instant view of our leaders. I dare not fail them."

Another series of screams from beyond the kitchen made him pause. Then, there was silence.

Major Kedrov nodded knowingly. He examined the expressions on the faces of Dr. Kapitin and Dr. Petrovsky. "Do not be concerned, gentlemen. In my work the result always justifies any action taken. Simply remember one thing. This discovery was made in the Soviet Union, because of the hospitality of the Soviet Union. Therefore, logically it belongs to the Soviet Union. So you must—"

"Major Kedrov!" It was the KGB agent Shvernik, who was hurrying toward him. "He has confessed—admitted Professor MacDonald left the country—"

"Left the country?" Kedrov echoed with disbelief.

"That's right," Shvernik said breathlessly. "According to this Leonid, the professor learned there was a special flight leaving Sukhumi Airport earlier this evening and that there was room for him on it. The professor found Leonid, pulled a gun on him, and forced him to drive to the airport. He was afraid to confess at once, afraid we would not believe he had been forced to do it. But under extreme interrogation—"

"Never mind," said Major Kedrov harshly. "Where in the hell did he go? What was the destination of the flight?"

"Venice, Italy, sir."

"Venice? We have no business in Venice."

"The Italian Communist party—"

"—got their mayor elected," Kedrov said. "I remember. Look, Shvernik, get on that phone and call Sukhumi Airport. I must be positive there was such a flight and that MacDonald was on it."

The KGB man dashed to the phone, put through his call, identified himself, and spoke to the dispatcher. Was there a special flight to Venice this evening? Yes, there was—Flight SU-509, a Tupolev, to Italy. Was an Englishman or American, a Professor MacDonald, on the flight? Yes. His papers were in order, and he had boarded and was on the plane when it took off.

"Hold it a minute," Major Kedrov called out, before Shvernik could hang up. "Ask him one more thing. Where is the plane right now—can it be recalled?"

Shvernik repeated the question into the telephone. He waited, listened, then said, "I see. Thank you." He hung up. "I'm sorry, Major. The Tupolev is over northern Italy, in a landing pattern and getting ready for descent. It is too low on fuel to bring back. It cannot be recalled."

Major Kedrov slapped the palm of his hand on the coffee table. "Damn!" He walked around the table, thinking hard. "The plane went to Venice because . . ." He looked up. "The Italian Communists are in control of the city. Well, now. That's something."

He strode purposefully to the telephone, lifted the receiver. "Operator. Major Boris Kedrov, KGB. Priority call. Give me long distance. . . ."

▶ ▶ ▶ ▶

Not until the three-engined Tupolev had touched down on the Marco Polo Air Terminal runway, bouncing and bumping, and the hydraulic retractable landing gear had jolted him against his seat belt, and the jet plane had gradually slowed and begun coasting toward the terminal—not until then did the tension begin oozing out of Professor Davis MacDonald's body.

Even when they had approached the city from above, and he had looked down upon the garlands of gay lights far below on this cloudless night, he had not felt secure. He had still been in the capsule of a Russian plane, guided by two Soviet pilots and one Soviet engineer, his neighbors up ahead thirty-five drinking and noisy Russian bureaucrats. Because the plane's capacity was 128 passengers and there had been little more than a fourth of the seats filled, he had been able to have three seats to himself in the back, somewhat isolated from the others. Still, all the while aloft, he had felt like a Russian captive and threatened.

But now, bringing up the rear in the crowded aisle of passengers going forward to leave the airliner, he was beginning to feel better. In minutes, he was at the exit. A stewardess wished him well and welcomed him to Venice. MacDonald thanked the stewardess, and wished her well, and then stepped onto the metal platform of the portable stairs. Holding the railing, he descended.

One more step, and his feet were on Italian soil.

His heart quickened. Safe, at last. Safe with the secret that would astound the entire world.

In front of him, a yellow bus waited at attention. Members of the Russian cultural delegation were climbing into it. MacDonald also entered the bus and gripped an overhead rail, ignoring the others. In seconds, the bus doors closed. The bus rumbled across the airstrip and, in a few minutes, halted before a brightly illuminated building.

MacDonald had moved toward the nearest door and was the first person on the ground. As the other passengers left the vehicle, MacDonald remained motionless, observing the air terminal with pleasure. It was a two-story blue-and-white building, the second story recessed. On top of the terminal was a large blue sign with one spotlighted word lettered in white. The word was VENEZIA.

Safety, he thought. Thank the Lord.

Just ahead of him he could see the members of the Russian delegation strung out, walking alongside the air terminal toward the rear entrance. Briefly, MacDonald held back again, so that a short distance separated him from the Russian travelers. Somehow, this apartness gave him an even greater sense of security and freedom.

Standing there, he recalled for the first time that he had been here once before—not at this airport, but in Venice, in what now seemed another age. Unbelievably, it had been over fifty years ago. It was during his last year in medical school, the summer vacation, and he had been confused about his future. He had accompanied his widowed mother—it was chic that year to travel with one's mother, especially when she was a renowned physicist and was received in the best homes—from London to Paris by boat train via the Dover-to-Calais crossing. They had spent an exciting week in Paris and then had taken the overnight train from Paris for a three-day stay in Venice, before continuing on to Florence and Rome. One memory of Venice had never left him: emerging from the railroad depot into the hot, bright sunlight. He had stood at the head of the stairs agape at the shimmering broad canal filled with gondolas and motorboats, and been awed by the expanse of indigo water stretching as far as the eye could see in either direction. It had been magical, a liquid fairyland.

Another memory: His mother had become unwell their second day in Venice. Nevertheless, they had gone on down to Florence. There she had become dreadfully ill. The remainder of the trip had been canceled. He had taken her back to London. Two weeks later, she had died of cancer. Two months after that, he had decided that when he finished medical school he would specialize in gerontology, challenged by the idea of extending the human life-span.

His mind had gone back to Venice. Besides a remembrance of his first view of the place from the railroad-depot staircase, what other fragments remained? The Piazza San Marco with its pigeons and vendors and cafés. The Campanile di San Marco, or bell tower, rising to the sky in the Piazza. The curious but delicately harmonious Palazzo Ducale, or Doges' Palace, with its Byzantine and Arabian (overlaid with Gothic and Renaissance) architecture, the structure Ruskin had called the central building of the world. Where had they stayed in Venice? It had been a hotel with a familiar name. It came to him. The Grand Hotel. Again he thought of his mother. If he had discovered C-98 before that long-ago visit to Venice, his mother might be meeting him there tonight, alive and healthy at the age of 101 or so. Well, he could do nothing about the past. But for all the tomorrows facing humanity, he had a gift. Most mothers on the earth would live on and on to 150, enjoying the pleasures of their great-great-great-great grandchildren.

He realized that he had been walking again and had arrived at the Marco Polo Air Terminal. He went through the doorway into a wide corridor, where the last of the Russian travelers were being cleared by a sturdy Italian official wearing an open-collared sport shirt, perched on a stool behind a counter. As the last Russians continued on, turning left and passing out of sight, MacDonald approached the official.

"Passport, please, and *carta de sbarco*," the official requested.

MacDonald remembered that he had filled out the disembarkation card on the plane. He found it in a pocket with his passport, and handed both over. The official kept the disembarkation card, then opened MacDonald's passport, held on his photograph, glanced at him, and returned the passport. "Show it to the young lady at the door before you leave the terminal," he said in English.

"Thank you."

MacDonald moved on, and turned left into a large hall that was divided by a railing, beyond which was a rotating luggage turntable. The Russians were all clustering about it. MacDonald started toward the opening in the railing, meaning to join them, and then realized that he had no luggage. Straight ahead of him, two sloppily uniformed Italians were standing beside a low-slung table beneath a sign reading, DOGANA DOUANE/ZOLL CUSTOM. MacDonald deduced that these were certainly the customs inspectors. Just past them was another raised counter manned by a young, plumpish blond Italian lady in a light blue blouse. Above her was a sign reading, INFORMAZIONI.

Before proceeding, MacDonald tried to organize his next actions. At the passport counter, he would inquire if there were any planes scheduled to depart for Paris tonight. Small chance at this hour, he knew, but he would inquire. If he was too late for any plane, he would go into Venice and try to locate the Grand Hotel—or any good hotel—and take a room until morning. He would make a reservation on the earliest flight to Paris. Then he would telephone the Plaza Athénée hotel in Paris, where Dr. Edwards, his associate, was staying, and he would announce the incredible news of his discovery. After that, he would ring room service for a light supper, and then he would lie down for a much-needed sleep. This momentous day—the excitement of the discovery, the celebration with champagne, the fearful escape from the Russians, the air trip—had been a terrible strain, and his entire being ached with exhaustion. He would need as much rest as he could get tonight and in the week to come, when he would be writing his paper, for once he appeared before the assembled Gerontology Congress, in six or seven days—he could no longer be certain of the time—and read his paper to the delegates and the world, he would never know quiet or rest or solitude or peace again.

Clutching his passport, MacDonald started toward the customs officers. They watched him with interest—perhaps because he had no bags—and then one of them unsmilingly gestured him past. He came to the counter, confronting the young blond Italian lady.

She smiled at him. "Your passport, Signore?"

MacDonald handed her his passport. She opened it, examined it, fixed on his photograph, looked up to match it to his face. "You are Davis MacDonald?"

"Yes."

"Very good. You can go now."

Pocketing his passport, he hesitated. "Can you tell me, Miss, are there any flights to Paris tonight?"

"No, no. There are no departures at this hour. Everything is closed down. You can get a flight in the morning."

"Thank you. How do I get to Venice from the airport? Are there taxis outside?"

"Water taxis," she said. "*Motoscafi*. The motorboats. It is twenty minutes on the canal." She gestured off to her left. "Any of those men outside there—they have public transportation—they will take you to Venice."

As he went through the terminal exit into another roomy hall, two youngish men flanking the doorway—one short, in a rumpled tan suit, the other burly, wearing cap, white shirt, gray slacks—accosted him.

"You go to Venezia, Signore?" the short one asked.

"Yes."

"We have the water taxi. You come with us. You have luggage?"

"None."

MacDonald followed them out of the building to an asphalt court in the middle of which was a semicircle of grass bright with marigolds and snapdragons. The two boatmen led MacDonald to an abbreviated wooden pier.

"I'd like to go to the Grand Hotel," said MacDonald. "Is there still such a hotel?"

"Si, si. Near the Grand Canal," said the short boatman. "Via Ventidue Marzo. Very, very fine hotel."

"I have no reservation," said MacDonald. "Well, we'll see."

Nestled against the pier, a rakish brown motor launch, mahogany and chrome, tied by a rope to a piling, bobbed gently in the water.

The short boatman went quickly down into the craft, then reached up to help his passenger. MacDonald stepped gingerly on the edge of the boat, made his descent down two wooden steps. Over his shoulder, he saw the burly one untie the craft and step aboard.

"You go inside there," the short boatman was saying to MacDonald. He indicated a spacious cabin. "You relax. We come to Venezia soon."

MacDonald bent low, went inside the lighted, well-appointed cabin, and settled himself on a leather couch. He observed with interest as the burly boatman stood behind the pilot wheel, with his partner on his feet beside him. The engine erupted with a cough, and the motor launch backed up through the water, stopped, lurched into a half circle, and plunged forward smoothly.

MacDonald felt eager to get to his Venice hotel, arrange his flight reservation for tomorrow, get Dr. Edwards on the telephone in Paris, and burst out with his tremendous tidings. At last, the undulating rhythm of the boat, the monotonous beat of its engine calmed him, and he settled back. He felt inside his jacket for a cigar. There were three. He extracted one, peeled its wrapper, bit off the tip, and found his silver-plated lighter.

Smoking, he squinted out the boat window, its blue curtains drawn back. Through the thin spray, very near, were neatly spaced groups of wooden pilings, each group of three pilings banded together by metal—all of them moss-covered, reassuring, like guideposts to Venice—and each with yellow lights from lamps showing the way to Venice. Behind the pilings were retaining walls, and soon mudbanks and green marshes of grass and weeds.

After a while—five minutes, perhaps ten—Mac-Donald swiveled around in his seat, ducked his head, and peered through the opposite window. There were many more lights illuminating buildings: residences, warehouses, an apartment house with squares of brightness. The outskirts of Venice, he was certain.

Ahead, the canal had widened considerably and entered a broad lagoon. To the left a tiny island, to the right a shoreline filled with more residences—brick buildings, plaster buildings—some hidden in the shadows of night.

Now into one more canal, then sliding under an iron bridge which bore a sign that read, PONTE VIVARINI.

Emerging from this canal, they were in open water once more. Suddenly, past the curving landscape, far off to the right, there was a dazzling array of lights, a mammoth sparkling bouquet of lights, and he reasoned that this must be the historic center of Venice itself—the heart of the city, his destination—and he waited expectantly for the launch to turn in toward it. Instead, to his mild surprise, the motor launch spurted straight ahead, picking up speed, prow rising from the water as it drove between the columns of wooden pilings on either side. He looked off to his right, past the two standing boatmen behind the prow, and he saw that they were proceeding with certainty toward the center of a vast lagoon, with strings of lights forming narrow lanes through the water.

MacDonald hadn't the faintest idea where he was, but he was sure his pilot knew the way to Venice, and that they would be circling inward toward the city's concentration of lights any moment. Waiting for the happy landfall, he sat back and smoked with contentment.

In minutes, the motorboat was slowing, rocking to a stop, quietly gliding, and finally it banged against something wooden, shuddered, halted. His watch told him the trip had taken thirty-two minutes. The passport woman at the airport had said it would be twenty minutes. Well, he thought, nothing is ever on time in Italy, or so he had read.

Now he heard voices, the boatmen calling up to someone above them.

MacDonald squinted through the window again. There were steps leading up to a pier, and just beyond, the outlines of a large old two-story building with several windows here and there showing yellow lights.

"Signore," he heard someone summon. It was the short boatman, holding the cabin door open.

Stooping, MacDonald left the cabin. Once he was in the open part of the boat the burly boatman reached for his arm and propelled him up the craft's steps to a landing. Here there were six or seven steps to the top of the pier. At the top stood two men, one in a business suit, one in a uniform, and the man in the business suit was silently beckoning him.

Confused, bewildered, MacDonald turned around to the boatmen. "Where am I? This isn't Venice."

"*Arrivederci,*" the burly boatman called out, pushing the motor launch away from the pilings. It was drifting away, and MacDonald saw in a panic that already the gap of water between himself and the boat was too wide to cover.

He turned back to the pier steps, heart tripping.

He waited.

"Come up here," he heard someone order him. "We have a gun pointed at you."

His legs leaden, MacDonald slowly began to climb up the steps. As he attained the pier, he found the two men directly before him. The squat one in khaki uniform, a white strap running from his shoulder to one hip, plainly an Italian, possibly a member of the *carabinieri,* was pointing a small-caliber pistol at him. The other man, curly black hair, beady eyes, a pointed nose on an angular Slavic face, attired in a natty double-breasted dark blue suit, wore an expression of amiability.

"What is this?" demanded MacDonald, voice quavering. "I'm supposed to be in Venice. Where am I?"

"You are on the island of San Lazzaro," the one in the business suit said, with the trace of a Russian accent. "You are eight minutes outside Venice."

"What does this mean? Why am I here?"

"For your own safety, my friend. You are far too valuable a property to be anywhere but here."

MacDonald felt panic. "What are you going to do with me?"

"We are going to hold you in protective custody, Professor. Then, after a few days, we are going to send you home. Yes, home. We are going to send you back to the Soviet Union."

▶ ▶ ▶ ▶

In the morning, neither the warm sunlight slanting through the barred windows nor the delicious breakfast served a half hour ago could comfort him. The cold fact of his situation remained. He had not escaped. He was not free. He was a prisoner.

MacDonald, in mussed shirt and wrinkled trousers, still slumped before his breakfast tray, which sat on what resembled a bridge table, felt confused and helpless. Normally a calm and pacific man, who handled each of life's new experiences thoughtfully and logically, he had never suffered or enjoyed high drama in his existence. Except for his visits to foreign countries, his interviews with native octogenarians, his work was largely mental and his routine somewhat sedentary. The events of the last sixteen hours following his discovery of C-98—his flight from Sukhumi, his abduction in Venice—were events he had always assumed happened in the cinema or suspense novels. Now, to have had them happen in real life, and to himself, of all people, was almost too unreal to accept.

Yet here he was, an innocent, harmless scientist with one of history's greatest secrets locked in his head, being held captive by a foreign nation in a medieval monastery on an island in Italy. The consequences of this captivity—imprisonment for the rest of his life in an alien land—were too frightening for him to imagine.

He recalled that last night, at gunpoint, he had been led from the pier across a court into the entry of what he had been told was a monastery. He had been prodded up four short flights of stone steps to the second floor. There, after passing through a long corridor hung with framed tapestries, he had been brought to a gilded doorway where another armed member of the Italian carabinieri, fiercely moustached, stood guard.

The door had been unlocked, and MacDonald had gone inside, followed by his civilian Russian host.

"This is a library housing Armenian manuscripts as well as other rare treasures," his captor had told him. "You will find it roomy and comfortable. We've moved in a cot for you. You will take your meals here. A monk will deliver them. If you have need for the water closet, tug at that maroon bell rope in the corner. It will summon the monk assigned to you, and he will take you down the hall. Since we have real concern for your health, you will be escorted outside twice a day to take a walk and enjoy fresh air. Do not be foolish enough to consider another escape. You are on an island, in the midst of a lagoon, and you will be under constant surveillance. Our Italian allies have provided us with eight members of the carabinieri—four in the building here, four on the grounds—to guard you. As for your quarters here, you can see that the two windows are grilled, and both doors are securely locked. Accept your lot, and try to enjoy it. Do not fear what is ahead. If you cooperate, you will become a hero of the Soviet Union. For now, welcome to San Lazzaro. Have a good sleep. I will see you tomorrow."

And here it was tomorrow. And he had not had a good sleep.

Rising from his chair, MacDonald scanned the library room once more. Hanging from the ceiling, an ornate brass chandelier. On either side of the second door, ancient books behind glass. To one side, a white marble bust on a pedestal. Nearby, a showcase containing an 8th-century manuscript of the Koran, a gift to San Lazzaro from one of Napoleon Bonaparte's scientists. Next, the low-slung cot on which he had slept.

His eyes went to the two windows. Each was covered by heavy bars. On the ledge of one window, four fat gray pigeons were perched. MacDonald remembered, from his first visit, the density of pigeons pecking at kernels of corn in the Piazza San Marco. These four, he decided, must be on a holiday.

For want of something better to do, MacDonald went to his breakfast tray, picked up a white roll, tore a piece from it, and broke that into smaller pieces as he walked to the window. The window was on a latch. MacDonald opened it. The pigeons, accustomed to tourists, did not fly off. MacDonald held out a palm filled with bread crumbs, and immediately the pigeons waddled to his hand and began eating. When they had finished, two of them waddled away, fluttered their wings, and flew off.

MacDonald inspected the iron bars covering the window, gripped one. It was immovable. Leaning forward, brow pressed against the bars, MacDonald was able to make out a grass yard at what seemed to be the rear part of the monastery. To his right there was a dirt walk leading to three or four steps that went to a small hillock where two uniformed men sat on a green bench beneath a large olive tree. Each wore a white strap from shoulder to hip. Carabinieri. Each held a rifle.

MacDonald turned away from the window in despair. The place was escapeproof.

A slight rattle drew MacDonald's attention to the main door. It was being unlocked, opened, and a tall, thin, boyish-looking monk with a thatch of brown hair entered. He wore a full-length black robe with a narrow leather belt held together by a single pearl clasp. At his neck was an open starched white collar. His black sandals were mesh and sporty. He was not the same monk who had silently delivered breakfast earlier.

"I have come for your breakfast tray," he said in English. Reaching MacDonald, he stopped. "I am Padre Pashal Nurikhan," he said. He appeared eager to offer friendship, to allay MacDonald's apprehension. "You may call me Pashal. Easier to remember. I am assigned to serve you meals and to take you on your daily walks. If you require anything, you need only ring for me."

"I require more information," said MacDonald, testing the monk. "Where am I? What is this? What is going on?" MacDonald paused. "Or aren't you allowed to talk?"

"I can speak," said Pashal, "but I have not much to tell you. Because I do not know anything, except that I observe you are being held by force. Are you a criminal?"

"Absolutely not," said MacDonald indignantly. "I am a scientist, a respected one. I'm British by birth, although an American citizen now. I was undertaking experiments in the Soviet Union when I made a—an important discovery. The Russians wanted it for themselves. I felt it belonged to the world. I left the Soviet Union last night, taking the only plane I could get, one that happened to be going to Venice. Apparently, when the Russians learned where I had gone, they contacted their Communist allies in Venice. When I got off the plane, they were waiting for me. They brought me here. They are going to hold me, and return me to the Soviet Union. *They* are the ones who are criminals. You seem a perfectly decent fellow. How did you get mixed up with that lot? Or are you one of them?"

"No, we have nothing to do with the ones who hold you," said Pashal, obviously distressed. "I can only explain what I saw last night and heard this morning. There was a telephone call to our father superior, the abbot, and then they came in a motor launch from Venice—Colonel Cutrone, the *commandante* of the carabinieri, and Mr. Ragazzi, the head of the local Communist party, who won the recent municipal election, and Mr. Aleksandr Veksler, the Soviet cultural attaché in Venice—it is he whom you met last night. They also came with a force of eight police guards. They told our father superior they must have his cooperation for a week. They said a foreigner had stolen something important from the Soviet Union and was on his way to Venice. They expected to catch him. They wanted to keep him incarcerated here at the Mechitarist Monastery of St. Lazarus—what visitors call San Lazzaro—until he could be returned to the Soviet Union. They wanted to leave Mr. Veksler and the eight carabinieri on San Lazzaro for a week to ensure security. Also, none of us—there are forty-five of us in the monastery—would be allowed to leave the island while the prisoner was here. Our father superior was appalled that this holy place should be converted into a prison. But he had to oblige. Honestly, what else could he say or do? We live by the sufferance of the Venetian government. Our abbot had no choice but to cooperate. That is all I know of the circumstances. I am sorry for you."

"I understand," said MacDonald. "I see now that you are as helpless as I am." He stared at the monk. "Or are you? Could you get me off here to the mainland?"

"Even if I dared, I couldn't. There is no way. For this week, every monk is a prisoner too."

"Yes, this is foolish of me." MacDonald sighed. "I
guess I'll just have to make the best of a bad thing."

As Pashal Nurikhan started for the breakfast tray,
MacDonald caught his arm. "One thing more. Can you
tell me about this place—San Lazzaro? Exactly what is
it?"

Pashal seemed happy to oblige, reciting his answer
like one who had done so hundreds of times before to
tourist groups coming over from the city. "Our Mechitarist Congregation—Armenian Catholics—was founded
by Maning di Pietro, known as Abbot Mechitar or Abbot
Counselor, in Constantinople in 1701. Fourteen years
later, fleeing Turkish persecution, Abbot Mechitar escaped to Venice, and two years later the Venetian government gave him the island of San Lazzaro as a gift.
There was this two-story building on the island—it had
been a monastery in the twelfth century, then turned
into a leper hospital, then abandoned, and with Abbot
Mechitar it became a monastery once again. While many
people have not known about San Lazzaro, there have
been some distinguished visitors who have come here
in the last two centuries. The most distinguished was
Lord Byron, who came to study the Armenian language
and who wrote an Armenian–English grammar book on
these premises."

"What do you do on the island?" asked MacDonald.

"We are one of the leading Armenian centers in the
world. We have an important school here. We have a
church. We have a printing press—in fact, eighteen
modern presses, run by four of the brothers. We print
Italian guidebooks, and—this may amuse you—we print
Italian comic books to raise money to support ourselves.
Otherwise, we are one of the most tranquil places on
earth. In 1717, when we took over the island, it was only
6,000 square meters in surface size. In 1850, the emperor
of Austria, who controlled Venice, enlarged our island
with new soil, making it its present 30,000 square meters

in size. These 30,000 square meters have been a garden spot. None of us ever dreamed they would be used for a prison. I hope—"

That moment, Aleksandr Veksler, in the same dark business suit he had worn the night before but now wearing a pink sport shirt, came into the room.

Observing that he had interrupted a conversation, he frowned. "You may go now, Padre," he said. "I have some business with our guest. We must be alone."

Hurriedly, the monk took up the breakfast tray and, with a quick nod at MacDonald, departed from the library room.

Veksler waited for the door to close, and then he gestured to the chair behind MacDonald. "Perhaps it would be better if you sat down. I want to have a little talk with you."

MacDonald felt defiant and considered remaining on his feet, but he decided that this was childish, and he lowered himself into the chair.

Veksler drew another chair from beneath the windows and settled in across from MacDonald. "I have been authorized to make a proposition to you, a very generous one." For the first time, MacDonald became aware of a sheaf of paper and a pen that the Russian had in one hand and was now holding up. "I have brought you paper and a pen," he said. He laid them on the table beside MacDonald. "I am going to leave them with you. As to the proposition . . ."

The Russian pulled his chair nearer to MacDonald and leaned forward, speaking softly. "The pen, the sheets of paper are for your C-98 formula. If, in the next few days, you will write out your formula for us, we will have our scientists immediately analyze it by computer. If they think you have honestly given us your formula, and it appears to be workable—that is, it could double the human life-span—you will be handsomely rewarded. You will be given great comforts, honors, and complete freedom inside the Soviet Union while we actually test it on human beings. That is our pledge to you."

"Inside the Soviet Union," MacDonald repeated. "Do you mean that?"

"Our premier has taken a special and personal interest in you and your discovery. Those were his very words several hours ago."

"I am an Englishman by birth and a naturalized American," said MacDonald. "I work in New York, and my home is an hour's drive outside the city. That's where I choose to live. I don't intend to spend the remainder of my life in Russia."

Veksler stiffened. "I am afraid there is no choice for you. You made your discovery in the Soviet Union, and the Soviet Union alone has the right to possess it and to dispense the formula as it wishes."

"That's insane," said MacDonald heatedly, "trying to monopolize a discovery that was made for all mankind, that belongs to all nations of the world and people everywhere. My God, can't you see? You'll get the formula to C-98 anyway. Everyone will have it. Not only the United States and Great Britain, but France, Germany, Spain, Italy, Liechtenstein—and China, China too, and Japan, and the countries of Africa—and yes, the Soviet Union. It can belong to no one nation, no one group, exclusively. No, I will never allow it."

Veksler's countenance had gone frosty. "In your place, I would think it over very carefully. If you are uncooperative, if you resist, things could go badly for you. Once you are back in the Soviet Union, we would be forced to confine you. And to use—to use every means at our command to make you come to your senses."

MacDonald considered the threat. In reality, what could they do to him? Starve him? Torture him? Bring him to the brink of death? No, he decided, they would not dare risk it. In view of his age, they would fear kill-

ing him. His only value to them was in being kept
healthy and alive in the hope that his confinement alone
might eventually encourage him to give them the formula.

"You don't frighten me," he said calmly. "It's all in
my head. As long as it is, you need me alive and well.
Kill me, and you kill all your hopes—your hopes of even
sharing longevity with the rest of the world."

"You might be surprised."

"I'll take my chances."

Veksler came to his feet. He gestured toward the pen
and paper. "You think it over. Believe me, if you are
wise, you will give us the formula right now. If you wait
until you are back in the Soviet Union, we may be less
generous and less patient with you."

Rising, MacDonald asked, "How long are you keeping
me here in this monastery?"

"Six days, at the most. We thought of sending a special
plane for you tomorrow. But that has been vetoed. We
do not want to give you the slightest opportunity to make
your predicament public—en route to the airport or at
the airport. Instead, we have diverted a Soviet freighter
and asked it to call at the deep-water dock not far from
San Lazzaro for one passenger. It will then sail back to
the Black Sea and Sukhumi." He crossed the room to the
door and turned back briefly. "Take the easy way, Professor. Write down your formula. Believe me, you will
not regret it. I shall look in on you again in a few days."

He was gone. MacDonald was alone.

He remembered the day, so long ago, when his mother
had died. The future had seemed bleak. He felt the same
loss now. Only the loss was his own life. And the future—there was no future at all.

▶ ▶ ▶ ▶

On this, the third day of his confinement, the solitude
had oppressed him, and when the monk, Pashal Nuri-

khan, had appeared with the lunch tray, MacDonald had asked if he might take some fresh air before eating.

Pashal had no objection. "Except the food—it will be cold."

"No matter," MacDonald said. "I really have no appetite. Maybe the walk will help."

The routine had been exactly the same as that of the previous two days. They had gone down the four short turnings of the staircase and crossed to a door that led them out into the enclosed courtyard in the center of the monastery. In silence, they had walked under the overhang, past green metal chairs and around the colorful garden, which featured two small palm trees and was profuse with pink hydrangeas and purple geraniums.

Ten minutes later they emerged from the monastery to the outdoors and began their hike that would cover the grounds surrounding the aged two-story building with its red tile roof. The noon day was windless and abnormally bright. The sun blazed down, and it promised to be hot. MacDonald inhaled deeply, but the fresh air did not dispel his lingering depression.

"It is beautiful today," the monk said.

"Not for me," MacDonald replied bitterly.

Pashal tried again, pointing off to the east. "The Lido island—you can see it clearly today."

"The Lido?" MacDonald repeated blankly, uncertain whether he had been told about it before.

"It is the large island opposite Venice. There is a city of 20,000, many apartments for upper-middle-class Italians. Automobiles are permitted. There is the casino, and there are many rich hotels—mainly the Excelsior, with its cabanas—for tourists."

MacDonald supposed he should show interest, but he did not. His mood was too low.

They traversed a dirt walk between dense foliage and a scattering of trees, going alongside the monastery to the rear of San Lazzaro. There, as before, sternly forbidding, were the two guards from the carabinieri, each with a rifle slung over a khaki-clad shoulder, each watching him intently. There again, just past them, were the stone steps to the rise which held the green bench and the full-grown olive tree that Lord Byron himself had planted long ago. As they walked on, there was once more the small, quiet ancient cemetery of the Mechitarist fathers.

They turned a corner and strolled on between the far side of the monastery and a six-foot brick wall that held off the sea. As they neared the front of the monastery, the neighboring island, dominated by a huge ugly building, came fully into view, and MacDonald remembered that this was San Servolo and the building was a mental hospital.

MacDonald jerked his thumb toward it. "That's where I'll wind up—or in one like it in Russia."

"I cannot believe it," the monk said, trying to cheer him. "Sooner or later they will have to let you go."

"Do you want to wager on that?" MacDonald said.

The monk, uncomfortable, tried to change the subject. Shading his eyes, peering off, he said, "Look, today you can see Venice more perfectly."

Indeed, at some distance to the northwest, like a needle pointing out of the lagoon, there was the Campanile, the bell tower, of Venice, and to its right were the majestic outlines of the Doges' Palace.

For a protracted interval, MacDonald considered the miniature of Venice, haven of freedom, his one hope, so very near—eight minutes by motorboat—yet, now, so impossibly far and out of reach.

He turned desperately to the monk. "Pashal," he said in an undertone, "you must help me. For the sake of humanity, you must help me escape."

Pashal backed off nervously. "There is no way for me, Professor. I am helpless."

"But you could help. You could have a motorboat

ready, and when we went for our next walk, I could make a run for the boat and get away."

"You would never manage it. They would catch you easily. I would be punished severely, maybe put in jail for life." He shook his head. "No, please, it cannot be done."

"Then get in touch with someone for me," MacDonald persisted. "There are telephones. I see them being used. When you are not seen, call the American consul in Venice, tell him my situation. He would do something. You can try."

"Believe me, Professor, it is too dangerous. I would be caught, and it would be the end of me. I am sorry, but—"

"Never mind," MacDonald said curtly. "I understand. Let's get back to my cell."

In a few minutes, preceded by the monk, MacDonald was approaching his library room. As the monk held open the door, he said, "Let me take your tray and heat the *pasta e fasioi* and the *pollo.*"

MacDonald nodded as they entered, and the monk went ahead of him to retrieve the tray. That moment, MacDonald realized there was a third person in the room. At the grilled window the Soviet cultural attaché, Aleksandr Veksler, stood, hands clasped behind his back and fidgeting. The Russian waited until Pashal had taken the tray and hurried out with it, and then he came slowly forward to meet MacDonald at the table.

Veksler offered a half smile. "Well, now, I hope the Professor is feeling better."

MacDonald made no comment.

Veksler resumed. "You will always have such freedom available—to walk anywhere, to talk to people, to do as you wish. All this you will have in your new homeland, once you choose to cooperate."

MacDonald remained silent.

Veksler eyed him briefly, then reached down and

snapped the rubber band that held together the sheaf of
paper he had left behind three days earlier. "I see the
pages are still blank," the Russian said. "You have written down nothing."

"Nor will I," said MacDonald.

"Stubbornness may be a good trait in a scientist, Professor, but in a prisoner it can lead to death."

"I am not afraid. As long as the formula is in my head,
you will not harm me."

"Do not be so certain," said Veksler. "I can assure you
we will try various forms of persuasion. It is a foolish
risk for you to undertake. I remember one occasion, several years ago, when we had to interrogate a dissident
scientist about his friends. We were advised to use every
means to make him talk, yet were warned to keep him
alive. The interrogators, unhappily, were unable to
judge his strength, and our scientist died on us during
the second hour. You see, Professor, there are no guar-
antees."

"There is one *I* can make," said MacDonald. "Whatever becomes of me, you are not going to get the formula
from me—not now and not later."

Veksler shrugged. "We shall see."

He had started for the door when it opened and Pashal
came through with the warmed-over lunch.

Veksler stopped him to inspect the contents of the
tray. "Um, bean soup," he murmured, "a half spring
chicken, mixed salad, fresh white bread, butter. Not bad,
considering." He looked at MacDonald. "I am sorry to
say your fare on the freighter that is coming for you a day
earlier than expected will not be quite as good. Yes, I
meant to alert you, our freighter will be here, near San
Lazzaro, the day after tomorrow." He watched the monk
set down the tray, adding, "Still time enough for you to
reconsider how you wish us to treat you."

"If I write down the formula," MacDonald said on
impulse, "will you call off the freighter and let me go on
to Paris?"

"You are in no position to bargain," said Veksler.

"Neither are you," said MacDonald.

"You are not merely foolish," said Veksler, "you are stupid."

With that he turned on his heel and followed Pashal out the door.

MacDonald heard the door close, heard the key turn, and at last walked glumly to his lunch tray and sat heavily before it. He tore a piece of bread in half, dipped it into the soup, and chewed on it. He spooned the thick bean soup, reluctantly consumed a portion of it, and decided he'd had enough. He had no stomach for food while his poor exhausted mind conjured up fantasies—perhaps realities—of what might await him in the Soviet Union. Again, as it had almost ceaselessly for nearly three days, his mind turned to escape, countless unworkable schemes locked in his brain, as he was locked in this room.

He glanced at the grilled window where the noisy familiar pigeons were waddling about on the ledge outside. As he held on them, it struck him as ironic that those idiotic birds were free as the air, while he, with all his brilliance, was confined to a cage.

If there were only some way to be as free as those pigeons, some way to fly out of here to freedom. If there were only some way to get word of his captivity to the outside world. If there were someone, some way, to carry his cry for help out of here. To carry news of his plight, carry it . . . carrier . . . carrier pigeon.

Carrier pigeon!

My God.

He had cultivated the friendship of those damn pigeons on the window ledge, faithfully fed them twice a day, and now they owed him something.

It was perhaps a futile and impractical idea, a ridiculous and hopeless idea, but it was an idea where there had been none before. The odds were a thousand—more likely ten thousand—to one against its working. Were these pigeons from Venice itself? Did they commute daily from their home in the Piazza San Marco to nearby islands like San Lazzaro? And even if they did, would anyone in Venice recognize his desperate cry for help? It was a pitifully romantic idea. But it was an idea, an action. It was *something.*

He glanced off at the pigeons. There were four of them, waddling or perched on the ledge, waiting for his crumbs. He realized he had better make haste while they were still there.

He eased the rubber band off the sheaf of paper that Veksler had left him. He placed the rubber band on the table, took the top sheet of blank paper, carefully tore a half-inch strip from the bottom of the page. It would be too long to fit, he decided, and he ripped it in half.

Setting the strip of paper on the table, he prepared to write his SOS.

What to say that made sense and could be squeezed into three or four microscopic lines?

He thought about it for a number of seconds. He must identify himself. He must state his situation. As well as the time factor. He must ask for help and beg the finder to contact Dr. Edwards in Paris.

Could he manage all this legibly and clearly in four tiny lines? He must try.

His pen touched the narrow strip of paper, and he began to write: *Am British scientist illegally imprisoned on San Lazzaro by Communists.*

He paused, considering what to say next, finally framed it in his mind, and resumed his miniaturized writing. The message was complete. He reread it. Not quite complete. He must give some indication of why he was a prisoner, why the Russians wanted him, why at any cost he must be saved. There was barely room for a hint, space for no more than six to ten words. He sought them, found them, and meticulously fitted them into the last blank space on the strip of paper.

Now, quickly, he folded the strip once, then again, then a third time. He stuffed it into his shirt pocket with the rubber band.

From his lunch tray he tore off a corner of bread, broke it into crumbs. Rising, trying to show no signs of anxiety, he approached the window where the alerted pigeons were waiting. As he had done yesterday, and the day before, he put his right hand through the bars of the grille, spilled a few of the crumbs onto the ledge. Immediately, two of the pigeons went for the food, and a third crowded in to join them. The fourth pigeon, a fat dark gray one, was watching his hand. MacDonald moved his hand toward the lone pigeon, offering his palm of remaining bread crumbs. The pigeon strutted toward his hand, hovered over it, suddenly darted its beak toward the crumbs and began to eat them.

Cautiously, MacDonald slipped his free left hand through the next pair of bars, lowering it over the occupied pigeon.

For a moment, MacDonald held still, motionless. Then in a flash he dropped his left hand toward the pigeon, grabbed it about the back of its head and its breast. The startled bird was all motion, trying to squirm loose, get away, but MacDonald had its wings pinned down.

Swiftly he drew the pigeon into the room, held it with its bottom up and its flailing claws exposed. With his right hand he dug into his shirt pocket, pulled out the rubber band and the tightly folded message.

The next and last was the most difficult part—securing the paper slip to one of the pigeon's legs—but he applied himself to it with grim concentration. He managed to roll the paper around the pigeon's leg without dropping the rubber band. Then he got the elastic around it, doubling it up and twisting it until it looped tighter and tighter around the paper and the pigeon's thin leg. At last the message held fast.

For a fleeting second, MacDonald contemplated his handiwork. He now had a carrier pigeon. He prayed it was a San Marco pigeon. But would anyone in a million years—let alone two days—notice it, retrieve it, act on it? The odds mocked him. It was the most futile endeavor he had ever undertaken. But one thought buoyed his spirit. Minutes before, the world had been blind and deaf to knowledge of his discovery and incarceration. With this winged creature, the word would go out of his cell for the first, the last, the only time.

Gripping the squirming bird, MacDonald strode back to the window. He held the pigeon high, then pushed it out between the bars, preparing to cast it off into the free air. From the corner of an eye, he saw a movement on the ground below. It came from one of the khaki-clad carabinieri guards. The guard was lifting his rifle.

MacDonald's heart hammered. With a gasp, he threw his arm forward in a pitching motion, opening his hand, releasing the pigeon. The bird dipped, flapped its wings, rose, and was airborne to the northwest. Below, the guard had whipped his rifle to his shoulder, was aiming, training his gun on the lofting pigeon.

The rifle rang out.

Almost simultaneously, the pigeon seemed to have exploded in midair, a flurry of feathers and wings. The bird shuddered, wobbled, began to sink, beating its wings weakly. It was dropping fast when it disappeared from MacDonald's sight.

MacDonald looked down at the guard once more. The Italian was waving what was first a triumphant and then a threatening fist at him.

Sick with grief and defeat, MacDonald turned away, trudged back to his chair, and clumped down into it, eyes on the door, waiting for them to come and board up his window.

After that, there would be only darkness.

II

▶   ▶   ▶   ▶   ▶   ▶   ▶

For Tim Jordan, the first moment of revival (after a bad night, and his nights were gradually getting worse) usually came when he walked out of the Hotel Danieli Royal Excelsior into the glaring sunlight of Venice and faced the beginning of a new day.

The spell of the city almost always worked for him, and it was working right now as he stood unsteadily before the hotel entrance in the teeming Riva degli Schiavoni. Ahead of him, a jam-packed *vaporetto* had just arrived, bumping against the floating wooden landing and rocking it. The water bus was disgorging a stream of passengers—Venetians, German and French and American tourists. Moored on either side of the shaky landing were several motorboats for rent, and a motoscafo was taking on the last guests of the Danieli who were seeking the pleasures of the Hotel Excelsior beach on Lido island before the lunch hiatus.

While this was for Tim Jordan the beginning of a day, he knew that the day had awakened long hours ago. When he could, especially when he had been drinking the night before, he slept late, not joining the life of the city until noon and not getting to his desk until one o'clock. This was one of his noon days, because he had stayed up late the night before, drinking and brooding in solitude, sleeping hard and straight through, and he had not been able to get out of bed until less than an hour ago. Now, outside at last, he felt the thin, quivering band of a hangover behind his forehead, and his brain felt mussed and his legs were rubbery.

He had spent some time, late this morning, after shaving, staring at himself in the bathroom mirror, and he had not liked what he had seen. He could remember himself at the time of his marriage six years ago—his youthful appearance had been frozen in the wedding picture Claire had always kept on her dressing table—when he had stood a lean, athletic five feet eleven. In the time since her death, but especially during the nearly two years past in Venice, his body had changed, become a little hunched and paunchy and soft. And not only his body, but his face also. What a ruthless biographer the human face was! The bathroom mirror had read the story of his latest years to him. His hair was still black, neatly parted at one side, and his facial features were still narrow and angular, but the rest of what had happened reflected three years of sorrow, self-pity, ennui, and dissipation. The brown eyes this morning had been bloodshot and puffy, the forehead creased, the cheeks blotched and sagging (or so they seemed), the full chin less firm. And to add to this Dorian Gray disintegration, he had cut himself while shaving.

Now he held his hands up before him. They were still unsteady. It was a sad condition for a man just turned thirty-eight, he thought. But seven cognacs last night and three years without commitment before that had worked their creeping erosions. He wanted to tell his employers, the directors of the Venice Must Live Committee, "Gentlemen, change your priorities and make your first one: Tim Jordan Must Live." Save Jordan before the tides sweep him under, save your secretly sinking public relations representative.

He smiled wryly at this nonsense, gave his head a shake to rid it of cobwebs, and started on his daily walk. It had been his habit, ever since he had moved to Venice two years—actually, twenty-one months—ago, to take a leisurely stroll around the area, a half hour or so, winding up at a café in the Piazza San Marco for breakfast, before going to his office. Even when it rained or he was too hung over to stand up straight, he never missed the walk. It always had a salutary effect on him. He never tired of viewing the ancient Byzantine buildings and medieval monuments, of mingling with the bustling crowds of sightseers in zigzag streets, of exchanging gossip with many lively Venetians whom he now counted as friends. It was life-generating and important. It was also exercise.

He climbed the arched Ponte della Paglio, jostled by perpetual hordes of people coming and going; observed the tourists with their cameras at the stone railing photographing the enclosed overhead passageway—known as the Bridge of Sighs—which connected the Doges' Palace with the dungeons. He pushed his way down toward the Piazzetta, the small square with its twin columns celebrating a protector of Venice and one of its patron saints.

On his way, Jordan looked at the cluster of black gondolas roped to poles in the lagoon under a red banner reading, SERVIZIO GONDOLE, searching to see if Luigi Cipolate, his favorite gondolier and bar companion, was about. He spotted Luigi just as the gondolier saw him. Jordan waved and called out, *"Strigheta!"*—Luigi's nickname, meaning Little Witch, because his long nose and curved chin seemed to come together like those of a witch.

"Timothy!" the gondolier called back. "Good to see you so early!"

Jordan grinned and considered detouring for a short chat with his friend. It was tempting. Luigi was one of the more interesting, independent, traditional gondoliers. Only half the gondoliers owned their own boats, and Luigi was one of them. It had cost him about 5,000,000 lire—around $6,000—to buy the boat; its stainless steel, aluminum, and brass fittings; its chairs, cushions, rug. Luigi owned his own apartment, too, decorated by a wife and son, in the Dorsoduro quarter near the recently restored old church of San Nicolò dei Mendicoli. He was one of the few gondoliers who continued to wear the regulation costume of straw hat, white cotton sailor shirt over a striped T-shirt, and blue trousers. He was also one of the few who sang for his clients as his oar pushed the sleek gondola through the canals. His repertoire consisted of "O Sole Mio," "Santa Lucia," and "Ciao Venezia."

About to join Luigi, Jordan glimpsed the time on the clock tower and decided that any protracted conversation now would make him too late for work. He waved to Luigi again and headed for the Piazza San Marco. Passing between the Libreria Vecchia, with its shops and the Gran' Caffè Chioggia beneath, and the shimmering white Doges' Palace, he tried not to be distracted. Soon he was in the shadow of the towering Campanile, and at once the Piazza San Marco lay before him.

The sight was awesome, and never failed to inspire him with wonder. The vast outdoor square, surrounded by the golden Basilica and three colonnaded buildings on its four sides, no billboards or vehicles visible, the enclosure filled with three cafés, three orchestras, animated groups of visitors, numerous vendors, and pigeons everywhere.

Feeling better, Tim Jordan moved forward, pigeons fluttering out of his path, until he reached the dark, narrow, crowded Mercerie, the main shopping street of Venice which led from the Piazza into the city proper.

Pushing along slowly, head swiveling to see what new merchandise the shopwindows were displaying, Jordan reached the first corner, where he barely avoided bumping into the priest who had emerged from the side street.

"Don Pietro," Jordan greeted him with warmth. Pietro Vianello—the "Don" was a courtesy title for priests—was one of Jordan's favorite conversational companions. "What are you doing so far from home?" Don Pietro had a church in the San Giacomo quarter of Venice, near the railroad station, at the far end of the city.

The priest, bald except for a fringe of wispy hair, cherubic and rotund, scowled uncharacteristically and removed a rolled newspaper from a fold of his black cassock. "I have come to San Marco to see if any of Venice is left for us," he said with mock anger. He held up his copy of *Il Gazzettino*. "Have you seen the new municipal tax that Accardi and his gang of Communist thugs are trying to impose on gift items? If he has his way, it'll be the end of tourism, and the death of Venice. If those Communist thugs don't sink Venice, then the snails on your Venice Must Live Committee will manage it."

These were two of Don Pietro's pet subjects. A Christian Democrat, he distrusted the Socialists and detested the Communists. A native Venetian, he also feared the destruction of his city by the annual winter floods.

"I can do nothing about the Communists," said Jordan patiently. "After all, your parishioners elected them."

"Not *my* parishioners," said Don Pietro.

"Well, somebody elected them."

"Nobody elected them," argued the priest. "They stole the election. That is my suspicion."

"As for our Venice Must Live Committee," said Jordan good-naturedly, having been over this ground before with his clerical friend, "they may be snaillike, but they are moving. They installed the Pirelli dam across the Lido entrance to the sea last winter—"

"They did not use it to keep out the tides. We were flooded in January."

"It wasn't ready yet—installed, but not ready. It should be all set to use this winter."

"I hope I live to see the day."

"You will, I promise," said Jordan. "Now I'd better get to work."

The priest's scowl disappeared. "I have missed you. Come by for tea some afternoon soon. We can have a real argument."

Jordan left him. He was still not in the mood for work. He decided he would walk a little farther, at least as far as Nurikhan's Glass Shop, before turning back for breakfast. Sembut Nurikhan's modernized glassware store was a short distance, just off Ramo San Zulian in the small square called Campo San Zulian. The Armenian proprietor was perhaps Jordan's oldest friend in Venice. Shortly after Jordan's arrival in Venice, when he had still been interested in the showy Murano glass and eager for a reliable place where he could buy gifts for his sister and her husband in Chicago and an elderly aunt in Los Angeles for whom he had affection, Nurikhan's Glass Shop had been recommended to him. Although the store's owner, Sembut Nurikhan, a smallish, somewhat professorial and dapper man in his fifties, had seemed remote on first meeting, Jordan had been drawn to him. He was that rarity, an honest and forthright being, and in the months that followed, Jordan had dropped in on him more frequently, eventually dined with him and his attractive Egyptian wife once a month, and the relationship had become closer.

Jordan had arrived at the shop, with its two front windows trimmed in aluminum. On display in the windows, dramatized by overhead spotlights, were pieces of glass sculpture by Seguso and Nason resting on slabs of black Swedish marble. Jordan went to the doorway and looked inside. The store was filled with customers, and under a

baroque Venetian chandelier stood the proprietor surrounded by a circle of Japanese tourists. All that Jordan
could see of Nurikhan was his finely etched gray-haired
head, gold-rimmed glasses on his thin nose, and the
oversized polka-dot bow tie.

"Sembut," Jordan hailed him. "Just wanted to say
hello."

The glass store owner materialized from between two
customers. "Tim, five minutes and I'll be free."

"No time today. Got to get to work. How's everything?"

"Personally, fine. My brother, not so good. Come back
for lunch when you can."

Jordan nodded his promise and started away to retrace
his steps to the Piazza San Marco.

It was a quarter to one when Jordan returned to the
Piazza. He picked up the *International Herald Tribune*
from Gino, the shabby vendor at the portable newsstand,
then crossed into the sunlight, going past the outdoor
Caffè Lavena, continuing onward to the next outdoor
café, which was Quadri's, nearer the center of the Piazza. About a third of the small circular gray tables were
occupied by tourists, but the ones in the front row were
empty.

Jordan pulled back a yellow wicker chair at the nearest table and sat down to enjoy the sun and some breakfast. A waiter in the aisle came over quickly and welcomed him with familiarity. "The same as usual, Signor
Jordan?"

"The same, except today I'll have some orange juice.
Then the hot tea, no lemon, rolls and butter."

With the waiter gone, Jordan settled back, crossed his
legs, and unfolded his newspaper. The lead story on the
front page announced that the Pope had elevated Cardinal Bacci to head a new council for the propagation of
the faith that would police and oversee those elements
of the clergy that were straying too far from the orthodox

line. Bad news for the liberals. Cardinal Bacci was characterized as a flinty modern-day Savonarola, an extreme zealot. Jordan shifted his attention to a story at the bottom of the page. A Chicago White Sox pitcher, in his rookie year, had last night hurled a no-hitter against the New York Yankees.

Jordan heard his name and looked up. Approaching him was a lean, blond young man with sensitive, delicate features. He had the odd but not uncommon Venetian name of Memo—Oreste Memo—and he played the violin in the Quadri orchestra. He and Jordan had refreshments together about once a week. When the orchestra took its break, he would come down from the bandstand, remove his light summer jacket, and sit with Jordan. The last time they had been together, Jordan remembered, Memo had told him he was composing the score of a speculative musical on Eleonora Duse for which a friend of his in Milan had already written the book.

"Hi, Oreste," Jordan called back. "Want to join me for some tea?"

"Wish I could," said Memo breathlessly, "but I'm almost two hours late and I don't want the boss to fire me. Heavy date last night, all night—one of your American college girls, very acrobatic. I was so exhausted I overslept. Supposed to begin fiddling away at eleven, you know, so this isn't going to make the old man happy. Be seeing you."

He hastened up the aisle toward the bandstand, where the other musicians were assembled.

The waiter was setting down Jordan's breakfast. Jordan folded his newspaper, laid it on the next chair, and drank his orange juice.

Presently he was buttering his rolls, and doing so transported him to another time and place. It was something Claire had always done for him at breakfast—buttered his rolls or toast as she chattered away. She had been doing that very thing the fateful morning that continually came to his mind. He could close his eyes and picture her unblurred: honey-colored hair, blue eyes, tilted nose, sweet lips, clever, insecure, filled with love and the need for love. And on that morning, three months pregnant. They had both been entertaining high hopes. They had plans to leave the rented apartment in Chicago and buy a house in the suburbs. They had a hundred dreams about the child, children. They had talked about Jordan's doing what he wanted to do. He had been an engineer for a large Chicago firm, which bored him, and he had begun to write popular science articles on weekends, which did not bore him, and one day he would do full time what he enjoyed.

He had gone to work, and an hour later had received the call from the police. Claire had been standing on a corner of Michigan Avenue waiting for the traffic light to change. A car had swerved out of control, jumped the curb, smashed into her, killed her instantly. Just like that. Pointless. Madness. Claire was dead.

For almost all purposes, he was dead too.

He sat here now, in the sun of the Piazza San Marco, absently staring at the pigeons, the tourists feeding them, munching at his rolls, drinking his tea, not wanting to remember the months of despair and mourning that had followed.

Still, his Claire-less life unreeled in memory. He had quit the engineering firm. He had moved to New York, not wanted to drink, did drink, not wanted to write, did write. His science articles had appeared, were liked, gave him an erratic livelihood. He had been half alive, without ambition or goal, when he had gone apathetically to a charity party on the mezzanine of The Plaza, accompanied some single woman as her escort, gone to the party sponsored by something called the Venice Must Live Committee. He had not been to Venice, or anywhere, had not known it was dying. He had been only partially attentive to the celebrity entertainers, and the committee director who had spoken about the beauties of Venice that might soon be lost to civilization, about how Venice was sinking into the sea even as its monuments were eroding. He had been introduced to someone, a Dr. Rinaldo, who had recognized his name from his published by-line and had been impressed. The man had asked him some probing questions about his career, and he had answered them unseriously, with self-deprecation and cynicism. Dr. Rinaldo had suddenly asked, "How would you like to come to Venice and work for us? We need a communications or press officer, and we have the funding for such a job. You seem to possess all the qualifications. Imagine being paid to live in Venice! Try it for three months. You'll love it."

He had tried it for three months, and now it was twenty-one months. He had loved it and not loved it. He could have loved it entirely, with passion, with Claire. But he could not love it entirely without her, because he no longer loved himself.

One bright spot, eleven months old. He had needed an assistant in the press office of the committee, located in the Procuratie Vecchie building right behind him looking down on the Piazza San Marco. Six young female applicants had been sent to him, and he had hardly looked at five of the women as he had interviewed them. But he had looked at Marisa Girardi—an absolutely stunning raven-haired, dark-eyed Venetian beauty. She was then twenty-six years old, educated in Padua, currently employed as publicity head for the local branch of an international fabric house. She had appeared bright, efficient, intent, and sexy, definitely sexy. He had hired her without a single misgiving.

After her first week on the job he had invited Marisa out to dinner at Harry's Bar. They had eaten sparingly—grilled scampi for her, veal scallops for him—had drunk straight Scotches before, during, and after dinner, and had got fantastically high and extremely personal and intimate.

Leaving through the swinging doors, they had stood in the street near the vaporetto station, both immobilized, uncertain as to what came next, he knowing how he felt but not knowing how to bring it up.

Marisa had said, "I would invite you to my apartment, but I live there with my mother and brother. Where do you live?"

"I have a permanent suite in the Hotel Danieli. I live alone."

"Why don't we go to your place?"

The moment they had entered the living room of his suite, and he had shut the door behind him, she had turned, put her arms around his neck, kissed him with her full crimson lips parted, her tongue teasing his as her large, firm breasts pressed against him. Her lips had moved to his ear. "I want you, Tim," she had whispered.

Inside the bedroom, lit by one lamp, he had undressed with his back to her. As he removed his last garment, his jock shorts, he turned toward the bed. She was lying on it stark naked. The size of her distended brown nipples on her enormous breasts, the soft wideness of her hips, the prominence of her long vaginal mound affected him instantly. He had felt his penis grow, and rise, and swell. In several dozen previous sexual encounters in his Claire-less years, he had barely risen to each occasion, finding the bouts as exciting as jogging. But this night he had attained a total erection.

He had started to kiss her nipples. "Don't waste time, darling," she had whispered.

He had found her moist vaginal opening, and as his penis slowly slid inside, he groaned, "I'm not going to last long."

Her hands were on his ribs, drawing him down. "Tomorrow night it will be longer, and the night after even better. Oh, darling, good . . ."

Marisa had been right. It had been longer and better. It had been good. It had been daily for two weeks, and with familiarity it had settled into twice a week. He had not been in love with her, but had appreciated human warmth and companionship. How she truly felt about him he had not known for certain. She had been undemanding. Lately, he had seen her less and less during his after-work hours. The pointlessness of his existence had sucked him into some kind of emotional quagmire, where one wanted to be alone with a bottle of cognac until one felt senseless and buried in a blackness of sleep.

He opened his eyes to the sun of Venice and the unreal activity and babble in the Piazza San Marco.

He saw that he had finished his tea, and consumed his rolls except for the half of one he always automatically saved for the pigeons. They knew him as a friend, and they came to him after breakfast when he was ready.

Breaking up the roll, he dropped the pieces at his feet. Then he reached into his jacket pocket, took out the small bag of granola he had bought at the grocery near the Danieli yesterday, and scattered the mixed grain around the bread. With amusement, he watched the pigeons quickly gather, twelve or fourteen of them. They were mostly dark gray, speckled a lighter gray on their breasts and tails. Their heads dipped jerkily as they pecked at the bread or grain and gobbled it down.

The pigeons of Venice had fascinated Jordan from the very day of his arrival in the city. He had learned, mostly from Marisa's younger brother, Bruno, several versions of how pigeons had first come to Venice. According to one account, in medieval times a Doge, on Palm Sunday, to celebrate the dove that had told Noah of the end of the Flood, released a number of pigeons that had been housed in the vestibule of the Basilica. According to another tradition, Venetians had decided to import pigeons to their city to celebrate that day in 1204 when a carrier pigeon had brought a message from the Orient describing the victories won by Doge Enrico Dandolo in the Fourth Crusade. In modern times, the 200,000 pigeons had been fed maize twice a day by the doorman of the insurance company, Assicurazioni Generali, that occupied the building on the clock-tower side of the Piazza. Then, in 1971, the frescoed ceiling of the Church of Angelo Raffaele had collapsed because of the pigeon droppings and nests that blocked the gutters of the church. In 1972, the mayor of Venice had decreed that 150,000 of the city's 200,000 pigeons should be moved to other cities. Some were removed—bird lovers saw that their number was few, and even this loss was quickly replaced by the prolific reproduction of the birds.

And Jordan, for one, was glad of it. For him, the pigeons were synonymous with Venice and therefore a part of his love for the city.

He continued watching his birds eating the last of his bread and grain. Now they were done, and done with their benefactor, and moving away, spreading back out to the center of the Piazza in search of new benefactors. Three lingered behind at his feet, and then two of these flew off and there was one. That one stood wobbling, shaking, when suddenly, unexpectedly, it toppled over and lay on its side, still as death.

Jordan reacted with astonishment. He had never seen a sight like this before. He could not understand. He came forward in his wicker chair, then went down on one knee, grasped the pigeon under its fat belly, tried to right it, but it fell on its back. That moment, he realized two things—that the pigeon was dead, and that he had blood on his hand. He bent closer, inspecting the bird, and plainly saw what seemed to be a bullet wound on the side of its belly. And an instant later, he saw something else. Tied to one of the pigeon's legs was a small folded strip of paper, held loosely in place by a rubber band.

Incredible. What kind of game was this? Or could this have been a carrier pigeon?

His hand went out to the pigeon's inert leg, pulled off the rubber band, and caught the piece of paper. He brought the paper with him back to the chair, carefully unfolded and opened it, and flattened the miniature strip on his table. There was something in a tiny handwriting. He squinted more closely at it, and realized to his surprise that it was not in Italian but in English. Slowly, he read the message:

Am British scientist illegally imprisoned on San Lazzaro by Communists. Planning to send me to USSR in 2 days. Save me. Call Dr. Edwards Plaza Athenee Paris to tell world. Prof. Davis MacDonald. Aug. 18. Have discovered Ft. of Youth. Reds want it.

Jordan blinked, blinked again, and not knowing what to make of this melodramatic plea, he reread the message.

Written August 18. That was today, this very day.

By someone on San Lazzaro—he knew San Lazzaro, had seen the island hundreds of times on the way to the Lido beach—by a Professor Davis MacDonald, a name that had no meaning to him, although faintly familiar.

Who was this MacDonald? What was his so-called Fountain of Youth? What kind of Communists were trying to send him to Russia?

It made no sense, unless you took it literally. That some Communists would kidnap a British professor here in Venice, and hold him a prisoner on San Lazzaro, because he had found the place that gave eternal youth: that sounded absolutely impossible, surely less real than some concocted Hollywood script.

Then Jordan realized he had been taking the message literally, and that he was a fool. A thousand to one, a million to one, this was a practical joke conceived by some nut who had nothing better to do. It was a joke, a bit of fun, a hoax, and he felt embarrassed at having taken it seriously for even a minute.

Irritated with himself, he lifted the slip of paper, stuck it into his jacket pocket to give Marisa a laugh, paid his bill, got up, and was starting to leave for his office in the building behind him when he remembered the poor dead bird. He stopped, picked up the pigeon in one hand, and carried it up the aisle of Quadri's Gran' Caffè to the bandstand. He sought and found his musician friend, Oreste Memo, hidden by a row of green planters that surrounded the ledge of the stand. Memo was busy polishing his violin.

"Oreste," Jordan called.

The musician saw him, sprang to his feet, and came toward him inquiringly.

"Oreste, I found a dead pigeon," Jordan said. "What do I do with it?"

"Give it to me. I'll dispose of it."

Jordan handed the bird over. "Careful. It's sticky around the belly. Someone shot it."

Memo took the pigeon. "That's horrible. Who in the devil would do a thing like that?"

"God knows," said Jordan. "Thanks. Now I'm the one who is late for work."

He headed for the black gate that opened to the stone staircase leading to his upstairs offices, and one thought accompanied him.

The pigeon carrying the desperate message—if it was all a joke, why would anyone on earth want to shoot the pigeon carrying it?

All at once it didn't seem funny.

And maybe not a joke at all.

▶ ▶ ▶ ▶

As he passed through the yellow-painted anteroom, in which four *commessi*, or doormen, in dark gray uniforms sat with several persons waiting for their appointments,

Jordan was conscious once more of the exotic environment in which he had been toiling for almost two years. This 15th-century Renaissance building on the Piazza San Marco had, five centuries ago, housed the offices and private apartments of old Venice's Procuratori, the nine men elected for life to assist the Doge in his administrative work. In 1831, the Assicurazioni Generali, the foremost insurance company in Italy, had bought the building for its international headquarters. Five years ago, just after the Venice Must Live Committee was formed, the insurance company had donated a dozen of its offices in this building for the use of the committee. Jordan occupied one of these offices, Marisa another, and Gloria, the secretary they shared, maintained the office between them.

His mind still on the message that he had taken from the pigeon's leg, Jordan made his way up the corridor to the glass door to his office and went inside. Marisa, in a tight pink sweater and flared blue skirt, her shining black hair down to her shoulders, was busily poring over the contents of some folders in the open drawer of his green file cabinet. On his entrance, she pivoted to meet him, tilting her head back to offer him her lips. He gave her a perfunctory kiss.

"How are you, darling?" he asked. He moved thoughtfully to his oak desk beside one of the three windows overlooking the Piazza.

Marisa eyed him quizzically. "How are *you?* Something on your mind?"

"Always something on my mind," he said lightly, pushing around the memorandums on his desk.

Marisa came closer. "I hope sometimes it is me."

"I'm sorry, Marisa. I've just been tied up lately. I want to see you."

"When?"

"Why—why, tonight. If you're free tonight, we can have dinner at Harry's."

"For you, I am free."

"Fine. We'll arrange it before I leave. Anything urgent today?"

"Generally quiet. The correspondent for *The New York Times* in London called. He wanted some recent photographs of our miniature Pirelli-Furlanis inflatable dam, especially shots showing it in action. I'm digging them up now. He would not tell me what they are for."

"All right. Keep digging."

Marisa stared at him a moment. "Something *is* troubling you. Can I be of help?"

"Thanks, but no. I'll see you later."

She was about to leave the office when his voice caught her. "Marisa, please tell Gloria to hold off incoming calls and all visitors for the next hour. I don't want to be disturbed."

No sooner had she gone, and he was alone, than his mind fastened on the so-called message for help from the so-called Professor Davis MacDonald. In retrospect, it seemed more sinister than cranky. Yet its implications were so melodramatic, so far removed from his humdrum workaday world, that he could not accept it as genuine.

His hand had gone into his jacket pocket and come out with the message. He lowered himself into his swivel chair and placed the slip of paper on the desk before him.

Am British scientist illegally imprisoned on San Lazzaro...

His eye skipped to *Call Dr. Edwards Plaza Athenee Paris to tell world.*

Why not? The worst he could do was make a gullible fool of himself. It would not have been the first time. On the other hand . . . if the message was authentic . . .

His instinct told him to act.

He pressed down his intercom button and buzzed his secretary. She answered. "Gloria, get me the Plaza Athénée Hotel in Paris."

"Anyone in particular?"

"Just the switchboard. I'll take it from there."

Jordan thoughtfully fingered the piece of paper, saw a push button light up on his telephone, and waited. Seconds after, Gloria could be heard on the voice box. "Mr. Jordan, I have the Plaza Athénée in Paris."

Jordan pressed down the lighted button and picked up the receiver. "Operator, I'm calling from Italy. Do you have a Dr. Edwards registered in your hotel? If so, I'd like to speak to him."

"*Attendez,*" said the operator. A pause. Then, "I am ringing."

Two, three, four rings, no answer. A fifth ring. Someone had picked up the phone at the other end. A low feminine voice said, "Hello."

"Hello," said Jordan. "I'd like to speak to Dr. Edwards. I'm calling long distance. Is he in?"

"You are speaking to Dr. Edwards," replied the feminine voice, with mild exasperation. "I'm Dr. Alison Edwards."

Somewhat taken aback, Jordan was immediately apologetic. "I-I'm sorry. I don't know why I assumed Dr. Edwards was a man. Professor MacDonald's message didn't give your first name."

"Did you say Professor MacDonald?"

"Yes, I have a message from him for you. You do know Professor MacDonald?"

"Certainly. I work for him. I'm his research associate. Did you see him in Russia?"

"No, no, it's nothing like that," said Jordan hastily. "I'm calling from Venice, from Italy. I've never set eyes on Professor MacDonald. But I do have a message from him—or I think I do—I'm not sure."

There was a tinge of impatience in Dr. Edwards' voice. "I'm afraid I don't understand you, Mr. . . . ." Her voice dropped off.

"My name is Timothy Jordan," he said quickly. "It is a little complicated. I think I'd better explain. By accident—today—fifteen minutes ago—I got a message, signed Professor Davis MacDonald, asking the finder of the message to get in touch with Dr. Edwards at the Plaza Athénée in Paris."

"Whatever are you talking about, Mr. Jordan? It makes no sense at all."

"It will or it won't, once I tell you what happened. You'll have to be the judge. Now, here is what happened. I'm an American living and working in Venice. I'm the press officer for the Venice Must Live Committee—"

"The what?" she interrupted.

"An organization that is trying to save Venice from sinking, being destroyed. This noon, on my way to work, I stopped in a café to have some tea, and I started feeding the pigeons—"

"Mr. Jordan or whoever you are, is this some kind of joke? If so, I don't have time—"

"Please listen to me, will you?" he said with a flare of annoyance. "This could be deadly serious. Your Professor MacDonald could be in trouble. Now, please, *listen.*" There was a silence on the other end. Jordan resumed. "I was feeding some pigeons—yes, Venice is filled with pigeons—that's part of what happened—and one pigeon fell over dead in front of me. When I examined it, I found a note tied to one of its legs. The note was signed Professor Davis MacDonald. You say you work for him?"

"I do. He is one of the most eminent scientists in the world. But all you are telling me—pigeons—a note from him—in Venice . . . I mean, I can't—"

"It's true, Dr. Edwards. It just happened to me exactly as I'm telling you. I read the note, and—look, I have it right in front of me on my desk. I'll read it to you."

"Please," she said with bewilderment.

Receiver to his ear, he bent closer to the strip of paper. "It is written in ink, and it reads—these are the exact words—'Am British scientist illegally imprisoned on San Lazzaro by Communists.' "

"Illegally imprisoned by Communists? On—what? San Lazzaro? What's that?"

"A little island with a monastery just a few minutes outside the city of Venice. Here, let me read the rest of it. I'm reading. 'Planning to send me to USSR in 2 days. Save me. Call Dr. Edwards Plaza Athénée Paris to tell world.' It is signed, 'Prof. Davis MacDonald. Aug. 18.' Then—"

"But it still doesn't make sense. Professor MacDonald is in the U.S.S.R. I heard from him just before coming to Paris. I'm terribly confused."

"Wait, Dr. Edwards. There's more to the note. Two more sentences. Let me read them. He writes—or someone writes—'Have discovered Ft. of Youth. Reds want it.' " Jordan paused. "That's the entire note I found. That's why I called you."

"Fountain of Youth," she said in a hushed voice. "Read that to me again, that line."

" 'Have discovered the Fountain of Youth.' "

"My God, if this isn't a hoax, he's trying to say—he's made the discovery."

"What discovery? Now I'm the one who's in the dark."

"The secret to the prolongation of human life, to human longevity. He's a renowned gerontologist. You mean you've never heard of him? He's been experimenting on this for twelve years. He's currently in the Soviet Union, in the area of the Caucasus Mountains near the Black Sea, doing his research—and now he's saying . . . My God, this is tremendous news, no news on earth could be greater, if, if he really wrote that note—"

"If he wrote this note," repeated Jordan. "That's the question. Would anyone else besides you and Mac-Donald know of his research?"

"Oh, yes. Many people know of it through scientific journals. through his writings."

"Then someone else could have written this note as a practical joke."

"Possibly. Still . . ." There was hesitancy in Dr. Edwards' voice. "Mr. Jordan, I am a scientist. I have a precise and logical mind. Before we examine the authenticity of this note, let us logically figure out how the professor could have written the message, assuming he did write it. Let me think." There was a brief silence. "All right. I believe I have a logical scenario. The professor is in the Soviet Union. He makes his discovery. The Communists want it—in fact, he says in the note they want it—for themselves, I would guess. Professor MacDonald wants it for the world. That would be in character. He leaves the Soviet Union for wherever he can go. In this case he comes to Italy. The Russians learn he has left. They chase him or intercept him near Venice. They keep him on this island, before taking him back to the Soviet Union. Are there Russians in Venice? Is that logical?"

"A few, since Venice elected a Communist government recently."

"In the note—he speaks of being imprisoned by Communists. Could he mean Italian Communists?"

"He could," admitted Jordan, "but it doesn't seem likely. I can't see Italian Communists behaving this way. It's possible, but hard to believe."

"Still, if the Russians made them a promise—said, Look, we'll share his long-life discovery with you if you hold on to him until we can return him to the Soviet Union—that could have happened."

"It could have," conceded Jordan. "But it's hard for me to accept. It's all too fantastic. It sounds as if someone is having fun with whoever finds the note."

"It sounds real enough to me," said Dr. Edwards slowly. "I mean, everything in the message is factual or possible. He uses my name. He knows I am going to be at the hotel I'm at in Paris. He announces his discovery, when in fact his recent letters to me hinted he was onto something big. It very much sounds as if Professor MacDonald wrote that note."

Jordan remained skeptical. "But the information in his message—would anyone else know the same facts? Would anyone else know your name, that you were going to be at the Plaza Athénée in Paris right now? Would anyone else know he could be on the verge of so great a discovery?"

"Yes, any number of people would know all that."

"Then the note could have been written by someone else who happened to be in this area?"

She hesitated. "I suppose so. Although why anyone would do such a thing I can't imagine."

"Don't try to be logical about human motives, Dr. Edwards."

"I guess you are right."

Jordan glanced at the slip of paper again. "The note says he is being sent to the Soviet Union in two days— the day after tomorrow. What are you going to do?"

"I don't know," she wavered. "Could you—can you go to the local police in Venice and get them to investigate?"

Jordan considered the move. "No," he said, "I don't think that would be wise. If it is a hoax, I'd be laughed out of Venice. I'm willing to help a damsel in distress to a point, but I don't want to be made ridiculous. On the other hand, if it is not a hoax, I might be getting myself and the professor into real danger by going to the Italian police, who may have cooperated with the Russians in a kidnapping. What about you? Why don't you go to someone in authority in France? The note asks you to 'tell the world.'"

She was silent once more. Finally, she spoke. "I'm hesitating, because—well, if it proved to be a hoax, I don't mind being ridiculed, but what I'm afraid of is—if he is still in the Soviet Union going about his normal work, and this got out—the big plot, imprisonment, derring-do—and it weren't true, it would endanger his position there. At the same time, if I went to the Sûreté or Interpol or some of the important United Nations people the professor knows, and the news was leaked—the Communists on San Lazzaro would be alerted, and might rush him back to the U.S.S.R. before anything could be done, and then claim they'd never had him. It seems there is no way to act safely."

"Not as long as we don't know if this note is authentic or not."

Suddenly, the tone of Dr. Edwards' voice heightened. "I know what to do," she said with decision. "I'm going to find out whether that note you have is authentic."

"How?"

"By looking at it. Of course. I know Professor Mac-Donald's handwriting. If I see your note, I'll know whether he wrote it or not. If someone else wrote it, then this is all nonsense and we can forget it. But if I can verify that the note is in his hand, then we'll know it's all true, and we won't have to be afraid to take some action. Since our timing is so important, I'll take the first flight I can get to Venice. Hold on, let me find out when there is a flight. I'll ring the concierge on the other phone."

Jordan sat with the dead phone in his hand and pondered what fate had got him mixed up in this improbable affair with this strange lady.

In a minute, she was back on the line. "Hello, are you there?"

"I'm here."

"There's a flight in two hours from De Gaulle. Alitalia. It takes an hour and a half to get from Paris to Venice. I'll be there at four-thirty. Can you meet me at the airport with the note? It would be kind of you. We could solve it then and there. If Professor MacDonald wrote that note, and made his discovery, it would be a matter of life or death for the whole world."

"I'll be there," said Jordan. "Hey, whom do I look for?"

"Look for the prettiest young woman leaving the jet-liner."

With that she hung up.

Jordan dropped the receiver into the cradle of the phone, stared at it a few seconds, then lifted it up again. He punched the intercom and pressed down Marisa's number.

"Marisa? About dinner tonight—I'm afraid I'm going to be tied up—an emergency—I have to be at the airport to meet a visiting fireman. . . . What is a visiting fireman? I'll explain it the next time I see you. For now, let's say it is someone important. Okay?"

▶ ▶ ▶ ▶

She was indeed the prettiest young woman off the airplane.

Originally, when he had spoken to her on the telephone and she had told him she was a scientist, Professor MacDonald's research associate, he had conjured up a picture of a stereotype. He had envisioned her as a cold, efficient virgin, fortyish, wearing bangs, horn-rimmed spectacles, compressed lips, and lots of jaw. This picture had gone up in smoke when, just before hanging up, she had frankly told him that she was pretty. During the next hours in his office, marking time until he would meet her, he had tried to frame a new picture and it had come to nothing. He had decided, upon arriving at Marco Polo Airport, that he would be watching for a glacial blonde who was probably an aggressive feminist.

Now, posted outside the air terminal looking in, Jordan smoked his straight-stemmed pipe and kept an eye out for her as he watched the first passengers from Paris go through customs with their hand baggage.

Then he saw her—was certain it was she—because she had the kind of good looks that made you turn your head on the street. She was rather tall, maybe five feet six, erect, poised, graceful, carrying a short beige jacket and wearing a blouse of some material that clung to her pointed, shimmying breasts and a short skirt. She was neither glacial nor blond. She was animated and brunette. She had a short gamin haircut, smooth brow, big eyes behind her oversized lavender sunglasses, a pert nose, full red lips, and she was in her ripe mid-twenties. He had seen her before in a half dozen lush paintings by Boucher—Marie Louise O'Morphi.

She was coming directly at him, carrying an Hermès overnighter in one hand and a brown leather purse under her other arm.

"Mr. Jordan," she said. No question mark. "I'm Alison Edwards."

"I know," he said. "How did *you* know?"

She looked him over. "You're just what I pictured. Maybe a little flabby, less muscular."

"Well, you're not," he said with a laugh. "Not what I pictured, I mean."

"The 'Doctor' in 'Dr. Edwards' always puts people off. It's formidable. I'm not. Right now I'm scared and nervous, and trying to hide it."

"Nothing to worry about yet. Here, give me your bag." He took it. "I have a boat waiting. I think we'd better be moving."

Once they were shut inside the cabin of the motor launch, seated facing each other, the craft cast off, rocked around, and was soon cutting the water toward Venice.

Her face had become anxious. "Do you have the—the note?"

"I left it in my suite. I thought it better if you saw it and discussed it in privacy."

"Do you have any new thoughts?"

He glanced at the pilot. "If I did, I wouldn't discuss

them here. Actually, I don't. Everything depends on what you say about the handwriting."

"Yes," she said. "That'll tell."

"Have you ever been to Venice?"

"No. I've always dreamed of coming here—under different circumstances. In fact, this is my first time away from the States." She peered outside across the prow of the motorboat. "Exactly where are we going?"

"Hotel Danieli, right in Venice. I keep a year-round suite there. I reserved an adjoining room for you."

"Oh, I don't think I'll be here long enough for that. I made a reservation on the last flight back to Paris a few hours from now."

"Then you think it's all a hoax, and your boss is safe and sound in—in wherever he is in the Soviet Union?"

She evaded the question. "I put through a call to him, to see if he was really there, just outside Sukhumi, a town in western Georgia. It was hopeless. You never get through. I've tried before. Never once got a call through to him. We stay in touch by mail." Her eyes—brown, he guessed—held on him through the lavender sunglasses. "Fact or fiction. I don't know what to think."

"You'll know in twenty minutes," he said, and he sat back to smoke, wondering why he wished he were less flabby and more muscular.

In twenty minutes, as he had predicted, they were at the Danieli, ready for the moment of truth. They stepped out onto the boat landing alongside the Danieli, went into the lobby, climbed one flight of broad red-carpeted marble stairs to the first floor, turned right and crossed to the second flight of stairs, climbed them, and near the top of the staircase entered suite 226.

The familiar large sitting room—brown diamond-patterned carpet, beige walls, three-cushioned green sofa, two green armchairs facing the sofa, small brown refrigerator with its tray of bottles and glasses, leather-topped desk, another sofa—was cool and darkened, since the maid had closed the heavy green wooden shutters against the sun. While Alison Edwards washed her face and touched up her lips, Jordan deposited her over-nighter on the light brown bedspread in her adjacent bedroom. Then he crossed the sitting room to his own larger bedroom, unlocked the suitcase resting on his double bed, and retrieved the note signed by Professor MacDonald.

Back in the sitting room, he pushed the shutters on each window aside and allowed the day's last sun to stream in. Remaining at one window, he shaded his eyes and squinted in the direction of San Lazzaro, which was blocked from sight by the island before it. Could one of the most prominent scientists in the world, with a discovery that would shake the foundations of mankind, actually be imprisoned on a piece of land in the midst of this placid lagoon and this busy tourist paradise? It seemed most unlikely.

As Alison Edwards came into the room, he turned toward his desk and motioned for her to sit down.

"Okay, here it is," he said.

She had removed her sunglasses, and her wide brown eyes followed his hand as he laid the slip of paper on the desk before her.

She stared at it as if mesmerized, reached out and took it by each end, and brought it up closer to her eyes. She studied it in silence, her features rigid. She raised her head toward him. Her face was sheet-white.

"It's his," she said almost inaudibly. "It's in Professor MacDonald's handwriting and it's his signature. I've seen his handwriting a thousand times. There's no mistaking it. This appeal for help was written by Professor MacDonald, no other. It's for real!"

The single hand now holding the note began to quiver, and she looked as if she might cry. Gently, Jordan took the note from her and slipped it into his pocket.

She was on her feet. "He's actually a prisoner on San

Lazzaro. They're going to send him back to the Soviet Union in two days. The world will never see him—or his secret—again. Mr. Jordan, we've got to save him." She clutched Jordan's arm. "What should we do?"

▶ ▶ ▶ ▶

A half hour later, her question still echoed in his head. What should we do?

We.

Any further involvement with her, any part at all in this mysterious and potentially troublesome enterprise gave him pause. It was not his sort of thing, not at this time in his rattled life. He was not seeking commitment. Yet maybe in some hidden reach of his heart, he was seeking—*something*.

"Dr. Edwards," he had said, "let me think about it. I'm going downstairs. I'm out of tobacco. I won't be long. No more than a half hour. Then we'll sit down and calmly discuss the best course."

He had left her, very much alone and very wretched, himself feeling a minor betrayer, since he would be weighing his role in Professor MacDonald's fate and since he might return with a verdict that would cast her out on her own and helpless.

Troubled, he had made his way downstairs through the hotel lobby and outdoors, and dutifully bought his pack of tobacco, although he did not need it, and continued to the Gran' Caffè Chioggia in the Piazzetta. There, seated isolated in the third row, facing the façade of the Doges' Palace, still dazzling in the late daylight, he erased the diverting sights of Venice from his vision and turned his mind's eye inward.

Jordan pictured Alison Edwards, and he liked what he saw. It was an incomplete picture, but there was enough of it to attract him. His first instinct was to help someone who was pretty and who was lost. Of Professor Mac-

Donald he could form no clear picture, except that of some sort of savant, a blurred cross between Einstein and Schweitzer, who had made a remarkable, life-changing discovery and had been imprisoned for it and had communicated his terrible predicament in a most improbable way.

But most sharply defined was the thing at stake.

The Fountain of Youth, MacDonald had called it in his note.

Jordan asked himself a single question: Was it worth a commitment that might seriously disrupt his euphoric, if discontented, life?

His mind immediately rejected any commitment. Selfishly, he wanted no association with others, especially not with the lives of two strangers. He wanted no changes, no ventures into the unknown. He wanted no action, no move that would make him more conspicuous in Venice, no effort that would alter the routine of his near-empty days. Certainly, he wanted no role of decision-making that would make others dependent upon him.

In this mood, he questioned what was at stake, was doubtful of its value. There were no details except that the essence of it was an extension of human life. Was that so important? Either a God in heaven or some accident of nature had given humans their three score and ten years on earth, and there was no voice to say life would be improved by tampering with it. If such a discovery had been able to save Claire from her insane death, that would have been different. But it could no longer affect her or anyone like her. Or himself, the survivor, Claire's survivor? Could it be meaningful to him? He had an instant answer. Today's answer. For him, a prolongation of life meant only a prolongation of pain. He preferred to wait out his time to seventy rather than 100 or 170. As far as he was concerned, the damn discovery meant only that old people would grow older. With one except—except if one of the old people were his father.

His father.

Immediately, the cynical logic in Jordan's mind faded and was supplanted by a feeling, the familiar other ache in his heart.

He had been raised in a small, peaceful Wisconsin town, an hour's drive north of Chicago, by his father, Michael Jordan, the only parent he had ever known and one whom he had admired and loved. Jordan's mother had died of pneumonia a year after his birth. The women in the house had been his older sister and a spinster aunt, who was his father's sister and junior, forever with a dishrag or dust mop in hand. His father, having sired him when past fifty, had already been advanced in years when Jordan entered college.

Jordan found himself smiling as he remembered his father. The old man had been the most popular teacher in the local high school. Michael Jordan taught English—not grammar, but literature—and every evening, seven nights a week, he worked on his opus, *The Land of Evermore,* the story of life in a utopia of the future. In dim memory throughout Jordan's childhood, and in better memory throughout his adolescence, his father had been making preparatory notes on his epic utopia and its story. About the time Jordan graduated from high school and had been accepted by a university, his father had finally felt ready to set his grand design on paper as a novel and had begun writing it.

Several times before his graduation from college, Jordan had asked to read what his father had written to that point. The first time, his father had told him the manuscript was not yet in shape to be read. The next time, his father had told him to read Plato's *The Republic,* Thomas More's *Utopia,* Tommaso Campanella's *The City of the Sun,* and James Harrington's *Oceana,* as a means of comparison before reading his own book. Enthusiastically, Jordan had undertaken the assignment. He had read three of the four books, with growing excitement at the opportunity of reading his father's life work, when a midnight telephone call had summoned him home to Wisconsin.

That afternoon while driving from the high school to his house, Michael Jordan had suffered a blackout, his car had gone out of control, and he had hit a tree. He would recover, but not as the same person. The doctor's diagnosis had been a hitherto undetected hardening of the arteries of the brain, with total senility perhaps a year off.

Soon his father had to give up his teaching post, and never again did he put pen to paper. Jordan had no heart to read his manuscript at that time. The old man languished briefly in a sanitarium, a vegetable, and then, aged seventy-four, he died in his sleep.

After the funeral, Jordan stayed on a week in the bleak and empty house, consoling his sister and his aunt, studying artifacts of his past, and one day he steeled himself, removed the unfinished manuscript from the old man's desk, and lay down on the porch hammock to read it.

By nightfall he had read all there was to read of it, mesmerized for hours by its scholarship, wit, movement, innovation, this blueprint for a new way of life, and then abruptly it was over in mid-sentence. Jordan had lain back, stunned. A towering work, one that could have changed the world—and here only a fragment of manuscript, one-fourth done, never to be finished, with no brain in the world capable of continuing what had been in his father's mind. The loss was as traumatic for Jordan as the loss of his father, although he knew these two losses were one and the same. The ache in his heart had begun.

Had his father not suffered senility at seventy-two, had there been the means of prolonging his life as a healthy and productive person, how the world might have changed for the better.

In the same way, Jordan could see, Professor Mac-Donald's own work might change the world for the better. Indeed, it would prolong the lives of thousands, even millions, of Michael Jordans who might be on the verge of enriching humanity.

And he himself—he was still an extension of his father. Not yet senile, not yet dead, except as he willed these conditions prematurely upon himself. Given a new life, a prolonged life, he might find a way to live his Claire-less life to its destined end. With time, he might become a great writer, as his father had almost been, and he might find another woman and even have the child he had wanted by Claire.

The moment had come for decision, and the choice had been simplified.

To go back to the young woman in the hotel, to Dr. Alison Edwards, and tell her that he was in no position to get involved further. To tell her nicely, reluctantly, that she was on her own. To advise her to do the only sensible thing that could be done—namely, take the professor's note to the police, the carabinieri, and assume that they were decent and honest and would help her save MacDonald. But he knew, instinctively, that this would mean that the professor's discovery would not be for the world.

Or to go back to Alison and tell her that he was ready to help her as far as was humanly possible and then hope for the best.

An outside chance to save the Fountain of Youth.

Timothy Jordan stood up, paid his bill and left the Gran' Caffè Chioggia to return to the Hotel Danieli—and commitment.

▶ ▶ ▶ ▶

They sat in the sitting room talking it out, discussing every possibility on earth no matter how farfetched, and they were still there weighing their options.

By now she had calmed down, regained her composure and poise, and was being very sensible. By now
they had had two Bellinis apiece from room service, and
the blend of champagne and peach juice had helped
settle them. And by now he was comfortably Tim, and
she was Alison.

She was deep in the sofa and he in the armchair across
from her. She was saying, "Poor man, look what you got
yourself involved in, an innocent bystander who liked
pigeons."

"At least it's a challenge," he said. He did not mention
his father. "Maybe that is what I've been needing."

"Nobody needs anything like this," she said. "It is just
too much."

He kept his eyes on her, without speaking. He knew
next to nothing about her personally, yet the past hour
had made him feel profoundly close to this beautiful
stranger.

Alison had straightened on the sofa, and she looked
Dr. Edwardsish—competent, intelligent, together.

"I've got my head on," she said, "and I think we've
done enough exploring of possibilities. I am ready to
make a choice and a decision. If we discard all romantic
ideas, our talk really narrows down to two possible logical actions. Don't you think so?"

"Spell them out, Alison. Let's see if we're on the same
wavelength."

"Very well," she said matter-of-factly. "Either we go
to the authorities, the Venice police, and hope they are
no part of this plot and will be on our side. Or we go to
the monks on San Lazzaro and confront them with the
professor's note. One or the other might net results.
Which do you suggest?"

"Neither," said Jordan.

"Neither?"

"To me, the direct approach seems hopeless. As hopeless as calling in an outside organization like Interpol.
We agreed that if you called Interpol or anyone else, they

couldn't just come here and barge into San Lazzaro. An outsider would contact the Soviets or Italians, who would deny the kidnapping while whisking MacDonald away, and then they would invite the foreign investigators to look for themselves. Well, it would be the same if we went to the police or to the Armenian monks. No one could abduct someone like MacDonald right here in Venice, keep him a prisoner, without both police complicity and the voluntary or involuntary cooperation of the monks. So if we go to either of them with the note, they will say it is a crazy forgery, say they have no knowledge of MacDonald's whereabouts, move him off San Lazzaro, and invite us to see for ourselves. At best, the police might pretend to look into the matter, investigate, and then tell us they had found no trace of a Professor MacDonald, imprisoned or otherwise. No, Alison, the direct approach won't do."

"But we've got to do something," Alison said desperately. "We're running out of time."

Jordan was lost in thought. Gradually, he began to speak his mind. "It's no use going to the police. Let's forget them. That leaves the monks on San Lazzaro. I know all about them. They're a decent lot, good-hearted, charitable. I've been over there sight-seeing and have visited with some of them. Besides, one of my best friends here in Venice—an Armenian who owns a glass shop—has a nephew who is a member of the order on San Lazzaro, and he's always telling . . ." Abruptly, in mid sentence, Jordan stopped speaking. He sat up, staring at Alison. "By God," he said, "maybe that's the way. Sembut. Sembut Nurikhan."

Alison showed her bewilderment. "What are you saying?"

"Listen," said Jordan excitedly, almost coming off the chair, "I have an Armenian friend here, a good friend, named Sembut Nurikhan. He has an older brother in Mestre—that's the nearest mainland city—who has been very ill. The brother's youngest son became a member of the Mechitarist Congregation on San Lazzaro. For his brother's sake, and because he likes the boy, Sembut keeps in close touch with his nephew, helps him with money and in other ways. Don't you see, Alison? This gives us a contact on San Lazzaro." Jordan stood up. "I know Sembut telephones his nephew at least once a week, to report to the boy on his father's condition and to find out how the boy is doing. That means it is possible to get a phone call through to San Lazzaro. I'll go to Sembut and explain the situation honestly. Tell him what's happened."

"Can you trust him?" Alison interrupted. "After all—"

"Completely," said Jordan. "I'll get Sembut to call his nephew. Try to find out for us what's going on—and if there is some way his nephew can help us, or get someone to help us. . . ."

Alison was still worried. "Will he be able to talk on the phone?"

"We can only find out."

"When?"

He took her by the arm. "Right now."

▶ ▶ ▶ ▶

Night was beginning to fall when they hurried up the alley called Ramo San Zulian and into the Campo San Zulian. The store windows in the small square were lighting up for the evening's business, but as far as Jordan could see, Nurikhan's Glass Shop was darkened. That instant, Sembut Nurikhan stepped out of the store into the thoroughfare and began to draw down the metal shutters that protected his front entrance.

Holding Alison's arm, Jordan hailed his friend and accelerated his pace.

The Armenian proprietor halted what he was doing,

adjusted his gold-rimmed glasses to make out who had
called his name, and then broke into a smile. "Ah, Tim,
it is you. I was closing the shop early to go to Mestre to
visit my brother. He is confined to bed, I am sorry to say.
He appreciates company. You came to see me?"

"Yes. I must speak to you, Sembut. I'm sorry to delay
you, but I need your help. This is an urgent matter."

"Of course. . . ." His magnified eyes strayed to Alison.

"Sembut," said Jordan, "I want you to meet a dear
friend of mine from New York, Miss—Dr. Alison Edwards."

"My pleasure," said the shopkeeper gallantly, shaking
her hand. "Well, come inside where we can talk."

"Thank you," said Jordan.

He and Alison waited for the Armenian to unlock the
front door, and then they followed him into the glass
shop. Nurikhan locked the door from the inside. He
apologized for the lack of lighting. "I do not want customers to disturb us. Do you want to sit down?"

"Not necessary, Sembut. Let me get right into it."

"Please."

"Something bizarre happened to me today at Quadri's,
after I finished breakfast. . . ."

As briefly as possible, Jordan recounted the events of
the day from the time that he had found Professor
MacDonald's note tied to the dead pigeon's leg to the
time that Dr. Alison Edwards had arrived from Paris and
authenticated the note.

As he listened, the Armenian proprietor's face, usually
phlegmatic, plainly reflected his astonishment.

"And so," Jordan concluded, "the Mechitarist monks
have Professor MacDonald a prisoner on San Lazzaro,
and they are sending him back to the Soviet Union the
day after tomorrow. Now you know the situation."

The proprietor searched Jordan's face. "You are, as
you Americans say, pulling my leg, are you not?"

"Why would I, Sembut? No, every word I have told

you is true. They've kidnapped and are holding this man."

The proprietor's skepticism was evident. "I cannot believe this. There must be some mistake. I am at San Lazzaro often to see my brother's boy, Pashal, and I know all of the monks. They are gentle human beings, recluses, concerned only with the Lord. They would kidnap no one on earth. They would not imprison another soul."

"Wait, Sembut," Jordan interrupted. "I'm not saying the monks had anything to do with this. I suspect it was all done by the local Communists, who control the police, as a favor to their comrades in Russia. Dr. Edwards and I don't know exactly what happened, but we strongly suspect the Communists here wanted a place to hide Professor MacDonald until he could be sent back, and they selected San Lazzaro because it is isolated, not often visited, and they forced the abbot and the few resident monks to cooperate. You know how dependent the abbot is on the city administration."

"That part is true," agreed the shopkeeper. Most of his initial skepticism had vanished. "But why on earth would anyone want to arrest and hold a man you call an eminent British-American scientist?"

In relating his story, Jordan had purposely not uttered a word about Professor MacDonald's specialty and his momentous discovery. He hesitated. Instinct told him not to speak of it now or ever, unless he had to do so. He glanced at Alison and thought she knew what he was thinking and agreed with it. Jordan decided to answer his friend's question as ambiguously as possible. "They are holding Professor MacDonald because he has made some secret discovery in the field of biology. The Russians want the professor because they want his finding exclusively for themselves."

Sembut Nurikhan appeared satisfied. "And me? Where do I fit in this story?"

"Someone has to free the professor. We can't go to the carabinieri. They are probably working hand in hand with the KGB as comrades. We can't ask for outside intervention, because the moment the Communists learned of it, they would remove the professor from San Lazzaro to God knows where. Our only hope is to get some friendly monks on the island—or one monk—to act mercifully and help the prisoner escape. I know none of the monks well enough. Then I thought of you. . . ."

"You want my nephew Pashal to help. That is it?"

"Yes, that is it."

The shopkeeper tugged nervously at his bow tie. "You want me to telephone San Lazzaro and—what? Ask to speak to my nephew? Ask him if anything unusual is happening?"

Jordan nodded. "Something like that. If he can talk, find out if MacDonald is actually being confined there. If your nephew knows about this or confirms it, find out if he has access to the prisoner or if he knows anyone on the island who has access to him. From then on, we can play it by ear." Jordan briefly placed an arm around his friend's shoulders. "This would be an important favor, Sembut. We know it's a long shot. But we can't think of anything else. And—well—you never can tell."

Alison edged forward. "Mr. Nurikhan, we'd be most grateful."

The Armenian shopkeeper made a motion of surrender. "I will try. You both come with me."

He led them between tables crowded with glassware to the rear of the shop and into the cubicle that served as his office. He flicked on a lamp, settled gingerly behind a rolltop desk, and drew the telephone toward him. Jordan and Alison hovered close by.

The shopkeeper raised his head, his eyes meeting Jordan's. "If what you have told me, Tim, is true, this will be difficult." He shrugged. "Let us find out."

He lifted the receiver off the telephone, and with care he dialed a number.

He listened. "It is ringing," he said. He waited.

He was alert. Someone had answered the phone.

"Hello," he said in English. "This is Sembut Nurikhan in Venice. I—" He paused, listened. "Ah, yes. It is good to speak to you too, Vartan. I am calling to have a word with my nephew, with Padre Pashal, if I may. I want to discuss his father with him. . . . Thank you. I will hold."

The shopkeeper cupped his hand over the mouthpiece of the telephone and addressed Jordan. "That was a friend of Pashal's. He has gone to the refectory to fetch Pashal. At least they are answering the phone."

He now held the receiver tightly, pressing it to his ear.

Suddenly, the shopkeeper sat up. "Ah, it is you, Pashal. How are you?"

As his nephew, on the other end, answered, Nurikhan signaled Jordan to listen with him. He held the receiver back a few inches from his ear, took Jordan by the sleeve, and pulled him down behind him, so that Jordan's own ear was near the receiver and within hearing of the voice.

"As long as you are well, Pashal," the shopkeeper was saying. "I'll tell you why I call. I have been discussing your father with Dr. Scarpa. A new cardiac treatment has been recommended. I thought I would come over to San Lazzaro tomorrow so that we can talk about it."

Jordan could hear the young voice on the other end— tinny, anxious. "Impossible, Uncle Sembut. The abbot is allowing no visitors tomorrow or the following day. When it is possible to visit, I will call you."

"No visitors tomorrow," repeated Nurikhan. "I have never heard of such a thing before. Why is this?"

The distant voice dropped. "I cannot talk about it now."

Nurikhan cast a sidelong glance at Jordan, who nodded. The shopkeeper nodded back and spoke into the mouthpiece. "Perhaps *I* can talk about it. You need only confirm if I am right or tell me if I am wrong. I have heard—from someone—you are holding a prisoner on San Lazzaro."

There was a silence on the other end. Then Pashal uttered one word. "Yes," he said.

"A British professor?"

"Yes."

"Do the police know about this?"

"Yes."

"You mean they are part of it?"

Pashal's voice was reluctant. "Yes."

"A moment, Pashal," said Nurikhan. "Do not go away." He covered the mouthpiece with his free hand, and looked up at Jordan. "You heard, Tim. It is as you guessed. What do I say next?"

Jordan was ready. "Ask—ask your nephew if the prisoner is accessible to him or to one of his brothers."

The shopkeeper removed his hand from the phone and spoke into it. "Is the prisoner accessible to you, Pashal?"

A long pause. "Sometimes." Another pause. "To two of us."

Jordan whispered, "Will the prisoner be accessible to your nephew tonight?"

The shopkeeper repeated the question into the phone.

Jordan heard Pashal's answer. "No. I have different duties tonight."

"Tomorrow night?" Jordan whispered to Nurikhan, who immediately repeated the question into the phone.

"Yes," Pashal answered.

Jordan gripped his friend's shoulder. "Ask your nephew if I came quietly tomorrow night, could he turn the professor over to me outside the front door or on the pier?"

Nurikhan held back, troubled. At last he directed himself to the phone. "Pashal," he said softly, "if someone came discreetly to San Lazzaro tomorrow night, could you turn the professor over to him?"

Jordan looked at Alison. She was holding her breath. He bent closer to the receiver, then heard Pashal's voice distinctly. "No. I cannot. Too dangerous."

Jordan wanted to yank the telephone from his friend's grasp and plead with the young man, let the monk know the secret MacDonald carried, what it meant to civilization, what it could mean to Pashal himself and to his father. To his father. Jordan had his friend's shoulder again, drawing him partially nearer. "Listen to me, Sembut. Neither you nor your nephew know what is at stake. I had better tell you. You worry about your brother, his father, because he is gravely ill. What would you give to save him? You can. This is your chance. You can give your brother many more years of health and life." He looked at Alison desperately, floundering.

"Seventy more years of life," said Alison quickly. "That was Professor MacDonald's goal. He wrote of doubling the human life-span."

"You heard her," said Jordan to Nurikhan. "She is Professor MacDonald's associate. The professor is one of the world's leading gerontologists. Why do you think the Communists are holding him a prisoner on San Lazzaro? Because Professor MacDonald has just found the means of prolonging human life. The Communists want the secret for themselves. The professor wants it for every human on earth, including your brother, the boy's father. The professor could save him."

Ignoring the telephone, Nurikhan stared at Jordan. "This is possible?" he said with incredulity.

"It is the truth," said Jordan. "A fact. If your nephew will help us, I guarantee that his father will be one of the first to be treated by Professor MacDonald."

Nurikhan continued to stare at Jordan. "You would guarantee it?"

"You have my word," said Jordan fervently.

Nurikhan sat blinking, taking in both Jordan and Alison and, finally, the open phone. He spoke into the phone. "Pashal," he said quietly, "you heard? My friend is a truthful and honorable man."

The shopkeeper was listening to his nephew on the other end. When he spoke into the phone once more, it was in Armenian. Then, for an interval, he listened, nodding at the telephone. One more word in Armenian, and he slowly hung up.

He turned in his chair and faced Jordan. "He will risk it. Be at San Lazzaro pier tomorrow night at exactly ten o'clock."

▶ ▶ ▶ ▶

All through the following day, Jordan had tried to block the evening's rescue attempt from his mind. He was not a man of action, of adventure. He was, as a creative engineer turned creative writer and public relations person, essentially a dreamer and passive creature. To dwell on the rescue he had so mindlessly agreed to undertake in the evening would have thrown him into a fit of anxiety.

But now—carrying Alison's overnighter, as he followed her through the revolving front door of the Hotel Danieli and started toward the waiting motorboat his gondolier friend, Luigi Cipolate, had rented for him— Jordan was assailed by the reality of the situation, and he was taut with apprehension.

He saw the gondolier standing beside the motorboat. He glanced at his watch. "Nine forty-five," he said to Alison. "Right on schedule. But we can't waste a moment."

They reached the gondolier. Jordan greeted him, then considered the motorboat. It was a low-slung arrow of a craft, capable of carrying six passengers.

"You like it?" asked the gondolier. "The fastest small one I could find."

"*Strigheta*, old pal, thank you."

The gondolier assisted Alison into the boat and next took Jordan's arm to assist him. "You can still change your mind, Timothy," he said. "To take your lady out for a pleasure ride in a motorboat, it is unromantic. Come, I take you in my gondola."

Jordan smiled. "Next time, pal." He saw that Alison was safely seated, and he positioned himself at the wheel. He started the engine as Cipolate untied the rope from the piling and dropped it into the boat. "I'll see you in an hour or less," Jordan promised, and he backed the boat off between the pilings and into the open lagoon.

Quickly, they were pointed toward San Lazzaro and under way. After slowing once for a vaporetto that plowed across his prow, Jordan cut loose, and the boat's nose lifted out of the water and it skimmed across the lagoon like a water bug.

Although the night retained the warmth of the day, the spray refreshed Jordan, and all his senses were awakened.

He saw Alison out of the corner of his eye, and her poise and lack of anxiety continued to amaze him. A basic scientist's personality, he thought—low-keyed and cool. She was wearing a blue velvet cap, a striped gondolier's shirt, and new jeans, all purchased during her first wanderings through Venice that afternoon, when he had left her to do what had to be done. Jordan had not wanted her along on this rescue attempt, but as he had developed the escape plan, he had seen that her presence was necessary.

He had gone over the plan with her two or three times. Originally, because no planes to Paris were available at this hour, he had hoped to put Alison and Professor MacDonald on a late train to Paris. But it had not worked out. The last train for Paris departed earlier. That left only one other means for a safe and hasty departure—a rented Fiat. It had turned out that Alison had her own car in the States and drove all the time. Actually, Jordan had realized, a rented car would be the only way to cap the escape successfully. Had there been a train, they might have been overtaken by the police in their wagon-lit compartment.

The plan had been simple, and its completion depended entirely on a matter of timing. Assuming that Pashal delivered the professor to the San Lazzaro pier as promised, assuming that there were no unexpected interferences or delays, there would be just time enough to get the pair to the rented Fiat before the police could block them. Jordan had tried to anticipate what would happen from the moment that he had Professor MacDonald in his motorboat and sped past Venice toward the Piazzale Roma, where they would find the car that would take them over the causeway to the mainland city of Mestre. Calculation of time had been difficult, because Jordan had possessed no knowledge of how closely MacDonald was being guarded. If no one checked on him during the night, his disappearance would not be known until morning, when he would be safely in France. If someone checked his room or cell during the night, his disappearance might be discovered in a half hour or an hour or several hours, yet allow a sufficient head start to get him to Mestre before the swift motor launches of the Guardia di Finanza had been alerted and could intercept Jordan and his own boat.

Throughout the day, Jordan had occupied himself with preparations.

The first thing this morning, he had telephoned the office and told Marisa that he was tied up and would not be in today, but he had assured her that he would be at his desk tomorrow. Then, after giving Alison instructions on where to shop for herself, he had caught a vaporetto to the Piazzale Roma and had made arrangements for the rented Fiat to be ready by ten-thirty this evening.

Returning to his hotel, he had called room service for a cheese sandwich and while eating lunch had skimmed yesterday's edition of the *International Herald Tribune*. When the motoscafo ferry service between the Danieli and the Hotel Excelsior at the Lido resumed, he had caught the first launch for the short crossing. Midway, the launch had passed the clump of land that was the island of San Lazzaro. Standing on the narrow open deck of the boat, between the pilot and the rear awning, Jordan had examined San Lazzaro with greater care than he had in the past year. There was the two-story ancient monastery with its red tile roof, squatting in silence, no sign of life anywhere in the front. The monastery entrance sat back about fifty feet—maybe more—from the wooden pier, with its stairs leading down to a platform above the waterline.

An hour later, when he had returned from the Excelsior to the Danieli, again passing close to San Lazzaro, he had studied the scene once more, and by the time it had receded from view he felt that he had his night's destination clearly mapped in his mind.

Back in the Danieli, there had been one more thing that niggled at him. The idea of it, the melodrama of it, embarrassed him, yet he felt it was necessary. He had gone to the concierge's desk and waited for his longtime friend and sometime confidant Carlo Fabris, the head concierge, to get off the phone.

The concierge had finally finished with the phone. "Yes, Mr. Jordan?"

Jordan had lowered his voice so that other tourists along the counter would not overhear him. "Mr. Fabris, I want to borrow or rent a gun—something small, compact, an automatic, with a full clip of ammunition. Is it possible to have it before six o'clock?"

Mr. Fabris' good-natured, beefy, sunburned countenance had expressed neither surprise nor curiosity. "Do you have any preference as to make?"

"None whatsoever."

"Then no problem. It shall be delivered to your suite by six o'clock."

Although Fabris, perfect concierge, never questioned unusual requests made by hotel guests, Jordan had felt that this most uncharacteristic request did deserve some kind of explanation. "The gun—it's for a contest. Some friends at Mestre are having a sharpshooting contest with targets."

Fabris had tendered a benign smile. "I hope you win."

The gun had been discreetly delivered in a brown paper bag to Jordan's suite at a quarter to six.

That had been four hours ago.

Now, at the wheel of the motorboat speeding toward San Lazzaro, adhering to the illuminated deep-channel lagoon route, he dropped one hand down to his jacket pocket and felt the secure bulge of the revolver. He could not imagine using it, and then he could. In minutes he would be entering the guarded lair of Communist agents who were holding a genius of the free world in captivity. If all went smoothly, as he prayed it would, the gun would be as useless as pabulum. But if something went wrong, well, he was armed with a defensive weapon.

He met Alison's eyes briefly. He smiled, and she smiled back, but both smiles, he knew, were more like nervous twitches.

Off to his left, beyond the yellow illumination of the lagoon's traffic lane, he saw the hulk of a building loom up and enlarge.

"San Servolo," he said to Alison. "The island just before San Lazzaro. We'll be there in a few minutes."

He remembered that San Servolo was the site of a mental institution and that any boats he had ever taken past it always slowed down. He presumed that was a Venetian law, and he quickly reduced his craft's power.

Leaving San Servolo, he saw San Lazzaro before him, and he wheeled his motorboat toward it and kept the speed down. He glimpsed his watch. The time was six minutes to ten o'clock.

He made out the wooden pier jutting into the water.

"We're here," he said quietly to Alison.

He shut off the engine and let the boat glide forward, stepping sideways to catch a piling and hold the craft from bumping. He pulled at the piling, dragging the boat forward against the lower platform.

"Okay," he said to Alison.

She was already on her feet behind him, preparing to perform what they had worked out earlier in the evening. She took up the rope, ran it around the piling, and knotted it loosely.

In the dim light shining down from a lamp above the pier he made out the time once more.

"Three minutes," he said, his heart going harder. "Wait here at the rope. The second MacDonald and I are back down here, untie the rope and pull it free. I'll do the rest."

He was wearing sneakers, and he stepped off the motorboat onto the platform without a sound. He went gingerly up the slippery first steps, more solidly up the rest. At the second step from the top, he halted. He held up his wristwatch again. Two minutes. Less.

Would Pashal emerge with Professor MacDonald?

How would he manage it?

Would anyone else be alerted?

He held his breath and concentrated on the front door of the monastery. Except for crickets, a bird, the night was still. He stood frozen, expectant.

Suddenly a sliver of light, then a beam pierced the semidarkness from the monastery front. The door was opening. One figure slipped out, followed by another, as the door was partially closed.

Jordan came up the remaining steps, attaining the top

of the pier, and hastened across it toward the forecourt. At the end of the pier, they met him.

The tall, thin young monk came first, his Adam's apple continuously jumping.

"Pashal?" Jordan whispered.

"Yes."

"You have him?"

"Here is Professor MacDonald." He backed aside, revealing a much shorter elderly man, white hair, wire-framed spectacles, white moustache, his face a mixture of confusion and fear.

Jordan grabbed the professor by the arm, drawing him toward the wharf. "Go to the end of the pier, down the steps—carefully, they're wet. Get into the motorboat. Dr. Edwards is waiting. I'll be right behind you." He turned quickly back to the monk. "Pashal, we don't know how to thank you. I'll never know how you did it, but what you've done will have God's blessings forever. Good-bye."

As he wheeled to leave, the young monk's strong hand clamped on his shoulder.

"Wait," Pashal Nurikhan whispered.

"What is it?"

"I must have some explanation," the monk said urgently. "I had to take him to the bathroom, that is how I got him past Antonio, his carabinieri guard outside his room. When I return without the professor—I have concocted a story to protect me—you must help—"

"Tell me, but hurry."

"I will say a stranger came with a gun as we left the bathroom, forced me out here. I tried to overcome him. He knocked me down and fled in a motorboat. So, please, now. Knock me down, so it looks real—now. . . ."

Jordan recoiled. "Just hit you? I can't—"

"You must," Pashal whispered fiercely, "to protect me. Then I will stumble back and shout what has happened and collapse."

"Hey, hold it," said Jordan. "If you alert the whole damn monastery, I'll have no time to get them to the Piazzale Roma and out of the country. The second you yell out, the Venice boat patrols will be called—"

"It is not my business what happens after you go. We have made a deal. MacDonald will save my father if I save MacDonald by bringing him to you. I have done my part."

"Yes, Pashal, but don't you see, getting him out of Venice was also . . ."

That instant, the illumination from the front door of the monastery widened, engulfed them like a searchlight. Terrified, they both spun toward the monastery.

In the doorway, filling it, was a bulky uniformed man, rifle slung over his shoulder. His hand had gone up to his mouth. "What's going on out there?" he bellowed.

Frantically, the monk had Jordan by the lapels. "Hit me," he implored.

On reflex, Jordan's hand snaked to his pocket, yanked out the pistol, and he slammed the butt flat against Pashal's head. The monk cried out in pain, clutched at his bleeding temple, and went down to his knees, groaning.

For a split second, Jordan looked up. The uniformed guard had shouted, "Who is it?" He was pulling the rifle off his shoulder as he came out of the doorway on the run.

Jordan whirled toward the empty pier, tucking his pistol into his pocket. He rushed across the pier, stepped down, gripped the rail as he maneuvered his descent of the slippery steps. The motorboat was there, rocking in the water, with Alison at the rope and MacDonald in a seat.

"Let's go!" yelled Jordan, leaping into the motorboat, staggering behind the wheel, as Alison freed the rope.

Jordan had the engine coughing, coughing, and at last it started with a roar. He reversed the boat, pulled the wheel around sharply, arcing the craft away from the pier. He pointed the boat for the lights of Venice and opened up the throttle.

As the boat practically leaped out of the water, Jordan turned his head, saw the guard silhouetted on the pier, his rifle up to his shoulder.

"Get down, get down!" he shouted at Alison and MacDonald.

The other two dropped to the boat bottom, and Jordan fell to a knee as the first shot whistled overhead. Then came a second shot and a third, like handclaps, past his ear.

They were hurtling toward Venice, and his last glimpse of San Lazzaro was that of lights going on everywhere in the monastery. In seconds, the island had disappeared from sight.

Jordan rose to his feet behind the wheel, signaling the others to get up.

"We got you free of there," he said breathlessly to the professor, "but I haven't the faintest idea what's going to happen to you next."

III

▶   ▶   ▶   ▶   ▶   ▶   ▶

The city hall of Venice, located on the Grand Canal—
one passed it en route to the humpbacked Rialto
Bridge—consisted of two palaces, the Palazzo Loredan,
built in the 12th century, and the Palazzo Farsetti, built
in the 13th century by Doge Enrico Dandolo and later
the residence of the aristocratic Farsetti family. The
buildings were connected by a covered passageway over
the Calle Loredan, which otherwise separated them.

In the more than a century since these palaces had
been converted into the *municipio,* or city hall, they had
been the scene of many historic occasions. But none,
perhaps, exceeded in importance the emergency meeting that had been called by Sindaco Accardi—Mayor
Accardi—so recently elected headman of this city of
100,000 inhabitants by Venice's sixty councillors, of
whom forty-one were members of the local Communist
party and who in their turn had been elected by the
people in the last municipal election.

It was predawn, four o'clock in the morning, and the
brightest lights that partially illuminated the darkened
Grand Canal came from the mayor's office on the first

floor, above the ground floor of the Palazzo Farsetti. In this spacious office, six men and one woman, several of them just roused from their beds, had assembled. The last to arrive had been Aleksandr Veksler, the Soviet Union's cultural attaché, accompanied by a forbidding bull of a man with a Mongolian face named Major Boris Kedrov, who less than a hour ago had landed at Marco Polo Air Terminal in a special Soviet military aircraft assigned to him by the premier himself.

Mayor Accardi's office seemed ill suited for an emergency meeting. The office was exquisite and graceful, as if designed for easy small talk and long, pointless anecdotes. On the felt-covered walls with their floral patterns hung three framed pictures: a portrait of Cato by Molinari, a portrait of Antony and Cleopatra by Molinari, a portrait of Podestà Angelo Corner by Maganza.

Mayor Accardi, a portly man of fifty-five with a double chin, had a face as smooth and round as an infant's bottom. His thinning hair was plastered straight back, and by habit he always smiled even when he did not feel like smiling. He sat down in the high-backed swivel chair behind his overpolished, uncluttered 19th-century desk, waiting for the others to be seated in a semicircle before him. Momentarily distracted, Deputy Mayor Santin, almost all nose, almost chinless, adjusted the giant map of Venice and environs, tacked to a plywood board, propped on a sturdy easel to his left. Finished, Deputy Mayor Santin picked up his pointer and went back to his red upholstered chair.

Everyone was assembled. Mayor Accardi surveyed the cast of characters, reading from left to right. There was his secretary, Mrs. Rinaldo, a nondescript widow, her gray hair mercilessly drawn tight into a bun, her pencil poised over her shorthand pad. The next chair was occupied by Deputy Mayor Santin. Beside him sat Colonel Cutrone, commandante of the carabinieri, the federal police force in the area. He was an impressive man—full head of hair, darkly attractive, resembling a young opera bass in the role of a military officer. At his left, fidgeting, was Questore Trevisan, superintendent of the local Venice police force—short, bandy-legged, his most striking feature two poached-egg eyes set in a vacant face. Next, chain-smoking, Ragazzi, unofficial leader of the Communist party in Venice—square countenance, intense, brooding, with muscles like bands of steel. Then came the two foreigners, the Russians: Aleksandr Veksler, his close-set eyes fixed on the map of Venice, and the newly arrived Major Boris Kedrov, who appeared curiously uncomfortable in an ill-fitting navy blue suit.

Mayor Accardi pushed his desk lamp aside, took in the group once more, and addressed them in a conversational tone.

"Gentlemen, you all know why we are gathered here at this ungodly hour. We are here to review what has happened in the case of Professor Davis MacDonald, to discuss the actions already taken, and to decide what further actions we should take. Normally, this meeting would be conducted by Prefetto Gasparini, but he is on a visit to America, attending an international law-enforcement convention in Chicago, and in his absence the home secretary in Rome has invested me with the authority to organize our effort.

"Very well. As best I could, I have collected the relevant facts in the case, and now I shall briefly review these facts. As those of you in this room know, from my preliminary phone calls last night, Professor Mac-Donald, a naturalized American citizen, was a guest of the Soviet Union when he made a startling and earth-shaking discovery—the means of prolonging human life, increasing the human life-span from the average seventy years to the probability of 150 years."

"A discovery made," Major Kedrov interrupted, "because of the cooperation of the scientists of the Soviet Union."

"Exactly," Mayor Accardi quickly agreed. "However,

instead of sharing his find with the Soviet Union, this Professor MacDonald slipped out of Russia, intent on taking the discovery to his American masters, to do with it as they pleased. Our Soviet comrades"—he nodded amiably at Veksler and Kedrov—"were quite understandably upset by and concerned about Professor MacDonald's unfair and hostile behavior. They knew MacDonald had taken a special Soviet flight with Venice its destination. They called upon us, as allies and friends, to detain MacDonald for them upon his arrival. We were only too happy to cooperate with our comrades, and I requested that Colonel Cutrone apprehend MacDonald and keep him in protective custody until our allies could return him to the Soviet Union and convince him that the U.S.S.R. was a partner in the discovery and deserved to share it.

"Colonal Cutrone did his job well. MacDonald was apprehended and detained under guard on San Lazzaro until he could be returned to the Soviet Union. Then, by some means or other—precisely what means we have not yet learned, although there was some mention of a carrier pigeon, which sounds unlikely—MacDonald was able to inform some persons on the outside of his situation and arrange for them to attempt to remove him from San Lazzaro. This attempt to help him escape was carried out six hours ago. Mr. Veksler was in charge at the monastery when the escape was undertaken." The mayor nodded at the Russian. "Perhaps you can fill us in on the firsthand details, Mr. Veksler."

The Russian twisted in his chair to speak to the others. "We had arranged with the Armenian abbot to give us two of his young monks to look after Professor MacDonald—this aside from the company of armed guards Colonel Cutrone so kindly provided. We were given the most trustworthy and obedient monks to take care of the professor, to serve him, to walk him, to take him to a bathroom down the hall when he needed use of it. Last night, at approximately nine-fifty, the professor rang for his monk and asked to be accompanied to the bathroom. The carabinieri guard outside the door saw MacDonald and his monk go down the hall and around the corner, toward the spot where the bathroom is located. As far as I can reconstruct what happened next, when MacDonald and his monk, Pashal, emerged from the bathroom, a masked figure stepped out of the shadows and poked a gun into the monk's ribs. He commanded the monk to lead them out of the building by some route in which they would be unobserved by the guards. When the monk, Pashal, objected, the masked intruder said he would kill him. Afraid for his life, the monk led the two out the front door to the pier, where a motorboat was waiting. Meanwhile, the carabinieri guard posted outside MacDonald's room became worried. The rule was that MacDonald was to be back in his room in five minutes. The guard realized that more than ten minutes had passed. He decided to investigate and find out what was delaying MacDonald and his monk. He could not find them in the bathroom or anywhere on the floor. He went downstairs, saw the front door ajar." The Russian paused, craned his neck toward the commandante of the carabinieri. "I believe you have his report, Colonel Cutrone, on what followed."

"*Si*," said Colonel Cutrone. He spoke in a measured tone. "Our man, Antonio, the guard, he went to the door and looked outside. He saw, at the pier, the monk, Pashal, with another man. Professor MacDonald was nowhere in sight. Antonio called out to the two he saw. Neither replied. Instead, the other man, the stranger, pistol-whipped Pashal, knocking him down. Antonio pulled his rifle off his shoulder and began to run toward them. The stranger immediately fled across the pier and into a waiting motorboat. By the time Antonio reached the edge of the pier, the motorboat had turned away toward Venice—"

Major Kedrov interrupted. "There can be no mistake that the boat was going to Venice?"

"No mistake at all," said Colonel Cutrone. "Antonio had his rifle up and fired three shots before the boat was lost in the dark and out of his sight."

"Did he hit either of them?" asked Major Kedrov.

"He could not tell. Actually, there were three in the boat—three men, he thought. They all ducked down very low as the boat pulled away. One he definitely identified as Professor MacDonald, being familiar with him."

"And the other two?" asked Major Kedrov.

"Very little to go by. No identification from the guard. It all happened too swiftly. There was darkness, and the lighting was poor. The boat went away fast, throwing up spray. However, the monk Pashal—when he recovered consciousness, he gave a vague description of the one with the gun. He had been too frightened to take a good look until they reached the pier. He said the stranger had a crooked nose and thick lips and spoke with some kind of accent, possibly German."

"Was he tall or short?" Major Kedrov asked impatiently.

"He was shorter than Pashal. It is not much, but it is something."

"I do not trust your monk's description," said Major Kedrov. "It would be a waste of time to hunt for the abductor. The one to hunt for is Professor MacDonald. We know exactly what *he* looks like." He tapped a portfolio on the floor leaning against the chair. "I have the professor's photograph from our files."

"We can use that immediately!" Trevisan, the Venice police superintendent, exclaimed.

"You shall have it," said Major Kedrov. He addressed Colonel Cutrone again. "I want to hear the rest of what happened last night. After the guard fired his shots, what happened next?"

"Everyone acted with dispatch," said Colonel Cutrone calmly. "Antonio did not even bother with the injured monk. He rushed back into the monastery and awakened Mr. Veksler, who telephoned me at my apartment in Venice. I saw the gravity of the situation at once. These were dangerous minutes when MacDonald might slip away. The vital thing was to contain him in Venice. I quickly contacted our *stazioni*—our branch buildings and carabinieri—at Mestre, the Lido, Cannaregio, Castello—all of them, everywhere. I alerted our barracks at San Zaccaria. Within fifteen minutes, maybe less, we had thrown a net around Venice. By ten-thirty, every exit had been stopped—the fugitive could not go by auto from Piazzale Roma, by train from the depot, by air from Marco Polo, by sea from the Lido and the other outlets. Our water patrols were almost everywhere, instantly. Gentlemen, we have our professor trapped in this city."

"Now we must catch him," said Major Kedrov.

"We shall," said Colonel Cutrone. "That is why I called our mayor and suggested this emergency meeting. To plan a concerted action that will flush out our— our fugitive."

Major Kedrov came to his feet. He looked at the others. "All of you, you understand the importance of the secret Professor MacDonald is carrying?"

Mayor Accardi pulled his swivel chair to his desk. "Yes, Major. Mr. Veksler, through Colonel Cutrone, has apprised each of us of the facts about the discovery."

"MacDonald has really discovered how to eliminate the leading fatal diseases," Major Kedrov went on compulsively, "and how to slow down the aging cells with shots that inject a formula he calls C-98. There has never been anything like it in the world. Imagine how it will be if you can live to the age of 150."

"We know how it will be with *you*," Mayor Accardi said shrewdly. "You want MacDonald and his formula for yourselves. It will make *you* happy." He made a broad gesture. "But what about *us?*" Then he added quickly, "Of course, we cooperate with you willingly, because we are political allies, comrades. But for this show of friendship, I wonder what will happen to us?"

The question hung in the air a moment. All eyes were on Major Kedrov. He considered Accardi, then moved closer to the desk. "You," he said, "you will be taken care of. Everyone in this room will have a special priority. Once our scientists have the formula from Mac-Donald, and after our leaders—the premier, Politburo, Lenin Prize winners—are given their shots, you will be next. When we say this discovery belongs to the Soviet Union, we also mean the allies and friends of the Soviet Union. Have no concern. I give you my pledge."

"It is understood and accepted," said the mayor.

Major Kedrov turned to the others. "The real business at hand, I repeat, is that we must go about catching MacDonald. How do you propose to do it?"

"I will answer you," said Colonel Cutrone, rising. He took the pointer from the deputy mayor and walked to the map. "The first thing to be done is to see that Venice is airtight. Last night, working against time, I stopped up every obvious exit. But we must be aware of two facts. The first, that Venice has many less obvious exits. See"—his darting pointer touched numerous spots on the map—"here and here and here. We have our net, but there are still holes in it. The second fact to know is that we are dealing with a daring and cunning enemy. The ones who staged the rescue last night were clever. We cannot underestimate them. So if there are holes in our net, you can be sure they will discover them soon." He looked at the Russian major. "Therefore, our imme-diate primary job is to see that MacDonald does not get away. To make certain, I am taking action as soon as it is daylight. I will call the home secretary in Rome and I will request and obtain additional carabinieri from all nearby cities—Padua, Milan, so forth. By noon today, or a few hours later, every obscure exit involving land, sea, air will be closed. It will be impossible for MacDonald to escape."

Colonel Cutrone left the map, tossed the pointer to Deputy Mayor Santin, then went to the desk.

"Your Honor," he said, "to contain MacDonald, but far more important, to contain his secret—to see that he does not send it to the outside world by some other means—will require, I am afraid, a certain amount of sacrifice from you, your town councillors, and the city's merchants." He paused. "All traffic into and out of Venice must cease at the crack of dawn."

Mayor Accardi appeared startled. "What are you saying? That cannot be!"

"It *must* be," said Colonel Cutrone emphatically. "No one in Venice at this moment will be allowed to leave. We can watch for MacDonald at every exit, but we cannot watch for some unknown person carrying his formula out of here. No one leaves for five or six days—we should flush out MacDonald in that time, if lucky earlier—but no one leaves. That means tourists wanting to go home, that means laborers who commute to the factories at Mestre—everyone is stuck until we let them go."

"There'll be riots."

"Let there be riots. We may give special dispensation to a person or two we know, who would have to get direct permission, written permission, from you personally. But basically, no person may set foot outside of Venice until our matter is settled. But that is not all. No one must be allowed to come in—"

Mayor Accardi jumped out of his chair. "That is madness, Cutrone! You go too far. This is the height of our tourist season. Our economy is based on the tourists who pour in now. Keep them out and you ruin us!"

"It will not ruin you. Five or six days won't hurt you at all."

"But why is this necessary? Not let people out, that I understand. But not let them in—?"

"There are many reasons. One is that some of Mac-Donald's important friends might get in, and we'd have no way to keep them from helping him or announcing his discovery to the world. Another is, once thousands more people enter our city, we cannot let them out for the duration of this hunt, and it will give us too many people to deal with, to screen. Your Honor, it has to be done my way or it cannot be done at all."

Mayor Accardi sank back into his chair, dragged out a handkerchief, wiped his damp brow. "All right. It will be done." He sighed. "This is reaching 150 the hard way."

"Cutrone," someone called from the semicircle. It was Ragazzi, the local Communist leader. "How do you explain this to the people—to our 100,000 Venetians, to our 50,000 or more tourists suddenly confined here? You can't tell them you are looking for a scientist who has found the secret of longevity. The capitalist world would fall on us, force us to free him. What will you tell them? You must have a reasonable explanation for what will seem to most an unreasonable quarantine. What will be your explanation?"

Colonel Cutrone nodded. "*Si*, I have already thought of that. I ransacked my mind for a plausible cover story. At first I thought we might say we are searching for a desperado who has stolen one of our priceless Venetian masterpieces, a Titian perhaps, and we must catch him before he gets away. Then I decided that most people would not think such a robbery justified our drastic action. Rejecting that story led me to a cover story I feel will hold up." He surveyed the others. "An American spy, working against our Communist government, has stolen our plans for a secret weapon, defensive weapon, an anti-guided-missile device. He—"

"One moment," Kedrov interrupted. "I don't like calling him an American spy. That might bring inquiries from the United States government and press."

"The United States won't know about it."

"Are you suggesting a news blackout?" said the Russian.

"An entire communications blackout. No private telegrams or letters are to leave Venice this week. No wireservice stories. I think we can all agree on that."

"But afterward," Kedrov persisted. "We must look ahead. When we've caught our—our so-called spy—and lifted the travel and news bans, word would get out that our spy was American. It might make the United States Department of State, the Pentagon curious. No, I don't like that."

"Very well," said Colonel Cutrone. "Let's make our fugitive a foreign spy, nationality unknown, a foreign spy who *posed* as an American scientist."

"Better," said Kedrov.

"So this foreign spy has stolen the plans for Italy's big secret weapon," Colonel Cutrone resumed. "He had flown into Venice to await his contact. Meanwhile, we learned what had taken place, we surrounded the spy in Venice, and now we have him trapped here. We ask the forbearance and cooperation of the entire population and all visitors until we catch him. How does that sound?"

"I like it," Major Kedrov rasped. "I believe it."

"Yes," said Mayor Accardi. "Security of the nation. Very good." His fat face clouded for an instant. "Only one thing bothers me. With the city closed down, with communication ended, what will the outside world think? We've got to tell them—the world press, other businesses, governments—we've got to tell them something."

"I was coming to that," said Colonel Cutrone. "We want to say as little as possible, but—yes, we must say something. There will be a brief, a terse announcement given to the wire services after daybreak today, minutes before we impose the communications blackout. We will have Mayor Accardi announce to the world that an emergency measure has just gone into effect—no traffic into or out of Venice the next few days—no further communications—until a foreign spy trapped in the city, a spy known to have stolen Italian military defense plans, is caught. As soon as he is arrested, Venice will be opened up again. That should satisfy almost everyone."

"Not everyone," said Mayor Accardi. "Not the press on the outside—"

"To hell with the press," said Colonel Cutrone. "They are not our concern right now."

"Agreed," said Kedrov.

"Now let's get back to the immediate business at hand." Colonel Cutrone ran his fingers through his bushy hair, thinking, as he walked slowly back to the map. "Our hunt, to begin with daylight, will be two-pronged. First, we will enlist the population to join us in the search. We will release our cover story to the press, and to be passed around the city by word of mouth. A spy with an Italian secret. It will touch the patriotic fervor of the entire citizenry. We will also release the photograph of Professor MacDonald that Major Kedrov has brought along. We will make several thousand reproductions—for our exit guards to have handy, for merchants, for concierges, for everyone who can help. We will also print posters with MacDonald's portrait for the populace to see wherever it turns." He hesitated. "One problem."

"Yes? What is it?" Mayor Accardi wanted to know.

"This MacDonald," said Colonel Cutrone. "How do we identify him to the public? Do we say the man we want is Professor Davis MacDonald, who used his work as a gerontologist and scientist as a front for his espionage? Or do we give him another name?"

For some seconds the questions remained unanswered.

Major Kedrov was the first to offer answers. "I see no advantage to using his real name. I see disadvantages. Some persons may know of him, of his reputation, and it would cast doubt on our cover story. Further, if the press leaked the story, MacDonald's friends in high places would deny our cover story."

"There need be no press leaks, not with the news blackout," said Colonel Cutrone. He looked at Kedrov. "So we should give our fugitive another name?"

"Definitely."

"Very well. Another name, similar but different. I once had a foreign friend, a British police officer—dead now—whose name was MacGregor. Shall we call our spy MacGregor—E. MacGregor?"

The conversion of MacDonald to MacGregor was agreeable to all parties.

"Of course," said Superintendent Trevisan, "one or two persons may recognize the face in the posters as MacDonald."

"What difference," said Colonel Cutrone, "if there is a communications blackout? Later, we can say they were mistaken in identifying the foreign spy as MacDonald."

"True," said the police superintendent.

"So our first offensive against MacDonald today will be to bring the public in as collaborators," continued Colonel Cutrone. "We have the great majority of our 100,000 population, plus many tourists, ready to report to us if they spot MacDonald anywhere in the city. Our second offensive takes place here—" His finger drew a slow circle around the perimeter of Venice. "A city two miles long, a mere hour and a half's walk to cross it leisurely. To our advantage, 177 canals, covering twenty-eight miles, where MacDonald need not be sought intensively. There are relatively few closed boats. On the other hand, there are 3,000 alleys or small streets in this warren, adding up to ninety miles. To our disadvantage is the matter of time—these alleys and streets will have to be searched. The number of private residences to be entered? I cannot tell exactly, except that we have almost 30,000 house numbers in the city. Here you see what we call our busiest thoroughfare, the Grand Canal, which divides our city. It is 10,400 feet in length. Every foot will be patrolled. Gentlemen, we have 150,000 carabinieri in Italy. In the next day or two, as many as we choose to requisition will be in Venice, hunting and seeking our man."

He stood back, contemplated the map, and faced the others. "*Si*. We will join our carabinieri with Trevisan's *questurini*, as well as with outside police who will be transferred here today, and except for those on a shift of guard duty at the exits, we will use our army to move from the outer edges of the city inward toward its center. Our raiding squads will methodically enter and examine personnel in every apartment, shop, café, *palazzo*, public building. We will continue this hunt-and-search operation every hour, slowly closing in until we have caught Professor MacDonald in our vise." He looked out the window. "Day is coming. It is time to begin. We will not fail."

▶ ▶ ▶ ▶

When Tim Jordan awakened, the bedroom was dark, and he thought it was still the middle of the night. Then he picked up his small travel clock off the lamp table beside the bed and saw that it was five minutes after ten in the morning. The bedroom was dark, he realized, because he had drawn the heavy green draperies, after closing the wooden shutters, to keep the sun from disturbing his sleep.

He remembered, with a start, the events of last night, and that Professor MacDonald had shared his bed. He rolled over and saw that the opposite side of the bed was empty. That meant MacDonald had been up earlier. He hoped MacDonald hadn't done anything risky.

Worried, Jordan swung out of bed, bare-chested, bare-footed, wearing only his pajama bottoms. He padded to the door that stood between the bedroom and sitting room, and opened it a crack. He put his ear to it. He could hear first Alison's voice, then MacDonald's, and he felt relief.

"Hey," he called through the door, "are you both all right?"

"We're fine," Alison called back.

"Have you had breakfast?"

"We're waiting for you," said Alison.

"You can order for me and yourselves," said Jordan. "Call room service, Alison. Keep the professor away from the phone. In fact, after you order, keep him out of sight. In your bathroom. We don't want the room-service waiter to see him. Order orange juice, scrambled eggs, hot tea, and rolls for me."

"All right," Alison said. "What do you think is going on out there, since last night, since we—you know what?"

"I don't know, but I can guess. Look, put in your order while I shower. Be with you in a minute. Then we'll organize ourselves."

He went to the bedroom draperies, tugged at the cords, pulling them back. Then he unlatched the double windows, reached out, and pushed back the shutters. What was revealed of the Venice morning was an overcast sky, a gloomy day, a choppy lagoon, the moored boats all rising and falling crazily and the water washing up on the street below.

Presently, standing on the rubber mat in the bathtub, invigorated by the shower, he allowed his mind to stray back to last night. The rescue had been both successful and disappointing—successful in that he had actually pulled it off, freed MacDonald, but disappointing in that MacDonald's captors had learned about the rescue too soon and blocked any possibility of his getting safely out of Venice. Leaving San Lazzaro under gunfire, Jordan had taken MacDonald and Alison straight to the side boat entrance of the Hotel Danieli. Since they had to traverse only a small corner of the lobby, he had hoped that they would go unnoticed. He had told them to hasten straight upstairs to his suite. Once they had gone, he had backed the motorboat out of the canal and turned it over to Cipolate. When he had rejoined MacDonald and Alison in the suite, he had found the professor unnerved by the experience. Jordan had soothed him with some cognac, diverted him with small talk about Venice while avoiding any discussion of his still-dangerous predicament, and at last got him to go to sleep. After Alison also retired, Jordan had stayed up late, drinking, thinking about his own position of jeopardy and involvement with a man he knew so very little about. After a few drinks, his thoughts had gone to Alison. He had realized how little he knew about her too, and how attracted to her he was in a way he could not define. Eventually, drowsy from the cognac, he had put himself into bed and blacked out instantly.

And here he was in the morning, in the shower, aware that he would be responsible for getting MacDonald safely out of Venice—and without the faintest idea of how difficult this might be to achieve.

After drying himself, he dressed, choosing a blue sport shirt, lightweight navy slacks, crepe-soled shoes.

In the sitting room, he found Alison leaning against the edge of his desk watching the room-service waiter set the breakfast tray on the coffee table. MacDonald was nowhere to be seen. Jordan gave Alison an approving wink. "Be right back," he said. "I want to pick up the morning paper. See if there is anything in the news."

He hurried downstairs and approached the concierge's counter. The head concierge, Fabris, and two of his assistants were huddled over an Italian newspaper.

"Good morning, Mr. Fabris. Do you have the *Herald Tribune?*"

"Good morning, Mr. Jordan. Not yet, I'm afraid. It is delayed again. Even with Communism, we have the strikes." Fabris indicated the newspaper his assistants were reading. "There is great excitement today. The Italian press is full of it. You have seen *Il Gazzettino?*"

"No. I just got out of bed."

Fabris reached under the counter and came up with a folded copy of the newspaper. When he set it down, only the top half of the front page was visible. The blaring Italian headline was at least three inches high. Jordan translated it:

MILITARY SPY HUNTED IN VENICE

A second bank of headlines read:

POLICE DECLARE CITYWIDE EMERGENCY
ALL TRAFFIC HALTED INTO AND OUT OF VENICE
FOREIGN AGENT WITH DEFENSE SECRETS SOUGHT

Confused by the espionage headlines, relieved that their own caper had not found its way into print, Jordan lifted and opened the paper to the full front page. Hitting him square in the face was a huge half-page photograph, an enlarged portrait of Professor Davis MacDonald. The bold black caption read:

IF YOU SEE THIS MAN, CALL THE POLICE
A recent photograph of E. MacGregor, a foreigner who posed as an American scientist to steal blueprints of Italy's newly invented antimissile rocket. MacGregor has been trapped in Venice and is the target of the greatest manhunt in Italian history.

Jordan emitted a low whistle. He understood what had happened at once. The authorities had determined to hide MacDonald's identity, the news of his fantastic discovery, their motive for wanting it, and had deliberately concocted and released this false story.

"Something, isn't it?" Fabris said.

"You mean they're shutting down the whole goddamn city because of some spy?" asked Jordan.

"Look on page two. The most drastic emergency measures I have seen in my forty-five years in this community. No one can come into the city. No one can leave. Until they apprehend the criminal. No one can leave? Do you know what will happen to us when our guests— American, English, French, German, Japanese, all the others—when they get word of this? They can't go on with their vacations. They can't go home. They are stuck here for who knows how long. They'll be descending on us by the hundreds, screaming bloody murder. What can we say to them?"

"I just can't believe they won't let anyone out," Jordan said.

"Read the whole story," said the concierge. "They mean it."

Jordan folded the newspaper. "I'll take this along," he said. "Put it on my bill."

He hastened upstairs, his head buzzing at the magnitude of their problem.

He entered the suite, ignored MacDonald and Alison, who were eating at the breakfast tray on the glass-topped coffee table, and gave his attention to the white plastic plate inside the door. He flipped up the switch, and immediately a screen on the white plate lit up illuminating the words—

Non Disturbare

Don't Disturb

Pas Déranger

Nicht Stören

"This lights up similar panels outside our front door," Jordan explained. "We don't want the maid or valet or anyone else walking in on us."

He was aware that Alison had been searching his face. "What's the matter, Tim?" she asked.

"This is the matter," said Jordan, shaking open the newspaper and holding it up in front of him.

"My picture," MacDonald gasped. "How did they— But of course. My passport picture. The Russians got a copy when I applied for a visa."

"Oh, no!" Alison exclaimed. "It looks like an FBI Most Wanted picture. What do those Italian words say?"

Jordan sat down in the armchair across from the two, and he slowly read the lead story and haltingly translated it, giving them the essence of each paragraph. When he had finished, he threw the newspaper onto the sofa and met their eyes. For all her cool, Alison appeared frightened. MacDonald was unable to hide his upset state.

"What does it all mean?" MacDonald asked.

"It means they'll go to any length to get you back," said Jordan grimly.

"Tim—" It was Alison. "We've got to do something. What do we do next?"

"I don't know. I-I can't think on an empty stomach. Give me . . ."

Alison handed him his plate of eggs and passed on the rolls and butter.

Jordan began to eat as he mentally reviewed what he had just read aloud. He looked up. "Did I say I don't know? I do know—I know exactly what we should do next. We've got to keep Professor MacDonald out of sight. No one, absolutely no one, must know he is here." Jordan stopped abruptly, staring at the breakfast tray. "Alison, you didn't order for three people, did you?"

"For two, Tim. Give me some credit for being smart. I ordered twice as much as I wanted and gave Davis half."

"You're sharp. I won't underestimate you again." He turned to MacDonald. "Your only chance is to remain invisible until we find the means of smuggling you out of the city."

"I'll do whatever you say," said the professor.

"To begin with, you'll remain right in this suite while we try to find a way to spring you free. You are never to answer the door, even when you are alone. Now, here's the normal traffic in the suite. Room service with food and drinks. Whenever the waiter is due, you lock yourself in the bathroom. Laundry. They always return the laundry by depositing it in the bedroom. I'll put a stop to that. A maid and valet come by daily to make the beds, put in fresh towels, clean up, sweep. I'll put a stop to that too. Besides leaving on the red light outside—that means no one is to intrude on our privacy—I'll speak to the head housekeeper, tell her no one is to come into my suite or Alison's bedroom until we say it's okay."

"Won't she be suspicious?" asked Alison.

"I don't think so. I'll tell her I'm working on top-secret engineering plans for the Venice Must Live Committee and the plans are all over my rooms and I can't allow anyone to see them. I'll tell her to leave towels and bed linens outside the bedroom doors."

"How do you explain no one coming into my bedroom?"

"Easy. You're a nymphomaniac. When I'm not in bed with you, someone else is."

Alison blushed. "Tim, really!"

"It's the only happy thought I've had today. All right, I'll tell the housekeeper you're my assistant, helping me with the plans, and we work in your room too. Now, we all understand that every precaution must be taken so that Professor MacDonald is not seen."

MacDonald set down the coffee cup. "You are very kind, Mr. Jordan. You don't know me, you don't owe me anything, yet you are taking all this time and chance. You don't have to do this, but"—he hesitated and threw up his hands—"if you didn't, I'd be lost. I suppose they'd catch me within a day. I'm grateful for your Good Samaritan streak."

Jordan smiled. "I'm not a Good Samaritan. I'm afraid I'm not a good anything. To put your sense of guilt at rest, I'm in this to the end for three good reasons. First, I wanted a commitment to something, to shake me out of my boredom. Second, when I first set eyes on your research associate, I liked her legs. Third, and most important of all, I think your discovery belongs to all mankind."

"Thank you," said MacDonald.

Jordan finished his eggs and took his tea. "One thing, Professor. As long as I'm involved, I'd like to know what I'm fighting for. Despite our talk last night, and the few hints Alison has dropped, I have only the vaguest idea of what you've discovered, of why the Russians are after you. I'd like to know just a bit more."

"You mean how I came to discover C-98, as the formula is called?" asked MacDonald.

"No," said Jordan. "I'm sure it is too complicated for a poor layman to understand."

"Unless you are a scientist, it is extremely complicated."

"I really want to know what your formula will do. Also, what are its implications?"

Professor MacDonald considered the questions. At last he spoke. "I will do my best to simplify it for you. Injections of C-98 into a human being will eliminate or arrest cancer, heart disease, vascular ailments, pneumonia, and perhaps a hundred or more other afflictions of the flesh. Above all, it will attack the so-called death genes that cause the degeneration of cells and the aging process. I'm convinced it cannot contain the action of these genes forever, but on the basis of my animal experiments, the shots should give a person who might normally live seventy years an assured life-span of 150 years. Equally important, the shots will be a rejuvenator.

Although old age comes at 120, the aged will not be senile, ailing, decrepit. They will reach their later years full of health and vigor. Of course, my shots won't prevent people from dying in their earlier years as the result of accident, murder, suicide. The shots will prevent people dying from diseases and old age, at least until the ripe age of 150 or thereabouts."

Jordan was dazed by the immensity of the discovery. "Absolutely incredible," he murmured.

"Isn't it?" said Alison. "I think it is the greatest discovery in the history of the human race."

"The broad implications of a means to prolong life are endless," said MacDonald. "People will have more time to enjoy life, their mates, their children, their friends. They will have more time to learn, to develop their skills, to explore and learn specialties. They will have more time to help others, to improve the environment, to gain more wisdom that will bring us more inventions. They will have much of a century and a half each to go into outer space. The oldest will not be shunned as lepers, but will have the health and strength to exist equally, compete equally with the young. There is no limit to the revolution in living the prolongation process can bring to the world." He paused. "The question is— will it ever reach the people of the earth?"

Jordan stood up. "That's a question I'm going to try to answer today."

"How?" Alison wanted to know.

Jordan began to gather up the breakfast dishes and set them on the tray. "I'm going to scout the city, try to find out how tight the police security system really is. Sometimes the Italians can be notoriously inefficient and disorganized, no matter how grandiose their plans. I want to see how rigid they are about letting people leave the city. Alison, you can help me. You don't know your way around Venice, but you can pick up information. I'll direct you. I'll rent a motorboat for you, and you can go to the airport and observe what the police are doing at Marco Polo. I'll cover the railroad depot and the Piazzale Roma, where all the automobile traffic starts. As for actually getting Professor MacDonald out of here, well, I know a lot of Venetians, and I'm going to tell some of them I have to get to Paris on business and ask them to suggest some way—any way—for me to leave Venice."

He carried the tray to the door, deposited it in the hallway, and returned thoughtfully.

He looked down at MacDonald. "Professor, I have an assignment for you. It may take us several days before we can smuggle you out of here. You'll have to stay in hiding. You'll have time on your hands. I'd like you to put that time to good use. I'd like to make a suggestion."

"Anything you say."

"This formula of yours for longevity, C-98—do you have it on paper?"

"No. I thought that unwise."

Jordan went to his desk, picked up his straight-stemmed pipe and pouch, filled the pipe and lighted it. He said finally, "I don't think it's unwise. Putting your formula on paper, I mean. True, there is a certain amount of risk involved. But considering your circumstances now, I think it is worth a gamble."

"You want me to write it out?"

"I think that would be a good idea," said Jordan. "Let me put it this way. We want to get you out of here. We are going to try. But what if we fail? What if the Communists catch you? If it is all in your head, they've got you and they've got the secret to themselves. But if whatever is in your head is also on paper, left with Alison or me, well, if they took you away, we'd be free to release your formula to the world. This would undercut the Russians. Everyone would have the formula. And once everyone had it, the Russians would have no reason to hold you prisoner any longer."

MacDonald considered this. "It makes sense," he conceded.

"It makes sense because of one more thing I have in mind. What if the next few days turn into a stalemate? They can't catch you, and you can't get out? Well, it occurs to me that if we can't get you out physically, we might find the means of getting a piece of paper out. Once the paper was delivered to the Gerontology Congress, or to anyone, and announced, the secret would be public. Your formula would belong to the world, and you would be safe. What do you say?"

"You're right. I'll do it."

"There's paper in the desk drawer, and a pen. How long do you think it'll take you?"

"To write out C-98? Umm, as I told you, it is complicated, even for another gerontologist. Oh, three, four, maybe five days of concentration."

"I hope we have you out of here before then, but just in case. Will it take many pages?"

"I'll need plenty of work sheets. But the actual formula, perhaps one or two pages."

Jordan was pleased. "Good. The sooner you start, the better. As for you, Alison . . ." He glanced at his wristwatch. "I'll order a motorboat to pick you up at the side canal entrance of the lobby in a half hour. You go to Marco Polo. Observe the patrol-boat activity along the way. At the airfield, have your motorboat wait for you, and scout the vicinity on foot for maybe a half hour or an hour. See how heavy the security is, the number of guards. See if any planes are landing or taking off, passengers coming in or going. Just gather a whole report on that."

"Will do."

"Since Professor MacDonald can't order room service while we're both out, we'd better leave some food for him." Jordan took out his wallet. "Maybe you can pick up a few things, Alison, keep them in the refrigerator. You just go out of the hotel, the first street to your right—

it looks more like a dark alley—is filled with shops, several of them groceries." He offered her some money, but she refused it. He tucked his wallet into his hip pocket. "All right, I'm off. Catch up with you later this afternoon."

Leaving his room, he saw the valet and told him not to bother to do the suite, then inquired after the housekeeper. The valet pointed to the landing below the staircase. On the first-floor landing, Jordan confronted the buxom housekeeper and made his urgent request that no one enter his suite for the entire week. The housekeeper was aghast, she had never heard of such a thing, it was impossible, against the hotel regulations. Jordan persisted, explained in detail about the secret blueprints in his rooms, Dr. Edwards bedroom, and at last the housekeeper was intimidated and agreed to give out the immediate order that no one was to enter the rooms this week under any circumstances.

Relieved, Jordan continued on to the grand marble staircase leading to the lobby, descended it, and found bedlam.

Standing before the reception desk in the Oriental Gothic lobby, he was surprised by the crush of hotel guests—tourists of every age, garb, and nationality. Angry knots of tourists were milling about, complaining of the madness of the city officials in confining them, not permitting them to leave Venice. The greatest concentration of rebellion was centered on the concierge's counter. Carlo Fabris and his four assistants were beleaguered.

Fighting his way through the crowd to the head concierge, Jordan could hear snatches of the protest in English, German, French. "But we're on a scheduled tour. In a week we'll miss five cities! . . . I have to leave! I'm meeting my husband in Bern! . . . There's a party for me in Rome tomorrow night! . . . We can't stay! Our charter leaves Paris tomorrow!"

Jordan had reached the side of the counter. Fabris

noticed him, backed away from five or six apoplectic guests, and came to Jordan mopping his brow.

"It is Dante's hell," the concierge said.

"You can't blame them," said Jordan.

"I don't, I don't," said Fabris, "but they should not blame *us*."

"Mr. Fabris, I need a motorboat in about thirty minutes for Dr. Alison Edwards."

"It is arranged."

"To Marco Polo Airport and back."

"You are sure? There is no one arriving or going today. There is nothing there."

"She left behind a piece of luggage."

"Fine, very well."

Turning away, Jordan saw a dirigible of a woman squeeze out of the telephone booth, and he grabbed the door and jumped in before anyone else could take the phone.

He dialed his office and asked his secretary to connect him with Marisa Girardi.

"Marisa?"

"It's you. I wondered what happened to you. Have you ever seen such a thing before? Everyone is angry—"

"I know. I'm at the Danieli. All hell has broken loose."

"I don't understand it. For a mere spy. They are overreacting."

"Could be."

"We have lost three of our feature stories. We had a writer coming from Munich tomorrow. One from New York and one from Paris the next day. No air traffic to Venice. No landings. All planes are being diverted to Milan."

"Maybe they'll lift the quarantine tomorrow," said Jordan.

"Not unless they find the spy. We are not dealing with ordinary Venetians. They are easygoing. We are dealing with Venetian Communists. They are stubborn like mules. You are coming in today?"

"I can't. I'm tied up. That's why I called. You can take care of everything."

"Sure, but— Tim, when do I see you again? You canceled our dinner last night. Can't we see each other tonight?"

"I-I'm not sure. I have some friends from back home who are stuck here now. I should look after them tonight."

"They may be stuck here a long time. Bruno heard the mayor say the quarantine could last for days."

Jordan was instantly alert. Marisa's twenty-two-year-old brother, Bruno, was the star photographer for Venice's leading daily newspaper, *Il Gazzettino*.

"What's Bruno doing with the mayor?"

"He's with the mayor and Colonel Cutrone day and night. *Il Gazzettino* assigned him full time to cover the spy manhunt."

"Maybe what your brother heard the mayor say is right. My friends may be stuck here for a while. I suppose I really don't have to meet them tonight."

Her voice was eager. "Does that mean we can see each other?"

"I want to see you. Let's make it dinner at Harry's Bar, eight o'clock."

"I'll be there."

"And by the way, you can invite Bruno to join us. I'd like to hear his inside version of what's going on."

"That is nice of you, Tim, but I am sure he is too busy."

"Well, tell him to at least join us for a short drink."

"I'll try."

"I've got to go now," he said.

"Don't get yourself arrested," she said cheerfully.

He gave the telephone a rueful look. "Who'd want me?" he said, and then he hung up.

He left the telephone booth, pushed and elbowed his way through the lobby, and emerged from the Danieli's revolving door into the windy, overcast afternoon. He walked to the vaporetto station, removing a 1,000-lire note from his wallet, and went to the ticket vendor.

"Piazzale Roma, please."

"Sorry, Signore, no service to Piazzale Roma today."

In Jordan's memory, this was unheard of. So the police were serious, efficient, organized after all.

Shrugging, he left the station and walked on around to the quay. The boat pilots and gondoliers were standing about, gossiping. Business was poor today. The nasty weather.

Jordan summoned the man lounging near the first free motor launch. He pointed to the launch. "Yours?"

"*Si.*"

"I want to go to the railroad depot and the Piazzale Roma."

"You waste your time. No one can leave."

"I don't want to leave. I just want to see what's going on."

The man jerked a thumb toward his launch. "Get in."

As they rode through the lagoon and swung into the Grand Canal, Jordan stepped out of the cabin and seated himself in the open rear of the launch. The craft rocked ahead in the choppy waters and Jordan held on to the rail, concentrating on the police activity in the canal itself and along both shores.

Traffic was almost always heavy at this time of the day, but what made the difference now was that at least half the water vehicles were patrol boats. Jordan could make out the white-and-battleship-gray craft with the word POLIZIA painted on the side that belonged to the Squadra Mobile of the local *questura*. Then there were the all-white patrol vessels with GUARDIA DI FINANZA painted on them, the swift craft that usually kept on the lookout for smugglers. Then there were the smooth mahogany launches belonging to the carabinieri. Every passing vessel was filled with armed police.

On his left, before the Basilica della Salute, the huge

monument to the Virgin Mary, he saw a gathering of several dozen carabinieri in their khaki uniforms and boots, all wearing swords and carrying nine-millimeter Berettas. He examined the terrace of the Gritti Palace Hotel. Only one policeman, the rest diners. Jordan realized that they were going under the first of the three bridges that traversed the Grand Canal, the wooden Accademia Bridge, and to his right Jordan recognized the Casina delle Rose, where Gabriele d'Annunzio had made his home in 1915. At the huge 17th-century Palazzo Rezzonico, once owned by Robert Browning, once a residence for James McNeill Whistler, there were uniformed men in the open doorway. At the boat landing stage before Ca' Mocengo, where Lord Byron had dwelt for three years, there were the questura, the local police, in blue uniforms and white holsters. On the quay next to Ca' Corner-Martinengo, where James Fenimore Cooper had stayed in 1838, there were numerous and ominous plainclothesmen carrying light machine guns and scrutinizing pedestrians.

As they rode on, Jordan continued to study the shore above the Grand Canal. What he saw was unsettling. One out of every two persons seemed to be armed and in uniform.

He sat back, bemused, felt the coolness of the Rialto Bridge overhead, observed the bustle at the Pescheria, Venice's fish market for five centuries. On his right, the Palazzo Vendramin-Calergi, a Venetian Renaissance edifice, where Richard Wagner had lived and died, came into view. But Jordan was, in these minutes, not interested in past history, only in current history. He waited to see what was happening at two of Venice's leading exit points.

The motorboat was slowing.

"*Stazione!*" the boat driver shouted back.

Jordan left his rear seat, crouched low, went through the cabin, and came up alongside his pilot.

"I'm not getting off here," Jordan said. "Just keep going past it slowly."

On the top of the stone steps of the Stazione Ferrovi-aria, Venice's modern railroad depot, uniformed police were picketed two or three yards apart. Travelers were approaching these guards, appealing to them, gesticulating and begging, and being turned away.

"Okay, I've seen enough here," said Jordan. "Take me to the Piazzale Roma."

This was the large square where most persons, leaving Venice, took an automobile, taxi, bus to depart from the city across the causeway known as the Ponte della Libertà, which took them to Mestre and the mainland of Italy.

As the motor launch picked up speed once more, Jordan said to the pilot, "You can pull in when we get there. I'll walk around for ten minutes."

Jordan bent back into the cabin and sat puffing on his pipe until they arrived at their destination.

On shore, Jordan could see that the situation at this end was hopeless. The police were everywhere in the area. They were planted in front of the city-owned Garage Comunale and before the privately owned Garage San Marco, not permitting any automobiles to leave. Jordan hiked on and soon saw that the road leading to the causeway out of Venice was filled with police, and cars attempting to leave the city were being resolutely turned back.

Discouraged, Jordan returned to the embarkation point, got into his motor launch, telling the pilot, "Okay, I've seen enough. You can take me back to the Danieli."

Less than an hour later, Jordan entered his hotel suite to find Professor MacDonald dozing on the sofa and Alison seated at the desk making notes.

"Hello," Jordan said. "Did you make it to Marco Polo Airfield?"

"I wish I hadn't."

"What do you mean?"

"It's depressing, Tim. All the way there, we kept passing police boats—clearly identified as police boats—and when we reached Marco Polo, I walked around pretending I didn't know what was going on and saying I was expecting a friend from Paris. I was told there was an emergency, and all airlines had been notified, and no planes would be landing or taking off from Marco Polo. That was certainly evident. A few Alitalia planes grounded, no crews, and very little personnel in sight. But a lot of men there, all in uniforms and with side arms. I started to count the police. When I got to forty-two, I stopped. There must be a hundred or more."

"Nobody is going to leave Venice by air, that's for sure," said Jordan. He sank down into a chair, shaking his head. "And nobody's going to leave by train or car, that I just found out."

"Which doesn't leave us many options."

"None that I can see immediately. Still, knowing this city, knowing these people, there must be a way out."

"Professor MacDonald has been trying to think of someone on the outside he might contact to come in and help him."

"Good luck," said Jordan. He leaned forward. "Do you and the professor have any money?"

"I have four thousand dollars in traveler's checks, and a bank account in New York I can write checks on. Maybe up to six thousand dollars. Davis—Professor MacDonald—has close to five thousand dollars in traveler's checks. Why do you ask?"

"In case I can bribe someone. I wanted to know our defense budget. Of course, the professor's checks are useless. We don't dare cash them. That leaves you and me. I can throw in enough to give us twenty thousand dollars."

"We wouldn't touch your money," Alison said.

"You may have no choice. Besides, I'd consider it a

down payment on a chance to live to the age of 150. I hope I can find someone who will want the money in return for leading the professor out of here."

"I hope so, Tim."

"In fact, I'm seeing someone tonight, someone who is close to the police and might be able to give us more information. I'm sorry I won't be able to have dinner with you."

"I didn't expect it," Alison said hastily.

"What are you going to do with yourself?"

"I thought I'd go out and shop for as long as the stores are open. I have to get the professor some clothes. He needs a change—trousers, jacket, shirts, underthings, socks; I was just writing down the sizes he gave me before he fell asleep. And I'm afraid I'll need a few more items for myself."

Jordan stood up. "Don't buy anything too expensive. Because when you leave here, you will probably be leaving with only the clothes on your back."

"I'll remember." She hesitated. "Tim, do you think we can find a way out before—before they find us?"

"I don't know," he said, starting for the bedroom to get ready for dinner. "All I do know, Alison, is that it's going to be close. Very close, I'm afraid."

▶ ▶ ▶ ▶

At five after eight in the evening, Tim Jordan pushed through the swinging doors of Harry's Bar.

As ever, he felt as if he were walking into a riot. It was the best restaurant in the world, Jordan had long ago decided, but it took stamina to survive until one had a table. Harry's Bar was always crowded in season, but tonight it was packed to overflowing because of the threatening weather outside. The small round lacquered tables, with their undersized chairs, were doubly occupied, while the waiters, holding their trays aloft, were trying to squeeze through aisles that no longer existed. To the immediate left, customers were standing three deep at the bar.

The head bartender, Alberto, mixing a drink, saw him and called above the hubbub of voices, "Good evening, Mr. Jordan. The usual?"

"The usual," Jordan called back.

He planted himself behind the others at the bar, to wait for Marisa, and waiting, he scanned the crowd. Largely, a rich and elegant turnout—numerous celebrities, many faces that were familiar to him. The Contessa Elvira De Marchi, descendant of one of Venice's oldest families, her long nose and chin like a collage pasted on wrinkled parchment paper, was holding court at a table for eight. The Contessa blew a kiss to Jordan, and he blew a kiss back. Nearby, one of his favorite people, Dr. Giovanni Scarpa, like an austere fugitive from a Carpaccio painting, seated with some of his wealthy patients, greeted Jordan with a rare smile. At another table, Jordan recognized the darkly beautiful, but slightly aging, Italian film star Teresa Fantoni, whom he had never met but who was known to him from her early Fellini pictures.

"Mr. Jordan!" It was Alberto handing him his drink across the bar. Jordan, reaching between the heads in front of him, precariously had his drink. Alberto was pointing toward the rear of the room. "Miss Girardi, she is here—against the wall, holding your table."

Jordan looked off, saw Marisa with her hand raised, and then he began to make his way toward her between the tables. His progress was slow, and so he could overhear snatches of conversation at each table. The subject was the same: the closing down of the city and the massive manhunt taking place.

Marisa had someone else at their table, and Jordan was relieved to see that her companion was her younger brother, Bruno. He was relieved because he had been afraid Bruno might not come by, and a talk with Bruno had been Jordan's real objective tonight. Besides, he liked Bruno, who was less temperamental than his sister, more ambitious and energetic. Except for the pockmarks on his cheeks, he resembled a perfect curly-haired male angel.

"Aren't you a dream tonight," Jordan said, bending to kiss Marisa. "Hi, Bruno. You don't look right without a camera."

"Here it is," said Bruno, lifting his brown leather camera case from the floor and then lowering it again.

Jordan settled down in a chair. "You both ready for another round? What is it—Bellinis?"

"Maybe not," said Bruno. "I have to go to work in a few minutes."

"Don't be a spoilsport," said Jordan. He gulped down half of his drink, caught the eye of their waiter, and made a gesture indicating a round of refills. Now he addressed Bruno once more. "Marisa tells me they haven't got you shooting bikini beauties on the Lido this week."

"The paper has assigned me full time to the hunt for the spy. Double shift. Sixteen hours a day I am at city hall or the carabinieri headquarters."

"You must be exhausted," said Jordan.

"Not at all. It is very challenging. Biggest story since I've been on the paper. The only bad thing—normally, my photographs would be going out on the wires to France, England, America, everywhere—it would make my reputation—but this quarantine has stopped all the wire services."

"For what reason?"

"It does not seem right to me either, Tim. But the decree is no wire stories or pictures are to be sent from Venice. No mail to leave Venice, none, until the spy is caught."

Jordan finished his Scotch and water as the waiter placed fresh drinks on the table. "What if the spy is *not* caught?" Jordan asked Bruno.

"Oh, they'll catch him," said Bruno airily, "especially now that his picture is out everywhere. They are systematically sweeping the city—room by room, almost. If they don't catch him in a day, they'll catch him in three or four at the most. There is a lot of pressure on the authorities, from airlines, travel bureaus, newspapers on the outside, from businessmen on the inside—everyone wanting to know why no traffic is permitted. The police must catch their man, and fast."

"Are the local police getting any help from—from anyone outside Italy?"

"Outside Italy? Why should they?"

"I mean, the plans for the defense weapon that were stolen, that could be of real interest to Italy's Communist allies. Like the Russians. I'd think they'd want to help out."

"No, I have seen no Russians," said Bruno, sipping his peach-and-champagne drink. "Except, of course, for the few who've been around for the cultural convention."

"So you don't think the spy can get away?"

"How can he? The normal number of police was tripled today. The city is sealed airtight. No one can leave."

"No exceptions?"

Bruno thought about it.

Marisa spoke to her brother. "You told me there were some exceptions."

"Yes, but they hardly count. Mayor Accardi said in certain cases, where someone has something pressing outside the city, and the someone is known to the mayor and applies to him personally, a special exit permit will be issued. That limits it, doesn't it?"

Jordan drank his Scotch, wondering how to approach Bruno with what he had in mind. "Bruno," he said tentatively, "suppose I had to go to Paris tomorrow or the next day. Do you think they'd let me go?"

"Not a chance."

"But why not? I've met the mayor socially. Why wouldn't he let me go?"

"Because you might have memorized the secret plans the spy has stolen."

"I see. Well, let me try something else on you. What if Marisa and I had to take some visitors out to the Centro Sperimentale di Idraulica in Voltabarozzo to show them our miniature mock-up of the Pirelli-Furlanis inflatable dam? It is something we've done regularly up to now. Do you think they'd let us go?"

"Maybe that is different," said Bruno. "It is near here. It is a place you have been to often on business. They could control you. They might give you a special permit to Padua, but maybe only if you were accompanied by police guards."

"But Paris, or anywhere else—?"

"No, not from what I've heard. Forget Paris."

"I can't forget Paris," said Jordan intently. "That's really the reason I wanted to see you tonight. I have a friend—an old college friend—who *has* to be in Paris this week. For him, it's a matter of life or death."

Bruno was shaking his head. "I told you—"

"Wait, listen to me," Jordan said. "My friend is a courier for an underground separatist movement. He is carrying a large sum of money, illegally, undeclared, to deliver to a rebel leader who will be in Paris for only a week. If my friend is delayed, it will be thought that he has failed, and the leader will disappear and the entire movement be abandoned. So my friend must get to him. It is a good and just cause. I thought with your police connections, you might know some guard who would look the other way—"

"Impossible."

"—for his share of $10,000."

Bruno had stopped shaking his head. His eyes held on Jordan, widened.

Jordan said quickly, "Yes, $10,000 in American dollars—$5,000 for the guard, $5,000 for you."

Marisa put a hand on Jordan's arm, but spoke to her brother. "I'm afraid of this, Bruno. . . ."

He ignored her. His eyes were still on Jordan. "That is a lot of money," he said.

"Yes, it is," said Jordan.

"In cash?" said Bruno.

"In cash."

Bruno looked down at the table, speaking in an almost inaudible voice. "I don't know if it can be done. My police connections—yes, a few are my friends. I am thinking of one particularly. He is a captain in charge of a carabinieri detail guarding the Ponte della Libertà, which leads to Mestre—"

"And to Paris. It would be simple."

Bruno bit his lip. "Not simple, but not impossible. The captain has a big family and bigger debts. His wife is pregnant. He worries." Bruno paused. "He might be interested."

"Will you try?"

Bruno slid out of the booth, lifted his camera case, and hung the strap over his shoulder. "I must go to work."

"Will you try?" Jordan repeated.

"I don't know," Bruno said. "We'll see."

And without looking back, he left Harry's Bar.

▶ ▶ ▶ ▶

Once they were alone, Jordan and Marisa had two more drinks. After that, they ordered dinner. They both had the *tagliatelle verdi*, and after the green noodles they both had *cotoletta alla Milanese*.

Now, in Harry's Bar, Marisa finished her veal cutlet and turned to Jordan. "I'm sorry, Tim, but I still don't like your involving Bruno in whatever you are up to."

"It's a good cause, Marisa."

"I don't care. I don't want Bruno in trouble."

"Well, he's a grown man. It's for him to decide."

"I suppose so. I suppose that sum of money will tempt him."

Jordan swallowed the last piece of his own veal. "With his contacts, it may not be so dangerous."

"Bribery is always dangerous." She continued to stare at Jordan. "You know, Tim, I don't believe your story at all. I mean about your having a separatist friend who has to get to Paris. You're not a good liar. I know you too well. I have a suspicion—just a suspicion—you are harboring that spy everyone is hunting for."

He solemnly held up his right hand. "I swear to you, this has nothing to do with a spy."

"Then I don't understand."

"I won't lie to you again. I'll only say I have someone very important—who has to avoid the police—and who has to get out of Venice as quickly as possible. When I can, I'll tell you the whole thing."

"Fair enough. Maybe Bruno will help you."

"I hope so. Now, then, Marisa, the dessert. Do you want one?"

"Yes."

"What do you want?"

"You."

"Me? But you have—"

"I want to make love with you. It's been over two weeks. My body is hungry for you."

"I want to love you too," he said. It had been the furthest thing from his mind, but considering her now, picturing the voluptuous body naked, he began to feel a desire for her. "We can't go to my suite. My friend is staying there."

"The one who isn't a spy," she said with a smile. "But we can go to my apartment. No one is there. I told you, Mamma is in the hospital for tests. And Bruno won't be back for two or three hours. We can have it to ourselves." She gathered up her shawl. "Do you think you can keep me occupied for two or three hours?"

He started rising. "The last person in Venice who was able to do that was Casanova. But even if I turn out second best, I'm willing to try. Let's go."

▶ ▶ ▶ ▶

Minutes after they closed themselves in Marisa's darkened bedroom, and undressed each other, and lay down on her double bed, he had lifted himself and settled down between her widely spread legs and entered her slowly and deeply.

Despite the stimulation of her lubricated vulva, her rotating hips, her increasing breathlessness, he had lasted a long, long time, far beyond his normal endurance.

Now, feeling the wetness of perspiration on his body, momentarily distracted, he had a glimmer of what was accounting for his ability to go on like this. He realized that his body was engaged, but much of his mind was elsewhere, on the problem of how to save Professor MacDonald.

MacDonald in his head brought someone else into his head.

Alison.

He could feel Marisa's soft thighs against his sides, and immediately in his mind's eye he saw Alison's shapely long legs leading up to her magnificent nude torso, and he pictured, felt, himself between her legs, inside her, tightly held, enclosed hotly inside her.

The thought in his head and the intense friction below came together, and he stiffened, gasped, exhaled in an orgasmic spasm.

He dropped to his side, on the bed, bringing her close to him.

"Was it good?" she whispered.

"Great," he said, trying to catch his breath and feeling guilty for the image that had brought on his orgasm.

"Tim, I'm ready too," she said.

He disengaged himself from her and reached down to touch and rub her distended clitoris.

She was ready. In the next ten minutes she had four prolonged orgasms, and at last she pushed his hand away and lay back limp and exhausted.

"Can I say I love you?" she said.

"Don't," he said, reaching for one of her cigarettes and lighting it. "Just say you care for me a lot."

"I love you," she said. "I wish you could stay all night. Can you? Bruno goes to his own room."

"I can't," he said, getting off the bed. "My friend is waiting for me. I've got to tell him about my discussion with Bruno." He peered down at her and saw that her eyes were closed. "Marisa, are you still awake?"

"Mmm."

"One thing I forgot to ask Bruno. Will you ask him if the police are going to visit the hotels? I suppose they are—but if they do, try to find out from him when they are going to do it. Will you remember?"

She opened her eyes. "I will ask him in the morning."

"I just want to be sure my friend is safe, until Bruno can help get him out of the city."

"Then tell your friend not to make long-distance calls. Bruno told me they are monitoring all calls."

"Thanks, darling." He went to the edge of the bed and bent down to kiss her.

As she returned his kiss, her hand reached out and stroked his penis. "Good night, lover," she said. Then she closed her eyes again and turned on her side to sleep.

Not until five minutes later—after he had dressed, had quietly let himself out, had taken the steep staircase down to the ground floor, and stood in the street before the apartment building—did it strike him. As he had left Alison, earlier, she had said, *Professor MacDonald has been trying to think of someone on the outside he might contact to come in and help him.* As he had left Marisa,

just now, she had said... *tell your friend not to
make long-distance calls*... *they are monitoring all
calls.*

What struck him was that if MacDonald was seeking
help from the outside, he would likely try to locate some
friend in London or New York by telephone. His call
would be monitored, reported to the police, and he
would be traced and grabbed at once.

Perhaps it had already happened. Perhaps not yet.

Jordan began to run through the deserted street toward the Hotel Danieli. It was drizzling lightly, and
when he reached the Piazza it was slippery, and he
slowed to a trot as he hurried to the hotel.

When he reached his suite, he burst inside. Alison,
curled up on the sofa reading a book, was startled.

Trying to regain his breath, Jordan sputtered, "The
professor—did he phone anyone on the outside
tonight—any long-distance calls?"

"He was trying to think of someone to call. He just
did. He's in the bedroom now, trying—"

"He can't!"

Jordan dashed toward the bedroom, pushed open the
door. MacDonald was seated on the edge of the bed, the
telephone receiver at his ear. He was saying into the
mouthpiece, "Operator, I'd like to put through—"

Jordan was across the room, snatching the receiver
from MacDonald's hand. "Sorry, operator, but forget it
for now," Jordan said into the phone. He firmly set the
receiver down on the cradle.

Taken aback, MacDonald blinked at Jordan uncom-
prehendingly. "I was just calling—trying to call New
York—"

"No long-distance calls, now or at any time."

"But it is my only chance," MacDonald pleaded. "I've
just remembered an acquaintance, a man I have a social
friendship with—he's a delegate to the United Nations
from Britain—and if he heard my situation, he could
alert the U.N., and then the whole world would descend

on Venice to free me. The Communists would be help-less."

Jordan heard him out tolerantly. "Sorry, Professor, it won't work. The Communists aren't stupid enough to let a call like that go through. They're having every long-distance call from Venice monitored right now. The min-ute they realized what you were talking about—knew it was you—they'd cut you off, trace your location, and have the police in this suite in five minutes to apprehend you. You'd be finished. I'm afraid there is no way you can communicate with anyone outside of here."

MacDonald found it hard to believe. "They're moni-toring all long-distance calls?"

"Every one," said Jordan, "to prevent you from doing exactly what you were attempting to do."

MacDonald lowered his head into his hands. "Then I'm afraid my situation is hopeless."

"Not quite," said Jordan. He took MacDonald gently by the arm and helped bring him to his feet. "Come into the next room and let me pour you a drink. I'll catch you up on what I've been doing."

They went into the sitting room to join Alison, who had been listening at the doorway.

"Have you found a way?" inquired Alison anxiously.

"Possibly," said Jordan, halting at his makeshift bar atop the refrigerator. "Let's just relax a moment. What'll you have?"

"The same as you're having," said MacDonald.

"Me too," said Alison.

Jordan poured three cognacs, handed one to Mac-Donald, placed the other two on the coffee table. He sat down, waiting for the others to be seated.

"All right," said Jordan. "Let me tell you of a conver-sation I had tonight." He paused. "Professor, did Alison repeat to you my talk with her about raising money for a bribe?"

Alison spoke up quickly. "I haven't told him about that yet."

"We'll need $10,000," said Jordan. "Alison has $4,000 on hand. I'll be glad to kick in the other $6,000—please don't protest—as I told Alison, I consider it an option on living to the age of 150. Now let me tell you what happened at dinner tonight."

After identifying Marisa Girardi merely as his assistant at work, and her brother, Bruno, as the leading photographer for *Il Gazzettino,* he recounted what he could remember of his entire conversation with Bruno in Harry's Bar.

When he had finished, MacDonald said, "Then you think there is hope?"

"Bruno would not promise anything. But he was interested. Very. And he is close to this captain in the carabinieri, who heads a company of guards on the causeway to Mestre. Bruno made it clear this captain needs money badly. I'm sure Bruno will find a means of approaching him. I'm not sure what his answer will be."

Alison sipped her cognac. "When will you know?"

"I can't say. Bruno is aware of the urgency. I told him my separatist courier had to be in Paris in less than a week."

MacDonald was still worried. "What if the police captain refuses to cooperate?"

"I'll be thinking of an alternative plan, making inquiries. I'm confident something else will turn up. But I'm betting on Bruno. I feel he'll get his friend to come along."

"In a few days," said MacDonald.

"Yes. Our situation isn't too bad. You're safe here, Professor. No one knows where you are. So we just have to sit back and wait for the moment we can smuggle you out of the city. Now, what do you say to another drink?"

▶ ▶ ▶ ▶   ∘

Tim Jordan lay on his side, in a fetal position, in the bed. He could hear the windswept rain beating against the wooden bedroom shutters. It was coming down in torrents. Every once in a while it was counterpointed by a crackle of lightning. Beside him, in the bed, another sound, the professor erratically snoring. Then another insistent sound. On his bedside table, his travel clock, ticking away. At last glimpse, the clock had read two-sixteen in the morning.

His eyes were shut, the lids heavy from cognac and fatigue.

He tried to erase the thoughts floating through his mind and to sink into what he hoped would be dreamless sleep.

But yet another sound intruded.

With difficulty he opened his eyes, listened, raised his head. It was his bedside telephone, two feet from him, ringing.

His hand darted out, captured the receiver, brought it to the rim of his blanket.

He tried to keep his voice down. "Hello?"

"Tim? Marisa. Did I wake you?"

"No. Is anything the matter?"

Her tone was one of concern. "You asked me, before leaving tonight, to find out from Bruno in the morning if the police were going to investigate the hotels in Venice."

"Yes?"

"Bruno just came home. He was having something to eat in the kitchen and that woke me. So I got up to talk to him, and I remembered what you wanted to find out. I asked him if he knew about the hotels. He knew. I thought I should call you immediately."

"What did he say, Marisa?"

"It is not good for your friend. The police have already started surprise raids on every hotel in Venice. They are scheduled to move in on your hotel, the Danieli, and all the hotels in your area at seven o'clock tomorrow morning."

"Tomorrow morning?"

"I mean *this* morning, Tim. Five—four hours from now."

Jordan lay back on the pillow, deeply disturbed. "Bruno is sure of this?"

"No question. Colonel Cutrone gave the assignment to his officers a little while ago. Bruno overheard the officers discussing it. Seven o'clock this morning. They will fence in the Danieli. Let no one out. Interrogate everyone inside. Search everything. You had better do something quickly for your friend."

"I'd better. Thanks, Marisa."

He hung up, threw off his half of the blanket, and jumped out of bed. Taking off his pajamas, he could hear the rain outside the window even louder. He tried to think as he hastily dressed. Buttoning his shirt, he went around the bed, turned up the lamp on MacDonald's side, and then shook the professor, who finally opened his eyes.

"Are you awake yet?"

"I guess so. . . ."

"Listen. I just got a call from a friend. She tipped me off that the police are raiding the Danieli—this hotel—in a few hours, to question every guest. If they find you here, you're cooked. I've got to get you out of here in the next two hours."

MacDonald was sitting up, shivering. "But where? Where can I go?"

"I don't know. I'll think of something. You get dressed. Pack all your effects. Leave nothing behind. I'll give you a canvas bag. And, Professor—shave off your moustache. Every little bit helps. Now hurry."

He left his bedroom, crossed the sitting room, opened the door to Alison's bedroom, and entered. He turned on the light next to her bed. Her lovely face was deep in the pillow, only a bare shoulder exposed above the blanket.

He touched her shoulder, and at once she was awake. She tried to focus on him, did, and sat right up, holding her blanket to her throat.

"What is it, Tim? Is something the matter?"

Without wasting words, he told her what was going on.

She was agitated. "What can you do?"

"I'm going to try to find some place to take him. I can't risk another hotel. It'll have to be a private place. It'll be safe to move across the city. It's raining heavily outside, and at this hour the streets are practically empty. He'll have my raincoat. He can partially cover his face. You can stay on here."

"No, I'd prefer to come along, if someone will take me too."

"If you insist. Okay, put on your clothes. And check out both bedrooms and the sitting room to see that no evidence of MacDonald is left behind."

He went out of her room and stood in the middle of the sitting room trying to clear his head and fasten on someone he could trust who would help him.

He needed a hiding place, a sanctuary.

Sanctuary.

Churches always provided sanctuary.

Church. Priest. Friend.

His old friend Don Pietro Vianello, whom he had seen only yesterday noon on the Mercerie.

Jordan started for the telephone.

IV

▶ ▶ ▶ ▶ ▶ ▶ ▶

It was ten minutes after seven o'clock in the morning, and Tim Jordan, fully dressed, sipping his breakfast tea, sat in the sitting room of his Hotel Danieli suite waiting for the police.

Once again, restlessly, he got up and walked to his open window to see whether they had arrived yet. Outside, the lagoon was calm. The rain had stopped. Soon the sun would break through. It would be a hot and muggy morning. Before him, the usual sights. There was the six-foot-wide pier, two motorboats moored on one side, two gondolas on the other, with a sign over it reading, SERVIZIO MOTOSCAFI/TAXI. Nearby was the vaporetto landing station with its glass ticket booth and its own sign above, reading, LINEE 1   5   8. Then there was the one-funnel, two-deck steamer, the *Altino*, one of the vessels that made the twelve-minute commuter's run to the city of Lido every twenty minutes. In the street between the Danieli and the lagoon, an elderly man had set up a brown umbrella beside the three-lamp street post and was now stacking prints on an easel in preparation for the day's tourist traffic.

So far Jordan had not seen what he had expected to see. He stepped out onto his small balcony, gripped the iron railing, and peered directly below.

There they were, all right. A group of a dozen or more carabinieri in their khaki uniforms, white straps, side arms, black boots, cordoning off the hotel entrance. For the time, no one could enter or leave the hotel without examination and interrogation. Jordan imagined that the teams of searchers had covered the ground floor by now, had worked their way up to the first floor, and would soon reach his suite on the second floor.

He sat down once more before his breakfast tray, finished the last of his tea, and stared at the entrance door. He was quite alone in the suite, thank God, and ready for the hunters.

The experience of last night had been unnerving, and the aftereffects still had him on edge. The telephone call to the priest, to Don Pietro Vianello, had been difficult to make at that awful hour. And indeed, he had awakened Don Pietro. He had been blunt with the clergyman. He had said that he was trying to protect a friend who was being sought by the police. He had said that he needed sanctuary, for a brief period, for his fugitive friend. He had added, fervently, that his friend was innocent, that he would swear by him, and that he required a hiding place just long enough to be vindicated. Jordan had promised Don Pietro he would give him all the details at a more reasonable hour.

Don Pietro had only spoken twice after that.

"You swear by him?"

"Yes."

"Bring him."

They had watched from their window for the approach of a vaporetto, finally seen one approaching from a distance, and they had hurried downstairs. Before descending into the empty lobby, Jordan had inspected Mac-Donald (who appeared younger without a moustache), made certain the raincoat collar shielded his face. With Alison carrying a duffel bag of MacDonald's old clothes and papers, they had gone past the night concierge, who had hardly looked up from his magazine, and emerged from the hotel into the slashing rain. They had run to the station platform, caught the vaporetto headed for the Rialto station. Looking around the almost-empty water bus, Jordan had been afraid that they might be conspicuous. The few passengers coming and going had paid no attention. At the boat's destination, they had left it and gone on foot in the downpour the rest of the way, over the Rialto Bridge to the Santa Croce quarter.

Don Pietro, bald head and cherubic face shining, had been watching for them from the lighted doorway of the *canonica*, or rectory. They had come out of the rain into the hallway, all three soaked to the bone. Jordan had hastily introduced MacDonald, then Alison, asking if the priest had room for Alison also.

"No problem," the priest had said. "My flat is upstairs. There are two spare rooms. I will fetch you some dry nightclothes." He addressed MacDonald. "My nightgown will come to just below your knees only." He addressed Alison. "I will get you a nightgown from my mother's wardrobe."

"I must go back to the hotel," Jordan had said. "I have some business there early in the morning. After that I will return here for lunch—if I am invited."

"You are invited."

"And, Don Pietro, I will then offer you an explanation."

"I hope so," Don Pietro had said.

Now, sitting, waiting in his hotel suite for the searchers, Jordan lit his pipe to calm his nerves and thanked his lucky stars that it had gone smoothly in the early-morning hours. They had crossed a great part of the city undetected. They had received a hospitable reception from their generous host. MacDonald had safe sanctuary, hopefully until Bruno shortly delivered the escape route.

So now there were only the investigating police to contend with. And as far as they knew, he was merely a longtime resident of the Hotel Danieli, a familiar and crazy American who chose to live and work in this sinking city, so far from his own golden America.

He must simply remain calm and pretend ignorance of what the authorities were after.

It seemed an eternity, this waiting, and then, as he looked at his wristwatch, which showed seven-twenty, the expected knocking came on his entrance door. Knocking, followed by the buzz of his doorbell.

He hastened to the door and admitted the three of them.

They were carabinieri, all right, in full regalia, one of them an officer.

The officer said in precise English, "I am Captain Dorigo. I have a search warrant." He displayed an Italian document. "We are searching every room of the hotel."

"For what?" asked Jordan.

"There is an American spy named MacGregor—"

"I have read about him."

"Then you understand." He removed a five-by-seven-inch photograph of MacDonald from his jacket pocket and held it up before Jordan. "Here he is. Do you know him? Have you seen him?"

Jordan shook his head. "No."

"You have your passport?"

Jordan had it ready. He pulled it out of his trouser pocket. Captain Dorigo took it, flipped the pages. "Timothy Jordan," he read. "American. Engineer." He handed back the passport. "Why are you in Venice?"

"I work here. I have a job. I have been here almost two years."

"As an engineer?"

"No. I'm public relations director for the Venice Must Live Committee."

"Ah." The captain's countenance was less harsh now. "I think I have seen you about." He studied Jordan. "You are all dressed, I see. Most guests we have found in their nightclothes."

"I was going to work early. I couldn't get out of the hotel."

Captain Dorigo surveyed the sitting room. "You have another room?"

"Actually, two." Jordan pointed to the two bedrooms.

Captain Dorigo wandered to the center of the room. "Why two?"

"To spread out my work. I use the second bedroom as an office. Also, for my girl friend when she stays for the weekend. You will find some of her things in the closet."

The carabinieri officer signaled his two men. "Aldo, you search that bedroom," he ordered, gesturing toward Alison's, "and Filippo, you take his bedroom. I'll look around this parlor room."

As Aldo and Filippo disappeared into the bedrooms, Jordan kept a watchful eye on the captain, who was moving around the room, poking at a pile of magazines, opening and shaking some books, going toward the refrigerator.

Jordan pivoted, to take in the rest of the room. Alison had combed through it last night, and he himself had done so this morning, to make certain there were no telltale clues to MacDonald's presence. Jordan decided it was foolproof. He relaxed and walked to his desk, to see how it would look to the search team.

On one side of his desk was a pile of writing paper, all blank. Then five sharpened pencils in a Venetian pencil holder. Then a pile of publicity releases on the accomplishments of the Venice Must Live Committee. Then— something unexpected caught the corner of his eye.

The silver-metal wastebasket at the nearest leg of the desk. There was something in it. He racked his brain. He had put nothing into the wastebasket. It was something MacDonald or Alison had dropped into it.

He edged closer to the wastebasket. What lay at the bottom of the basket were shreds of paper, large shreds—a sheet that had been torn in half and then in quarters. The ball-point-pen writing on it was barely legible. Jordan squinted, trying to read what was on one shred of paper. He made out a portion of a word, a name, "cDonald," and beneath it some numerals, with square roots.

He felt panic. The blood rushed to his head. He made an effort to hide his agitation. Plainly, MacDonald, trying to put his formula for C-98 on paper yesterday, had torn up one sheet and discarded it. And the too-familiar wastebasket with this giveaway inside it had been overlooked by all of them.

Frantically, Jordan glanced up to see what Captain Dorigo was doing. The captain's back was to him as he leaned into the bedroom to say something to his subordinate in Italian.

It was risk time again, the whole ball game at stake.

As quickly as possible, Jordan bent down, reached into the wastebasket, scooped up the shreds of paper, lost one, retrieved it, brought the handful up, and shoved the pieces deep into a trouser pocket. His hand was still in his pocket when Captain Dorigo turned around and came to the desk.

Jordan nimbly stepped away, to make a place for the officer. The captain stood over the desk, thumbed through the blank sheets of paper, pulled the pencils out of their holder and turned the holder upside down, lingered over the press releases, reading the top one, shuffling through the entire pile.

Now he was yanking out the desk drawers, rummaging through them.

Aldo was back from Alison's bedroom. Captain Dorigo's questioning look held on him. Aldo shrugged. Seconds later Filippo emerged from Jordan's bedroom. He spoke only one word in Italian. *"Niente,"* he said.

The captain confronted Jordan. "We are through with your quarters," he said crisply. "We are sorry to have inconvenienced you. I wish you luck with the Venice Must Live Committee. Good morning."

As they left the suite, Jordan called after them, "I wish you luck with your spy."

The door closed.

Jordan exhaled and listened for his heartbeat to return to normal.

Then he realized there were perspiration patches on his shirt, and he went into the bedroom to change and to flush the shreds of MacDonald's notes down the toilet.

▶ ▶ ▶ ▶

Jordan had walked all the way, a long walk, from the Hotel Danieli, stopping briefly at his office on the Piazza San Marco, continuing to the Church of San Vincenzo in the Santa Croce quarter, going by foot because he wanted the time alone to organize his thoughts and examine options for MacDonald's escape.

He reached the *campo*, or square, with its several trees—rare in this part of Venice—a few minutes before noon. The modest mustard-colored Church of San Vincenzo, with its painted cross over the door and its Romanesque bell tower, had been built in the 12th century. Don Pietro Vianello, after serving six years as a *vicario*, or assistant, at Mestre, had been promoted to full priest of this church and had served here almost fifteen years. Extending from the church was the tile-roofed two-story rectory, and Don Pietro lived upstairs.

Jordan strode across the square to the rectory door and went inside the entry hall, almost bumping into Don Pietro, who was shuffling through the interior door from the church, leading Professor MacDonald and Alison on a guided tour. "And here in the canonica, as we call the rectory," he was saying, "is an area we use as a *patro-*

nato, meaning a place we use for youth activities and even as a village hall." He became aware of Jordan. "*Buon giorno,* Tim. I was afraid you had dissolved in the rain."

"I survived the rain," said Jordan. He greeted Mac-Donald and Alison with a nod, adding, "I had a harder time with the police this morning."

"The police?" echoed Don Pietro.

"Don't worry, they weren't after me particularly," said Jordan. "They were searching through the entire Danieli, all the hotels in that area, trying to turn up their fugitive spy."

The priest frowned. "So I hear." He cast a nervous glance at MacDonald, then said, "My mother will have lunch ready. We will go upstairs."

Single file they climbed to the upper floor, entered a central hall—"the *portego,*" Jordan explained, "found in almost all Venetian homes"—and moved into a dining room, which had a balcony looking over the small square. The old oblong table was set, and Don Pietro directed them to their places. Almost immediately, a plump elderly lady, with gray hair and warts on her face, came in carrying a large platter heaped with spaghetti and tomato sauce.

Respectfully, Don Pietro introduced her as his mother, Lucia, to Alison and to MacDonald. To her son, she intoned, "*Sia lodato Gesù Cristo.*" Don Pietro answered, "*Sempre sia lodato.*" Jordan translated this for Alison beside him. "She offered the formal religious greeting, 'Let Jesus Christ be praised,' and her son replied, 'Always praised.' She is a wonderful lady. She keeps house here for Don Pietro."

The mother had gone and was already returning with another platter filled with *fegato alla veneziana*—liver fried with onions. After she had left the dining room, and as the platters were being passed around, Don Pietro said to all of them, "Yes, I am fortunate to have her here to help me. The situation is difficult for parish priests in Italy. If a priest has a widowed mother, as I have, or an unmarried sister, he usually has her live with him, to cook, to clean, and in return he is able to take care of her. But my colleagues who are not so fortunate as to have a mother or sister must find an unemployed woman to be a *perpetua*, which is what we call such a housekeeper. It is not a simple matter. Such a woman, as we say, must be ready to marry the priest's job without marrying the priest. Usually she must be over forty-five years old, and preferably ugly, to—uh—let us say, to avoid being a temptation."

Professor MacDonald seemed fascinated. "Is it expensive to hire such a woman, Father?"

"Everything, everything is expensive here," Don Pietro grumbled. "Most perpetue work by the hour and live out. They must be paid 2,000 lire an hour, to which must be added contributions toward their health insurance, their pension, their taxes. Yes, that is expensive when you realize that a priest like me is paid only 49,000 lire a month—translated into American dollars, that is fifty-seven dollars a month. Of course, to be honest, I have other sources of income. I celebrate Mass every day, and offerings are made—altogether maybe 3,000 lire a day. Also, I receive payment for teaching religion. In every school, each class must have one hour of religious instruction a week. The other money I receive, such as for officiating at weddings and funerals, this money goes to support the expenses of my church, such as heating, electricity, candles, repair work. So you see, it is not easy."

With that, Don Pietro devoted himself to his liver and spaghetti.

Jordan cleared his throat and spoke to the priest. "Don Pietro, this reminds me of something I meant to bring up with you last night. You are doing us a tremendous favor. Any expenses you incur, by keeping Professor

MacDonald and Dr. Edwards here, will be reimbursed by us. It is only fair—"

"It is nonsense," Don Pietro, his mouth full of food, declared. "You are my friend. What I do, I do out of our friendship. I would expect the same from you. We will not speak of such a matter again."

As the lunch proceeded, and drew to a finish, Don Pietro continued to talk about himself and his daily life. To Jordan it was as if the priest were deliberately avoiding any mention of Professor MacDonald's presence, either because he did not want to know the truth or because he did not wish to embarrass his guests.

The coffee had been served, and Don Pietro had already discussed his upbringing by his religious father, an organist, his education at a *scuola media* until he was fourteen, at a *liceo classico* until he was nineteen, and finally at the Seminario Patriarcale where he studied theology and where he had prepared for the priesthood. Now he was giving MacDonald a rundown on his daily activity, from his eight o'clock morning Mass to his teaching at the Instituto Turismo across the Grand Canal to his after-dinner evening meetings with parishioners who were about to get married or who had just had children.

Don Pietro stopped his autobiographical monologue. "Enough. I will drive you from here with my ceaseless reminiscences."

Jordan smiled. "You couldn't drive us from here, Don Pietro. You have a captive audience."

"How long will you be with me? I only inquire because I must take leave of you tomorrow, for a few days. In fact, I will be gone five days. Of course, you can stay. My mother will watch after you, but—"

"Thank you," interrupted Jordan, "but we won't need five days. Maybe only a day or two more. You are very kind."

MacDonald had pushed his chair back. "I've eaten too

much. The meal has made me sleepy. If you don't mind, I'd like to go to my room for a nap."

Don Pietro watched him leave the room in silence. Once the three of them were alone, the priest turned in his chair, set his arms on the table, and looked directly at Jordan. His expression was intent, his voice business-like.

"Now we must be more practical, Tim," he said. "I told you the professor can stay on here, and he can, but now that I can speak more freely, I must inform you that there is one important qualification to my hospitality. Last night you asked my help. I gave it, not only in the name of the church, but as your personal friend. Last night you said you would explain why you must hide this man. However, like everyone in Venice, I am perfectly aware that there is a spy, an American, a man who has stolen military secrets, who has been trapped by the police in this city. It is only natural for me to suspect, since the professor is an American and wanted by the police, that he may be the much-sought spy. If this is true, then I must tell you, I am not in a position to harbor a criminal. You can understand."

"I do understand," said Jordan. Throughout the morning he had been preparing for this confrontation. His mind had entertained many explanations, but just before crossing the bridge to the Church of San Vincenzo, he had decided that the best explanation was the truth. "Believe me, my friend, if the professor were a criminal, I would not ask you to give him sanctuary. Don Pietro, he is not a criminal."

"Why does he hide from the police?"

"Another story completely. One you will find hard to believe. But you shall have the whole truth, I promise you. Professor Davis MacDonald is one of the foremost gerontologists in the world. Dr. Edwards is his research associate in New York. While visiting and working in the Soviet Union, Professor MacDonald made a discovery unparalleled in human history." Jordan paused dramatically. "I hope you are ready for this. Professor MacDonald discovered a formula that will allow human beings to live to the age of 150."

Don Pietro's face showed no comprehension. "To 150?"

"With his formula we can double the human life-span, both yours and mine."

"But—but is that possible?"

"It is done. He did it."

"It is difficult to—"

"He did it for the world. But the Russians want it for themselves. Let me tell you exactly what happened. . . ."

Omitting no detail he could remember, Jordan recounted MacDonald's adventures from his escape to his arrival in Venice to his imprisonment on San Lazzaro to his rescue to the police manhunt and the flight from the Hotel Danieli.

"So there it is, my friend," Jordan concluded. "That is why I brought him to you for safety—until I find a means of getting him out of the city."

The priest was shaking his head. "If I did not know you better, I would think you are having sport with me."

"Every word is the truth," said Jordan solemnly.

Don Pietro was awed. "To have lived to see such a miracle."

Alison joined the conversation. "It *is* a miracle, don't you agree, Father?"

"A miracle from above," said the priest. "If the Lord did not wish his children to live longer, he would not have permitted it." His eyes went from Alison to Jordan. "And now the forces of Satan want it for themselves."

Jordan nodded vigorously. "The Communists are doing everything possible to get their hands on Professor MacDonald."

"Godless Communists," Don Pietro muttered. Then, raising his voice, he said, "They shall not have what

they are after—neither Professor MacDonald nor his discovery. You will have the little I can offer—the protection of my church—but surely that is not enough. How
long can the professor be safe here? Sooner or later those
heathens will come to search. Do you have some plan to
get the professor out of Venice?"

"One plan," said Jordan. "I have no idea if it will
work. I'll try to find out today if any progress has been
made."

"How long would it take to execute your plan?"

"I don't know. I suspect it may take several days."

"Too dangerous," said the priest. "Something should
be done immediately."

He pushed himself to his feet, paced the room, coming
to a standstill before the balcony. For a silent interval,
he seemed to be contemplating the cloudless blue sky
above. At last, his right hand hit his right thigh in some
kind of resolve. He came around in front of Jordan, who
had risen.

"One miracle," he said, "deserves another. It may be
another is in the offing."

Puzzled, Jordan said, "What do you mean?"

"We shall see," said Don Pietro briskly. "I am busy
now. I have much to do. You go about your day. Meet
me here at eight o'clock tonight. We will have dinner.
Then we will talk."

▶ ▶ ▶ ▶

Jordan and Alison Edwards, after crossing the Rialto
Bridge—its marketplace nearly empty, since the vegetable boats could not make deliveries from the mainland—
had been walking side by side down San Salvador,
which led to the main street, the Mercerie, where Alison
wanted to shop.

Except for the sights that Jordan had pointed out, and
Alison had remarked upon, there had been little discus-

sion. Once, Alison had speculated upon Don Pietro's mention of another miracle.

"What do you suppose he meant, Tim?"

"I haven't the faintest idea."

"He *did* say there was an urgency to get the professor out of Venice immediately—he used the word 'immediately.' He said it wouldn't be wise to wait for your plan to happen. He must have some escape plan of his own in mind."

"It would seem so. But I'm not depending on it. I'm going to *Il Gazzettino* right now, and hope Bruno is there. I want to know if he's done anything yet."

"Now maybe we have two chances."

"Maybe. . . . There's the newspaper building, up ahead. I'll tell you what. Instead of hanging around waiting for me, I'd suggest you continue on to the Piazza San Marco. When you enter it, turn right and go to the second outdoor café—the farthest one, Quadri's—and sit down at a front table and have some ice cream or a drink and wait for me. I won't be more than a few minutes behind. Then I'll take you shopping. I know the best places."

After giving her these exact directions, he watched her leave. She was wearing a clinging shirred chiffon skirt, and he loved seeing it move so gracefully and provocatively against her long legs. When she was out of sight, he reluctantly put his mind on the business at hand. He headed for the 15th-century Gothic façade of the land entrance—there was also a canal entrance to the rear—of the newspaper building in the Calle delle Acque.

Inside, he greeted the *portiere*, or doorman, who was seated behind a counter on which lay a card with the numbers of all the telephone extensions inside the building.

"I'd like to see Bruno Girardi, if he's in. Tell him Tim Jordan is downstairs."

The portiere made several calls, then on the last one spoke at greater length in Italian, and hung up.

"Mr. Girardi says he will meet you in the portego of the second floor."

Jordan took the small elevator to the second floor and went to the central hall. Bruno was not there yet. Circling the hall, Jordan could hear the typewriters clacking behind the metal partition. It always surprised him that this local edition of the Venice newspaper had a staff of fifty, but then there were twelve provincial editions providing news for readers in towns as distant as Trieste and Verona. Indeed, Bruno, one of the four photographers, was always overworked.

"Hi, Tim." It was Bruno, a Hasselblad camera hanging from one shoulder.

"I just thought I'd pop by," Jordan said, "and find out if you've contacted the party of the third part."

"Yes and no. Yes, I have spoken to him about a meeting, and we will have a drink tomorrow. No, I have not broached your proposition to him yet. I must wait for the meeting. Then I will judge what to say. I must proceed cautiously."

"I understand."

"He may be eager for this opportunity. Or he may be afraid of it. I cannot predict."

"Assuming all goes well, how long do you think it can be before—well, before my friend can leave?"

"I would guess two days, three at the most."

"You'll let me know. Just call the Danieli. If I'm out, leave a message where I can reach you."

"You will hear from me, Tim."

They parted, and Jordan rode the elevator down to the ground floor and made his way to the Mercerie.

As ever, the Piazza San Marco was breathtaking in the sun. He stood enjoying it a moment, then entered the crowded arcade, balancing himself between the pushing tourists until he reached the rear of the bandstand. He turned left, going down the aisle, waving at his friend the first violinist and composer, Oreste Memo, and searching the tables for the sight of Alison.

He saw her in the front row, tossing food to the pigeons. He took a seat beside her. "Having fun?"

"I guess it is fun. I've been so worried I'm not sure what's fun anymore."

He watched her break off part of her roll again and fling it to the gathering pigeons. He said, "That's how I got to meet you. Doing that. Feeding the pigeons."

"Aren't you sorry you fed the pigeons that day?"

"I'm glad. It got me involved in a challenge. I was pretty low. Now I'm fairly high. Alive, I mean. Also, it got me involved with you."

She cast him a sidelong glance. "Is that a plus? Getting involved with me, I mean."

"Very much so."

"I guess it is for me too. Being involved with you. I haven't had much time to think about it. But I like your company." She shifted in her chair toward him. "Tim, this is unreal. Here we are, right in the middle of the most romantic place in the world, flirting with each other—and at the same time we're fugitives, the Most Wanted people in Venice."

"Nobody wants *us*. Nobody knows we are involved, except the glass-shop owner and Don Pietro."

"You know what I mean."

"I suppose you're right. It is unreal. But then the tension gets so great, you have to divert yourself with other things. I mean you can't worry, and be apprehensive, and rack your brain about an escape route every minute. You've just got to let go sometime in the day. We were onto a good subject. How we enjoy each other."

Her almond eyes held on him from behind her oversized lavender glasses. "I don't think so," she said. "Not today. Let's change the subject. What's that tall tower across from us?"

Good-naturedly, Jordan accepted her determination to be impersonal. He tried to see the bell tower through her eyes. It was, indeed, awesome, set in the corner of the Piazza, its rust brick sides rising toward the sky. "Il Campanile," he said, "the tallest building in Venice. Completed by Doge Pier Tribun in the year 912. At night, a bonfire was built in the belfry and the tower was used as a beacon. It once had a spiral ramp running from the ground to the top—323 feet to the top—so that horsemen could ride up to the belfry. Emperor Frederick III of Germany rode a horse to the top. In 1609, Galileo was up in the belfry presenting the city councillors with his latest invention—the telescope. I'll give you another interesting fact, Alison. Do you know the Campanile once fell down?"

"Fell down? But there it is."

"The original just collapsed one morning—July 14, 1902, to be exact. There had been warnings this might happen, so no one was killed or even injured. Except a cat called Mélampyge, named after Casanova's dog. All that was left was the base. The city council decided to rebuild it on the same spot and in its old shape. Nine years later it was completed. And there it is."

"How do you know all that?"

Jordan shrugged. "I was an engineer. I am a public relations man. I continue to be a Venice lover." He called to a nearby waiter and ordered a chocolate ice cream soda. Then, for Alison, his hand swept the Piazza San Marco. "Want to know about the Piazza San Marco?"

"Oh, yes."

"Long ago, it was a swamp—canals and marshes. Nuns used part of it as a garden. Then a series of Doges began converting it into a huge city square. Doge Ziani—he reigned until 1178—began to fill in the canals and throw up the buildings. Between 1500 and 1600, the Piazza took its present form." He pointed off toward the Mercerie. "See the clock tower. It was constructed in that period. Look on the upper terrace, at the big bell. The two bronze Moors on either side of it mechanically strike the bell on the hour. It's quite a sight. Across from it, filling in the end of the Piazza, is the Basilica of San Marco, all golden and glittering in the sun. There are over 43,000 square feet of mosaics covering the inside and outside of the Basilica. See those four magnificent horses on top, at the front? They are Greek, third century. They've been everywhere, it seems. Whenever they were moved, an empire fell. They were in Rome, then in Constantinople, then brought here, where they stayed until Napoleon Bonaparte took them away for eighteen years. They were finally returned to Venice by the emperor of Austria. On the opposite end of the Basilica—"

"Where?"

Jordan pointed off to his right. "That's the newest of the structures that enclose this square. Napoleon put up that wall in heavy traditional style. He also put up the statues of those Roman emperors, leaving one blank space for his own statue. The building across from us, stretching the length of the Piazza, has shops downstairs, an old library and museum upstairs. The one behind us, constructed in the 15th century, is the Procuratie Vecchie. It used to consist of offices and apartments for the nine councillors of Venice. Now it is an insurance company. My office is up there, right behind us." He paused. "Have you had enough of places? Are you ready to talk about people?"

She did not answer. She watched as the ice cream soda was served to him. Finally, she spoke. "There is one person you haven't mentioned. When you sent me on, you were going to see your contact who is supposed to help us."

"Because there was not much to report. Bruno has arranged a meeting that is crucial to our chances. We'll know in a few days."

"Unless we know something else tonight."

"I can't imagine what Don Pietro has in mind."

She continued to watch him sip and spoon his soda,

and her face softened. "You're really very nice," she said.

"Oh?"

"To do what you've done and are doing. I know I've said it before. But I can't say it enough times. I don't know another person who'd give up his work and at great risk devote himself to helping a pair of strangers."

"Don't be fooled. I'm not all that nice and decent. I'm doing it mostly for myself."

"Yes, you've said that before, but I don't believe it."

He smiled, pushing aside his soda and fumbling for his pipe. "You don't know me, Alison. You don't know a thing about me."

"I realize that. It's shocking. We've lived so intensely together in the last seventy hours, so closely, yet we know hardly a thing about each other."

"Let's start now," he said. "With you."

"I'm not very good at autobiography. It seems I've done nothing but go to school and work in libraries and laboratories. My background doesn't seem interesting."

"How old are you?"

"Twenty-seven."

"Pretty young for the likes of me."

"How old are you?"

"By the calendar? Thirty-eight. By the emotional age clock? Ninety-eight."

"Well, you appear young, and you are young."

"Only since I met you. MacDonald isn't the only one who can arrest aging. You do well enough. Or do you still dislike this kind of talk?"

"I'm afraid of it, but I like it fine, if you mean it."

"I do mean it. I'm not an artful liar or seducer. But why are you afraid of intimate talk, compliments?"

"Because I might believe it, and give myself. When you give yourself, you are disarmed, vulnerable to disappointment, hurt, rejection. That scares me. So I try to remain remote—and safe."

"Have you been much involved with men?"

"Not much. But enough to know what I want. I want devotion, security, the safety of knowing I can give myself totally. Until now it has all been Grade B. The usual student mismatchings in Boston, in Berkeley, and two unsatisfactory affairs in New York. In the last three years, abstinence, dedication to work, to Professor MacDonald's work."

"I should imagine men are after you constantly."

"They are."

"And you avoid them."

"Yes."

"For the same reason you want to avoid me?"

"Yes."

"Well," said Jordan, "I can understand that. It gives me some insight into you."

She was studying him. "You haven't been exactly spilling over about yourself. Why is your emotional age ninety-eight?"

"I've been through hell," he said, "and it is unpretty. In fact, it's rotten. I was married, you know."

"I didn't know. What happened?"

"I loved her and she was killed. Like that, killed, wasted. On a street corner in Chicago—a car gone out of control. It was all over."

Alison reached out and touched his hand. "I'm really sorry. How long has it been since, Tim?"

"Just under four years. Almost two of them here in Venice. I was an engineer. It bored me. I turned to writing. Better. I was offered a job to come to Venice and work for the people who are trying to save the city from going under. They've installed a mammoth inflatable underwater dam to keep the tides from flooding the city. I'm supposed to promote the effort."

"Has there been anyone since your wife?"

"No," he said flatly. "I'm not counting sexual gymnastics. You mean if I loved anyone, even a little? No. Except . . ." He hesitated. "I have someone here in Venice. A young woman. Venetian. She's my assistant. It's not serious. It's companionship. We both know it." He took out his wallet and put down some lire. "There you have Jordan in a nutshell. Not too edifying a saga. Surely not the story of a person who wants to live 150 years. But suddenly I want to live 150 years."

"Why?"

"I don't know. I can only say I got the feeling right here, today, in the Piazza San Marco, talking to you." He sat back, examining it. He had not had this feeling, this desire to live and use life well, since the hour of Claire's death. Yet he had it now, and he suspected that it had to do with his being attracted by Alison Edwards. He was interested in her—even excited by her, if he allowed it—the first woman to interest and excite him since Claire. The idea of *feeling* for someone would have been impossible a week ago. Now it was a reality.

Abruptly, he stood up. "Let's take you shopping," he said. "You can leave things to be mailed after the city is opened again. This may be your last day in Venice—if Don Pietro delivers his miracle tonight. Let's shop and let's wait for word from the Lord."

▶ ▶ ▶ ▶

At five minutes after eight in the evening, Jordan and Alison arrived at the rectory door beside the Church of San Vincenzo and were met by Lucia, Don Pietro's mother.

"I am sorry, but Pietro is not back yet," she said in Italian. "But he was expecting you. He reminded me you would be here for dinner. Come, wait in his study. Professor MacDonald is already there."

The elderly woman led them up the stairs and showed them the way to her son's cramped study, adjacent to his bedroom. Professor MacDonald was seated beside the priest's desk, turning a page of a worn leather-bound English-language Bible.

The professor welcomed them as Lucia went to fetch

another chair. When the chair was brought in, and they were all seated, the professor tapped the Bible. "I was just reading up on Methuselah," he said. "Old Testament, Genesis. He lived to the age of 969 and died in the year of the Flood. Allowing for legend and exaggeration, he still must have lived a very long time to have his age noted at all. I was speculating to myself whether those ancient Israelites could have discovered or created some form of C-98, which was then lost in the Flood and lost to history until I rediscovered it."

"Anything is possible," said Jordan.

"Is the search for me going on as intensely as ever?"

"I'm afraid so, Professor." His hand took in the room. "But you're safe enough here, at least for the time."

"For the time," the professor echoed skeptically.

"It won't be long," Jordan assured him. "I went to see my photographer friend this afternoon, the one who is going to try to pay off the police guard."

"Any news?"

"Not much, but some. The photographer, Bruno, has arranged a quiet meeting with the captain. He will feel him out and then make the offer. We may know something by tomorrow. Meanwhile, Don Pietro may have something else. I—"

"I have, I have something else," said the cheerful voice from the doorway. It was Don Pietro, waddling toward his desk, offering an incongruous sight. Gone was his black cassock. In its place he wore the clerical dog collar with a short-sleeved shirt and baggy brown slacks. "*Buon giorno,* Signorina Edwards. *Buon giorno,* Signor Jordan." He plopped down behind his desk, beaming at all of them and fixing finally on MacDonald. "For you, Professor, I have news. The small miracle has happened. You may be traveling tomorrow."

"Tomorrow?" said MacDonald excitedly. "You've arranged something?"

"I've arranged something," said Don Pietro, pleased

with himself. "It needs only the stamp of approval of the highest local authority."

"Well, tell us," Jordan urged him.

Don Pietro held up a plump hand, as if to slow him down. "You recall, my friends, that when I spoke to you this morning of a trip I must make tomorrow, I told you I would have to be gone for five days. The fact is, a party of six of us, Bishop Uberti and five parish priests of Venice, myself one of them, have been summoned to Rome to meet with an eminent cardinal on important matters concerning change within the Church. This summons came about quite suddenly, hours after the emergency had been imposed upon the city. Bishop Uberti applied to Mayor Accardi for special dispensation, special permits for each of us to leave Venice for Rome by train tomorrow, the only train leaving here. Since Mayor Accardi knows each of us personally, and furthermore, since he is eager to soften any hard-line Communist image by accommodating the Catholic Church when he can, he readily gave us our special departure permits. Our party leaves from the railroad station at noon tomorrow. But with one change. I am not going to Rome." He wagged a fat forefinger at MacDonald. "You, Professor, are going to Rome in my stead."

Alison could not conceal her joy. "That's wonderful!" She jumped up and hugged MacDonald. "Oh, Davis, I'm so happy. You're going to be free. The world's going to have your discovery."

"Thank you, Alison." The professor pulled free of her and pressed closer to the desk. "Can this really be done? Will it be safe?"

"How safe?" added Jordan to the priest. "How are you going to pull it off?"

"There is nothing to 'pull off,' as you put it," said Don Pietro. "Each of us has a special signed travel or exit permit from Mayor Accardi. The guards are expecting the bishop and five priests at eleven-thirty tomorrow morning and will pass us right through to the train. We will be the only passengers from Venice on the train. Among the five priests will be Professor MacDonald, instead of myself. It is as uncomplicated as that."

"The guards won't have your name or picture?" asked Jordan.

"They know only that the bishop and five priests will be coming through. Professor MacDonald will be dressed in a hat and cassock on loan from my vicario, the one who assists me, who is approximately of Professor MacDonald's size and bulk. The professor will go through the guard line with the others unnoticed. There is no element of danger. By evening he will be safely in Rome. There is the miracle I promised."

"I don't know how to thank you enough," said Jordan with relief.

"Your thanks are premature. Bishop Uberti and I must go to the patriarch of Venice tonight and request his approval. It is only a formality. He will approve, of course. But even then, there is no reason for thanks. We all serve a common cause and command. To outwit the atheistic Communists. To give to the world a benefit that the Almighty in heaven above has bestowed on mankind." He stood up. "Dinner is waiting, and our best wine. We celebrate the miracle of tomorrow."

▶ ▶ ▶ ▶

All through the night, before sleep, and again upon awakening in the morning, Jordan suffered one emotion: a sense of loss.

Alison had elected to remain behind at Don Pietro's after dinner, in order to see Professor MacDonald off in the morning, and Jordan had gone by himself to the Piazza San Marco and listened to the music until it was closing time.

He could see the scenario of his immediate future

clearly. After reaching Paris, the professor would turn the world upside down with the announcement of his discovery. The Communists in Venice, seeing that they had lost, would lift the blockade on the city. Alison, free to go, would leave to return to Paris and then New York. And Jordan would once more be left alone, rudderless. In victory—loss.

Now, midmorning, hastening over the bridge to the Church of San Vincenzo to say his farewell to the professor, he sighted Alison in the square waiting for him.

"I'm sorry, Tim" was the first thing she said, "but you missed him by just a couple of minutes."

Jordan looked at his watch. "They weren't supposed to leave until ten-thirty. It's only twenty after."

"I guess they left early. Don Pietro is walking him over to the bishop's house. It is nearby here. The whole party will leave together for the railroad station."

"Well, as long as he's safely on his way."

"Thanks to you."

"I think Don Pietro would take another view of it. He would say thank God."

"You should have seen him, Tim, outfitted in a cassock. You'd have sworn the professor had been a priest all his life. He'll have no trouble getting by." She pointed off. "Look, Tim, there's Don Pietro returning. . . ."

Don Pietro was applying a large handkerchief to his forehead. "Hot, too hot in the sun. Come on inside. I'll treat you both to iced tea."

He continued toward the rectory, and Jordan and Alison caught up with him in the cool hallway.

"How did it go?" Jordan asked.

"He was just stepping into the gondola to join the others when I left," said Don Pietro. "There will be no problem."

"What time does he get to Rome?"

"About seven o'clock this evening."

Jordan turned to Alison. "Probably too late to catch a flight to Paris. He'll take a morning flight, be in Paris by noon. Do you know where he'll be staying?"

"He'll be taking my room at the Plaza Athénée," said Alison.

"Let's call him in Paris at noon tomorrow," said Jordan, "just to make sure everything's all right. We won't have to worry about our call being monitored."

"We'll call him—Paris—tomorrow," agreed Alison.

Don Pietro cleared his throat, as if to get their attention. He appeared strangely uncomfortable. He said hesitantly, "Uh, I should tell you, it will be no use to call him in Paris tomorrow. He will not be there."

"I don't get it," said Jordan. "Where will he be?"

"Uh, in Vatican City. He will be detained for a short time in the Vatican so that one of our superiors can speak with him."

"What are you talking about, Don Pietro? I don't understand."

"It was the patriarch's decision last night, when the bishop and I went to see him for his approval. The patriarch felt that in helping MacDonald leave the city, the Church was taking a great risk. In return for the risk, the patriarch thought it only proper that MacDonald have an opportunity to hear of the Holy See's interest in his discovery."

"I still don't understand," Jordan said. "What interest does the Church have in the professor's discovery? You're not being very lucid."

Don Pietro was distinctly more uncomfortable. He squirmed inside his cassock. "I-I will try to explain. It was felt that once the Holy Father learned of this momentous discovery, he would want the Church to convince Professor MacDonald that the Vatican is the proper medium through which to dispense his C-98 to the entire world. After all, the Vatican is neutral, serves all of mankind—"

"Wait a minute," Jordan interrupted. "Are you saying what I think you're saying?"

"That the professor should allow us, the Church, to handle the formula, pass it out in an intelligent and decent way. It would be done correctly, for the good of humanity."

Jordan did not like what he was hearing. "For the good of humanity?" he repeated. "And the Church is getting nothing out of this?"

Don Pietro lifted his shoulders. "I will not attempt to deceive you, my friend. I will be honest. In a secondary way, the Church would profit from the opportunity to dispense C-98, of course. The act would earn tremendous goodwill for the Church, especially in a time when the faithful are dwindling. Overnight, we are the ones selected by the discoverer as the agent to give succor to mankind. After all, Tim, what difference does it make who is selected to pass out the formula? It has to be someone. Why not the Church?"

"And you think Professor MacDonald will go for that?"

"We are all certain he will approve."

"What if he doesn't?"

"But he will. He will be persuaded to see this in the proper light."

"And if he isn't persuaded? You will let him go on to Paris?"

"Tim, Tim, he will be convinced. Once Cardinal Bacchi has talked to him—"

"Cardinal who?" Jordan interrupted harshly.

"Bacchi."

"That reactionary madman!" Jordan exploded. "I've read about him, heard about him, trying to turn the Church back to the Middle Ages, to impose super orthodoxy on orthodoxy, to stamp the entire world with his brand of Catholicism. You're going to turn that inquisitor loose on Professor MacDonald?"

"Come now, my friend, be reasonable. You are exaggerating. . . ."

"Don't tell me I'm exaggerating." Jordan whirled away from the priest, facing Alison. "Don't you see?" he said to her. "Now we're getting to the fine print. Bacchi is the kind of man who could keep MacDonald in the Vatican indefinitely, make him a prisoner again, until he cooperates. Bacchi is the kind of man who will use C-98 to proselytize, employ it as blackmail to hold over the world—You want to live to 150? Well, join up or no soap."

"Please, Tim," Don Pietro protested behind him.

Jordan ignored the priest. "Alison, believe me, turning MacDonald over to the likes of Cardinal Bacchi is a greater risk than keeping him here in Venice. Bacchi and his crowd are fanatics—well meaning, I'm sure—but so certain that their medieval beliefs are infallible that they are capable of doing anything to have their way. They could hold on to MacDonald forever, until he gave in. It may not happen. But it could happen. I don't see rescuing the professor from one set of ruthless fanatics—Communists—to turn him over to another set of fanatics—that Opus Dei group in the Church. We can't take a chance."

Alison was frightened. "Whatever you think is right, Tim."

Jordan had her by the shoulder. "Wait for me at the hotel." He started for the door. "I've got to get Mac-Donald back. I hope it's not too late."

He was through the door, in the sunlight, in the square, when he heard Don Pietro's shrill voice cry after him. "Tim, don't, don't—don't interfere!"

▶ ▶ ▶ ▶

Luckily, Jordan had caught a motorboat cruising in a canal, had hailed it, had offered the driver a bonus to get him to the railroad station as fast as possible.

During their speedy passage, Jordan had speculated on the possibility of catching Professor MacDonald in time. The clerical party had had a good head start, but they had gone by gondola, and now he hoped his motorboat would close the gap between them. If he failed to catch the professor in time, he felt it could be a disaster. The Church itself, he knew, would never condone what might happen, and might never know. Cardinal Bacchi and his minority group of Savonarolas could work quietly and meanly to achieve their ends.

Now the railroad station was in sight and growing closer. Then, just as the driver eased the craft in alongside the wharf, Jordan, at the bow, spotted them up ahead. The six members of the clerical party were at the top of the white stone stairs, before the entrance to the station. Two guards, one an officer, were inspecting their exit permits.

For a split second, as he paid off the boat's driver, Jordan had a pang of indecision. A few moments more and the professor would be free, free of the Communist net, and it might be the only opportunity for regaining his freedom he would ever have. If he remained here, the Communists might win by attrition, surely close in on him or catch him unless Bruno came through with another escape hatch. At the same time, he might be walking into a trap set by religious fanatics, who could detain him indefinitely. On the other hand—Jordan always was mindful of his own paranoia—the good priests might merely talk to MacDonald, try to persuade him, and failing to do so, they might free him. Could the gamble be taken?

Jordan's mind was already made up as he leaped out of the motorboat and hurried up the pier.

He wanted to run, to be sure to catch MacDonald before he finished the inspection and went through the glass doors into the depot. But Jordan was afraid to run, afraid to attract the attention of the many police scattered about the area.

With effort, he contained himself, moving in long, fast strides to the station's stairway and then up the steps two at a time.

Ahead, he could see that MacDonald, in a long black cassock, had just been allowed to proceed by the police guards and was going to join four others who had already been passed. One clergyman was left, his permit being inspected by the officer. The one who was left was dressed more regally than the others, and Jordan guessed that this was Bishop Uberti.

At the top of the stairs, Jordan slowed down and, trying to be as casual as possible, walked toward the two policemen and the clergyman. The police officer had just handed the one who was presumably the bishop his paper, and nodded, when Jordan called out, "Bishop Uberti."

The clergyman, about to start toward the others in his party, halted, responding to his name, and looked inquiringly at Jordan.

"I can't cross the line," Jordan said. "Can you come here for a moment? I must have a word with you concerning your mission."

Perplexed but curious, the stout bishop changed his course, moved past the guards, and came to Jordan. "Do we know each other?" he asked.

Jordan took him by the elbow and propelled him out of earshot of the guards. "I am a friend of Don Pietro's," he said in an undertone. "I am also a friend of the professor's. I brought them together."

"You are the American—Jordan?"

"Yes. The professor wrote out his formula. He left it at the hotel. I was to bring it to him, but I missed him." He patted his trouser pocket. "I have it here. He has it all in his head, but this will make it easier for him to remember. I want him to have it before he leaves."

"I'll take it and give it to him," said the bishop.

Jordan had been prepared for this. "I'm sorry. Except

for me, no one may touch the formula but the professor. His own rule. If you'll send him over here, I'll hand it to him and he can go."

The bishop wavered, undecided a moment, staring down at Jordan's pocket. "Very well," he said. "I'll send him over, but hurry it up."

He left Jordan, spoke a few words to the officer guard, then continued on to the glass doors of the depot where the priests were gathered. Jordan watched him speaking to MacDonald. He saw MacDonald nod, look toward him, and then begin to retrace his steps, walking back past the guards.

Nervously waiting, Jordan glanced over his shoulder at the floating boat station below. There were no unoccupied motorboats in view. A half-filled vaporetto, heading down the Grand Canal toward the lagoon, was just arriving at the station, the gate in its guardrail opening to discharge several passengers.

Jordan turned back just as MacDonald reached him.

"I'm almost free," MacDonald said. "The bishop told me you wanted to see me. What is it?"

"Listen to me. Just listen, and do as I do." Jordan had one arm around the professor's shoulder, and was starting him slowly down the flight of stone steps, as he pretended to dig for the nonexistent formula in his pocket. "You were not almost free. You were being led into a different trap. They were taking you to Rome, with no promise to release you until you gave the Vatican the exclusive right to C-98."

"That—that's unbelievable. Would they really do that?"

"They could do it. You can't chance it. We'll find another way. Right now, I've got to get you out of here fast."

The two had reached the foot of the stairs.

"But the bishop—he'll—" MacDonald began to protest.

"He can do nothing. He doesn't dare alert the guards, let them know he was helping you escape. See that vaporetto—the water bus—just about to leave. It would be natural to run, to catch it. Let's run."

At the platform of the station, Jordan broke into a trot, followed by MacDonald.

They came to the edge of the station just as the boat was parting from it.

"Jump on!" yelled Jordan.

He let MacDonald go past him. MacDonald leaped from the station to the boat, caught his foot in the hem of his cassock, and went sprawling on the hard wooden deck. Jordan vaulted aboard after him, regained his balance, and hastily joined several Venetians who were helping MacDonald to his feet.

"Are you all right?" Jordan asked anxiously. He drew MacDonald toward a bench and saw that he was limping.

"My leg," grunted the professor, "it's very painful. I hope I didn't break anything."

Jordan eased MacDonald down on the bench, and as he did so, he looked back at the receding railroad depot. There was a single figure, the bishop, hastening down the steps, running toward the boat station, shouting. But they were in the middle of the canal, out of reach, and Jordan turned away from the station.

"We'll have to get you some help for your leg," Jordan said to MacDonald.

"Maybe we'd better," MacDonald said, wincing. "But where do we go?"

"Considering your leg," said Jordan, "we have little choice. There's only one place to go—to a small clinic I know."

"But if they recognize me?"

"A small clinic owned by a dear friend," said Jordan. "We'll get off at the next station. Do you think you can make it?"

V

▶   ▶   ▶   ▶   ▶   ▶   ▶

There had been two narrow escapes as they had tried to make their way, haltingly, to the doctor's clinic in the square of San Zan Degolà.

Going on foot, they had twice almost run into police patrols, on each occasion detouring into a claustrophic side street in the nick of time. Increasingly, also, Professor MacDonald's injured leg impeded their progress. At last, Jordan sought and found a free gondola. They were able to move through the city, using the network of canals, more easily and safely.

Now, as they neared their destination, Jordan was speaking to MacDonald, who was still wearing the black cassock.

"This gondola will take us practically to his doorstep. He's been my doctor ever since I've been in Venice."

"What's his name again?" asked MacDonald.

"Dr. Giovanni Scarpa. He's one of the most popular physicians in the city. Has patients as far away as Mestre. In fact, he's so busy he has no time for exercise. You know how he gets his exercise? He keeps a car, a motorcycle, and a bicycle at the garage at the Piazzale

Roma, and if the weather is good, he uses the bike to pedal to his patients, to keep in shape. He's a Mutua doctor—Mutua is the name of Italy's National Health Insurance—and he takes workers who belong to the plan, even though it means less income for him, because he feels everyone deserves the best medical help possible. You may find our *Sior dotor*—'Mr. Doctor,' as the Venetians say—a little remote, cold, businesslike, but he's a good, warm, concerned man inside. And extremely learned. He and I have a mutual interest in rare books. He's quite a contrast to Don Pietro. For one thing, Dr. Scarpa is a freethinker, an absolute enemy of the Catholic Church. He believes strongly in birth control, population control, not only for Italy but for the world. In fact, his latest book—he's published several—advocates rigid birth control for Italy. It caused quite a controversy when it came out last year. . . . Well, here we are. Let's hope he's in."

The gondola had bumped up against the side of the canal, and the gondolier loosely secured it to the nearby iron rail. Jordan stood up, paid the gondolier, told him not to wait, stepped from the rocking boat to the semicircular cement stairs that led up to the square.

"Careful," he said to MacDonald as he helped him out of the gondola.

MacDonald limped up the stairs ahead of Jordan, who pointed to his left. "Scarpa's clinic, as well as his home."

It was a squarish two-story building, faced in yellow plaster, with an open terrace over the ground floor and a slanting red tile roof above it. They approached the black front door of the building.

"The doctor's offices and clinic are downstairs," said Jordan. "He lives upstairs with his wife and two children."

"After he examines me," said MacDonald worriedly, "do you think he'll allow me to stay?"

"I believe he will. At least, I'll try to persuade him,"

said Jordan. About to open the front door, he held back a moment. "Just one thing, Professor—"

"Yes?"

"I don't want him to know who you really are. Okay? I have my reasons."

"Very well, Tim."

They entered the cool, dark entry hall, setting a bell ringing, and continued into the austere waiting room, furnished with cane and brown imitation-leather armchairs and sofa arranged on a floor composed of red Verona marble tiles. The nurse's desk was unoccupied.

But almost immediately, from the open doorway of the examination room, she was heard, "*Chi è?*"

"She asks who it is," Jordan translated for MacDonald. He called back, "*Amici.*" Then to MacDonald, "Friends."

The nurse, a young but plain blonde in a blue uniform, came out of the examination room, looking a little annoyed. "The doctor's hours are not until two o'clock, and if you . . ." She recognized Jordan and stopped, breaking into a smile. "Oh, it is you, Mr. Jordan. That is different."

"Is *Sior dotor* in?"

"He has just returned from his morning house calls. He is in his office making some notes. I'll tell him you're here."

"Tell him I wouldn't have interrupted him this way, but it's an emergency."

The nurse disappeared into the doctor's office, only to reappear seconds later.

"Of course Dr. Scarpa will see you, Mr. Jordan," she said. "Please go right in."

Jordan took MacDonald by the arm and led him to a sofa. "Let me go in alone first, Professor. You get off your feet, rest that leg."

Once MacDonald had settled down, wincing as he sat, Jordan made directly for the open door of the doctor's

office and entered it. Dr. Giovanni Scarpa was standing,
occupied with some papers fanned out before him on his
desk. He was taller than the average Italian male, and
his height was accentuated by his thinness. Only a pa-
tina of black-gray hair covered his baldness. His face
was long and bony, and possessed a faintly clinical air.
His nose was sharp and long above a thin-lipped mouth.
At the sound of Jordan's approach, he raised his head,
and his dark eyes were warm.

"Tim," he said, putting out his hand.

"Giovanni, good friend," said Jordan, clasping the
other's extended hand, "and you are indeed a good
friend to see me without notice."

Dr. Scarpa's eyes took in Jordan's person, head to foot,
before he said dryly, "You look vigorous enough. But
looks can lie. Sit down and tell me what is wrong."

Jordan remained standing. "Oh, I'm fine. Nothing
wrong with me, knock wood." He rapped his knuckles
on the desk. "It is a friend of mine, a close friend. We
were running for a vaporetto just now, and he stumbled
and fell and injured his leg. I decided to bring him right
over here, to find out how serious it is. Can you have a
look at him?"

"Of course."

Jordan's relief was audible. "I'll bring him right in."

He left the office and returned to MacDonald, who
struggled to his feet awkwardly. "Will the doctor see
me?" asked MacDonald.

Jordan nodded. "This minute. Can I help you?" He
reached to take MacDonald's arm, then realized that the
professor was still wearing the black cassock. Jordan
hesitated. "Wait...." His hand touched the top of the
garment. "We'd have to explain this. The nurse didn't
seem to notice, but the doctor might ask questions. What
are you wearing underneath this thing?"

"My suit."

"Better, much better. Let's get you out of this clerical

outfit." Quickly, he helped MacDonald divest himself of the robe, then rolled it up and stuffed it into the side of the sofa. "Okay, that's better. Now let's go in to see him. I'll introduce you as Professor—Professor Dawson."

Jordan led the limping older man into the office as Dr. Scarpa came around his desk to meet them.

"Dr. Scarpa," Jordan said, "this is an old friend of mine from New York—Professor Dawson."

The Italian shook MacDonald's hand. "Professor of what?" he asked politely.

MacDonald looked at Jordan blankly, and Jordan answered, "Renaissance history. He's well known in his field."

Dr. Scarpa addressed MacDonald. "Tim explained to me that you had an accident. What seems to be troubling you?"

"It's mainly my knee—my left knee."

Dr. Scarpa's eyes had narrowed as they held on MacDonald's face. He nodded absently. "All right, let's find out what it is. Let's go into the examination room. I'll have a look and then take an X-ray."

He guided MacDonald into a small adjacent room and shut the door.

Jordan remained behind, alone in the doctor's office. Finding his pipe, filling and lighting it, he remembered that Dr. Scarpa had several recovery rooms with cots in the rear where he sometimes kept anesthetized patients overnight. He wondered if he could prevail upon the physician to keep MacDonald in one of those rooms for two or three days, until word came from Bruno that an escape had been arranged. Smoking, Jordan stood beside the doctor's neat desk, staring at a set of hypodermic-syringe containers. After several minutes, he heard the door behind him open and close, and Dr. Scarpa appeared at his desk.

"I had a look at the knee," he said. "I don't think it is anything serious. But we've taken a picture. We'll soon know for certain. I've left him in there for some heat therapy and"—he moved to the swivel chair at his desk and sat down—"because I wanted to speak to you alone."

This sounded mildly ominous. Jordan found a place on the couch across from the desk. "Yes, Giovanni, what is it?"

Dr. Scarpa's features were unmoving as a mask. His hands fiddled with a Florentine letter opener on his desk. His eyes were lowered. "Your friend in there," he said softly. "Examining him, I felt rather like your famous—or infamous—American doctor, Dr. Mudd."

Jordan was confused. "Dr. who?"

"Dr. Samuel A. Mudd, the American physician who treated John Wilkes Booth's broken leg in 1865 and was sent to jail for aiding Lincoln's assassin. Just now, in there, I felt like Dr. Mudd."

Jordan was momentarily speechless.

Dr. Scarpa went on. "I was aiding a criminal, an enemy of the state. Yes, Tim, I recognized your friend, the spy whose photograph is posted everywhere. He is no professor, no historian. He is a spy. All of Venice is trying to find him. Why did you lie to me?"

Jordan found his voice. "I didn't know what to say. He is a friend. He needed help. I said whatever came to mind. I'm sorry, Giovanni."

"You could compromise me. It could mean real trouble."

Jordan hesitated, then grasped a straw. "If you know the truth, why are you treating him now? Why don't you just pick up the phone and call the police?"

Dr. Scarpa's thin lips curved upward slightly in the semblance of a smile. "Because you are my friend, and he is your friend, and my instinct tells me you would not aid a criminal."

"Thank you, Giovanni. Your instinct is correct. The man is not a criminal. He is not a spy. That is some

nonsense the police dreamed up. His name is not Dawson. It is MacDonald. And he is a professor, an English
scientist who has his laboratory in New York. Why do
the police want him? For no criminal act whatsoever.
Quite the contrary. It is the police who are engaging in
criminal behavior. MacDonald was doing experiments
in the Soviet Union. He made a discovery the Russians
wanted. He came to Venice, en route home, and the
Russians asked your police to detain him. I don't think
he should be detained. So I'm trying to help him get out
of the city." He waited for the physician to absorb what
he had said, and then he added, "I know my story is
difficult to accept, but do believe me. It is true."

Dr. Scarpa looked up. "I believe you, Tim."

"I appreciate that."

The nurse had entered the office carrying Mac-
Donald's X-rays. She placed them before Dr. Scarpa and
left.

Picking up the X-rays, Dr. Scarpa came to his feet.
"Now we shall see what shape your fugitive is in." He
carried the negatives to the far end of the room, hung
them before a light box, and turned on the light. In less
than a minute he was through studying them.

He made his way back to his swivel chair. "Good
news, Tim. No fractures. Nothing of a serious nature.
Most likely just a pulled ligament. It will take care of
itself in a matter of days. Maybe three days or so. He
should stay off his feet as much as possible."

"Well, that brings up something else."

"Yes?"

"Considering what you've done already, I don't know
how much further I can impose upon you. I am seeking
a means of getting the professor out of the city. I need
some safe, quiet place to keep him until I complete my
plans. I was wondering if you'd mind keeping him for
two or three days—we'd see that he gets meals—in one
of your rooms in the rear?"

A buzzer sounded, and Dr. Scarpa lifted the receiver of his phone. "Yes?" he said in Italian. . . . "The mayor?" He glanced at Jordan and then said, "Of course I'll speak to him. Put him on." He waited, listened, said, "And good day to you, Your Honor. What can I do for you?" He listened again. "Well, I'm sorry she's feeling that way. But don't be concerned. It sounds like no more than a touch of the flu. But I'll certainly want to see her. You tell your wife I'll come by in an hour, in two at the most. . . . It is quite all right. Margot is one of my favorite patients. Tell her to keep warm, and to expect me."

He hung up and swung back to Jordan. "That was our Mayor Accardi. I take care of his wife. Now, wouldn't he like to know whom else I'm taking care of today?" With hardly a pause, he went on. "As to your last question. Yes, you may leave Professor MacDonald with me. We'll fix a comfortable place for him in a back room."

Effusively, Jordan reached across the desk to shake his friend's hand. "Giovanni, you're a godsend." He jumped up. "I've got to run now. I'll be back—bringing him some food at dinnertime."

▶ ▶ ▶ ▶

This was a trip, Tim Jordan thought, he had never taken before with a serious purpose. It was a trip he had taken several hundred times—although not lately—for pure relaxation and pleasure.

The crossing from the Hotel Danieli to the Hotel Excelsior on Lido island opposite always took about eleven minutes. Now Jordan's watch told him seven minutes had passed, with the island of San Lazzaro, so deceptively placid in the sunlight, already receding behind them. Up ahead was his destination, the Lido. Shortly, they would run alongside it. Then their CIGA motor launch, or motoscafo, would swing left into a short dead-end canal, move under two bridges, and slide up to the awninged pier at the rear of the Hotel Excelsior.

As they made their approach to the Lido, he was reminded, once again, that Alison Edwards, beside him in the open back of the launch, had never made this trip before.

"We're almost there," he told her, and pointed to the land and canal entrance ahead.

She leaned against him, toward the side of the boat, for a better look. The warm touch of her body made him tingle, and he was instantly aroused. He understood immediately the impulse that had inspired him to invite her along to the Lido. It was simply that he wanted to be near her all the time. Until now, it had only been the bottle he wanted near. But now it was a living woman, the first since Claire of long ago, and it seemed unbelievable to him that it was happening. Especially unbelievable that it was happening in a time of such turmoil and danger.

He realized that the day was only half done, and it had been packed with more incident and excitement than the entire year preceding it. After leaving Professor MacDonald safely with Dr. Scarpa, Jordan had returned to the Hotel Danieli, where Alison had been waiting for him in his suite as instructed. She had been filled with anxiety, wondering what had taken place after Jordan had left her with Don Pietro and raced off to rescue MacDonald from Bishop Uberti and the party of priests taking him to Rome.

Coke in hand, Jordan had sat down and allayed all of Alison's fears. MacDonald was safe, he had assured her. Briefly, he had recounted the events of the busy morning. He had intercepted MacDonald at the train depot in the nick of time. They had gone to Dr. Scarpa's undetected. The problem there had not been MacDonald's knee—his injury had been superficial—but the fact that the physician had recognized the professor from the posters he had seen. Happily, Jordan had reported, he had convinced his friend of the professor's innocence, and the doctor had agreed to provide a hideout until Bruno came through with his bribed guard.

Then Alison had asked the unexpected. "What if Bruno doesn't come through? What if the guard won't be bribed?"

Until this moment, Jordan had been so fixed on Bruno as the means of Professor MacDonald's liberation that he had not faced the possibility of failure. Alison had forced him to face it.

"You're right," he had told her. "I must find an alternative way out, just in case."

"Any ideas?"

"Not this second. But I'd like to look into some of the different routes out of Venice, find out how thoroughly they are being patrolled. The Lido, for one—the island across the lagoon—it stands between Venice and the open sea, the Adriatic—it is the best escape hatch aside from Mestre. I think I'd better get over there, find out what's going on."

He had meant to go by himself. He travels fastest who travels alone, et cetera. But he had been looking at Alison—gamin bob, oversized lavender glasses, absolutely ravishing pert profile—and on impulse he had asked, "Want to come along?"

"If I won't be in the way."

"Of course not. In fact, forgot to tell you, but I keep a cabana on the Excelsior beach the entire season. Although I haven't used it lately, it's there. You can use it while I poke around and make inquiries on the security setup. You can take a sunbath."

"It sounds too indolent and hedonistic, considering poor Davis's situation."

"You'll be seeing him between six and seven. I promised Dr. Scarpa we'd look in and bring the professor a bite. There's nothing you can do for him by sitting and fretting. But on the Lido, I might come up with something. And you can come up with a tan."

She had smiled, devastatingly. "You're persuasive, Mr. Jordan. Okay, I'm coming with you."

He was jolted back to the present moment by the contact of the motor launch against the wide Hotel Excelsior pier. After the pilot's assistant had secured the craft, Jordan helped Alison off the boat, then led her between the gaily striped poles that held up the awning into the cavern of the hotel arcade stretching beneath the upstairs lobby. He continued to lead her past the variety of display cases, until they reached the outdoor bar and restaurant.

As they faced the green Adriatic, Jordan indicated the rows of beach cabanas to the right and left of them. The cabanas, white canvas and brown-trimmed, each with a decorative glass ball on top, were as picturesque as ever.

Alison was enthusiastic. "Absolutely charming," she said. "Where do we go?"

"Mine's to the left," he said. "*Libra* 5."

He started her down a sidewalk running behind the row of cabanas directly on the waterfront, turned off into the sand between cabanas, and brought her under the awning that extended in front of his cabana.

"Here we are," he said. "A cot in the sun, a beach chair in the shade, a porch furnished with table, chair, tub of water to get the sand off your feet, and inside behind the flap a private dressing room."

"So this is how the rich live."

"On a special discount," he said. "Now let me tell you what I'm going to be doing, and suggest what you should be doing. For myself, I'm going off to see a friend of mine who works here, a lifeguard named Dante. He'll know the situation. You see, he lives near the Porto di Lido, and he'll know the security setup. He . . ."

Jordan could see that she was bewildered, and he decided to take a moment to explain.

"Let me give you an idea of the layout. There are two strips of land—islands, actually—that stand between Venice and the sea. To go from Venice to the open sea, you have to get past these two strips of land, you have to go through narrow channels. A person wanting to get out of Venice by sea would cross the main lagoon, go through one of these channels. On the north side of the Lido, at the farthest end, is a channel called Porto di Lido, where our Venice Must Live Committee set up the hydraulic inflatable dam that is supposed to keep seawater out of the lagoon and city, although it's never been used yet. At the opposite end of the Lido is a channel called Porto di Malamocco. And at the farthest end of the next strip of land, Pellestrina, is a third channel called Porto di Chioggia. Can you picture this, Alison?"

"I-I think so," she said hesitantly.

"These three channels, outlets to the sea, would be further means by which, through which, a person might escape by water. Just as the Piazzale Roma and its causeway is a means by which a person might escape by land. Well, we know the Piazzale Roma is being closely guarded. Now I've got to find out how carefully these three water outlets are being guarded."

"I understand."

"My lifeguard friend, Dante, will have a good idea. So that's what I'm going to be doing now. Looking for him. As for you, that's easy. While I'm gone, you're going to be getting some sun or water."

"In the nude?"

"They don't allow it, but even if they did, it's not necessary. There are two women's swimsuits in the cabana."

"How convenient."

"I told you I had a Venetian girl friend I see occasionally. She uses the cabana and keeps her swimsuits here. I think . . ." He ran his eyes down the curves of Alison's figure. "They just might fit you. Anyway, put one on and take a dip. I won't be gone long."

He was wrong. He was actually gone for over an hour. He had tried to find Dante on the nearby pier, but a new lifeguard was in Dante's place and had no idea where he had gone. Jordan had then visited the beach office under the Excelsior and learned that Dante had gone into the town of the Lido for lunch. Jordan was told that the lifeguard might be found in one of three restaurants. Jordan had then mounted the flights of stone steps to the immense Excelsior lobby, hurried through it out the front entrance, and hailed a taxi to the town. He had visited all three restaurants and found Dante in none of them.

Returning to the hotel, he had left word for Dante to call on him at his cabana when he came back, and then he had started off to rejoin Alison.

At first he did not recognize her and thought he had stopped at someone else's cabana. He had never seen her almost nude, had only imagined it, and the naked contours were all new to him. She was lying stretched out on the beach cot in the sun, on her back, eyes closed behind her oversized sunglasses, a ribbon of white bikini covering her nipples but not her breasts, and a wisp of matching bikini drawn tightly at her pelvic area.

Momentarily, Jordan became acquainted with this lithe, slender female body he had not seen before—the bony shoulders, overflowing breast tops, slash of navel, slim hips accentuating the rising curve of the vaginal mound, firm thighs, and shapely long legs.

He sat gently on the edge of the beach cot, awakening Alison.

He said, "I see one of her bikinis fitted you."

"Oh, you, Tim. I must have been asleep." Her hand went down to the string securing her bikini bottom on one side. "Actually, no, hers did not fit. She has too much hip for me. I went into the hotel, and they sent me to a women's shop a block away. I found my size." She started to get up. One breast began to slip free, and she caught and covered it, and finally managed to sit upright.

She looked down at the bikini bottom. "Maybe it's not my size. I feel naked."

"Is that bad?"

"Well, it is if you're the only one of two."

"Then I'll strip down, get into my trunks." He stood up. "Let's go in the water."

He had started for the cabana when she called out, "Tim, did you see your friend?"

"He was out to lunch. I left a message for him to come here when he gets back. . . . See you in a minute."

He went through the cabana door, ducked past the curtain, and began to take off his clothes. When he was naked, he pulled his blue Italian swim shorts off a hook and stepped into them. Then he looked down at himself, and did not like what he saw—or rather, what she would see. He was definitely flabby and would look twice her age. The damn shorts stuck to the skin like adhesive, forcing his stomach to protrude and hang down slightly. At his chest, too much fat. Oh, well, he decided, none of this could determine what she really thought of him. Inhaling, he sucked in his breath—and his stomach— and stepped outside.

She was standing in the sun, waiting for him. He felt her eyes on him as he approached her. He felt all belly.

"You don't look like the most dangerous man in Venice," she said, "but you're definitely cute."

Relieved, he stopped holding in his stomach. "A woman of exquisite taste," he said, taking her hand. Together, they started across the blistering sand toward the water.

As they went into the water, over the shoreline pebbles and stones, it was unexpectedly cold. But as they waded farther out, until the water reached their thighs, it began to seem warmer. Not until they were thirty or forty yards from the shore did the water cover her bosom.

"This is as far as I go," Alison said. "I can't swim."

"Okay." He fell back in the water and, using a splashy backstroke, circled her twice. When he came upright once more, he wiped his eyes and grinned at her. There was no response. Her mind was elsewhere, and her face crossed with concern.

"What's the matter, Alison?" he asked.

"I'm worried. Here we are out here, playing around, when the professor's in such deep trouble. I feel we should be doing something more."

"I'm doing everything I can."

"I know, I know you are, Tim. But it is just that—well, Bruno and his bribe are our only prospect, and it's not enough. As you said before, we've got to come up with another possibility."

"Believe me, Alison, I don't stop thinking of it. I'm sure we'll hit on another idea."

"We *must*. Every day they are closing in on Professor MacDonald. If this continues for even a week more, they'll have to catch him. He and his discovery will be lost to the world forever."

"All right, Alison. Let's go in now and see if Dante has turned up."

When they emerged from the water and started back to the cabana, Jordan saw the squat, muscular figure in straw hat, T-shirt, and red trunks. Dante was standing before the cot, signaling to him.

"Is that your lifeguard friend?" asked Alison.

"Yes."

"I'll go inside and change while you talk to him."

She ran on past Dante into the cabana, while Jordan shook hands with his friend.

Dante jerked a thumb over his shoulder. "I see you got a new girl friend." He smiled broadly. "Or another one."

"Neither," said Jordan good-naturedly. "Let's just say she's a business associate."

"They told me you were looking for me at lunchtime."

"I even went into town to try to find you at one of your regular eating places."

"I was invited to lunch at a lady's apartment. Those lunches always take longer."

"I bet they do. . . . Actually, Dante, what I wanted to find out from you wasn't all that important. Just something I was curious about. You still living out near the Porto di Lido?"

"As always."

"In light of the present emergency, what's the action out there?"

"Action?" Dante was plainly puzzled.

"I'm talking about the situation in Venice," said Jordan, "the way the police have surrounded and locked up the city. I wondered if they bothered about your area or the channel—the Porto di Lido."

"Have they bothered? In all my years I have never seen anything like it. On the water, from far in the lagoon right up to the channel, it is swarming with police boats on patrol."

"So it is sealed tight?"

"No one is let through. Everyone is turned away. I can't believe all of this is for a mere spy. There are so many spies. No one fusses about the others."

"But this one stole Italy's top military secret."

"Don't you believe it, Tim. Someone told me it's a thief they are after, one who has stolen a Titian."

"I read it was a spy," said Jordan. "What about steamer traffic—all those cruise ships that come into the lagoon this time of the year?"

"No more. None has even appeared. They have all been informed by wireless not to approach Venice, because they will be turned away. There is only one outside ship in the lagoon, I heard. It was here for sudden repairs, a Greek cruise ship. It will be allowed to leave in the next week, since none of the poor passengers have been permitted to go ashore. Everyone is confined to the ship, except some officers."

195 ▶ ▶ ▶

Jordan's mind had seized on the last. A Greek cruise ship leaving Venice in a week. But if no one, except officers, was authorized to board or leave the vessel, there seemed almost no chance to smuggle MacDonald onto it. Still, it was something to keep in mind.

"Well, Dante, my curiosity is satisfied," Jordan said. "I wanted to take my lady friend on a short excursion to sea, through the Porto di Lido, but I guess I'll have to postpone it." He nodded toward the Adriatic. "Unless we just tried to swim out from this beach."

"You wouldn't get far, my friend. The carabinieri are posted on the end of each of those piers armed with rifles with telescopic sights." He shrugged cheerfully. "We must face it. Our Venice is now a prison."

"Casanova escaped it."

"Ah, Casanova. That one was something special. Now we speak of mere mortals."

"I suppose we do. Anyway, I appreciate all your information. I'd better be heading back to the main prison."

"And I'd better get back on duty," said Dante. "See you soon."

Jordan watched the sturdy lifeguard leave. His thoughts went back to the plight of Professor Mac-Donald. He wondered whether MacDonald was still safely in the care of Dr. Scarpa. Then he was sure of it. Few men in Venice were more trustworthy or loyal to their word than Dr. Scarpa.

▶ ▶ ▶ ▶

In the huge, ornately furnished upstairs bedroom of Mayor Accardi's Renaissance-style home, not far from the Rialto Bridge, Dr. Giovanni Scarpa had finished his examination of Margot Accardi and was tucking his stethoscope into his small leather bag.

"Then you assure me I will live," said Margot Accardi, rising with difficulty from the chaise longue, securing her tentlike dressing gown around her. "The last time I had the flu—"

"It is not the flu, Margot," Dr. Scarpa said somewhat testily. "I have told you. It is no more than a mild cold that has settled in your chest. You may have a little discomfort, but if you stay indoors, keep warm, drink plenty of liquids, you should be your old young self in two or three days."

"Are you prescribing anything?"

"Not necessary," said Dr. Scarpa. He did not believe in promoting pills, even as a placebo, when they were not warranted. He believed in the natural restorative powers of the human body, especially when it came to minor ailments. "Just avoid overexertion. And, I repeat, take liquids."

Dr. Scarpa closed his bag, observed Margot Accardi lumbering to the bell rope next to the bedroom door. He remembered when she had married the future mayor. She had been a big-boned, handsome young woman with some pretension toward a career in opera. She had been too lazy to pursue singing seriously and had settled into a soft life of eating, shopping, charities. In the last two decades she had gained two chins, and her person was a mountainous monument to uncounted éclairs and products of Perugina.

"Speaking of liquids," she said, "we will begin now." She tugged at the bell rope. "I told Anna to have tea ready for us. Surely it won't hurt you to spare a few minutes for tea, Giovanni."

Dr. Scarpa sighed. Tea and gossip was the unfailing routine after every house call at the Accardis'. Dutifully, Dr. Scarpa brought a gilt chair to a position across from the chaise longue as Margot Accardi settled down on it and began to recount a rumor of Deputy Mayor Santin's wife and her flirtation with a virile young assistant bartender twenty years her junior.

In a few minutes the tea cart was rolled in between

Dr. Scarpa and his portly Scheherazade. He noted that the cart carried only a tiny pot of tea and a great heap of chocolate-covered cookies.

As Margot Accardi concluded her first gossip, poured the tea, and then served herself a plateful of cookies, Dr. Scarpa decided it was time to divert the conversation to something more topical.

"And how is your husband?" he inquired politely. "How is he coping with the emergency he declared?"

"I was just coming to that. We must both have ESP."

"Well, it is a problem that has affected everyone in the city," said Dr. Scarpa drily.

Margot Accardi's eyes brightened, and she came forward on the chaise longue, chins jiggling, and lowered her hoarse voice. "But the problem is not what everyone thinks it is," said the mayor's wife. "It is of much greater importance. Of world importance, really." Her voice dropped another octave. "This is absolutely confidential, Giovanni. You are the only person on earth I'd confide in. After all, you are my doctor."

"You can trust me, Margot," Dr. Scarpa said with a show of indifference.

"And I do. I'm bursting to tell someone. Guess what?" She made a dramatic pause. "Venice has not been closed down because Cutrone and his police are trying to catch a spy." Another pause. "In fact, there is no spy."

"Oh, no?"

"No spy whatsoever," Margot Accardi said with firmness. "They made that up because they can't let the world know the truth. There is someone loose here they are trying to catch—and will catch—but he's not a spy— he's an internationally famous scientist."

Dr. Scarpa tried to appear surprised, knowing as he did from Tim Jordan that the fugitive he was harboring in his clinic was a scientist. At the same time, he was pleased to hear Jordan's identification of the fugitive confirmed.

"A scientist?" said Dr. Scarpa.

"Not just *any* scientist," said Margot Accardi. "Perhaps the most celebrated scientist of our time—greater than Pasteur or Ehrlich—once the word gets out about his discovery."

This was new. "Discovery?" repeated Dr. Scarpa.

"Listen to me, Giovanni," said Margot Accardi, "because you've never heard anything like it in your lifetime. This scientist, Professor Davis MacDonald—his real name—he's a gerontologist."

"You don't mean geriatrician?"

"No, not someone who treats the diseases of old age. No, I mean gerontologist—someone who tries to prolong human life. Well, he's done it, this Professor Mac-Donald. He's made a discovery on how to prolong human life for each of us to the age of 150."

For the first time Dr. Scarpa's passive countenance cracked. He sat up. "Margot, I'm not sure I heard you correctly. Will you repeat what you just told me."

"About what? His discovery?"

"About this man's having found a way to make everyone live to the age of 150. It's not possible."

Margot Accardi's head went up and down, and her chins shook vigorously. "It's the truth, the absolute truth. My husband confided it to me from the beginning."

"Who told him?"

"The Russians. The discovery was made by Mac-Donald, an Englishman or American, while doing experiments in Russia. He wanted to keep his discovery from the Communists, and so he ran off with it. He came to Venice, and our Russian allies asked us to help catch him and take him and his discovery back to Russia, where it belongs. Of course, as comrades of the Russians, we will all be given priority in receiving these longevity shots."

Dr. Scarpa's hand was unsteady as he tried to set down

his teacup. "So now we have someone who is going to help us all live twice as long."

"As soon as we can catch him. My husband says he will. Won't that be glorious?"

"Won't it, though," said Dr. Scarpa bitterly. His agitation was so profound that he felt he must leave at once. He stood up. "Thank you for the—the news. I appreciate your confiding in me."

"You won't repeat it to a soul?"

"You know you can count on me, Margot. Now I had better hurry back to the office. I have an important—a very important meeting this afternoon."

▶ ▶ ▶ ▶

After leaving the motor launch that had returned them from the Lido to the pier near the front of the Hotel Danieli, Jordan had accompanied Alison past the police guards to the lobby of the hotel. She had wanted to take a shower and then take a nap before joining Jordan on his dinnertime visit to Professor MacDonald. He had wanted to check his mail slot to see if there was a message from Bruno before going out to buy some food for MacDonald's dinner.

He had found three message slips in his box noting three telephone calls from Marisa Girardi. Each one told him, *Please come to the office. Urgent.*

He had had no idea what office matter could be so urgent, unless this was Marisa's way of telling him that her brother, Bruno, had some word on his bribe attempt with the captain of the carabinieri.

Parting with Alison, he had promised to pick her up at five-thirty for their visit to MacDonald at Dr. Scarpa's. Before shopping for dinner, Jordan decided that he had better get over to his neglected office and learn what Marisa considered so urgent.

Now, on the second floor of the Assicurazioni Generali

building, greeting the guards in the anteroom, he entered the secretary's office. "Gloria, tell Marisa I'm back and ready for her."

He had no sooner settled behind his desk than Marisa appeared. He made an instant comparison. She was sexier-looking, but less sexy to him than Alison. She was more familiar to him, more obvious, but less interesting than Alison. She came straight across the office to him, kissed him briefly.

She stood over him, businesslike, and in a prosecutor's tone of voice asked, "My God, where have you been?"

"I was tied up with a few matters," he said evasively.

"But your job—there are some things I cannot handle, Tim. I haven't seen you at all since the night I woke you up to tell you the police were coming to the Danieli."

"That's it," he said quickly. "My old college friend, the one I'm trying to get to Paris to meet with the separatists. I've been busy trying to find a place for him."

She considered him. "Is that true?"

"Yes," he said too quickly. "Now about all those 'urgents' you left at the hotel. I hope they have to do with Bruno. Has Bruno come up with something yet?"

"I don't know, and I don't want to know. That's your private affair with Bruno. I want nothing to do with it. No, I haven't seen Bruno for two days. We keep different hours. He's chasing around with the police all the time."

"Then what can be so damn urgent?"

She shook her head, momentarily wordless. "Tim, you have a job. You work for the Venice Must Live Committee. Things happen here. You have to be here some time."

Chastened, he softened his expression. "All right. What is it? What's come up?"

"Schuyler Moore," she said.

"The columnist?"

"I'm told he is the most widely read journalist in the United States. I'm told that by him, anyway. Mr. Moore says he is with the American News Syndicate and because it is a wire service his column appears in 1,400 newspapers daily. He says he's the biggest."

"That's right. He's the biggest."

"Well, he came in to see you this morning. You weren't available, so I saw him. He had stopped in Venice for one day, on his way to Bucharest, and he got caught by the emergency. He's still stuck, and he must keep up his daily column, to file the minute he gets out of here. He doesn't know much about Venice, so he started asking around for some good story leads. Someone told him about the Venice Must Live Committee, how we are trying to save Venice from being flooded over or sinking into the sea, and that we had already installed an inflatable dam at the Porto di Lido to protect the city. This aroused his curiosity, so he came in to see us."

"You mean Schuyler Moore wants to write about our project?"

"Exactly. It was not easy. At first, he wanted to see the real inflatable dam in action. I said that was impossible. It has not been tried out yet. He wanted to know why not. I told him he had better get that answer from you."

"You could have told him. You could have been honest on that."

"It should come from someone like you, Tim. Anyway, I was on my toes. I told Schuyler Moore that in one sense, the dam had been tested—in fact, many times. I told him that we had a mock-up or large miniature model of the area, especially the Porto di Lido, built so that we could test a reduced version of the inflatable dam. This fascinated him. I told him it was at an experiment station called Centro Sperimentale di Idraulica and that it was located at Voltabarozzo, not far from here near Padua. He wanted to know if we would run a test of the dam in the miniature for him, if he wrote about it. I said I thought so, *if* he wrote about it. I described it, and he became more and more enthusiastic and finally promised to devote two daily columns to it, maybe

three." She paused. "Tim, that would be our biggest
publicity break of the year."

He agreed. "No question. One catch. What he wants
to see is outside Venice. And the city is locked up. How
do we get him out to Voltabarozzo?"

"I anticipated that. I took care of it."

He eyed Marisa more warmly. "You're really on the
ball for a dawdling Venetian."

She smiled. "I've been Americanized by you. I even
drink Cokes, eat hamburgers. What I did was phone Santin, the deputy mayor. I told him what we wanted to do
and how important the publicity was for us and for the
city. He spoke to Colonel Cutrone of the carabinieri. He
called me back. They know you. They know me. They
checked out Schuyler Moore and know him. They do
give some special permissions to leave the city temporarily, and they gave us such permission."

Jordan's heart leaped. He immediately saw that if he
could take Schuyler Moore out of the city, he might manage to take Professor MacDonald out with them.

Marisa was speaking again. "The one condition, for
our getting this permission to leave, is that we must be
accompanied by two guards from the carabinieri."

Jordan's hope was dashed. No MacDonald.

"Okay," he said. "When does all this take place?"

"The day after tomorrow. In the morning at nine. I've
arranged for a car."

Jordan frowned. "I had some other plans for tomorrow
and the next day. It'll be hard for me to get away. Look,
Marisa, you know as much about the project as I do. I'm
sure you can handle Schuyler Moore by yourself. You
can take him out there. I'd appreciate it if you'd do it."

"No, thank you," she said stubbornly. "I know the
project fairly well. But I can't explain and dramatize it
the way you can. I can't take the responsibility. You
really know how to handle it. Remember, you were an
engineer."

"But, Marisa—"

She had put her foot down. "No. It's you or no story."

He sighed. "Okay—day after tomorrow at nine o'clock. We'll pick him up."

She bent over Jordan and kissed him. "I knew you'd do it."

"I knew you knew. Go back to work, Marisa. I've got some errands to do."

She started to leave, then snapped her fingers, seeming to remember something, and whirled around. "I almost forgot. Dr. Giovanni Scarpa called on the phone asking for you. He called twice. He says he must see you at once. It is urgent."

Jordan groaned. "More urgents. Did he say anything else?"

"Only not to wait until dinner to see him. He would like you to come over to see him immediately. Do you have some ailment or problem?"

"In a way," he said with a forced smile. "Now beat it."

When she was gone, Jordan lingered, trying to imagine why Dr. Scarpa demanded to see him at once. Could the police have come by? Could Professor MacDonald be in further danger? Or what? Jordan had no clue, no imagined answer, and could only respond to Dr. Scarpa's summons in person to learn what was going on. He decided not to lose time picking up Alison. He would go by himself, as fast as possible. After all, the word for the day was—urgent.

▶ ▶ ▶ ▶

It was almost four-thirty in the afternoon by the time Tim Jordan arrived at the door of Dr. Giovanni Scarpa's yellow plaster two-story combination office and dwelling.

Inside, the nurse in blue uniform seemed to be ex-

pecting him, for she led him across the waiting room
directly to Dr. Scarpa's office. At the door, she said, *"Sior
dotor* told me he would see you immediately. You may
go right in, Mr. Jordan."

"Is he alone?" asked Jordan.

"Just a few minutes ago your friend woke up from his
nap—the professor with the injured knee—and *Sior
dotor* summoned him for a talk." She opened the door.
"Go right in."

Jordan entered apprehensively, closing the door behind him. He saw Dr. Scarpa behind his desk and Professor MacDonald seated on a pull-up wooden chair opposite him. Only one of them was talking. Dr. Scarpa,
elbows on his desk, fingers locked before him, was
speaking in a low, harsh voice. Neither one of them took
any notice of Jordan. Dr. Scarpa was intent on what he
was saying, and MacDonald was concentrating fully on
the physician's words.

Jordan stood uncertainly by the closed door, listening,
trying to comprehend exactly what Dr. Scarpa was saying.

". . . then the mayor's wife told me they were not hunting a spy," Dr. Scarpa was saying, "but a scientist—a
fact I already knew but did not mention—a special kind
of scientist, a gerontologist named Professor Davis
MacDonald. I assume that is correct?"

"It is correct," said MacDonald.

"And that you have made a discovery of how to prolong human life until approximately the age of 150 years.
Is that true?"

"It is true. I have discovered a formula I call C-98 that
arrests or eliminates fatal diseases and restructures an
essential part of the genetic system."

"You—you've really found this?"

"I have. Beyond a question of doubt."

"And what do you mean to do with this formula?"

"As soon as I'm free of Venice, I intend to give it to
the world, for the benefit of mankind for all time."

"Benefit of mankind?" Dr. Scarpa echoed. Then his voice rose sharply. "*Benefit* of mankind?" he repeated. "Of course."

"Professor MacDonald, was the nuclear bomb invented for the *benefit* of mankind? Was the bubonic plague, the black death, for the *benefit* of mankind? Professor, if you release your C-98, you will be unleashing the greatest disaster ever visited upon the human race. You mark my word, your formula to prolong life will ultimately destroy life."

MacDonald's voice also rose. "That's absurd."

Taken aback by Dr. Scarpa's accusation, Jordan made his way to the couch behind MacDonald and lowered himself onto it. He remained attentive, trying to comprehend what Dr. Scarpa meant.

"Professor MacDonald," Dr. Scarpa continued abrasively, "you listen to me. Perhaps I have a better picture of the consequences of your discovery than you have. I am a humanitarian, while you are a technician. I have devoted much of my adult life to studying the population explosion on earth and trying to confine the birthrate— this, this indeed for the benefit of mankind. But in one stroke you can obliterate my work and the work of all of us who are trying to contain overpopulation."

"Forgive me, Doctor, but you make no sense to me. By extending human life, prolonging it in good health, I will be saving life."

"Will you, though?" said Dr. Scarpa viciously. "A half century ago there were two billion people on earth. Today, there are over four billion. In another thirty or forty years, there will be eight billion people on earth. Already, with our short life-spans, without your damn prolongation-of-life formula, we have this natural growth overstraining our resources that supply food, that supply energy, that supply shelter. What keeps us going, even poorly, is that the four billion people now on earth, or most of them, will be dead in seventy or so years. But what if they did not die? What if they stayed on until their 150 years were up while new billions were added to them instead of replacing them? It would be, as one of your own gerontologists, Dr. Alexander Leaf of Harvard, said, 'terribly destructive socially and economically.' Take one simple factor—food. We can't feed four billion people today. If we extend their lives, and add four, eight, sixteen billion more, how are we going to feed them? Three to ten billion will starve—do you hear me?—wither and die for lack of food. There will be murders, riots, wars, and additional millions will die in the fight for food. Can you imagine wars for *food* and nothing else?"

"There will be food," said MacDonald calmly. "There will be synthetic food."

"Where is it *now?*" Dr. Scarpa demanded. "You are ready to prolong life now. Where is the food for that life today? You are going to condemn to death billions of people now and in the years to come. I won't even speak of the other consequences of your savage formula—the unemployment and subsequent misery it will create, the pollution and waste it will add to the world. The only leveler that exists today, that makes the world work, is death in our current life-span. If you postpone death, you send half of all humanity to certain execution. And I, for one, won't have it. I entreat you to bury your formula—never, never release it to the world."

"That would be impossible," said MacDonald. "Scientific progress cannot be inhibited by fanaticism. Each new scientific discovery tends to create its own problems. Newer scientific discoveries are made to solve them. Meanwhile, humanity will enjoy the golden dream it has entertained all its life—the Fountain of Youth for one and all in reality."

Dr. Scarpa sat silent, staring at MacDonald with hatred. "You are blind," he said, "blind and egotistical and stupid. I don't want to see you anymore, let alone talk to you. It would please me if you would go back to your room. Yes, please do so. Let me speak to Tim Jordan alone."

Professor MacDonald stood up, offended, glanced at Jordan, then limped swiftly out of the office.

Once he was gone, Jordan rose heavily, went to the pull-up chair, and drew it closer to the desk.

"Giovanni," he said, "you were too harsh with him."

"Not harsh enough."

"He is a genius. Whatever you say about his discovery, it is perhaps the greatest ever made in history. I do believe he is right. Science will find means to compensate for any harm his C-98 may bring."

"You are living in a fool's heaven," said Dr. Scarpa flatly. "I promised to give refuge to an innocent man wanted by the police. I did not promise to harbor a true criminal. Tim, I am sorry, but I cannot keep such a man under my roof."

Jordan was alarmed. "Giovanni, be reasonable. I have no place to take him. Only a few days—"

"No, in good conscience, I cannot protect him further."

"But if you send him out of here and we have no place to turn, the Communists are sure to capture him. They'll have him and his formula to themselves."

"All the better. Let them have him and his formula. It will mean the destruction of Communist Russia in a decade or two. Overpopulation—starvation—will destroy their system. Now, that would truly be a benefit to mankind. Yes, let them capture him. Let them have him and his time bomb."

Jordan felt helpless. "You won't reconsider? You are ready to turn him out, leave him to the mercy of the police?"

"Immediately."

"I guess it's no use arguing with you."

"No use whatsoever."

Jordan came to his feet. "Then one small favor only,

for our old friendship. Let him stay this one night, until I can figure out what to do with him."

For several moments, Dr. Scarpa did not speak. At last, he looked up. "Go now. Come back for him at nine tomorrow morning. Don't worry. I won't do to him what he would do to others. I won't let him starve. I'll see that the condemned has his last supper."

209

VI

▶   ▶   ▶   ▶   ▶   ▶   ▶

It was almost ten o'clock in the morning, a hot, humid Venice morning, and Jordan had had MacDonald in tow ever since leaving Dr. Scarpa's office a full half hour ago.

Now, in a side street off the teeming Mercerie, a few blocks behind the Piazza San Marco, Jordan scouted the terrain ahead. It was as dangerous as no-man's-land. At short intervals khaki-clad, armed local police, in pairs, passed in patrol, searching the faces of shopping pedestrians.

"It's a risk," Jordan muttered. "But I don't know what else to do."

Even if he made his destination, Jordan was aware, there were hazards involved. All last night, dreading the morning, he had reviewed in his mind friends and acquaintances he might trust to provide a hiding place until Bruno came through—if he came through—and he had been unable to think of a single safe haven. By the time he had picked up MacDonald, he had settled on a place of last resort. His plan was to take MacDonald to his office in the Venice Must Live Committee suite and try to secrete him there. He did not like his choice, but he could conjure up no other. The uncertainties were numerous. Suppose his secretary, Gloria, recognized MacDonald? Suppose Marisa recognized him? Suppose visitors, or other personnel in the building, came across him?

But at the moment, Jordan realized, the problem was not how unsafe his destination might be, but how much more dangerous the means of reaching it.

He watched the passersby coming and going on the Mercerie, then decided to venture into that main street by himself to see if the coast was clear of police.

"Just wait here a moment," he told MacDonald. "Let me see if we can make our move now."

He walked to the edge of the Mercerie and peered to his left toward the Piazza San Marco. No uniforms in sight. He swung to his right and looked off. At once he saw a familiar face and figure approaching from perhaps forty or fifty feet away.

She was a tall, flat young woman holding a black umbrella aloft and waving to a cluster, a human bee-swarm, of nondescript middle-aged people frantically trying to stay close to her.

This was Felice Huber, with a sensitive, elongated, Virginia Woolf countenance, a scholarly thirtyish woman of Swiss origin who was a tour guide for the Venice travel agency CIT. In a pre-Marisa period, Jordan had gone to bed with her several times, no copulation, strictly oral both ways, which was fine. They had remained friends, enjoying an occasional lunch and discussions about Magritte and other wonderful art crazies.

Jordan started toward her. "Felice!" he called out.

She saw him instantly, and her usual somber, sometimes unhappy, face broke into a smile. They met. She stopped, the bee-swarm stopping behind her, and he pecked a kiss at her cheek.

"You're looking wonderful," he said. "How've you been?"

"Unwonderful, same reasons," she replied. "And busy, as you can see. Today, for this English flock—Liverpool and Manchester—it is Program A." Mockingly she recited the tour advertising brochure. "Program A. Morning on foot. Short historical and artistic introduction of the city. Walk on Venice's main artery. Description of St. Mark's Square, political center of the Venetian Republic. Visit of the Golden Basilica and Ducal Palace, residence of the Doges and the most important seat of government in the *Serenissima*. Bridge of Sighs and prisons. Five thousand lire per person, including guide-lecturer, entrance fees, and tips. How does that sound to you?"

"So glowing that I'd like to invite myself to come along."

"You? You're kidding. You invented Venice."

"Actually, it's for a friend around the corner. His first visit. I've been trying to show him the city. But I'd rather have him hear it all from you." He reached for his wallet. "I'll pay you the 10,000 lire—"

"Cut it out, Tim. Get your friend and hop on. This one's on the house." She half-turned, hoisting her umbrella again and calling out, "All right, friends, stay together and follow me. We're approaching St. Mark's Square."

Relieved, Jordan backed off and hastened to get Professor MacDonald. He felt better. The perilous journey to the Piazza San Marco would now be safer—safety in numbers—the professor might be less identifiable caught up in a mass of pedestrian tourists.

He had MacDonald by the elbow. "A friend of mine is conducting a tour into the Piazza area. We're joining it. Make it easier to get to my office." He edged MacDonald to the main thoroughfare just as Felice Huber began to pass in front of them with her two dozen English visitors. "Okay, let's go," said Jordan as he pushed MacDonald into the group between a dumpy middle-aged woman wearing a floppy felt hat and a camera-laden, asthmatic elderly couple. Quickly, Jordan fell in step beside the limping MacDonald.

For the next five minutes, the pair pressed forward with Felice Huber's tour. Twice police came toward them, and passed them, without searching the group— in fact, ignoring it—and Jordan was pleased at his stratagem. At once, they came out of the confined darkness of the Mercerie, and the bright glare of the Piazza San Marco burst upon them.

Jordan stretched to look down the arcade toward his office entrance, prepared to break off from Felice's tour party and take MacDonald to their destination. But then Jordan saw that this would be impossible. In the arcade, not far from his office entrance, three uniformed members of the questura, or local police, were chatting with two officers of the carabinieri. To attempt to get past them would be suicidal.

As they proceeded into the Piazza, Jordan leaned closer to MacDonald, mouth almost to his ear, and said, "We were supposed to peel off here, but there are police at my entrance. We'll just continue with the tour, and when it heads back across the Piazza we can try again."

MacDonald was disturbed. "What if the police are still there?"

"I don't know, I don't know," said Jordan helplessly. "We'll see. But chances are they'll have moved on by then."

Felice Huber's umbrella was in the air again as she halted before the Basilica of San Marco and rallied her tour members around her. When she had assembled them, she directed their attention to the sweep of the populated Piazza and, in a singsong voice, began to re-count its origins and the highlights of its history. It was all too familiar to Jordan, and he did not listen as he drifted to the rim of the circle. He searched beyond Quadri's café, found it difficult from this distance to make out figures in the arcade near his office entrance. Then he thought he saw a flash of khaki and felt sure the police were still congregated there.

The circle of tour members was disintegrating, moving after Felice's umbrella toward the Basilica doorway. Jordan caught up with them, wormed his way into the middle of the group until he was beside MacDonald.

Inside, in the semidarkness of the church, erratically illuminated by reflections of gold treasures, flickering candles, lamplight, elbowing against other gawking tourists, Jordan felt more secure. With MacDonald and the others, he followed Felice to the front, where she stopped before the high altar and beckoned her charges to get as close as possible to her.

"This church, the Golden Basilica," she was saying, "is dedicated to St. Mark, or San Marco, the early Christian evangelist. At one time in his life, while in this area, he had a dream. In his dream an angel came to him and told him a magnificent city would rise on this site and in this city he would be venerated as a holy man. It all came to pass as he had dreamed. Later, when St. Mark died a martyr in Alexandria, Egypt, his body was stolen by two Venetian merchants. Hiding his corpse in a shipment of pork and herbs, they transported him to Venice. There was no basilica at that time. St. Mark's body was placed in a bronze coffin and kept in a chapel of the Doges' Palace. Presently, this basilica—then made of wood—was built in his honor, and his body was moved here. In the year 976, the entire basilica was destroyed by a fire. Afterward, St. Mark's body could not be found. Anyway, in the next hundred years a new basilica was built on the ruins of the old—this very building—and it was consecrated in the year 1094. At that time, the faithful of Venice gathered to pray for the recovery of St. Mark's body. During Mass, it is told, a marble slab broke open, revealing an ancient arm and finally St. Mark's body. He was reburied in a secret corner of this building, in order to keep him safe from vandals, and only two persons, the Doge and a canon, knew where he rested. When the Doge and canon died, St. Mark's body was lost once more. Well, seven centuries passed with no knowledge of where St. Mark lay. Finally, in 1811, while the basilica was being repaired, workmen came across his body—and he was reburied one last time beneath the high altar you see behind me. Now please follow me up the steps for a closer look."

Fifteen minutes later, they had finished inspecting the curiosities of the basilica and were trooping out into the sunlight.

Felice's umbrella directed them toward the lagoon. "Stay together," she called out, "and follow me."

Going past the stark-white Doges' Palace, Felice led the company to two giant columns in the middle of a small square overlooking the lapping waters of the lagoon.

"This is called the Piazzetta," she announced. "It is notable for the view and these famous ancient columns." She pointed to one reddish-gray granite column. "This is the column of St. Mark, topped by the bronze winged Lion of St. Mark sculptured by some Persian artists of long ago. The other is the column known in Venice as Todaro, or St. Theodore, and what you see on top is a representation of St. Theodore piercing a dragon. Originally these were two of three columns shipped to Venice, but one came loose and sank into the lagoon while being unloaded and it disappeared forever. These two had to wait in the Piazzetta for several decades before an architect could be found who would raise them. The architect who set them up in 1172 was Nicolò Barattieri. As one reward for the task, he was allowed to run a gambling stand situated between the two columns, and he made a fortune from it. Now, the other memorable thing about the Piazzetta, as I told you, is the view. Come, follow me."

Felice guided her party to the water's edge and aimed her umbrella at a small island out in the lagoon. "San Giorgio, once called the Island of Cypresses," she announced. For Jordan, as always, San Giorgio was unbelievably beautiful. It had the quality of a perfect red-and-white cardboard cutout planted in the water. "The Venetian Republic gave the island to a wealthy man named Morosini," Felice went on. "In the year 982, he sponsored the building of a Benedictine monastery on San Giorgio. It was a leading European cultural center until 1223, when it was brought down by an earthquake. Two hundred years later, Doge Pietro Ziani had it rebuilt. Today, the island is notable mainly for its church, the largest ever constructed by Palladio, and the two Tintorettos it contains."

Jordan's interest had waned, and absently he began to look at the others in the group. At once, his eyes rested on a short, portly Englishman in his middle sixties who was staring hard at MacDonald. Jordan wondered about the fat Englishman's interest in the professor, and then Jordan worried.

Momentarily, he was distracted by Felice's rising voice. "Off to the right of San Giorgio, to our south, you can see a longer, larger island. It is known as the Giudecca, probably named after Jewish immigrants who came to Venice in 1373 and were segregated on that island. The main feature of the Giudecca, besides its flower gardens and boatyards, is its Church of the Redeemer, built by Palladio in 1577 as a memorial of thanks for the end of the plague the year before. This plague had killed 50,000 Venetians, among them the aged painter Titian. The Giudecca was at one time a most fashionable resort for Venetian aristocrats. Only a few of their descendants live there today. The noblest private residence that has survived, and is still in use, is the Palazzo De Marchi. Lord Byron, during his stay in Venice between 1816 and 1819, was a guest there when he was having an affair with a draper's wife, Margherita Cogni, before he moved on to the Mocenigo Palace on the Grand Canal. The Palazzo De Marchi was inherited by the Contessa Elvira De Marchi, who lives there still. . . ."

Something caught and focused large in Jordan's head. Elvira.

Contessa Elvira De Marchi. A social acquaintance of his from his earliest days in Venice. She was gracious, she was generous, she was sympathetic. And devoted enough to call him Timothy. He had never presumed to ask her for a favor, but if he asked her for one now, he could not imagine her refusing.

Yes, of course, Palazzo De Marchi was the best hideout of all for Professor MacDonald until Bruno could arrange for his flight to freedom.

Then Jordan remembered the threat nearby, the portly Englishman who had been staring at MacDonald. He sought the Englishman again, and to his surprise the Englishman was not there. Jordan's gaze shifted, and he saw the Englishman squeezing through the group, approaching MacDonald. Roughly, Jordan separated the tourists behind him and made for MacDonald.

The Englishman was scrutinizing MacDonald as he spoke to him. "Pardon me, sir. Forgive my staring, but your face seems terribly familiar to me. Have we met somewhere before?"

MacDonald recoiled slightly. "No, I'm afraid not."

"Then perhaps I've seen your picture somewhere. I'm a physician from Liverpool. Are you also a physician, by chance—perhaps a renowned one?"

"No. Sorry, no," said MacDonald.

Jordan had the professor by the arm. "Pardon me, sir," Jordan said to the Englishman. "My friend and I have to go."

He pulled the limping MacDonald through the tour group and into the open, and headed him toward the vaporetto station.

217 ▶ ▶ ▶

"Thanks," MacDonald said with a sigh. "He almost had me there. Must have seen my face in some science journal."

"Or a poster," said Jordan. "Look, Professor, if I can get you from here to the vaporetto station, I think we can make it to a safe hideout. We're going to go over the bridge there, grab a newspaper at the stand, and then catch the ferry that crosses the lagoon from here to San Giorgio to the Giudecca. All the way over, I want you to bury your face in the newspaper, use it as a shield from other passengers. Once we get to the Giudecca, it's only a very short walk to the Palazzo De Marchi."

"Palazzo what?"

"The home of a charitable contessa. She's the only one I can think of at the moment who can save your neck. Now lower your head, keep going fast, and maybe we'll make it."

▶ ▶ ▶ ▶

There were two approaches to the Palazzo De Marchi, Jordan was explaining, one by boat on the canal that ran up alongside the palace and the other on foot on the sidewalk that separated the building from the Giudecca Lagoon.

They were approaching on foot from the vaporetto landing, walking as rapidly as MacDonald's bad knee would permit, heading for the palazzo's street entrance. To Jordan's relief, the street was almost empty. There were no police in sight—at least, not at the moment.

With the pressure off them, and still a few minutes before they reached their destination, Jordan felt that he could use the time to brief Professor MacDonald on the formidable old lady who might (if they were lucky) soon be his hostess.

"Professor, let me fill you in on the Contessa Elvira De Marchi," said Jordan, "just in case you're able to spend some time with her."

"Do that," said MacDonald. "I've met many politicians and millionaires—we depend on them for our grants—but I've never met royalty."

"Well, Venetian royalty is not real royalty in the feudal sense. Venice has always been a republic, and each Doge was a president. But from the start there was a kind of ruling class composed of wealthy merchants, mostly shipowners. Anyway, the contessa is a surviving descendant of one of those families. A really illustrious line. There was one Doge, a De Marchi, along the way, and one saint in the 15th century. Like her ancestors, the contessa is rich and religious."

"How old is she?"

"Oh, I'd say about seventy-five. She needs a cane, but she gets around very well. She's alert, bright, knowledgeable—she visits London almost every year—and she's a people collector. That's how I got into her orbit. Although generally, she scoops up celebrities, mostly American and British. Needless to say, her English is perfect. What else can I tell you? She's the daughter of a marchese. She's been widowed about twenty years. She has two children. One lives at the family summer villa near Treviso. The other spends a lot of time at the family house in Cortina."

"What does she do with herself?" MacDonald asked.

"Good question," said Jordan. "Far as I can make out, she goes to Mass every morning at eight. She likes to shop herself at the Rialto market. She doesn't do much around the palace. She has a Frenchwoman who serves her as a companion and maid. She also has a live-in couple for housekeeping and to serve at cocktail and dinner parties. What does she do? She's on the local board of several cultural organizations or charities—like UNESCO, like the Croce Rossa or Red Cross, like the San Vincenzo de Paoli, a Catholic group that helps the poor. Not that she's lavish with her own money. Most Venetian aristocrats are not celebrated for their financial generosity. They give time, not money. Our contessa is quite tight with a buck. Except when it comes to entertainment. She usually has a houseful of VIPs, and she treats them handsomely. That's my big hope for you, Professor. If she thinks you are a celebrity, she's more likely to take you in."

"You're going to tell her who I am?"

"I don't want to, but I'll have to," said Jordan. "I've got to impress her immediately. If I fail, we're in serious trouble. I don't know where to turn with you. Our backs are against the wall. I've got to make it with the Contessa De Marchi."

"Fingers crossed," said MacDonald.

"Keep them crossed," said Jordan, "and here we are at her front door."

The entrance was an enormous wooden door set into a 16th-century Renaissance façade of gray rectangular granite blocks. Jordan rang the doorbell.

A small, swarthy man, wearing a red vest over a black shirt and wearing black trousers, opened the door.

"I've come to see the Contessa De Marchi," said Jordan in Italian. "I'm an old friend."

"I'll see if she is free. Who shall I say is calling?"

"Signor Timothy Jordan. I need only a few minutes of her time."

"Please come in."

Jordan went inside, followed by MacDonald. They stood in a huge ground-floor hall, furnished only with a long bench along one wall, over which hung a wooden carving of a crowned eagle, the De Marchi family crest. There were two staircases—the smaller leading to the *mezzanino* floor, where the servants slept, and the monumental larger one rising to the first floor. At the top of this staircase stood a marble Madonna and child with a lighted lamp in front of them.

The servant gestured toward the bench. "Please wait here. I will find the contessa."

He went up the broad staircase. MacDonald immediately dropped down onto the bench with a grunt.

"I could use a series of shots of the eminent Professor MacDonald's C-98," he said wryly.

Jordan smiled. "You've been doing okay."

"I'm in a constant state of tension. I guess I'm scared as hell. I don't want to be caught."

"I'll do all in my power to see that doesn't happen."

"I appreciate what you're doing. I'm just afraid we're trapped. I can't let myself—and my discovery—be locked up in the Soviet Union for life. I think I might kill myself first."

"Don't talk like that," said Jordan. "You've got to be optimistic. After all, you're still free." He began to wander around the hall, determined to change the subject. "This ground floor is like the ones in all the big palaces. They were never lived in. They still aren't. The old Venetian merchants used to unload their ships, bring their goods directly to their palaces, and store them conveniently on the ground floor. The contessa's living quarters are entirely upstairs."

"Signor Jordan . . ."

Jordan saw that the servant had come partially down the staircase. He was friendlier now, and beckoning. "Please, sir, follow me. The contessa is happy to receive you."

"*Grazie.*" Jordan went to MacDonald. "You just stay put. I won't be long. I'll have a decision for you in five or ten minutes."

"I'll be waiting"—he tried to smile—"tensely."

Jordan climbed the stairs, went with the servant across the upper portego with its stucco walls decorated with paintings by Nicolò Bambini, and was finally shown into a tasteful, moderate-sized sitting room. One wall was hung with a tapestry depicting medieval horsemen, another wall held a bookcase filled with leather-bound sets, and a third wall displayed a marvelous Canaletto of a Venice sunset—and beside the dominating oil, even more dominant, regal, tall, thin as a rail, draped in an aquamarine dress, holding her brown lion's-head cane, stood the Contessa Elvira De Marchi.

She came forward, halfway across the room, to greet Jordan. "Timothy, how good to see you. It's been ages since you visited here."

Jordan took her aristocratic hand. "I've missed you. I'm always hoping to run into you in the Piazza."

"I get out less and less now. . . . Do sit down."

She settled slowly onto a flowered divan, and he sat in a straight-backed chair with gilt arms across from her.

"To what do I owe the honor of this visit, Timothy?" she inquired. "I suspect it is not a social call. If I may say so, you look too harried."

He smiled at her typical forthrightness. "You're very perceptive, Contessa. Actually, I'm in a bind, and I had to turn to someone who might be hospitable. I need your help."

She did not seem surprised. "In what way?"

He hesitated, trying to form what he would say. When he had entered the room, his intention had been to blurt out the truth, and trust her totally. But now he reasoned that if he could achieve the same end with somewhat less than the truth, MacDonald's situation would be more secure.

"Let me say this much," he began. "I have a friend visiting me from America, an Englishman, a prominent scientist who lives and works in New York. He happened to be in Venice for a day, when the city was closed down to all traffic—"

"Isn't it ridiculous, the way the authorities are behaving?"

"Yes. But it's made it difficult for my friend. For reasons I cannot explain, he is traveling incognito. He must not be recognized. He needs an isolated place to stay for several days. I was hoping against hope I might prevail upon you to put him up—three or four days at the most."

The contessa looked pained. "Timothy, this embar-

rasses me. You know how much I like to have visitors
here. You know how eager I am to help my friends. But
you've come to me just at the wrong time. I have a house
absolutely filled with guests. Cedric Foster arrived yesterday—I'm sure you've heard of him?"

"The best-selling novelist."

"The same. And he brought with him an entourage of
four, including his literary agent—his own companions.
I couldn't inconvenience someone as—well, as famous
as Cedric Foster by insisting he or one of his companions share a room with your friend—"

Jordan knew his approach had been wrong. Only truth
could prevail. It was a time for utter candor.

"I appreciate your predicament, Contessa. Now I had
better tell you the entire truth about my own. The man
I am speaking about is already renowned in his field.
But from the moment he leaves Venice safely, and reports a discovery he has made, he will become the most
celebrated, the most worshiped, the most famous man in
the world. Neither the President of the United States nor
the premier of the Soviet Union will be better known.
And you can be one of the persons responsible for his
fame."

Her eyebrows had arched. "Whatever are you talking
about, Timothy? Speak clearly."

Jordan knew he almost had her. She had taken the
bait. He must now draw her in. "Okay, clearly," he said.
"I have in my charge Professor Davis MacDonald. After
years of work, he has just discovered the means of prolonging human life, everyone's life, to the age of 150. Do
you comprehend what I am saying?"

She sat silently, eyelids blinking.

Jordan watched her. "It's true, Contessa," he said.

"It's fantastic," she murmured. "But then, why—"

"Why do I need a trusted person to give him a room,
to hide him out? That's what I'm about to tell you."

Then, crisply, withholding nothing, he recounted the

entire saga of Professor MacDonald to date. Throughout his recital the contessa sat stiffly, not a muscle moving on her wrinkled face.

When he had finished, she spoke. "Even Cedric Foster has never written a story quite like that."

"I've got to see that it has a happy ending, Contessa," Jordan said. "Right now there doesn't seem much chance. Except with your help. Without your help, we have no place to go. I've just about run out of ideas. The Communists are sure to get him in the next twenty-four hours."

"The Communists," she said vehemently. "They shall not touch him. Professor MacDonald is a great man, a genius, and his discovery belongs to the world. If I can help give it to the world, I shall." She pushed herself to her feet. "Where is this wonderful man?"

Jordan rose quickly. "Contessa, you're a dear. I'll never be able to thank you enough. The professor, he's downstairs in your entry."

"Well, my God, bring him right up and let's make him comfortable. I'll ask one of Cedric Foster's sycophants to vacate his room, double up with someone else, and the professor shall have a lovely bedroom to himself, with complete privacy."

"Contessa, just one thing. No one, but no one—certainly not your guests—must know what he has done or that he is here."

"You have my sacred word."

"I'll be by to see him tomorrow evening, to let him know how escape plans are progressing."

"Tomorrow evening? About tomorrow evening, Timothy. I'm giving a small dinner party for Cedric Foster. Since you're coming by anyway, why don't you plan to attend the dinner? You can bring one of your many ladies. I'd love to have you."

"I appreciate that. I'm not sure I'm in the mood for parties—"

"You need a diversion."

"All right, I accept. I'll bring the professor's assistant, Dr. Alison Edwards. We'll come by a bit early, so we can see the professor first. Now I'd better introduce you to our fugitive."

▶ ▶ ▶ ▶

The following morning, from the moment he had awakened early in the Hotel Danieli, Tim Jordan had determined to put Professor MacDonald out of his mind and for the first time in recent weeks concentrate on his work. After all, it was not often that the Venice Must Live Committee got a break like this, a chance to have its story told in 1,400 American newspapers by the most widely read columnist in the United States. This day, Jordan had known, he must give all his energies to the columnist, Schuyler Moore, and not be diverted by his role in MacDonald's escape.

Yesterday, after leaving MacDonald with the pleased and excited Contessa De Marchi, he had devoted himself to trying to locate Bruno Girardi. He had left telephone messages at *Il Gazzettino,* at the mayor's press office, at two restaurants he knew Bruno frequented, each time asking that Bruno contact him as soon as possible. By late this afternoon, he hoped, after he had returned from Voltabarozzo, he would have some favorable word from Bruno that he would be able to impart to Professor MacDonald tonight before the contessa's dinner party.

Until then, though, his devotion must be entirely to Schuyler Moore and the Pirelli-Furlanis Dam that was to save Venice from sinking into the sea.

There had been five of them who had met at the main garage in the Piazzale Roma. Jordan and Marisa had picked up Schuyler Moore at the Hotel Bauer Grunwald, taken a motorboat to the Piazzale Roma. There the two

young carabinieri guards assigned by Colonel Cutrone
had been awaiting them, as well as the Mercedes sedan
made available by the Italian Ministry of Public Works.
Jordan had driven, with Schuyler Moore beside him
in the front seat and Marisa squeezed between the two
guards in the back seat. Jordan had made the trip many
times before with journalists, and once again he had
reached Padua in forty minutes.

In Padua, he had driven the Mercedes to the Corso
Milano, and across from the Teatro Verdi had parked in
front of the modern building housing the Genio Civile,
the local branch of the Ministry of Public Works. While
the others waited, and accompanied by one guard, Jordan had gone inside briefly and from the chief of the
department had obtained the special pass that would
allow them to inspect the miniature model of the Venice
lagoon.

Now they were on their way to Voltabarozzo, the small
community outside Padua where the Centro Sperimentale di Idraulica—the Center for Experiments in Hy-
draulics—was located. As they rolled along the Strada
Statale, between rows of typical Italian dwellings on one
side of the highway and artificial canals and meadows
on the other, Jordan listened to Marisa describing the
area to Schuyler Moore. The columnist had twisted in
the front seat, facing Marisa in the rear to hear her better,
and Jordan had a closer and more careful look at him.
Moore appeared to be about forty years old, with a rather
squarish, slightly acned face. His hair was dark blond,
thinning, parted neatly on one side. Horn-rimmed
glasses perched on his short straight nose, and the lenses
somewhat exaggerated his small, doubtful blue eyes.
His mouth was small and constantly puckered. Until
now, he had not talked much, preferring to listen to Jordan's anecdotal highlights of Venice's history and Marisa's occasional interjections.

As Marisa caught her breath, Schuyler Moore spoke

up. "All very interesting and helpful," he said. "But until now you haven't told me a word about this flood-control apparatus we're going to see."

"On purpose," said Jordan from the wheel. "This is one of those things that are better understood when seen—even in miniature. It'll all be very clear once you set eyes on it. We just didn't want to confuse you."

"Fair enough."

"In fact, the Center is coming into view," said Jordan. In a few seconds he pointed out the window, adding, "There, to the left, up ahead, Mr. Moore. The Center complex forms a triangle. At one end of the triangle is a two-story office building. Next, an area for open-air experiments. Finally, the dominant part of the Center, the part that will interest you, the mammoth metal building that resembles a plane hangar—that's where the model of the Venice lagoon has been built. You'll see for yourself in a few minutes."

After they turned off the road, and parked, and got out of the car, Jordan guided Schuyler Moore up ahead of the others. As they approached the hangarlike structure, Jordan began to fill Moore in on the background. Moore quickly pulled a small, cheap notebook out of the pocket of his seersucker jacket, located his ball-point pen, and began to jot notes.

"There are many reasons why Venice is gradually sinking into the sea," said Jordan, "and there are many proposed solutions to save it, but we are only concerned with one, the best and most practical one. But first, why is Venice sinking? Answers. The world's ice masses melt, the world's oceans rise, and because of this the water level here is one inch higher every five years. Further, the city rests on a muddy foundation of soil. Then, more important, private industry in Marghera and Mestre pumped water out of the lagoon bottom, out of the subsoil, forcing the land to sink. But the main reason for the city's sinking—and in fact, its being slowly eroded and destroyed—is that high tides come in from the Adriatic through three channels and fill the lagoon. The lagoon, in turn, rises and engulfs, or floods, the city. Often, when the waters are at high tide, the sirocco, a windstorm or gale, sends the lagoon smashing over Venice. Almost every winter, floods put the Piazza San Marco under three inches of water. As you may recall, the disastrous flood of 1966 had the Piazza over six inches underwater, left oil from the central heating tanks six feet high on buildings, wrecked shops, homes, walls, paintings, boats, left 5,000 people homeless. And any future storm that generated a wind velocity of sixty miles an hour would put the city under nine inches of water. What can be done to prevent these annual floods? There is one solution. Now you shall see it for yourself."

After Jordan handed his permit to a guard, they entered the gray interior of the building, and what stretched before them for a great distance was a concrete layout of the city of Venice without a single one of its structures and landmarks. The slabs of concrete represented the ground, the soil, the land foundation of Venice, and gouged into the concrete were deep depressions representing the canals of the city. Even as they studied the layout, real water was being pumped into the model, and the canals were being filled.

"This model took two years to construct," said Jordan, "and was supervised by four teams of experts using bathymetric maps. The building covering this model is 16,000 square meters, and the model of Venice itself with its lagoon is 12,000 square meters—in all, roughly the area covered by the real Piazza San Marco."

Schuyler Moore was mesmerized by the water streaming into the toy canals. His small eyes shone through his thick spectacle lenses. He shook his head. "Truly astonishing," he said, and resumed making notes.

Jordan began pointing at certain locations. "The Piazza San Marco would be there. The Doges' Palace there. That's the Grand Canal in miniature, and then the Rialto Bridge. Now, way out there at the far left, at the other end—you can't see it well from here—is a large tank that represents the Adriatic Sea. Let's walk over there, all around the model, and I can show you fairly close up the source of Venice's problem and our prevention apparatus in miniature and exactly how it works."

Jordan led Moore, Marisa, and the two policemen along the side of the concrete model to the rear, where they ascended steps leading into a four-room electronic center. In one room, where an engineer was at work at a computer, they all gathered about Jordan at a wide window looking out upon the model.

"The equipment in use here," said Jordan, "is a 100,000,000-lire Siemens System 300. This controls the action of the nearby pumps that make the water flow and simulate the tide in either direction, entering Venice and leaving Venice. If the flow of the high tide in real life takes six hours, the flow of the same tide on this model occurs in six minutes."

Jordan gestured off. "There you can see the three channels, or openings, reduced, through which water flows from the Adriatic Sea into Venice. The nearest channel is the Lido, the next is Malamocco, and the farthest one is Chioggia. To prevent a high tide from entering through these channels and drowning the city, we contracted with Industrie Pirelli, which specializes in rubber, and Furlanis, which specializes in construction, to build flexible barriers or dams across each of those channels. One has already been completed and installed in the actual Lido channel outside the lagoon. You will see it in miniature on the model out there. Now, what is this flexible barrier or dam? It is a long container, resembling a kind of flattened-out dirigible, made of nylon fabric and a rubber compound. It is stretched across the mouth of the Lido channel and held fast on either side by anchor chains tied to metal pylons set in concrete.

The container or bag, deflated, lies fastened to the bottom of the sea, on the seabed, so that it does not interfere with ships passing into the lagoon. But suppose a high tide is coming, or a gale, and Venice is about to be flooded? Here is what happens. . . ."

Jordan signaled to the engineer, who nodded and bent over his electronic console. Jordan pointed below.

"Keep your eye on the Lido channel there. Water from the sea is mounting, starting to pour through the channel toward the lagoon and the city. An engineer activates hydraulic pumps, fills the nylon bag on the sea bottom with water, and inflated, filled, blown up, the top of the dam rises to the surface—there, look. . . ."

In the model before them, a miniature elongated bag rose out of the water, setting up a dam that stopped the high tide from going through the channel into the lagoon. The lagoon's water level was effectively protected by this inflated artificial barrier.

"You see," said Jordan, "the bag keeps out the sea, and Venice is saved from flooding and destruction. Now, as soon as the high tide recedes, or the storm has ended, and the sea and lagoon levels are the same, the bag barrier is automatically emptied of water, deflated, and it sinks to the bottom, out of sight, to permit shipping to resume from the sea into the lagoon and the industrial port."

"Remarkable," said Schuyler Moore, intrigued by the device. "Once there is a warning that the channel should be closed, how long does it take for one of those barriers to be inflated and rise out of the water?"

"It used to take thirty minutes," said Jordan. "But the pumps have been improved with a new invention, and now the flexible barriers can be filled and stretch from the seabed to the top in less than five minutes."

"And that can save Venice?" said Moore.

"It can."

"Has it been installed yet?"

"A real one has been installed in the Lido channel. It has not yet been installed in either of the other two channels."

"Well, the one that's been installed—is it being used at all?"

Jordan hesitated, weighing how much information he should give out to this journalist. But he knew Moore was shrewd, and one could not play games with him. If he was not given the truth here, he would learn it elsewhere.

"To answer your question honestly," Jordan said, "no—no, the Lido flexible barrier has never been used."

"Why not?"

"For the same reasons the device has not been installed in the other two channels. Business and politics. The political obstacles are that two new inflatable dams would cost between $16,000,000 and $20,000,000 to install, and after the Ministry of Public Works has approved, nine other government agencies such as the Ministry of Cultural Works have to give their approval. But the main problem is the lobbying of big business interests representing petrochemical, aluminum, steel, ammonia plants on the mainland. Right now, shipping goods to their doorstep at Marghera and Mestre is easy and cheap. They want to keep it that way. They don't want any inflatable barriers to hamper shipping. These industrialists are not sentimental or romantic. They don't give a goddamn about saving Venice as a museum. They would just as soon let it sink into the sea and have its area as a bigger harbor for importing and exporting. That's why the Lido barrier has been installed—yet never used. Its installation soothed the romantic museum faction. Its immobility satisfied the business and labor elements. That's why the other two haven't been installed at all."

Moore raised his head from his notes and squinted at Jordan. "I appreciate your frankness," he said. "If I quote that, will it give you trouble?"

"Probably. But let the truth be told. Let everyone know what the Venice Must Live Committee is up against."

Marisa stepped forward. "Mr. Moore, if you use that, please use it without attribution. Do not use Mr. Jordan's name."

He smiled at her. "Protective, aren't you? Of course I won't use his name."

"Let me show you around further, Mr. Moore," said Jordan.

For the next half hour, Jordan guided the columnist and the others around the interior of the Center, explaining more about the operation and its potential, and answering Moore's incisive questions.

At last, they had finished and gone out in the sunlight and started back to their car.

Walking alongside the columnist, Jordan said, "I hope you got a good story."

"A very good one, thank you. It'll take up two columns, which I'll file soon as they let me fly out of the city. What's going on here? I can't believe they'd quarantine a tourist city with a tourist economy at the height of the tourist season merely to catch some second-rate spy. Any idea of what's behind it?"

"There's probably nothing more behind it. I think they're quite serious about getting their hands on the spy."

"Well," Moore was saying, "I'd love to get to the bottom of it. But I'm afraid I'll have to use up my days here digging for something else."

"Do you have any other stories you're going to do?"

"Only one is set," said Moore. "The day after tomorrow, a travel agency is taking a dozen American and British industrialists on a preview tour of a new innovatively furnished petrochemical factory in Mestre. I was invited to cover it. Sounds dull, but what the hell."

"How are you getting to Mestre?" asked Jordan, suddenly interested.

"The same way I got here with you. Special dispensation from the mayor, and a couple of police guards."

"What agency is taking you on this tour?"

"I believe it is called CIT."

"Yes, that's one of the big ones." Then Jordan added casually, "Did they assign you a guide? I know most of them, and I can tell you if you got a good one."

"Some woman. I don't remember— Wait, I think I have a note on it in my pocket." He fished into the pocket of his seersucker suit and came up with several cards. He glanced at them, then held up one. "Here. CIT. The guide's name is Felice Huber. Is she any good?"

"The best," said Jordan enthusiastically as they reached the Mercedes. "You're very lucky."

And so am I, he thought, watching the columnist get into the car. Bruno Girardi had been one light at the end of the tunnel. Now there were two, and the second was named Felice Huber.

Jordan felt better, much better. The odds on hope had just improved. Two for one.

▶ ▶ ▶ ▶

It was late afternoon when Jordan returned to his suite in the Hotel Danieli. As he stepped into the sitting room, Alison, having heard him, came quickly out of her bedroom. Her face was tight with anxiety.

"Tim, there was an important phone call for you," she said without preliminaries. "Bruno Girardi got your messages and called. He wants to speak to you. He'll be in his office at *Il Gazzettino* until six o'clock."

"That's the call I've been waiting for," Jordan said. He held up his wristwatch. "Still time."

"Was everything all right today?"

"Bring you up on that later," he said, stripping off his jacket. "I want to catch Bruno."

"Mind if I listen?"

"We're in this together," he said, going to the sofa and pulling the telephone closer to him.

As Alison sat down at the desk, Jordan took up the receiver and asked the hotel operator to put him through to *Il Gazzettino*. Moments later, he had Bruno on the line.

"Bruno? Tim Jordan here."

"Yes. I meant to report to you sooner. But it seemed pointless because of the delays. Our—our party of the third part—our partner—he was jittery and broke two of our appointments. So I was waiting until I really saw him."

"He broke two appointments?" Jordan repeated for Alison's sake. "Have you seen him yet?"

"Yes, yes. I saw him at lunch today in the Piazzale Roma." There was a brief silence, and then Jordan heard Bruno speak to someone in the background. His voice came on again. "Someone stepped into the office. I'm alone now."

"Did you discuss the matter with our partner?"

"I discussed it fully. He was definitely interested, but thinks the sum involved only moderate for the risk involved."

"Did he want more?"

"He did not speak of more," said Bruno. "He was worried about the consequences if the—if the venture did not work out."

"Well, what was his decision?" Jordan asked impatiently. "Did he turn it down?"

"No, absolutely not. He wants to consider it. He wants to discuss it with his wife, for her opinion."

"Discuss it with his wife?" repeated Jordan. "Do you know his wife?"

"No. If she is a worrier type, she will influence him to turn it down. On the other hand, if she wants the extra money, she will persuade him to accept. I can say only one thing, Tim. I am sure the man and his family need money. So we shall see."

"How long?" pressed Jordan.

"What?"

"How long before we know?"

"Oh. I would say a day or two, no more."

"Will you keep after him? I can't wait longer."

"You leave it to me," said Bruno. "The second I have a favorable answer, I will find you."

"I'm depending on you, Bruno. Good luck."

Hanging up, Jordan summarized the conversation for Alison.

When he was through, she did not seem reassured. "What do you think, Tim?"

"I think I'd better make another phone call. Try to get us a backup position."

"Meaning what?"

"Meaning after I showed Schuyler Moore around the Center today, I asked him if he was going to do any more stories about Venice. He told me a small party of industrialists has been given permission to leave the city briefly the day after tomorrow and tour a new advanced factory at Mestre. Moore is going to cover it." Jordan reached for the telephone again. "The woman assigned to guide that tour happens to be a friend of mine."

"You think something's possible?"

"I'm sure going to try to find out. Alison, my personal address book is in the right-hand drawer of my desk. Toss it over."

She found the address book and handed it to him.

He looked up Felice Huber's phone number and put through the call.

There were two rings, and he heard Felice's voice on the phone.

"Felice, darling, this is Tim Jordan."

"I wondered what happened to you. Here I handed

you and your friend a free Program A tour yesterday, and you walked out on me. When we reached the Bridge of Sighs, I looked for you and you were the man who wasn't there."

"I had to find a toilet for my friend."

"Anyway, I'm glad to hear from you," said Felice. "What can I do for you?"

"See me for lunch."

"Nice. Business or pleasure?"

"Both. With you it's always a pleasure. But there is some business."

"It's a date. Where? When?"

"Tomorrow. Let's say twelve noon. Quadri's. Down in front of the orchestra. Are you free?"

"Umm, let me check the schedule. I've a tour group at two. Noon is fine."

"Look forward to seeing you, Felice."

Dropping the telephone into its cradle, Jordan lay back on the sofa, tired, and watched Alison as she wrapped her light pink robe more closely around her.

"Do you think she'll cooperate?" Alison asked.

"I don't know how tight the security is on her Mestre party," Jordan said. "If Felice can do me a favor, within reason, I think she might."

"And if you can pull it off?"

"We'd have a way of getting the professor out of Venice. Just in case Bruno doesn't come through. It would be the harder route. Much of it would depend on how resourceful the professor is. Do you think he is resourceful?"

"You'd better ask him."

Jordan started to get to his feet. "That's what I intend to do right now. The contessa's dinner party starts in two hours. Let's get to her palazzo an hour earlier, so we can have time to lay plans with MacDonald. Can you be ready to leave here in forty-five minutes?"

"I've had my bath, and I'm all dressed underneath.

236 ► ► ►

What do I wear on top? I've never been to a Venetian palace."

"Not formal. But no jeans either. Do you have a snappy cocktail-type outfit?"

"Just bought one off the Mercerie."

"You're set," said Jordan. "Meet you out here again in forty-five minutes."

► ► ► ►

When they had arrived at the Palazzo De Marchi a half hour before guests were to assemble for the dinner party, the contessa had personally met them. Without wasting a moment, she had taken Jordan and Alison up to the second floor.

"He's such a nice man," she had said along the way. "The professor and I talked for almost an hour this morning. I brought him some books in English, and then we chattered away. He wanted to know about my family, my background, and I told him what I could—I hope I didn't bore him—and then I asked him about his own beginnings and his experiments with C-98. At first he was somewhat reticent, but then he warmed up to me and tried to explain. I pretended to understand, but I'm afraid I was out of my depth with his scientific language."

"But you do understand what he has achieved?" Jordan had asked.

"That part was clear. People doubling their lives on earth, and in good health. It will astound the world."

"Provided the world hears about it."

"If I have anything to say in the matter, the world will hear about it. The professor is welcome to stay here safely, in hiding, until you find a means of smuggling him out of this Red-infested bedlam."

"Thank you, Contessa."

When they had arrived at the door to the guest bedroom, the contessa had tried to reassure Jordan and Alison. "As you can see, the bedroom is out of the way. The best hiding place."

"How many people do you have staying here?" Jordan had wondered.

"Four in Cedric Foster's party, plus Cedric himself. Then my live-in couple and my secretary. But have no fear. No one knows he is here. In fact, I don't even trust the servants to bring him his meals. I do it myself. Now you can go right in."

"You're the perfect hostess," Jordan had said.

"The perfect hostess serves dinner on time," the contessa had said. "Please don't be late."

Jordan and Alison had gone into the bedroom, a small room elegantly furnished in Empire style, and found Professor MacDonald stretched out on the bed, an open British paperback on his chest. Apparently he had fallen asleep, but their arrival awakened him.

MacDonald had sat up on the edge of the bed, while Jordan and Alison pulled up chairs.

Yes, he was comfortable enough, no complaints about that. But his nerves were edgy after all the recent running, and he was restless in confinement and eager for news about some escape hatch.

Now, listening to him, Jordan was pleased that he could speak of two lights at the end of the tunnel.

"I won't say I have good news for you, Professor, not yet," Jordan began, "but I do have slightly hopeful news. First of all, your own situation is better than it's been since the police set out to catch you. No one suspects where you are. The contessa sympathizes with you—indeed, is thrilled to have you—and she is a trustworthy person. And she just told us you can stay here as long as is necessary."

"I appreciate that," said MacDonald, "but I hope it's not too long."

"Professor, if I can get you out of Venice tonight or

tomorrow, I'll do so. The important thing is that your staying here safely buys me more time to find a means of escape."

Alison interrupted. "In fact, Davis, Tim has already come up with another possibility."

MacDonald looked at Jordan. "Really?"

"It's an idea. I'll have to see if it can work. To start with, let me bring you right up to date on where we stand. I got hold of our photographer friend, Bruno Girardi. He met with his carabinieri captain and laid out the proposition. The captain is, of course, interested. He can use the money. But he's worried about the risk. It was left that he's going to take it up with his wife. I can't say what will happen. But if her response is favorable, you should be on your way out of here very soon."

"And if it's not favorable?"

"Well, then, as Alison mentioned, a second possibility presented itself earlier today."

Professor MacDonald was extremely attentive, waiting.

Briefly, Jordan recounted his experience with the columnist, Schuyler Moore, at the Voltabarozzo Hydraulic Center in the early afternoon.

"When I learned," said Jordan, "he was accompanying a small tour outside of Venice the day after tomorrow, and I learned the guide would be my good friend Felice Huber—you remember her?—my mind started clicking. I phoned Felice after I got back to the city. I invited her to lunch tomorrow. That's when I'll find out if the second possibility can work."

MacDonald seemed lost. "I'm not sure I know what you have in mind."

"A group of American and English industrialists, businessmen, are being permitted to leave the city for a short time, go by bus to Mestre to tour some kind of new petrochemical factory complex. Well, Professor, if I can get you on that tour, out of here to Mestre, you'll be free."

"Could we get away with it?"

"I don't know. This is a longer shot than the Bruno one. I have to talk Felice into letting you join her tour. If she agrees, I don't see too much danger in getting you safely out of Venice. You'd be anonymous in a group. The group is not suspect, has high-level permission, and is, I'd guess, very VIP. The main problem presents itself once you get to the Mestre factory. There will be several carabinieri guards along to keep an eye on all of you. Somehow, you'd have to elude them, slip away without being seen, or hide somewhere in the factory until they were gone, and then make your own way to the Mestre railroad station or a car-rental agency. You don't know your way around there, but I'd give you some directions before you left. And almost everyone in the vicinity speaks English. I'm not saying it would be easy. It wouldn't. I can see endless dangers of being caught. Yet it is worth considering if Bruno's captain fails us."

"Somehow it frightens me, attempting this alone."

Alison tried to bolster him. "You did make it out of the Soviet Union, Davis."

"That was different," said MacDonald. "No one was looking for me when I left. Right now there are hundreds, maybe thousands, searching for me."

Jordan stood up and walked thoughtfully around the room. "One other thing occurred to me," he said. "Taking the columnist, Schuyler Moore, into our confidence. I'm sure he could be trusted out of his own self-interest. If he got you or the story out, he'd have the newsbeat of the century."

"How could he help?" asked MacDonald, bewildered.

"One of two ways," said Jordan, thinking aloud. "If I let him in on the whole thing, he could join you in trying to escape the tour group. You wouldn't be alone. You'd have a well-motivated, resourceful newspaperman to depend upon. Or if it proved impracticable for two of you to disappear from the factory tour, maybe Moore could do it alone. Then you need not even go on the tour. He would know about you, know the whole story of your discovery and the Communist hunt for you, and he'd be driven to make the escape on his own. He could get to the outside world, reveal what is going on, and half the world would be at Venice's doorstep forcing the Communists to release you. Does either of those ideas make sense?"

"No," said MacDonald with surprising firmness. "I don't like exposing myself to a newspaperman. He might make a deal of some kind with the Communists, turn me over to them in exchange for getting his story out."

"That seems unlikely—"

"No," MacDonald repeated. "Leave the newspaperman out of this. I'd rather try to escape from the factory on my own, if I have to."

Jordan shrugged. "Whatever you say, Professor."

"I say let's still wait for Bruno, and keep the Mestre factory tour as our alternative gamble."

Alison came to her feet, tapping her gold wristwatch. "And I say we're going to be late for the contessa's dinner if we don't get right downstairs."

Jordan smiled at her. She was utterly captivating in her white silk blouse and challis print skirt, and with her he now welcomed an escape of his own from the maze that had occupied him all these days. "You've got a date, young lady," he said, taking her arm. "And Professor, try to relax. I'm optimistic. I'll report to you tomorrow."

▶ ▶ ▶ ▶

It had been a lively, satisfying dinner at an oblong table under an intricate, dimmed Murano chandelier. Contessa De Marchi's food had been succulent: Parma ham with melon, small servings of pasta with clam sauce, delicate veal piccata, ice cream with delicious tiny cakes. The crossfire of talk—on world politics, travel to the Far East, the London literary scene, New York restaurants—had been ceaseless, largely dominated by the guest of honor, Cedric Foster, to whom the others deferred.

She rose and insistently moved them on to a nearby sitting room. Taking Alison by the hand, Jordan followed the contessa into the richly carpeted room. Alison was overwhelmed by the furnishings and decorations, admiring the Louis XIV table and the oval inlaid Dutch table, pausing to examine a showcase of Meissen plates and a wall filled with oil paintings of various saints.

As the guests chose their preferred places, Jordan sat with Alison on a divan. The servants were circling the room with trays of brandy, and Jordan took the opportunity to identify the guests in his mind once more. Unless a dinner party was given by a close friend, for mutual friends, Jordan found that he could never remember more than half the guests. At the moment, he could identify only six of the dozen persons. Besides the contessa herself, of course, there was the considerable presence of Cedric Foster, the best-selling novelist who had a penthouse in Manhattan and a twelve-room summer home in Maine. He was a tall, rather bulky man in his middle fifties. He had been handsome once, Jordan was sure, and was good-looking still, except that the advancing years had marked his features with folds and crevices, and blotches from too much drink. The brown hair on his head had begun to recede above his forehead. His carriage was erect, his attire natty, with Charvet shirt, Hermès tie, an English navy blazer, and sharply creased gray trousers. He appeared virile and wrote virile, but in the lilt of his speech, his movements and gestures, his overattentiveness to his younger male companion, there was a contradiction that definitely suggested the homosexual.

Right now, Jordan observed, as Cedric Foster took a snifter of Martell, he was plainly irked with his male companion seated a few feet from him. Jordan had noticed this irritation several times during dinner, and he saw it now. The companion, whose first name Jordan recalled to be Ian, was a slender, rather beautiful young man in his twenties, American and effeminate. And as at the dinner table, Ian was devoting himself to a darkly attractive, long-haired, vivacious young Italian publisher from Milan, a thirty-year-old named Sergio, who spoke charmingly broken English and flashed straight white teeth when he smiled, which was often. Less obviously, but most assuredly, he too was a homosexual.

Jordan could see that Cedric Foster's annoyance with Ian had deepened, and that he was jealous of his lover's enchantment with a potential rival. Jordan wondered whether Alison was aware of this byplay, and then he realized that her attention was being given to Teresa Fantoni across the room.

For Jordan, Teresa Fantoni needed no remembrance. She was famous. She was Italy's gift to the cinema, a glamorous motion-picture actress whose intense sensual beauty had given her international renown for two decades.

"God, isn't she gorgeous," Alison whispered.

"Wasn't she gorgeous," Jordan corrected her with no unkindness to the subject.

"She's still something to look at," said Alison. "I'd like to look like that at—what must she be?—forty, I'd say."

"You will, only better," he said, adding in an undertone, "especially with a shot of C-98."

He feasted his eyes on Teresa Fantoni. She was, indeed, something. Reddish hair drawn back tightly into a chignon, which accented her gaunt face with its high cheekbones, small broad nose and generous crimson lips. She was wearing a close-fitting sequined dress, deeply cut at the bosom so that a portion of each breast overflowed and was visible. She was pouting or brooding—Jordan could not tell which—and only half listening to the guest on her right, who was trying to engage her in conversation. The guest addressing her was Jordan's Venetian acquaintance Oreste Memo, the violinist in the Quadri café orchestra. When Jordan and Alison had been introduced to the guests, he had been surprised to find Oreste Memo among them. Working as a musician in a popular tourist café hardly seemed the ticket to attendance at a small, aristocratic dinner in a palazzo. Then Jordan remembered Memo's special status. He was a gifted modern composer, recently working on a promising musical play, and while he had not yet made it in the big time, Contessa De Marchi believed in his gifts and was his patroness.

These were the guests whom Jordan remembered by name, or who had some identity for him. The others in the room were blurs. One, Jordan knew, was Cedric Foster's American literary agent. There was a marchesa from Mantova, who was top-heavy and spoke in superlatives. There was a couple named Albrizzi or Barozzi or Grimani—one of those important old-family Venetian names. The remaining three were wealthy shipping people.

The servants had left the room and the guests were together, and now the contessa faced the social problem all rigid hostesses always faced. Had she allowed the guests to stay on at the dinner table, where they had become comfortable with their partners and were engaged in ongoing dialogues, the party would have stayed lively. But by uprooting them, stopping their conversations, marching them to a new setting, scrambling them into a new seating arrangement, she had stopped the party cold.

But she'll save it, Jordan thought. He had seen this situation a half dozen times before at the contessa's parties. Each time she had rescued her guests from the doldrums by dropping among them a sensational bit of gossip or posing a wildly provocative question that stimulated conversations to begin again.

Jordan watched her with amusement and saw that the Contessa Elvira De Marchi was about to do it once more.

"At the table, just before we left dinner," the contessa began in a loud, high-pitched voice, addressing herself to Cedric Foster in particular and the rest of the room in general, "Cedric and I were discussing fascinating people we have met recently, and how few there were. Isn't that right, Cedric?"

"Too few, unfortunately," said Cedric Foster sullenly, his attention still on Ian and Sergio.

"Well, let me tell you," the contessa went on, "a short time ago, within the last few weeks, I met the most utterly fascinating man I've met in years. What he had to tell me about himself, his work, has excited my imagination beyond belief. The man was an American scientist visiting Venice. A gerontologist, actually—that is, a scientist who is trying to prolong the human lifespan."

Je-sus, Jordan groaned inwardly, she's not going to dare talk about MacDonald, is she? Even if her account was disguised, it carried risk. But he knew his contessa. Trustworthy and decent as she was, she would flirt with any danger if it helped her make a successful party. Jordan glanced at Alison worriedly, and she met his eyes with a bewildered and helpless look.

The contessa, smiling sweetly at Jordan and Alison and the others, was going on.

"This gerontologist told me, actually sat here and told me, that he was in the last phase of an experiment that if successful—and he believed it would be successful— would provide us with a formula that would allow all of us, here and everywhere in the world, to live to the age of 150 years in health and vigor. Would you believe that?"

"I, for one, don't," said Cedric Foster somewhat nastily. "He was giving you a good dose of science fiction."

"But it's absolutely true!" exclaimed the contessa, turning toward Foster. "This scientist is a man of unimpeachable integrity, the winner of many of the world's great prizes. He told me it's the biggest secret in science today, this breakthrough, this being on the verge of producing something that will extend each of our lives to 150 and keep us young and trim in all the decades before."

"You believe this will happen?" Teresa Fantoni inquired from across the room. "He was not teasing you?"

"He was absolutely earnest, Teresa. He weighed every word he spoke to me."

"Did he speak to you of when this formula will be available?" asked Teresa Fantoni.

"Yes, I asked him that very question," said the contessa. "If his final experiment is successful, as he believes it will be, he says the formula will be available in the near future. It was my impression he meant it would be available to us in two or three years."

Cedric Foster had given his full attention to the contessa at last. He was showing more interest, less skepticism. "This man, Contessa—you really believe him?"

"If you knew who he was, you'd believe him too."

"Well, I'd like to believe him. What's his name?"

Jordan held his breath, staring hard at the contessa. She caught his concern, and reassured him with the wink of a smile, and then addressed herself to her guest of honor. "Cedric, I wish I could tell you his name, but I'm pledged not to reveal it. He does not want his momentous achievement—or near achievement—made public until it is ready. The press would hound him, and overplay it prematurely, and even distort it. I'm sorry, Cedric dear, you'll have to take my word and have to wait."

"You hear something good and there's always a catch to it," said Foster sourly.

"There's no catch to this, Cedric. It's simply secret, and it'll be out soon, and that'll be good news for all of us." She paused. "Or will it be? That's why I brought it up. To get your reaction to such a discovery."

Ian's small hands fluttered for attention. "How would you expect us to react, Contessa De Marchi? It would be a divine gift to everyone happy to be alive on earth. Who wouldn't want to live on and on and on?"

"That, Ian, is one of the questions," said the contessa. "I've given the possibility some thought. The social implications of almost everyone's living until 150 are simply staggering. For example, I can see how prolongation of life would work to the disadvantage of young people."

"How?" asked Ian.

"For one thing," said the contessa, "the young people now have one thing in their favor—their youth—their good healthy looks, their strength, their vigor in sex, sports, careers. But if life were doubled, if middle-aged people remained healthy twice as long, they would give the young competition in sex, sports, careers, besides also having the bonuses of experience, possibly more wealth, surely more wisdom. In short, the young would lose their only advantages. But the young would be handicapped even further. With longevity, older people would not be quitting or retiring from their jobs to make way for younger ones. Older people would go on working twice as long. It would be difficult, perhaps impossible, for the upcoming young to find jobs."

Teresa Fantoni strained forward in her seat. "Forgive me, Contessa, but what you speak of are minor considerations. Every human on earth would celebrate the opportunity to live in health twice as long. The old would simply take longer to become older, but sooner or later they would give way to the younger. There is no question. Prolonged life, without the—the signs of age, without infirmity, would be a blessing."

The contessa, Jordan could see, was happy. After-dinner sluggishness had evaporated. Her gathering had come to life. He could see her readying herself to take her provocation a logical step further. "Very well, a universal blessing," the contessa said to the actress. "Suppose that is true. Then a second question invites itself. If this discovery comes to pass, what would any of you— any of you who choose to answer—do with this miracle, this guarantee to live at least 150 years on earth?" She looked inquiringly around the room at her guests. She held on Oreste Memo. "You, Oreste—I see you are thoughtful. Are you considering what 150 years of life would mean to you?"

Oreste Memo passed his long fingers through his blond hair. "I've been thinking about it," he said haltingly. "I quite agree with Miss Fantoni. It would be a blessing, especially for creative people. Imagine if Michelangelo, Bach, Beethoven, Shakespeare, even Picasso, Gershwin, had each enjoyed 150 years, with their powers intact, to develop their creations. How mankind would have benefited."

"And for yourself, Oreste?" said the contessa.

"I hesitate to speak of myself, after speaking of the immortals. But in my case, time is what I seek. I compose, I write, and my mind dances with a thousand ideas for which I will have no time. I must give so much of my time to earning my keep that only the smallest amount of time is left for me to compose. But now, given twice as much time, it is possible I might fulfill myself and someday produce a work worthy of my dreams. Prolonged youth would mean prolonged time—all that I really desire."

"And give you an opportunity to court more of your young ladies," said the contessa mischievously. "Now, that too would be a consideration, wouldn't it, Oreste?"

Oreste Memo flushed, glanced apologetically at Teresa Fantoni, and stuttered, "I-I assure you, that would
be a minor consideration. I seek only one woman, a creative soulmate, to share my 150 years."

"Well spoken, Oreste," said the contessa. "And you,
Teresa, what would a slowdown of aging, a promise of
150 years mean to you?"

Teresa Fantoni was silent for a moment. "I am an actress, and in what has become a world of the young, an
actress needs youth," she said with undisguised passion.

"Sarah Bernhardt was active at seventy," the contessa
reminded her.

"She was a caricature of herself at seventy," said Teresa Fantoni. "I have seen film of her, and heard her old
voice on records, and she was an embarrassment. No, an
actress must not wrinkle and hobble and crumble before
the audience's eyes. She must embody, for the world, its
dream of eternal youth, romance, love, hope. If she cannot do that, she is dead. What more can I say than that I
would welcome a chance to play Juliet for another forty
to sixty years—and be believable and beloved."

The actress's passionate reply had laid a hushed silence on the room for seconds, finally broken by Cedric
Foster.

"She's right, entirely right," he said. "Who in the hell
wants to grow old so soon?"

"But Cedric," said the contessa, "you, as a novelist,
are perhaps the least affected by aging. You have a tradition in your field of continued productivity in advanced years. From Tolstoy to Maugham, writers in their
seventies and eighties have continued to produce works
of merit. After all, Cedric, with age come superior wisdom, experience, better judgment—"

"Don't give me that crap, Contessa," the novelist said
angrily. "That's crap, that's what it is—all the sedatives
to quiet the fears of the old, about the loss of their powers, about dying. Next you'll tell me it is fun to grow old,

gain peace of mind, be above the rat race. Growing old is rotten, it stinks, it's the final vicious trick played on man by an unkind God. To give us so much in youth, to promise so much, and then abruptly take it all away and boot us into oblivion. And I'm not speaking about writing alone. I agree with Miss Fantoni, old actresses are caricatures and old writers are blurb writers, essayists, reviewers, their prose witless, childish, respected only because they have stayed around so long. But it is not the loss of creativity with aging that I'm really talking about. I'm talking about the cruel loss of powers as a human being—with every added burdening year, being unable to remember, to walk quickly, or to make love like a magnificent animal—suddenly to find flab instead of firmness in face and body, to—to see the young look at you with pity—or amusement—and turn away from you to their own. No, Contessa, there is nothing good to say about growing old at seventy. But to be alive and well and young at seventy—to be strong at 100—to be optimistic at 120—that alone might enable one to forgive God."

Momentarily taken aback by the emotion in Cedric Foster's statement, more desperate than Teresa Fantoni's, the contessa turned toward Jordan, as if to question him next. But as she did so, Jordan could see, she had become aware of how the subject under discussion had dampened the mood in the room. Assessing this, judging the threat to the well-being of her dinner party, she was briefly troubled. Then she artificially brightened.

Clapping her hands, the contessa stood up. "Enough of geriatrics," she announced. "The time has come to savor the present. I'm going to put on some cheerful music, and I'm going to tell you of an adventure I had in London last summer."

With the music on, and the contessa diverting her guests with a humorous if pointless anecdote, the mood in the room lifted somewhat, but relaxation was never fully restored. Oreste Memo mooned over Teresa Fantoni, who sat remote, smoking cigarettes endlessly, lost in herself. Across the way, Cedric Foster, frowning, giving off an aura of bitterness, ignored his hostess's story and constantly glanced at his companion, Ian, giggling over the attractive Italian publisher's remarks.

After a half hour, Jordan took Alison by the hand and nodded toward the door.

Observing the amenities of leave-taking, Jordan and Alison quietly retreated from the room, followed by the contessa.

In the portego, at the head of the staircase, Jordan halted and considered the contessa with a slight smile. "Contessa, thank you, it was a lovely party."

"You enjoyed it?"

"Every minute," said Alison.

But Jordan could not resist one parting shot. "Contessa, you take big risks," he chided her. "You shouldn't. Too much is at stake."

"Oh, Timothy, no one believed it. No one can imagine it is all true, and that the scientist is under this very roof. It was just to liven up the party. It was for fun."

"It certainly livened up the party, but apparently for some of them it wasn't fun."

"Timothy, it is just that I don't mind old age—rather revel in the tyranny of it. I guess I forget how much others fear it."

"Anyway, promise me, no more games until the professor is safely out of Venice."

"You have my promise."

"Let no one see him—no one."

"You have my word. No one shall."

"You observed what he means to people. What he has is the last high left for humanity."

"You're right. I'll be careful, Timothy."

"I expect to be back here within forty-eight hours. When I come back for him, that will be when we are ready to make a break for freedom." He took the contessa's hand. "Pray for us."

"I'll pray for all of us," the contessa said fervently.

▶ ▶ ▶ ▶

At ten-forty the following morning, the Contessa Elvira De Marchi, wearing a silk robe, sat at the circular marble table in her small breakfast room between the kitchen and dining room on the first floor, finishing the last of her coffee and toast and reading *Il Gazzettino*. She had gone to sleep late the night before, assuring herself that she had hosted a successful party. She had awakened late, yet before her houseguests, and hastened to serve Professor Davis MacDonald his breakfast personally. Then, after a leisurely bath, she had made her way to this cubicle for her own light breakfast.

As she absorbed herself in a story on the progress being made by the carabinieri and the questore in their hunt for the spy, she heard approaching footsteps in the portego and then in the dining room. She raised her head just as the doorway was filled with the presence of Cedric Foster. He was as immaculate as ever in a loose cashmere jacket, ascot, sport shirt, and slacks.

"Good morning, Cedric," she said. "Coffee?"

"Please."

She rose, found a cup, brought it back to the table as he sat down. She poured. "Cream? Sugar?"

"Black. To match my mood."

She took her chair again, lifting up the newspaper. "Maybe I can improve it. Would you like me to read you a summary of the news?"

"Thanks, but no," he said, sipping his coffee. "I was up half the night. Couldn't sleep."

"I'm sorry."

"It was your story. I couldn't put it out of my mind. Kept turning it over."

"What story?" she said innocently.

"You know very well what story. The one that got me going. The one about the scientist you had just met who is on the verge of discovering a formula that will arrest aging. I kept speculating about it in bed, but I still don't believe it's true. That's not supposed to happen for another century."

"It's true, Cedric."

"You'd swear to it?"

"On the heads of my children and grandchildren."

Foster nodded. "Okay, I believe you. Where did you meet this scientist?"

"I thought I had made that clear. Right here in Venice."

"When?"

She hesitated. "Recently. Very recently."

"And he expects to have a formula that will keep us all healthy and prolong our lives?"

She did not know what impelled her next. Perhaps his own doubtfulness. Perhaps her own desire to reinforce her image of strict honesty and integrity. "Since we're alone now, Cedric, I can be more fully truthful. He doesn't expect to have such a formula." She paused, and added emphatically, "He already has it."

Cedric Foster's eyes opened wide. "Really?"

"Yes, he has it."

"Well, where is it? Why don't we all have it?"

"You will, with everyone else, but you'll have to wait until he can escape from here and be free."

Foster snatched at the last. "Escape from here? What does that mean?"

The contessa bit her lip. "I can't say any more."

Foster was after her. "You can't say that much and not say more. You mean he's the one who is wanted by the police? The reason for this whole emergency?"

"Cedric, please, I promised—"

"We're friends. You can confide in me. This scientist, he must be in the city right now. And you've seen him.

You've talked to him. You swore you talked to him and what he said about his formula was true."

"Yes, I talked to him."

"Then he must be here, nearby."

"He is nearby."

"Where?" Cedric Foster pressed her. "I must talk to him too. I must see him."

"You can't. I've given my word that no one will see him."

"You've given your word no one will see him. You mean you're his protector? You're in control of him?"

"Please, Cedric, I've said too much already."

"Wait a minute, Elvira, wait. Listen to me." There was the same passion in his voice that he had shown last night in speaking of the horrors of aging. "We're close friends, trusting friends, we've been friends for years. This is important to me. What you've been saying is so important to me, can have such an effect on my life, that it's difficult even to articulate it. This man can change my life, Elvira. He can save me, certainly save me from suicide."

"What are you talking about, Cedric? I've never heard you carry on this way. What's got into you?"

Cedric Foster, agitated, groped for words, then blurted them. "It's a crisis in my life, Elvira, the supreme crisis. I've not spoken of this to anyone. You are the only one I'd dare confide in. It's about Ian. You know we're lovers. I love him as I've never loved anyone on earth. He means everything to me. Without him, at this stage, life would be meaningless. But I'm going to lose him. I can see that. He's very young, half my age, and frivolous. I know his shortcomings. I know that in some ways he is not worthy of me. But I love him blindly, insanely—what else can I say? I must hold on to him, have him for my own. But I'm growing older, hatefully older, and soon I'll be too old for him. Already he is looking elsewhere, attracted by, flirtatious with, younger men. You saw him last night. It was a humiliation to me the way he ignored me and was openly attentive to that terrible Italian publisher, that young man Sergio. That's been happening more and more often, and one day soon, as I grow older, as I wither, as I become less and less attractive to him, Ian will surely leave me. And I will be lost. All will be ended for me. Can't you see my predicament, Elvira? Can't you feel human compassion for me and understand my need?"

His distorted face was close to her own. She could feel the brush of his warm breath. She pulled back, her mind an emotional pinwheel. "I-I'm sorry, Cedric. I do understand. I'm deeply sorry."

"But not enough to help me? To save me?"

"Be reasonable, Cedric, please be reasonable and understand my own situation. Someone brought him—the professor—to me, to help them hide him. I did so. Yes, he's here in this palazzo, under this roof. But I've pledged another friend, a dear good friend, given my word, that I would permit no one to see the professor. Much as I care for you, Cedric, I must honor my word."

Cedric Foster was in a frenzy of insistence. "But if he's here, right here in this building, as am I, what harm would it do anyone? But for me, it can save my life. If I could explain my desperation to the professor, surely he would understand and be sympathetic. He could administer his formula—simple as that—and I would be saved."

Fighting for time, bringing her coffee cup between them, she saw that it rattled in her hand and she set it down. "Cedric, you will see the professor soon. The Communists want him for themselves, and we're trying to get him out of here unharmed for the whole world. After that, the professor will see you, in Paris, London, New York, somewhere. I'll put in a word for you, arrange that he see you soon."

"When the whole world has him? When everyone is

tearing him apart to be first? You want me to stand in line with the whole world, wait years to be saved when I'm dying each day?"

"It's not at all the way you put it," she pleaded. "You'll have your opportunity like everyone—"

"No, I want it now, right now. Where is he in this building, Elvira? I'm going to see him. Take me to him this moment."

"I can't. I won't."

"Then I'll do it myself," he said, stumbling to his feet. "I'll find him myself, if I have to break down every door."

The contessa was standing, frightened but firm, blocking him. "Don't you dare!" she exclaimed. "Have you gone crazy or what? I won't let you. You're not breaking in on any of my guests, interrupting their privacy."

"I've got to," he said, voice quavering.

"You're not going to. I won't allow it. I forbid it. One move like that and I'll have the servants throw you out of here. Yes, I will. I'll throw you out of here."

Cedric Foster stood breathing heavily, staring at her as he recovered his composure. "All right," he said. "If you won't help me—I'll find other means."

"What means?"

"It's none of your business."

"Cedric, I confided in you. Don't you do anything to violate that confidence. Don't you dare do anything to harm that good man."

He pushed past her with determination. "I'll do what I have to do, and nothing will stop me."

He was gone, and she was alone and trembling.

My God, she thought, he's out of his mind. He's going to the police to make a deal. A promise of first priority for himself with the formula, and in turn he will bring the police here and lead them to Professor MacDonald.

It must not happen.

She had inadvertently betrayed Jordan, miscalculated

the madness of her houseguest, and now she was about to be responsible for the loss of C-98 to the world.

The room reeled about her. She felt a helpless old lady. Yet she must avert the disaster she had provoked.

She teetered beside the table, trying to rally her senses, trying to think.

VII

▶   ▶   ▶   ▶   ▶   ▶   ▶

The Piazza San Marco was bathed in sunlight once more. Pigeons and tourists were swarming everywhere throughout the vast square. A group of German visitors, carrying a wide homemade banner protesting their confinement, marched through the middle of the square attracting some attention.

From the shadows of the arcade beneath his office, Tim Jordan watched the panorama. At last, he started down the aisle toward the front of Quadri's café in search of his luncheon date. Passing the bandstand to his left, he slowed and peered under the awning to see if Oreste Memo was there. Oreste, in his white jacket with red epaulets, white bow tie, holding his violin, was talking to the accordion player and the bass fiddler. He saw Jordan and lifted his fiddle, and Jordan saluted him back and continued past the six rows of tables seeking his date.

Felice Huber had just arrived at one of the round gray Formica tables in the front row, had dropped her bulky purse onto a yellow plastic chair, and was about to settle herself in another one when Jordan spotted her. He went directly to her.

"You're right on time," he said.

"I'm Swiss," she said.

She tilted her dour, angular face to accept his kiss, and then he settled down opposite her.

"Hungry?" he asked.

"Yes."

He caught the eye of a waiter and beckoned him. She ordered two of the small salami sandwiches with mustard and an espresso. He ordered one salami sandwich and hot tea.

He considered her as she poked through her voluminous maroon leather purse for her cigarettes. She was absolutely a double for Virginia Woolf, he was again reminded. Her short brown hair matched her brown pleated skirt. Her muscular tanned legs were bare, and she wore scuffed brown sandals.

Finding his pipe, Jordan filled and lighted it, after he had put a match to her cigarette.

"Well, Felice," he said, "how's it going for you?"

"Rotten," she said. "Couldn't be worse."

"Emotional or financial?"

"It's always financial, Tim, you know that. And financial affects everything else. Those dumbheads running this city have really botched it this time. This was going to be a big summer. I expected to get ahead. Instead, they declared this embargo on all incoming tourists, and every agency—CIT, American Express, Cook's, Italtravel, Svet—is suffering, and the ones suffering most are the poor tourist guides like me. Thousands of tourists trying to get in are being kept out. The ones stranded here are running out of money or they've seen everything. The average tourist spends a day and a half in Venice, right? These people have been here almost a week and they've had it. There's nothing to be happy about, I assure you."

Jordan puffed on his pipe and studied her. "You still want to get out of it?"

"You know I do," she said unhappily. "I admit when I got into being a tourist guide three years ago, I was excited. I thought it would be glamorous. I couldn't wait to finish my training at the Scuola del Turismo and get going. First of all, as you know, I love art. It's my whole life. Second place, I love meeting new people every day. Then, it's a seasonal job. March to November. The rest of the time free to pursue my studies and writings on French art. And, of course, I thought it paid well enough."

"What do you make a day?"

"In season—between June and September—I can handle two or three tours a day. That means 100,000 lire. How much is that in your numbers?"

"About $120 a day, give or take rate fluctuations."

"Good money, you'd think. It wasn't and it isn't. Living is expensive here. The money is just enough for living fairly well. But the whole idea was to save, to get tuition to go to Grenoble, where I could study French art and become a teacher. The way it's going, I'll never get there. And now, after three years, the job itself just doesn't make it. The people you escort are boring or stupid or drive you crazy. The sights become repetitious. I sometimes think if I have to explain another Tiepolo or Tintoretto, I'll scream. Also, it's physically exhausting tramping about with those groups. One's legs just want to give out. But the worst part is the nervousness engendered by those fruitcake tourists. Job would need the patience of Job to handle them every day. You know, the Ufficio Turismo made a study of the sixty independent tourist guides in Venice. Ever hear what they found out? The most frequent illness among guides is a nervous breakdown."

"You don't look as if you're going to have a nervous breakdown."

"I will if I don't get enough to get out of here and get off to Grenoble. Want to help me rob a bank?"

Jordan laughed. "Where would we go with the money? No one can get out of this city."

The waiter appeared with the sandwiches, and after he had slipped the check under a paper napkin, he left them.

Felice Huber fell on the first of her sandwiches immediately, taking a bite, then remembering to spread mustard on both.

Watching her eat, Jordan was quietly aware of the reason he was meeting with Felice this noon. He felt unpressured. Professor MacDonald was in a safe hiding place. But Bruno Girardi's effort was still a question mark. Felice held the hope of an alternative escape route. He nibbled at his salami sandwich, drank his tea, and wondered how he might best approach her.

"I was just saying no one can get out of the city, Felice," he resumed. "I hear you're getting out of the city tomorrow."

She was surprised. "What a small town. Everyone knows everything. How did you know?"

"I guided a tour of my own yesterday. Showed a distinguished visitor our model of the inflatable dam out in Voltabarozzo. I had the columnist Schuyler Moore as my charge. He told me he was covering a factory in Mestre with you tomorrow."

"That's right. I didn't think he'd remember my name."

"How did you manage it?"

"Not easy," said Felice. "But I guess my boss did it the way you did it. Played on civic pride. Both Venice and Mestre still want favorable publicity. My boss had a terrible time with the authorities, but at last he got to the mayor, told him he had these important industrialists who were restless and eager to see the advanced technology in that newly built plant in Mestre, and the mayor finally gave a go-ahead."

"How many are in your group?"

"Eleven, I think. Schuyler Moore makes it twelve."

"Is security very tight?" Jordan asked casually. "I mean, for your group?"

Felice finished her first sandwich and started on the second. "Not especially. There's a list of approved names. Three carabinieri guards will accompany us. We're allowed two hours on the mainland."

"What if someone came along and requested you to add one more name to your list or group—one more industrialist? Would that be possible?"

She looked at him sharply. "I don't think so. Not officially. Of course"—she hesitated—"no one would notice if I added one more person to the list and the group unofficially. In any case, that would be tricky. If I were found out, I'd lose my job. Still, I suppose I might chance it for someone I trusted."

"Like me?"

"Well, yes, like you." She fixed on him. "Why did you ask?"

He squirmed slightly. "I thought of someone I know who would like that tour. I wondered if it was possible."

"It's possible. But I hope you don't ask."

"I probably won't," he said. As they talked, he considered trying to get Professor MacDonald a definite place on Felice's Mestre tour, but now he decided against it. Mainly because it might be pointless, since Bruno could come through today. Also because it was a truly dangerous and difficult means of escape, and he did not want to press it unless there was no other choice. Still, he wanted the option. "No," he repeated, "I probably won't ask. But I might."

"Then I'd consider it." She tried her espresso. "You mentioned last night you wanted to see me on business and pleasure. Was that the business?"

"It was, Felice."

"Of great importance to you?"

He gave a flick of his hand. "Not great importance.

Just to do someone a favor, if necessary. But no need pursuing this further now."

That instant, he thought he heard his name and glanced back over his shoulder. He saw a shapely young woman in slacks approaching rapidly, and then he realized that it was Alison Edwards. This was unusual, and he rose to greet her.

"I hate to interrupt you," Alison said quickly, "but something's come up and you're rather urgently needed at the hotel."

"All right, Alison," he said, puzzled. "Uh, I'd like you to meet Felice Huber. Felice, this is Dr. Alison Edwards, an old friend from the States." He sought the check. "I'm sorry, but I have to get back to the Danieli. . . ."

Felice balled up her paper napkin and rose. "Timing is perfect. We've finished lunch, and I have to get to the agency. Thanks for the sandwiches, Tim. Let's do it again soon."

"We will, Felice. And—thanks."

He waited until she was gone and then wheeled toward Alison, troubled. "What's going on?"

"Let's get back to the hotel fast. I'll tell you as we walk."

She had his elbow, allowed him to leave money for the snack, and then began to propel him across the Piazza, heading for the Doges' Palace and the turn to the Danieli.

"Something's gone wrong," she said as they hurried along.

"For God's sake, what?"

"I don't know exactly. I only know this. Fifteen minutes ago the Contessa De Marchi telephoned. She was looking for you. I told her you were out in the Piazza having lunch with someone. She begged me to get you and bring you right back to the hotel. She wanted me to do so at once. She said something has gone terribly wrong. She'll be waiting for you in the Danieli lobby."

"It was a perfect setup," said Jordan. "I can't imagine what could possibly have spoiled it."

When they entered the lobby of the Hotel Danieli, going between the police sentinels, there were numerous persons gathered around the concierge's counter. The Contessa Elvira De Marchi was not among them.

Jordan signaled Alison to follow him. "The real lobby is off to the left. It extends from the bar in back to the front of the hotel. If she's here yet, she'll be in there."

She was indeed there, almost lost in an armchair in a secluded corner of the lobby near the hotel's front windows. The contessa saw them at once, stood up, and then, as they reached her, sat down as they sat across from her.

Jordan could see that she was distraught.

"What's happened?" he asked at once.

"Cedric Foster found out I'm harboring Professor MacDonald in the palazzo," she said.

"How could he?"

"I'm afraid it was my fault," said the contessa.

Haltingly, she told Jordan and Alison what had taken place at late breakfast between Cedric Foster and herself in the past hour.

Jordan was dismayed. "Contessa, how could you have let him know MacDonald was under your roof? You'd promised—"

"Timothy, believe me," she pleaded, "it was accidental. I just blurted it out. You would have understood if you'd been there. It was the result of a highly charged, emotional scene. Cedric was a wild man, out of control. He confessed to me that he's afraid he will lose his lover—the young fellow, Ian—because he's growing older. He'll do anything to hold back his aging. When he found out Professor MacDonald was the one person who could save him, and was staying upstairs, he demanded

to see him. I refused. He threatened to break in on him.
I warned him I'd have him thrown out. Then Cedric
shouted 'If you won't help me, I'll find other means. I'll
do what I have to do.' And he ran out, left the palazzo."

"Dammit," said Jordan. "Obviously, you think he's
gone to the police?"

"I'm certain of that."

"But Foster is your houseguest, your friend."

"No matter. He was too upset, not at all rational. Getting that youth formula first, immediately, means more
to him than anything on earth. I have no doubt he went
to the police. He's probably with them right now, making a deal. If they will guarantee him a priority in getting
the formula, he will lead them to MacDonald. The minute I realized that, I telephoned you."

Jordan felt crushed. "It's probably too late to save
MacDonald now. The police are probably on their
way—"

The contessa straightened. "The police won't find a
thing. I kept my head. It was the least I could do to
rectify my blunder. I have Professor MacDonald with
me."

"Where?"

"In my motor launch, in the back, tied up right near
the Cipriani wharf not far from here."

"Thank God, Contessa," said Jordan gratefully. "But
is he safe?"

"Temporarily. Once the police start looking for me,
they'll spot my launch. It's one of the few privately
owned ones of its type in Venice."

"What about your driver?"

"He wouldn't know anything. He's an old man who
dreams, ignores so many people who go and come, and
does his job. But you'll have to move the professor to a
safer place as soon as possible, Timothy. That's why I
rushed over here to alert you. There may not be much
time."

Jordan looked blankly at Alison. "I just don't know where to turn."

The contessa came forward in her armchair. "Timothy, you have so many friends. There must be someone you can trust."

"I've used most of them." He shook his head. "And they've not all been dependable. It's hard to think."

The contessa was silent for long seconds, ruminating. She raised her head. "I've been thinking too. Last night at my place, at one point, someone told me how much he likes you, how much he's pleased to have you for a friend."

"Who?"

"Oreste Memo."

"The musician? Sure, we're old acquaintances, but—"

"He has great affection for you, Timothy. I've found him a most reliable human being. You might ask him—"

"I'm afraid I have no choice," said Jordan, rising. "It's an excellent suggestion. I'll try to see him now. You and Alison go to the boat. I'll find you. Just wait for me and hope I come back with good news."

The contessa was beside him. "Not too long, Timothy."

"Faster than a speeding bullet," said Jordan grimly, starting off.

▶ ▶ ▶ ▶

Fortunately, Jordan realized, the Quadri orchestra had just concluded its last number in this set and was preparing to take a time out as the orchestra next door at the Lavena café began its turn at playing.

Jordan waited in the aisle alongside the raised bandstand and saw Oreste Memo put aside his violin and mop his face with his handkerchief.

"Oreste," Jordan called out, "can I see you for a moment?"

The violinist removed his white jacket, laid it neatly on a chair, and then came down from the bandstand.

"I was just going to cool off with a bottle of Fiuggi," said Memo. "It's better to talk sitting. Will you join me?"

Jordan felt oppressed by time pressure, but he knew that the amenities had to be observed, especially when he would be making such an unusual request of Memo.

"Sure thing," said Jordan. "I'm thirsty too."

They settled down at an oval table just below the front of the bandstand.

"It was good seeing you at the contessa's last night," said Oreste Memo. "That was quite an evening."

"You mean the contessa's tried-and-true conversation-starters?"

Oreste Memo grinned. "I mean getting a chance to know Teresa Fantoni and to spend the evening looking down inside her low neckline. She's quite a package."

"She's magnificent," Jordan agreed.

A waiter went past them, and Memo ordered a bottle of Fiuggi water. "Well," he said, scanning the crowded café, "still a long day to go."

"Exactly what are your hours?" Jordan asked.

"Start at eleven. Finish at midnight, with a break every fifteen minutes, like now, of from ten to fifteen minutes. Actually, today is a shorter day for me. I requested the evening off and got it."

"You must do well here, Oreste."

"Well enough. I make 700,000 lire a month. That's over $850 a month. It takes care of me during the winter off and gives me freedom to do my serious work."

"Serious work? Oh, you mean your composing."

"I don't want to get stuck in this orchestra for life, fiddling away from *The Barber of Seville* every night. Not for me. I'm a member of the Società Italiana Autori ed Editori, and I get my compositions performed enough to be encouraged. Right now I'm working on a musical play called *Eleonora.* It's about Eleonora Duse, her affair with D'Annunzio, and her later years. It is really quite good. I have much hope. And you, Tim—have you been equally busy?"

The bottle of Fiuggi came. Oreste Memo poured. Jordan ignored his glass. "Busy enough. Actually, I'm on my way to an appointment, but I wanted to speak to you about something first."

"But of course. You need some money?" He laughed.

"I'll never turn that down," said Jordan, forcing a smile. He became serious. "It's something else. I remember you were kind enough, about a year ago, to have me at a cocktail party at your apartment."

Memo nodded. "It is a large apartment because I need room for all my Oriental rugs. I'm a fanatic about Oriental rugs."

"Do you still live there?"

"Still there."

"It's not far from here, is it?"

"Just a short way. In the Fondamenta del Traghetto di San Maurizio, right here in the *sestiere* of San Marco."

"Do you have canal access?"

"Nearby."

"I'll tell you why I'm bothering you with all these questions, Oreste. I need a favor from you. I'm rather shy about requesting it. Of course, you can say no and I'll understand."

"Tim, whatever you want, if I can help."

"Well, there's a certain person—I can't take the person to my hotel room, because I'm sharing it—I need a place to be alone with this person until tomorrow morning. I was hoping you could put us up for the night in a corner of your apartment."

Oreste Memo was expansive. "That is all you want? Such a need I completely understand. As the Spanish say, my house is your house. In fact, you are in luck. I

have a date tonight. Guess with whom? Teresa Fantoni."
He winked broadly. "I expect to be away all night."

"No kidding?"

He dug into his trouser pocket. "Here is a spare key.
Do you have a piece of paper?"

Jordan took a scrap from his jacket pocket. Oreste
Memo uncapped his pen and wrote on it. "And here is
my address. You can move in right now."

"You haven't asked me why I need your apartment."

"I don't have to. Why would any man want to borrow
a friend's apartment? Am I right, Tim?"

Jordan did not want to tell him he was wrong, but he
felt hugely relieved. He pushed away from the table. "I
don't know how I can repay you."

"Just wish me luck tonight, and have as good a time as
I expect to have."

▶ ▶ ▶ ▶

It was a balmy evening, soft and caressing, an evening
for happy lovers. But Oreste Memo, as he walked slowly
from Santa Maria del Giglio to his apartment, was not
one of them. His usually serene, Apollo-like countenance was clothed with frustration. The events of the
past hour had filled him with disappointment and
brought on his dejection.

Now, entering the Piazza San Marco on his way home,
he masochistically relived his so-called intimate evening with Teresa Fantoni.

Actually, the meeting had been promoted by his patroness, the Contessa De Marchi, who appreciated his
creativity and saw a great future for him. Last night, at
her dinner party, the contessa had taken Teresa aside
and spoken to her of his musical play, no details except
that it had a memorable role for an actress. The contessa
had suggested to Teresa that she meet with Oreste and
hear more about it. Teresa had agreed to do so. After

dinner, Oreste had deliberately sat himself beside the famous actress, intent on outlining his play for her. But her sensuous beauty, especially her pouting lips, her straining abundant breasts, her slim legs, had distracted him. He had wanted to see her privately to interest her in his play, but then, of equal importance, perhaps of more compelling importance, was his mad desire to take her to bed.

Last night he had been filled with confidence that once with her alone, he could seduce her. True, he was a nobody, and she was an international celebrity with the world at her beck and call. Still, Oreste knew that he had a way with women, a way of talking to them that was irresistible, and that more women were seduced by ear, by words, than by any other means. If she would agree to see him alone, he was certain he would have a success. Before the evening at the contessa's had ended, Oreste had his commitment. Teresa Fantoni had agreed to have a drink with him on the outdoor terrace of the Gritti Palace hotel at eight o'clock the next evening. Oreste had been overjoyed. Once she heard the role he had written for her in his play, once she heard his frank passion for her, his ardor, it would be a short distance from the terrace of the Gritti to the bedroom of her suite upstairs.

This evening, finishing his violin stint at seven o'clock and turning his chair over to his substitute, he had not bothered to go back to his apartment. Instead, he had gone into Quadri's indoor restaurant, made his way upstairs to groom himself, come down and fortified himself with a double Scotch, and then started to the Gritti Palace.

As he entered the lobby, he saw her emerging from the elevator. For a moment he held back to revel in what would soon be his. She was wearing a thin white silk cocktail dress that adhered to every contour of her figure. As she turned away from the elevator, her buttocks were clearly defined and he thought he could make out the line of her panties. He hurried to intercept her, taking her hand, bending to kiss the back of it.

"I have a table on the terrace," she said regally. "It is the most pleasant part of Venice, having a drink on the Grand Canal."

This was promising, this and the way she had dressed for him, and his confidence soared.

He followed her through the bar and outdoors, enjoying every step of the way as the maître d' and the waiters bowed and scraped before her, before this woman who was receiving him alone. They had a table on the rail overlooking the water, and except for another couple some distance away, they had this dream spot to themselves.

She ordered a martini and he a Scotch. Then she placed a cigarette in her long gold holder and he fumbled to light her cigarette. He searched for some conversational opener, something winning, a good note, but he could think of nothing because his attention was entirely absorbed by her breasts. She was either braless or wearing a half bra, because he could make out her nipples faintly, very large, very brown.

He tore his gaze away from her breasts and looked out at the canal. "You're right," he said, "it is soothing here."

"One of the few soothing sights left in Venice," she said, patting the barrette that held her sleek reddish hair. "Frankly, by now, I've had Venice up to my ears. I'm utterly bored by it. I came up here for two or three days on the Lido beach, to see some friends, but I never expected to be forced to stay here this long, to be a prisoner, held against my wishes. I should be back in Rome. I have a film starting soon, and so much to do before."

He was disappointed, because he adored Venice and he fervently wanted his adored one to love it too. "I'm sorry," he said. "Perhaps, if you have the time, I could show you some parts of Venice you've never seen."

"You are kind, but I am not the least bit interested."

"How did you like the contessa's party last night? I thought—"

"It was tiresome. I couldn't wait to get away. I like the contessa well enough. I've known her forever, and respect her. But she is a terrible hostess. Her parties are always a strain. She tries too hard. There is no ease, no comfort, no naturalness. Last night was a perfect case— the way she tried to liven up the party after dinner with that ridiculous story about the longevity scientist."

"Didn't you believe her? I was sure it was true."

"An absurd fairy tale. If someone found a way to keep people young, the whole world would know about it in an instant. I've read a good deal about these things. There have been breakthroughs in genetics, it's true. But science is still far, far away from giving us the gift of prolonged youth." She sipped her martini. "Too bad."

It was time, he saw, to start Operation Bedroom. "You are fortunate," he said, "to already possess the gift of eternal youth."

She looked at him with disgust. "Mr. Memo," she said, "save that for your plays."

"I mean it," he persisted. "You are young and you will always be young."

"Biologically untrue," she said. "But have it your way. I think I'll have another martini."

She ordered for herself and for him, then said a trifle testily, "About that play you are writing. The contessa told me you were doing a play that has a perfect role for me. Is that true?"

"I believe it is true. I had an image of you before me as I wrote it."

"Tell me about it." Then she hastened to add, "Not the whole thing. Just give me an idea of what it is about."

Oreste Memo cleared his throat. "It is about Eleonora Duse."

"Really?"

"I think it befits Italy's greatest actress of the past to be played by Italy's greatest actress of the present."

"You are most flattering."

"I'm sincere."

"All right. What about Eleonora Duse?"

"It begins in the last weeks of her love affair with Gabriele D'Annunzio. That is the beginning. Then it dramatizes the remainder of her story, a woman alone, brave, defiant, independent, against the world. Her American tour, when she would appear only in D'Annunzio's works. Her illness, which forced her retirement. Then, after twelve years in retirement, her financial difficulties that forced her into a comeback effort. Her return, overcoming the competition of Sarah Bernhardt, freeing herself from the ghost of D'Annunzio, winning the public again, a triumphal return, culminating with her death in the American city of Pittsburgh. There are moving scenes. There's—"

Teresa Fantoni held up her hand. Oreste Memo stopped in mid sentence, puzzled.

"Mr. Memo," she said, "I'm sure you know something about playwriting, but you know nothing whatsoever about women."

His confusion deepened. "I don't understand."

"You will. Hear me. When was Eleonora Duse born? She was born in 1859. You would begin her story when she breaks with D'Annunzio. That was 1899. So your play begins with Duse at the age of forty. Is that right?"

"Why, yes."

"Very well. So then her American tour. In 1902, when she was forty-three. Her retirement in 1909, at fifty. Her emerging from retirement at sixty-two. Her death in 1924, at sixty-five." She paused and stared at him. "Mr. Memo, are you asking Teresa Fantoni to play an actress from the age of forty to the age of sixty-five?"

"But you can do it."

"Of course I can do it. The point is I don't want to do

it. No actress in my years would play a role portraying a woman growing old from forty to sixty-five. Do you think that's what I want at this time in my life? To be up there on the stage, wrinkling and doddering, with no youth whatsoever? Impossible. I wouldn't dream of it."

"The public knows you are young and will only be acting."

"The public knows only that I am growing older, and it makes no sense to play a role that will assure them it is true."

"But you *are* young."

"Am I? How young?"

Dangerous territory. "I'd say thirty-five."

She made a face. "Thank you, but that has not been for some time. No, Mr. Memo, your play is not for me. It could hasten my ruin. I appreciate your thinking of me, but we had best forget it. Let's talk of happier things."

One of the happier things she was prepared to talk about was her new film now in preparation in Rome. In it she would enact the role of a twenty-eight-year-old nun who leaves her convent and has a love affair with an ex-priest. She went on and on, for twenty minutes, discussing her problems with the screenplay writer, the director, the producer.

Oreste Memo sat dismayed.

Her total rejection of the Duse part, her fixation with age, had shaken him. His design, Grand Design, for the evening had been nearly obliterated. There still must be something of it to save. He must be the Oreste Memo of old—fearless, bold, overwhelming.

He listened and waited, hypnotized by her breasts shaking gently beneath the white silk dress. She had finished an anecdote and was drinking from her second martini.

"Fascinating," he said to her. "Miss Fantoni, I'd be honored if I could take you to dinner from here."

"Thank you, but no. I'm tired." She set down her

empty glass. "I think I'll just go up to my suite, order lightly from room service, and get to sleep early. Maybe I'll be free to leave this wretched city tomorrow."

"Could I see you up to your room?"

She eyed him. "Whatever for? That's not necessary."

He saw that she might slip away. Boldness, boldness. "It is necessary for me."

"What do you mean?"

"I mean that every added moment I'm with you enriches my life. I've carried you in my head so long, enjoyed the pleasure of your presence in my head so long, loved you in my secret heart so endlessly, that now in person I cannot let you go."

She stared at him with disbelief. "That dialogue," she said. "You sound like a fugitive from a Pirandello play." She was on her feet. "I'm sorry, young man. Take your play and your amorous heart elsewhere. I wish you luck. Good evening."

She was gone.

And he, finished reliving the humiliation of her arrogant rejection, was trudging through the Piazza San Marco toward his lonely apartment, still lusting for the gorgeous bitch. But it was hopeless. There was no way he might ever seduce her.

Five minutes later, he had reached his place, climbed the stairs to his first-floor apartment, mournfully inserted the key, and gone into his long hallway. As he began to remove his suit jacket, he noticed to his surprise that he had left the lights on in his living room. Stepping to the archway, he saw his open bedroom door and was surprised again that the lights were on there too. It was unlike him to have left the lights on when he had gone to work late this morning.

Then he heard a voice from the bedroom. Startled, a little frightened, not knowing where to turn, he heard the same voice a second time, and he recognized it. Timothy Jordan's voice. At once, he remembered. So obsessed had he been with the conquest of Teresa Fantoni, his effort, his failure, that he had altogether forgotten his brief meeting with Jordan early in the afternoon. It came back to him now. Jordan had wanted to borrow his apartment for the night, to spend the night here in privacy with a friend, and he had said he would not need his apartment tonight and had given Jordan his extra key.

He realized he could not hang around any longer. Jordan was probably in bed with a woman, and his own presence would embarrass them both. He looked at the bedroom entrance wistfully. At least Jordan was being luckier than he had been.

About to turn away, Oreste Memo heard a second voice, a deeper, older voice, and it was male.

Next he heard both voices. Both male.

How strange. Tim Jordan was no queer. Memo knew of his continuing affair with his assistant, Marisa Girardi. Then what was this all about?

Automatically, Oreste Memo had moved into his living room, and the voices from the bedroom were clear and distinct.

They were discussing something about traveling.

Memo realized that this was none of his business. He had no right to invade their privacy. Even though this was his apartment, he had lent it in good faith to a friend. He had turned to leave quietly when a snatch of conversation held him in his tracks.

". . . and then you will be safely in Paris," Jordan was saying. "What will you do next? Wait for the Gerontology Congress to convene? Or immediately announce to the world that you've discovered the formula?"

"I will convene a press conference immediately," the older voice was saying. "I'll make my announcement of the discovery of C-98, read to the world the paper I had intended to read to the Congress—in fact, pass out copies of it—and I'll clarify it all by answering questions. But we're skipping too far ahead, Tim. First I've got to get out of here before the police and the Russians have me."

"All right, Professor MacDonald," said Jordan, rustling some kind of paper. "Assuming Bruno comes through, let's go over this map again and show you how to get to Paris."

Oreste Memo, wavering with disbelief in the middle of his living room, continued to listen. If there had been any confusion in his mind at the start, it was soon dispelled. For after they had methodically gone over the professor's escape route, they began to discuss in a relaxed way the potentials of the professor's discovery.

Memo felt the goose pimples growing on his arms and chest, and understood the implications of what he had been hearing.

Filled with purpose, he turned away and tiptoed out of the room.

He knew what he would do at once.

At last he had his Open Sesame.

▶ ▶ ▶ ▶

She had unlocked the door of her Gritti Palace suite, and she was wearing a pale blue dressing gown over some kind of short shift of a nightgown, and to Oreste Memo she looked like a sexy Roman goddess.

Teresa Fantoni stared at him, as if to discern whether he was drunk, and then, assured that he was not, she said curtly, "Don't just stand there. Come in. I can't have the whole hotel see me this way."

He came into her darkened suite, only one dim lamp on in her sitting room. His eyes held on her, penetrated the transparency of her garments. His eyes lovingly raped her as she closed the door and came before him.

"This is utter madness," she said, unamused. "I can't believe it. Is this one of your jokes, a ruse to get up here?"

"It is true. Every word I told you on the phone is true," he said.

He had called her, after leaving his apartment. He had rushed to the nearest public telephone and called her at the Gritti, and caught her in bed just as she was trying to fall asleep. He had burst out to her, almost uncontrolled, the news that what they had heard from the Contessa De Marchi last night was all true, exactly as she had told it. Minutes ago, he had met the scientist who had discovered the Fountain of Youth. He couldn't tell her more now—he was on a public phone, there were others around him—but he would tell her all about it if he could see her privately, come up to her suite. With some hesitation, she had finally told him to come right over.

They stood facing each other in the sitting room of her suite. She was studying him, her cat's eyes probing. "I still find it hard to take seriously," she said. "You're making this up."

"I tell you it is true," he persisted. "By accident, after leaving you before, I ran into him, heard him speak of his youth formula. The scientist, his name is Professor MacDonald. His formula is called C-98."

"I don't think you're inventive enough to make that up."

"Believe me!"

"This MacDonald, he's here in Venice?"

"Right here. He's a fugitive. Let me explain as much as I heard. I gather—I'm not sure—he must have made his discovery while visiting the Soviet Union, got out to Venice, and the Soviets asked our Communist government, our police, to get hold of him and return him. MacDonald is trapped, seeking a means to escape."

"So he's here," she said slowly. "He could give anyone the formula to keep that person young."

"No question."

She moved closer to Memo. "Where is he?"

He swallowed. "I-I can't tell you. I've sworn to a friend of his not to tell anyone. But listen, I can speak to him, to my friend, and have him intercede for you. I can perhaps arrange for you to be one of the first to be given youth."

She appeared overcome with emotion. "Oh, Oreste, you are so kind, so good to me." She was against him, her arms around his neck. She pressed her warm lips on his. "Thank you," she murmured.

For Oreste Memo the moment he had dreamed of, the incredibility of it, was overwhelming. He felt the stirring between his legs, the immediate expanding and growing of it pressed against her.

She clung to him tightly. Her lips touched his ear. He felt her warm breath as she whispered, "Not only are you kind to me, darling, but you are passionate."

"Teresa," he exhaled, "I want you."

She hugged him tighter. "Do you, darling? Do you really want me?"

The fragrance of her body, the softness of her limbs was almost too much to bear. "More than anything in the world," he gasped.

She released him, stepped back, untied her dressing gown, pulled it off, and let it drop to the carpet. She was wearing an entirely transparent nightgown that hung loosely to her knees. He could see the roundness of the firm protruding breasts and the brown circles of nipples, and he could see the broad patch of her vaginal mound, and he began to quiver.

"Oh, God, you're beautiful," he breathed. "I love you. . . ."

He reached for her, but she stepped back. "Take off your jacket. There. Now let me help you off with your shirt."

As she unbuttoned his shirt, he kicked off his shoes, loosened his belt, and stepped out of his trousers. He stood in his distended bikini briefs, breathing heavily.

She touched his shoulder. "Come, Oreste, dear, let's go to bed."

To bed with Teresa Fantoni! To bed with the female every male on earth worshiped! It was difficult walking as he went into the bedroom after her. Like the sitting room, the bedroom was darkened except for one dim lamp, on the stand beside the bed. She flung back the quilted cover all the way, pulled up her nightgown and was out of it, and threw herself on the bed, on her back.

"What's holding you, my baby?" she called out.

From the rim of darkness, he had been watching her with awe. Venus de Milo summoning him to her bed. He jerked down his briefs and staggered toward her. He knew he was a sight. His penis was standing straight out.

"My, my," she said, observing it, as he crawled toward her from the foot of the bed. Her legs, knees bent, were high and slightly apart.

"Teresa, my love . . ."

"Oreste, dear," she said caressingly, "where is he? Tell your Teresa where he is?"

"What? Who?"

"Professor MacDonald. You know what it means to me."

"I can't, I really can't."

He tried to separate her legs further, but she brought them together.

"You can, my heart. You can tell your Teresa."

"I wish I could." He reached for her knees. "Please, Teresa—"

"No, no. If you cannot trust me when I give myself to you—"

"I trust you, I trust you. Please, Teresa, I've got to go into you."

"You must tell me. I will repeat it to no one."

"He's in hiding."

"Where?"

Inflamed, he pleaded with her. "Teresa, I'm dying, exploding, let me—"

"Where? Just tell me where—"

"Christ, he's hiding—hiding in my apartment—"

"You darling."

Her legs opened wide, her red vulva opened wide, and he went down low between her legs, sinking into her, going into her inch by inch, and then rising and falling, pulling and pushing, as she spread beneath him, eyes shut, fingers loosely on his shoulders.

His movements had begun slowly, but gradually they increased in speed. Several minutes had passed, and he was pumping steadily, steadily, steadily, faster and faster as she lubricated. Again and again he sank into her soft wetness—paradise—his penis seeming to grow to near eruption.

He wanted it to go on forever, locked together like this in animal ecstasy, and then he glimpsed her placid face and once more realized with whom he was having intercourse—and the thought of it was too much. The love muscle between his legs, sliding inside her flesh, cleaving her, expanded once more, could contain itself no longer, and triggered a series of spasmic ejaculations spewing relief. He shuddered, cried out, letting go completely, and was encompassed by a red-hot aura that ever so slowly cooled.

It was over. He was empty. He was weak.

He lay atop her for minutes, at last rolling over on his side.

"You were a good boy," she said drowsily. "A very good boy. Now let your Teresa sleep."

He left the bed, washed, and dressed.

Before departing, he stooped over her on the bed. "Teresa, are you asleep?"

"Ummm."

"Teresa, I shouldn't have told you, but I did. I

couldn't help it. But it has got to be our secret, where the professor is."

"Our secret," she murmured.

"I'll ask my friend if he can talk the professor into seeing you."

"Thanks, darling. Good night."

He let himself out of her suite, and when he was outside the Gritti, and starting toward the Piazza, he was surprised at his lack of joy over his momentous conquest. Walking along, he wondered why he was not more pleased. After all, he had just laid Teresa Fantoni, the one and only. Then he realized there were two reasons for his lack of excitement. First, the sex act with the goddess had been one-way. She had proved a receptacle, nothing more. The intercourse had come from him alone, with no cooperation from her. In bed, she had not kissed him, touched him in love, not once moved her hips. His Venus de Milo could have been marble. It had been a lousy lay. Its only value was that it could be a conversation piece. That was what she was, that piece— a conversation piece. The second dampener. He had bought it, and paid too much. He had given away MacDonald's secret refuge, and if Teresa talked loosely tomorrow, there would be trouble.

He was almost at the Piazza, but now he stopped. He must go back to her, awaken her, impress upon her absolutely that she must keep their secret a real secret. Spinning about, he hurriedly retraced his steps toward the Gritti Palace.

As he reached the edge of the square, from which the Santa Maria del Giglio led past the hotel apartments to the hotel, he saw a lone figure emerge from the street.

He stopped in his tracks, his mouth agape.

She was wearing a brimmed hat, loose jacket, fashionable beige pants, and carrying an alligator bag. She was walking briskly.

She was Teresa Fantoni.

He fell back in the shadows, waiting to observe in which direction she would turn. When she turned toward the direction of the Rialto Bridge, he knew where she was going.

▶ ▶ ▶ ▶

The meeting in the mayor's office, on the first floor of the Palazzo Farsetti, the city hall, had been in progress for over an hour and was now winding down.

There were four of them engaged in the fruitless conversation. Mayor Accardi, his sausage fingers drumming his desk top, looked from Colonel Cutrone, head of the carabinieri, to Questore Trevisan, superintendent of the Venice police, to Major Kedrov, the Russian KGB officer, and finally he shrugged helplessly.

"Incredible," said the mayor, "that we've got no place in all this time. I still think MacDonald was taken to one permanent hideout, something obscure that has eluded our searchers, and he's dug in there until we give up."

Colonel Cutrone shook his head. "No, that is unlikely. We know he has a confederate, the very one who pulled him off San Lazzaro. This person must know Venice, and if he knows Venice he must have friends here. While I cannot prove it, possess no evidence, I suggest that these friends—one, then another, perhaps—are sheltering our fugitive."

"What makes you believe this?" Trevisan asked Cutrone.

"Mostly a gut feeling. Then something else. The lead that came to us at noon today. The American author—"

"Cedric Foster," the mayor prompted.

"Yes, Foster. He claimed to know where MacDonald could be found, if we promised him a priority. He sent us charging off to the Palazzo De Marchi. Except for the contessa and a few houseguests, we found no one there."

"The contessa was an unlikely lead anyway," said the mayor.

Colonel Cutrone pursed his lips. "I'm not so sure. I see no reason for Foster to make up his story. Despite the fact that the contessa told us she had been teasing him, she did know about MacDonald, did know we were hunting for MacDonald and not a spy."

"She has the best connections," said Trevisan. "Gossip travels quickly in Venice. One cannot keep a secret here."

"Nevertheless," insisted Colonel Cutrone, "she may have actually been protecting MacDonald. When she became alarmed about Foster's obvious hysteria, she may have arranged to have MacDonald moved to another friend."

"Do you want us to keep an eye on the contessa?" asked Trevisan.

"No—too late. She'll have nothing more to do with our quarry, I'm sure. But all of this brings me to one point, one possibility we've overlooked or neglected. Since I think we are dealing with a string of—an underground of—human beings—and if I am right—then we have a chance. Human beings are avaricious. A human being sold out the Saviour for money. One person, who might be helping MacDonald, might sell him out for money. Yes, gentlemen, I am suggesting a cash reward. It is something we should have done from the start. Our parsimony has hindered us. It is not too late for this. I feel the time has come to offer a substantial reward. I think that might smoke out our Professor MacDonald."

For seconds, silence lay on the room, as each of the others considered the proposal.

The mayor spoke first. "How much?" he inquired of Cutrone. "What do you have in mind?"

"A substantial sum."

"Eight million lire? Forty million lire? What?"

"One moment." Major Kedrov came around in his

chair. "I don't understand lire. You do not understand rubles. Let us speak in the language of the imperialist Americans, their language of money they have forced upon the world. Mayor, translate into dollars."

Mayor Accardi nodded. "I was asking Colonel Cutrone if he had a $10,000 reward in mind. Or $50,000."

"Nonsense," barked the Russian. "We want someone loyal to our fugitive to give him up. We must make the bait irresistible. I say offer $150,000 to anyone who leads us to him."

"One hundred fifty thousand dollars?" Mayor Accardi was aghast. "Major, we are not millionaires. We are a poor city—"

"Never mind," said Major Kedrov. "On behalf of the Soviet government, I guarantee you reimbursement for the sum. Yes, we will pay the reward. It is a mere pittance for what is at stake."

"If you really will—"

"It is guaranteed."

The mayor glanced at his police officers. They each nodded assent. The mayor brought his fat hands together. "Very well. The reward is established. One hundred fifty thousand dollars. Almost 130,000,000 lire."

"To be announced at once," said Major Kedrov.

"At once," the mayor agreed. He addressed Trevisan. "Questore, we must not waste time printing new posters. There is room on top of the old one—we have many extra copies in the print shop. Rouse someone and get him to the print shop immediately. Let him put in as bold lettering as possible, 'Reward for a clue leading to his arrest, 130,000,000 lire.' See that this is done in the next hour. Then have your people distribute the posters to the leading checkpoints. The rest we can distribute in the morning." As Trevisan hastened out of the office, Mayor Accardi said, "Good. It is done. We have accomplished something."

Colonel Cutrone was pleased. "It will get results."

The buzzer on the mayor's desk sounded, and he said,

"I guess Mrs. Rinaldo hasn't gone home yet." He picked up the telephone. "Yes?" He listened. "Really? Really? Tell her to wait in the reception room. I'll be right out. And you may go home now."

Hanging up, he said, "A nocturnal visitor outside. Wants to see someone in authority on an urgent matter. She'd called the police station and somehow got them to tell her we were all here. Excuse me, gentlemen, for a moment. Help yourself to some brandy on the table."

Mayor Accardi crossed his thickly carpeted office and went into the reception room. His secretary had already gone, and his visitor stood waiting in the middle of the room.

As the mayor approached her, he saw how beautiful she was. Her face was familiar to him, but he could not place it at first. "I'm Mayor Accardi," he said. "You were sent here, Miss—?"

"Teresa Fantoni," she said.

Of course. "What an honor, Miss Fantoni!" the mayor exclaimed, beaming. "How good to meet you, to have you in Venice. Can I be of help? You have a problem?"

"*You* have a problem," said Teresa Fantoni. "I'm prepared to solve it."

"Yes?"

"I've just learned you closed down the city because you wanted to capture—not some silly spy, but a man named Professor MacDonald, a man who has discovered the formula for prolonging youth and life."

Mayor Accardi was astonished. "How could you know? Who told you?"

"Never mind. It's not important. What is important is that you want him."

"We want him very much. We've just issued a reward of 130,000,000 lire to anyone who can lead us to him."

"I can lead you to him," said Teresa Fantoni flatly.

Mayor Accardi had not been prepared for this. "You can? You're sure of it?"

"I'm absolutely sure of it. But before I tell you where

you can find Professor MacDonald, I want to know what's in it for me."

"Why, of course, if it's true, if we apprehend him, you shall have the 130,000,000-lire reward."

"I don't want your damn reward," said the actress irritably. "I want something more."

"More?"

"Definitely more—to me. I want your pledge that after MacDonald is captured, before you send him to Russia—yes, I know all about that too—I will be the first, or one of the first, to receive a treatment of his youth formula. That is my price."

"I understand," said the mayor. "You have my word."

"I don't want your word. I want it in black and white, in writing."

"In writing? But—"

"On paper signed by you. Just a simple sentence saying in return for handing MacDonald over to you I am guaranteed a treatment of the youth formula within a week after his capture."

"Well, I suppose I can give you such a guarantee. Very well. We will make the transaction now." Taking his gold pen from his coat pocket, he tramped to the receptionist's desk, found a scratch pad in a drawer, tore off a sheet. Placing the sheet on the desk, he wrote out the brief contract, then signed it.

Teresa Fantoni, hovering over him, said, "Date it."

The mayor dated it.

Straightening, about to hand her the sheet, he thought twice about it and held it back. "Sorry, Miss Fantoni. Now your half of the bargain."

"You'll find Professor MacDonald this moment in the apartment of a musician named Oreste Memo, a resident of Venice. He is a violinist at Quadri's café."

"Oreste Memo. I'm not sure I know him."

"I assure you, he's very real, and he's hiding Professor MacDonald."

"Oreste Memo, good. You have his address?"

"I don't have his address. My God, you mean that's a problem?"

"No, no, forgive me, Miss Fantoni. No problem at all. The police will have his address in a moment. We'll have our man in an hour."

Teresa Fantoni smiled sweetly and removed the paper from the mayor's hand.

"Thank you, thank you," said the mayor, following her to the door. "You have performed a wonderful service tonight."

Her smile held. "So have you, Your Honor, so have you."

Minutes later, she emerged from the city hall and paused on the walk running along the Grand Canal to fold elaborately the piece of paper she had just obtained and then stuff it into her purse. Satisfied, she started back to the Gritti Palace hotel.

As she left, there was a movement in the shadowy recess of a building beside the city hall.

Oreste Memo stepped out into the moonlight and stood quietly watching her receding figure with hatred, gradually supplanted by guilt and self-loathing.

▶ ▶ ▶ ▶

The telephone in Oreste Memo's bedroom kept ringing, and Tim Jordan was uncertain whether he should answer it. Except for the apartment's owner, no one knew that he and Professor MacDonald were here. Not quite true, his memory quickly corrected him. Alison Edwards knew that they were here. He had slipped out in the afternoon to visit her at the Danieli, to tell her MacDonald was safe and to give her Oreste Memo's telephone number in case she needed it. But then he had also told her, if she had to call him, to ring three times, hang up, and repeat the call, ring three times, hang up, and he would know it was Alison and get right back to her.

But the insistent telephone beside Memo's bed had already rung at least eight or nine times.

If the call was for him, he decided, it could only be from Memo. If not, it could be for Memo from someone he knew, and Jordan could pretend it was the wrong number. Whoever was calling, it must be important. The telephone would not stop. Casting aside the newspaper he had been reading, glancing up at MacDonald, who had been taking off his shirt and getting ready for bed, Jordan reached for the telephone and picked up the receiver.

"Hello?"

"Tim? This is Oreste." His voice was breathless. "Thank God you answered the phone."

"What is it?" asked Jordan, instantly on the alert.

"Tim, get out of there this second. The police have been tipped off you and your friend are there. I can't waste time explaining how or why. I accidentally told someone where you and MacDonald were—"

"How did you know about MacDonald?" Jordan asked quickly.

"Never mind. I'll tell you when I see you. The main thing is for you to get MacDonald out of sight fast. The police are on their way to grab him. So get out of there."

With that, the phone clicked off.

Electrified, Jordan jumped to his feet. "Professor, the police know we're here. I don't know how, but they know, and they're coming over to grab you. Put on your shirt, your jacket, don't forget those notes, and let's go."

"Where to, Tim?"

There was no time to think. "To my office," he said. "Now, hurry."

In less than a minute the professor was ready. Jordan surveyed the room. Then, satisfied nothing had been left behind, he hurried MacDonald to the door. As he opened the door to leave, he heard the telephone ring in the bedroom.

It rang once, twice, three times. Silence.

Then it rang again three times, and it was still.

"Alison," Jordan said beneath his breath.

"It must be important or she wouldn't—" MacDonald began.

"Forget it," said Jordan, hustling him through the hall. "There's only one thing urgent now. To get you out of here."

They went hurriedly down the stairs and emerged into the street. Jordan directed MacDonald toward the Piazza San Marco, and they began going swiftly. Suddenly, at an intersection, Jordan heard a clatter, held MacDonald still, peered ahead past several tourists, and then he saw a company of uniformed police, six or eight or more, approaching on the double.

Desperately, Jordan shoved MacDonald into the narrow side street, reached to hold him up as he almost fell, and forced him into the alcove of a shop entrance. He turned in time to see the police rushing past ten yards away. Gesturing for MacDonald to stay put, Jordan casually walked to the corner and looked off. The police had reached Oreste Memo's apartment building and were pouring inside, some with their side arms in hand.

Jordan watched until the last of them had disappeared into the building. He ran back to the storefront and signaled MacDonald to follow him.

In the main thoroughfare again, they proceeded at a normal pace, unnoticed by the few window-shoppers and encountering no more police. As they reached the Piazza and turned into the arcade that led to Jordan's office entrance, Jordan whispered, "Take out your handkerchief and pretend to be blowing your nose. Just to keep you covered in case there are some police. It's a short walk. Come on, now."

They passed behind the Lavena café orchestra, which

was playing to a half-full house, jostled past strollers, and continued rapidly to the middle of the arcade.

A few minutes later they were safely in Jordan's office.

They both emitted weary sighs of relief. "Sit down somewhere and try to relax, Professor," said Jordan. "I'd better return Alison's call. After that, we'll have to figure out where to hide you in the morning."

He dialed the Hotel Danieli and asked to speak to Dr. Alison Edwards.

When she answered, he said, "Alison? Tim—"

"I just tried to call you."

"Yes, I heard your signal as we were going out the door. Memo tipped me off that the police had discovered where we were. So we had to get out in a hurry."

"Where are you now?"

"In my office. We barely made it. What's up?"

"I was trying to get hold of you because Bruno Girardi called. He has to speak to you. He wants you to call him at *Il Gazzettino* before eleven o'clock tonight."

Jordan lowered the phone receiver to make out the time on his watch. It was ten thirty-five.

"Okay," he said. "I'll call him. Did he give you any hint of what this is about?"

"No idea. Only his tone made it clear he must talk to you by eleven. Tim, do you think it's about you-know-what?"

"I'm hoping. I'm hoping it's something good. We need a break. I don't know how long we can keep up this disappearing act. It's getting tougher and tougher."

"Better be careful what you say."

"No one's on this line, Alison. They're only monitoring long-distance calls. They don't have the personnel for this. All right, I'll get after Bruno. And be in touch with you."

As he hung up, he saw Professor MacDonald's watery blue eyes behind the crooked wire-framed glasses, fixed on him.

"Are you all right, Professor?" Jordan inquired.

"A little frayed at the edges. I'm out of cigars. Do you have a cigarette?"

"I'm a pipe man, but wait. . . ."

Jordan went into his secretary's office, opened the top drawer of her desk, and found half a pack. He extracted a cigarette, brought it back to MacDonald, and lit it for him.

"Bruno wants to speak to me," Jordan said.

MacDonald, smoking awkwardly, frowned. "Let's pray he has news for us—good news."

"Let's pray," said Jordan, slumping behind his desk and lifting the telephone receiver once more.

He got through to Bruno almost immediately.

"Bruno? Tim Jordan. I just received your message. What's happening?"

Bruno's boyish voice dropped to a conspiratorial level. "Green light, Tim," he said. "Our carabinieri friend— his name is Captain Silvestri—he has received encouragement from his wife. He is prepared to go ahead as agreed."

Jordan, elated, waved his hand happily at MacDonald. "Great," he said into the phone. "When do we go?"

"Tonight. Midnight."

"That's fast. Little over an hour. We'll have to hustle. Where do we meet?"

Bruno's voice dropped again. "After you leave your motorboat, walk into the Piazzale Roma. On your right is the Garage Comunale. You've seen it."

"Yes."

"I'll be waiting for you on one side of the auto entrance. Then we'll walk across the square to a small indoor restaurant that is open until late. Captain Silvestri will instruct you from there."

"What about transportation?"

"I've rented a Fiat for you. It is all ready and waiting in the Garage Comunale."

"Good, Bruno. Very good."

"Now, about the money—the $10,000—"

"Look, Bruno, I don't have that much cash on me, and there's no place to change a large sum of traveler's checks. I can give you a down payment tonight. Maybe $2,000. The rest tomorrow. Will you and your captain trust me?"

There was the merest beat of hesitation. "It will be all right, Tim. I will trust you and my friend will trust you—until tomorrow. But bring the down payment so the captain can see you are sincere."

"I'll bring it." He paused. "Will it be dangerous?"

"Not tonight. That is why it is tonight. The captain is himself in charge at the Ponte della Libertà checkpoint. Tomorrow there would be others. But tonight is the safest."

"Midnight, then."

"Midnight," said Bruno, and he hung up.

Jordan smiled across his desk at Professor MacDonald. "We're on our way at last," he announced. "Tomorrow you're in Paris."

▶ ▶ ▶ ▶

It was a few minutes before the stroke of midnight when Tim Jordan entered the nearly desolate Piazzale Roma, going alone toward the Garage Comunale.

Over an hour before, after talking to Bruno on the telephone, he had left the professor drinking hot coffee in his office and had gone over to the Hotel Danieli. There the cashier was still on duty and Jordan had changed $2,000 in traveler's checks. Then he had gone up to his suite, found Alison in bed reading a paperback, reported to her about the arrangements for the impending escape, and finally entered his bedroom to make one last call.

The immediate problem was getting to the Piazzale

Roma safely. There was no gondolier or motorboat pilot he trusted, except for one. He had known that despite the hour, he could phone his old gondolier friend, Luigi Cipolate, and if it was humanly possible his friend would help him. Moreover, he knew Luigi had access to a motorboat—a motorboat was necessary because a gondola would be too slow traveling the fairly long distance to the end of the Grand Canal—since Luigi had frequently spoken of the motorboat owned by his son, which he himself sometimes used.

The phone had been picked up by Luigi's wife, who had reassured him that he had not awakened her and that Luigi was wide awake, probably having a beer in the kitchen. When Luigi had come on, Jordan had explained that he had a business associate he had to deliver to the Piazzale Roma by midnight. For various reasons, to be given one day when there was more time, he could not use public transportation and in fact preferred not to use a boat driver he did not know. He needed someone he could depend upon to be discreet. Luigi, as ever, had asked no questions. They'd need a motorboat to make it in time, he had said. He would borrow his son's. He would meet Jordan and his associate at the Servizio Motoscafi just in front of the Danieli. He would be there at eleven-thirty sharp.

Jordan had then gone back to his office to get Mac-Donald.

At twenty after eleven, as they prepared to leave, Jordan had suddenly wondered about something. "Have you finished writing out your formula for C-98 yet?"

"I have most of it down."

"Be sure to leave it with me when we part company at the Piazzale Roma. Just in case something happens to you."

MacDonald had shot him an apprehensive look and said, "I'll remember."

They had left Jordan's office and descended the staircase into the arcade. Only a few night people were in sight, and no policemen. Together, Jordan and Mac-Donald had walked down the aisle of the lightly populated Quadri's café.

There had been a scattering of people in the Piazza San Marco, mostly youngsters. As they started into the giant square, Jordan had cautiously surveyed their left flank. Among the people in front of the Basilica there were two in khaki uniforms, local police joking with several foreign girls.

Jordan had said, "Professor, bend your head close to me, as if you're engaging me in earnest conversation. That'll give them less chance for a full view of your face."

"I-I don't know what to say."

"Say the Lord's Prayer."

As MacDonald bent his head close to Jordan's and recited a complicated scientific formula, they had continued walking in stride past the towering Campanile. They had come to the Doges' Palace and the Piazzetta undetected and turned toward the Hotel Danieli, going a little faster between the columns of the Doges' Palace and the waterfront. They had gone up and down a bridge, and to their right they had seen someone trying to get their attention. It was Luigi Cipolate, and when Jordan acknowledged him, Luigi had run back to point out his motorboat.

Jordan had settled MacDonald low in the rear of the craft, and himself had stood beside Luigi as he maneuvered the wheel of the motorboat.

Although Jordan had been anxious the entire journey through the Grand Canal, the passage had been uneventful. Except for the approach of one small police patrol boat—its occupants had not even looked at them—and one churning vaporetto and a barge piled high with crates of canned goods, they'd had the Grand Canal to themselves.

Luigi's motorboat had arrived at the Piazzale Roma boat station at four minutes to twelve o'clock.

Jordan had gestured for Professor MacDonald to remain in his place. "I want to see them alone first," he had said. "I'll be back as fast as I can." To Luigi he had added, "Just stay put. If anyone comes snooping around, cut loose and drift around in the water until you see me. I should be back in ten or fifteen minutes."

Now he was in the Piazzale Roma, on his way to the meeting that would lead to MacDonald's escape from Venice.

There was a lone figure waiting in front of the entrance to the Garage Comunale. The stubby young man, curly-haired, darkly handsome, a camera case slung over one shoulder, was Bruno Girardi.

Jordan was relieved. It was going according to schedule.

"Hi, Bruno. Right on time."

"Good, Tim." He looked about. "You are by yourself. Where's your man, the underground courier you want to get through?"

"He's not far away. I thought I'd come alone first, meet Captain Silvestri, find out the plan."

"Everything is arranged." He pointed across the square. "He will be waiting for us in the all-night restaurant. He has told his men he is taking a coffee break. Let's go see him."

They started across the empty square. Entering the small restaurant, with its white metal tables, they found no one inside except a pudgy waitress setting out fresh salt and pepper shakers.

Bruno consulted his watch. "He told me he'd be here waiting."

"Do you think he changed his mind?"

"No." Bruno was confident. "I would have known already. He will be here. For the $5,000, he will be here. Let's take a table."

They seated themselves at a table. Bruno ordered black coffee, and Jordan ordered hot tea.

Setting down his camera case, Bruno asked, "What is your man's name?"

Jordan improvised quickly. "Pearson."

"All right. I didn't know his name, so I took the car out from the rental service—they know me—in your name. You'll have to reimburse me for the deposit."

"Okay."

"The papers are in the glove compartment of the car. There's the address of the company in Paris where Pearson will leave the car when he gets there."

"Very well."

The waitress came with the coffee and tea.

Bruno was silent until she was out of earshot. Then he said, "Does your friend know his way?"

"Not really," said Jordan. "He's never been here in this section before. I'll drive him across the causeway to Mestre. From that point on he'll use a marked map I've given him which shows what routes to take."

Bruno drank his coffee. "You are going to Mestre too?"

"If the captain doesn't mind."

"He won't mind. Are you coming back?"

"Yes, of course. Tonight."

"How?" asked Bruno.

"I hadn't thought of that. I suppose I'll take the first bus I can get."

"Tim, there are no buses coming into Venice. Have you forgotten? The city is closed down."

"You're right. I suppose I'll have to walk back."

Bruno shook his head. "No. I can borrow a motorcycle. It has room for another on the back. I'll follow you to Mestre, and after Pearson leaves I'll bring you back here."

"That's nice of you, Bruno."

Bruno grinned. "You're a member of the family. Be-

sides, you are paying me well." Then he said more seriously, "We need the money now. Mamma is running up
big hospital bills."

"Marisa told me she wasn't well. What's wrong with
her?"

"Nobody knows. They try to find out. She is weak. She
has stomach pains every day. They make tests." He
glanced at the door. "Where the devil is Silvestri?"

"You're still sure he'll show up?"

"He'll show up. Since he isn't here, I'll tell you the
procedure. We can confirm it again with him."

"Go ahead."

"Simple. Step one. You make the down payment. I'll
give it all to Captain Silvestri to show good faith."

"Okay."

"Step two. After our meeting, you will bring Pearson
inside the Garage Comunale. I'll be there and take you
to your car. Captain Silvestri will return to his post. Step
three. I will get the motorcycle and follow you to the
Ponte della Libertà. As you get to the causeway, you will
see the captain with perhaps three or four of the police.
You will stop. Captain Silvestri will hold his men off,
tell them he will attend to this personally. He will come
to you, pretend to see your permission pass to leave the
city. Then he will send you on, and I'll be right behind
you, and he'll send me on."

"Will there be any more checkpoints after that?"

"At the end of the causeway, there will be two guards
on the Mestre side. They will not bother you, since you
got that far. They are there to prevent cars from coming
into Venice. We will have a return permit."

"So we just keep going into Mestre? That's all there is
to it?"

"That's all." Bruno was scrambling to his feet.
"Franco—" he called out.

Jordan looked over his shoulder. From the doorway, a
small, thin police officer, in uniform and armed, was ap-

proaching their table. He had dark pinhole eyes, a long nose, and a foxlike aspect.

"Captain Franco Silvestri," said Bruno, "this is my friend Mr. Timothy Jordan, an adopted Venetian."

"How do you do," said the captain. He shifted a roll of what appeared to be posters held together by a thick rubber band from under one arm to the other so that he could shake hands. Taking a seat, he was apologetic. "Forgive my lateness," he said, placing the posters on the table. "I was just leaving for our meeting when I was called back because a messenger came from head-quarters with some new posters. Questore Trevisan wants them put up at once." As he began to remove the rubber band from the roll, he said to Bruno, "Is every-thing in order here?"

"I was outlining the procedure for Mr. Jordan. I will be going too, Franco, on a motorcycle behind them, so I can bring Mr. Jordan back. Is that all right?"

"Fine."

"I told Mr. Jordan when he reaches the checkpoint with his passenger, he is to stop, and you alone will come alongside to clear his permit."

"I will do that myself." He squinted at Jordan. "You are lucky. I am the only officer on duty tonight. There will be no problem."

"Thank you," said Jordan.

The captain continued to squint at Jordan. "Bruno tells me you will leave a down payment with him. And give him the balance of the 4,000,000 lire tomorrow."

"Exactly."

"Do you want some coffee, Franco?" Bruno asked.

"Not now," said the captain, beginning to unroll the posters. "I have to arrange to have all these put up." He had opened the posters and flattened them out across the table. "Why do we need more of these on the spy MacGregor? It's the same . . ."

Jordan's throat constricted as he saw once more the

large portrait of Professor MacDonald on the poster. Then he saw something else, which the captain saw at the same instant.

". . . no, I see, it's not the same," the captain was saying. "They've printed something new on top—a reward." He gave a low whistle. "One hundred thirty million lire to find this man. Now, *that* is a reward. Someone will be very rich." He stuck a finger on MacDonald's face on the poster. "This is the man I'd like to set eyes on. I appreciate your 4,000,000 lire, Mr. Jordan, but I'd trade that in for even a chance to get this 130,000,000-lire reward. Oh, well." He began to roll up the posters again. "I'd better be off. See you in ten minutes, Mr. Jordan."

After the captain had left, Jordan remained seated as Bruno rose and paid for the coffee and tea. At last, Jordan got up and slowly followed Bruno out of the restaurant. Trailing behind Bruno, Jordan realized to what extent the encounter with the police captain had shaken him.

When they reached the middle of the Piazzale Roma, Jordan took hold of Bruno's arm.

"One minute, Bruno."

"I'm going to get the motorcycle. You bring your friend. We can't lose time."

"Hold it, Bruno. I've changed my mind. I can't go through with it."

Bruno appeared not to have heard him correctly. "You can't what?"

"I'm not going through with it. I'll pay you something for your time."

Bruno was astounded. "You are not going through the checkpoint?"

"Not tonight. It's too complicated. I'll explain the whole thing tomorrow. I've got to leave now."

Jordan swung away and began to cut across the square toward the boat station.

"Tim, wait a minute," Bruno called. "This makes no sense."

"Tomorrow. I'll phone you tomorrow," Jordan called back.

He went as fast as he could go, without running, toward the wharf.

Luigi was waiting in the prow of the motorboat, smoking, with MacDonald huddled in the darkened rear.

Jordan stepped down into the boat. "Cut loose, Luigi. We're getting out of here. New plan."

Luigi moved to untie the rope that held the boat to a piling. "Where to?"

"I'm not sure yet. Start back to San Marco slowly, while I consult with my friend."

Jordan climbed to the rear of the motorboat and squeezed in beside MacDonald, who looked scared.

"What's the matter?" MacDonald wanted to know. "Did something go wrong?"

"At the last minute it did, godammit," said Jordan. "It was perfect, and then it blew up. We had it all arranged. Then the captain unwrapped some new posters— wanted posters of you—he'd just received. They're offering a reward now for you. It's splashed all over the poster."

"A reward for me?"

"A hundred and thirty million lire. A whopper. A hundred and fifty thousand dollars."

"Oh, my God—"

"The captain kept saying how much he'd like to lay his eyes on you—with your picture right in front of him—how much he'd like to get that 130,000,000-lire reward instead of the paltry 4,000,000 we had offered him. The minute he started talking like that, I knew our plan was cooked. Can't you see it? Me driving up to the checkpoint with you, and his coming alongside, looking in, and seeing you, the very face on the poster he was slobbering over a minute ago? He'd grab you, arrest you in a second. So I just told Bruno no soap—didn't tell him why—just took off as fast as I could. I'm sorry, Professor."

MacDonald tried to put up a brave front. "At least, now I know what I'm worth."

"A bad, bad break. We were almost there, almost had you sprung free."

"I hate to say this for what seems the hundredth time, Tim, but—what next?"

"There's one more chance. In the morning—"

"You mean—?"

"Yes. I've just got to find some place to put you tonight." He stared at the canal waters moving past them, then rested his sight on Luigi's thick shoulders up front. "Excuse me, Professor."

Jordan made his way through the boat until he was next to Luigi.

He hesitated, and then he spoke. "Luigi, can I ask you one more favor?"

"Anything that is possible."

"My friend in the back, he will be leaving Venice in the morning. I need some place to keep him until morning. I can't take him to the hotel. It must be a private place. Could you put him up for tonight? Just the next seven hours, then I'll pick him up. Am I asking too much?"

Luigi shrugged and offered a broad smile. "If he does not mind to sleep on the couch, he can stay."

▶ ▶ ▶ ▶

Later, in his Hotel Danieli suite once more, ignoring the questions from Alison for the moment, he went directly to the telephone and dialed.

The phone rang interminably and then a sleepy voice answered. Felice Huber was on the line.

"Felice, it's Tim Jordan. I'm sorry, I'm really sorry, to have wakened you."

"Forgiven. What is it?"

"About the tour of industrialists you're guiding to Mestre this morning."

"You want me to add one more name?"

"Yes."

"Is it that important to you?"

"Extremely important."

"What's his name?"

"David Pearson."

"Have him in the lobby of the Bauer Grunwald at eight o'clock in the morning." And with that she hung up.

VIII

▶ ▶ ▶ ▶ ▶ ▶ ▶

The Bauer Grunwald hotel faced a small square, the Campo San Moisè, only a short walk from the Piazza San Marco. As one approached it across the square, one saw the aged Church of San Moisè on the left and to the right a narrow canal with a stone bridge rising over it, always dense with foot traffic.

This early morning, Tim Jordan, after picking up a weary Professor MacDonald at Luigi's cramped apartment, came to the corner of the square cautiously. The distance he and the professor had covered from the point where Luigi had let them off had been relatively short, but at this time there would be more people in the square and possibly police. Now that the new poster had been issued, with its $150,000 reward for MacDonald, Jordan knew the chance that his charge would escape recognition was minimal. They were truly living on borrowed time, and detection of MacDonald seemed inevitable. An escape had to be achieved almost at once, or MacDonald would be lost to the enemy forever.

At the Campo San Moisè, Jordan had stopped, held the professor back momentarily as he scanned the area ahead. There was a hawker, at his portable stand, selling picture postcards of Venice. There were a few well-dressed people going into the hotel and emerging from it. There were shoppers traversing the bridge, and a family on top of it taking photographs.

There were no police in sight.

"Coast's clear," said Jordan. He inspected Professor MacDonald quickly. His only disguise was a pair of oversized blue sunglasses that Alison had acquired for him. Otherwise, the face was the face on the posters, except for the missing moustache. His general look was somewhat disheveled, his trousers badly needed pressing, and he did not quite appear to be a wealthy industrialist about to make a tour of a petrochemical factory in Mestre. But there was no turning back. Felice Huber's tour was definitely the only hope available. "All right, Professor," Jordan said. "Are you ready?"

"I can't see too well without my prescription glasses."

"Can you see where you're going?"

"I think so."

"Better stick to those sunglasses. They mask at least a portion of your face. Once you get to Mestre, and after you drift off from the tour and get away from the guards, you can put on your regular glasses. Remember, now, get out of sight of the guards. Find someone who will direct you to the railroad station. Do you think you can make it?"

"I can try." But the professor's voice carried no conviction.

"Okay. We'll walk into the hotel. Felice's industrialist party should be convening in the front lobby right now. You mingle with them. Be unobtrusive. Don't speak unless you're spoken to. Remember, you own textile factories in the South. Your headquarters are in New York. When Felice checks you out, your name is Pearson."

MacDonald nodded. "Pearson."

"You'll go by boat and bus. When you get to Mestre

and start the tour, hang back, as far from the police guards as possible. At the first opportunity, slip away."

MacDonald nodded again.

"Now to the Bauer Grunwald. I'm going to walk fast. Keep up with me."

They went into the square together, past the church, walking diagonally toward the extremely modern hotel front with its glass doors. Jordan opened a door, ushered MacDonald inside, and followed close behind him. In the lobby, the industrialists were easy to identify. They were loosely clustered—elderly, prosperous, richly dressed men—some chatting together, some smoking cigars.

Jordan saw the columnist, Schuyler Moore, at the farthest side of the group and fell behind MacDonald, not wanting to be recognized by Moore.

"Join the fringe of the group," ordered Jordan in an undertone. "I'll leave you now. I'll hang around outside until you've gone. God keep you, Professor, and good luck."

Leaving the hotel, Jordan stood uncertainly in the blaze of sunlight. High above, a helicopter was buzzing across the city, the long banner trailing behind it reading CINZANO. Emergency or no emergency, Jordan thought, it was business as usual. He cast about for a vantage point from which he might see the group's departure, yet remain unseen himself. Directly across from the Bauer Grunwald were several shops, including the ticket office of Alitalia, the Italian airline. There was a green awning, already rolled down to shade the broad front windows.

Jordan strode out of the sun and under the awning, opened the door, and let himself into the office. Little activity existed inside Alitalia. Since all travel out of Venice was immobilized, the airlines of the city had few visitors. At a counter to his left, a young couple was making inquiries of a clerk. Several other employees about the room were absorbed in their routine work. Jordan sidled over to one of the front windows looking out at the square, stood beside a large model of an Alitalia airplane, and gave his full attention to the Bauer Grunwald entrance.

Six persons, one after another, entered the hotel. No one came out.

Then a familiar female figure came in sight from the canal side, walking in loping steps from the bridge to the hotel entrance. It was Felice Huber, wearing a wide-brimmed hat, a peasant blouse, blue pants, carrying a purse the size of a briefcase. She hurried into the hotel.

While nervously waiting for the Mestre party to emerge and get on its way, Jordan absently observed the tourists and city dwellers passing to and fro before him. A middle-aged workman with a handlebar moustache appeared pushing a cart, which held a short ladder. Idly, Jordan watched him bring his cart up alongside the church, pull out his ladder, and set it up before a wall of the church partially covered with torn posters advertising operas at the Fenice and art exhibitions at the Accademia delle Belle Arti.

Now there was movement at the Bauer Grunwald entrance. Glass doors were swinging open, and Felice emerged into the square with a small clipboard in hand, and behind her the businessmen destined for Mestre streamed out and gathered together in the sun. Jordan stretched to locate Professor MacDonald and finally saw him, among the last to exit the hotel. So far, so good. Jordan wondered where the carabinieri guards were and then realized that they would be on the launch that would take the party to the mainland.

While waiting for her tour to assemble fully, Felice appeared to be distracted by something going on at the church. Jordan looked around to see what had caught her eye, and he realized she was holding on the work-

man, who was halfway up his ladder, unfurling a poster
he was about to glue to the wall.

Suddenly, Jordan's jaw fell open. The poster being
laid out against the wall was clearly visible, and it was
the poster featuring Professor MacDonald's portrait with
a heading above it in bold type offering a 130,000,000-
lire reward to anyone who told the police the whereabouts of this spy.

Jordan's lungs felt dry. His gaze returned to Felice.
She was drifting away from her group, wandering closer
to the church, until she stood behind the workman, staring up at the poster. She stood frozen in this attitude for
long seconds, gave her head a shake, and turned back to
join her party.

She began herding her businessmen into a semicircle
in the square, and then, starting from the left, going
right, she confronted each one, obviously requesting his
name, and checked it off on a sheet attached to her clipboard. In this way, she moved slowly around the gathering of men. Professor MacDonald was standing the
second from the far right. Felice was drawing nearer and
nearer to MacDonald.

Jordan's eyes riveted upon her as she came directly in
front of Professor MacDonald. She looked down at her
clipboard, said something, and automatically looked up
at him. MacDonald's lips moved. He was giving his
name. He was giving the name Pearson. Felice nodded,
started to check her sheet, when unexpectedly her head
lifted and she gave MacDonald a long double take.

Jordan's heart was in his mouth.

Everything depended on what happened next.

Felice backed up, not bothering to check the last man
in the semicircle. Jordan saw her casually glance over
her shoulder at the poster once more. Then slowly her
head turned and held on Professor MacDonald again.

She retreated further, and held up her hand, addressing herself to the group. Jordan could not hear what she

was saying, but he could guess. She was telling them to wait a moment. She had something to do, and she would be right back.

With that, she did what Jordan was afraid she would do. She spun away, and striding fast, she went to the bridge and began taking the steps two at a time.

Jordan suspected he knew where she was going, but he had to make sure.

He hastened out the door of Alitalia and went on the run for the bridge as he saw Felice disappear over the top of it. He too bounded up the stairs two at a time, and at the summit of the bridge he halted, winded, and watched Felice.

He saw where she was headed, and he saw her get there. Twenty yards away, on the other side of the bridge, right in the street, was a green metal stand, a public emergency telephone, with one big word painted on the top of it, and that word was POLIZIA.

For Jordan, the scenario was verified. Felice, always desperate for money, desperate to make enough money to get her out of tourism and into art school at Grenoble, had at last found the means of becoming rich and free overnight. She had recognized Professor MacDonald as the fugitive MacGregor in the police poster. She was informing on him. To hell with her friendship with Jordan. To hell with anything like that. Tonight she would be $150,000 richer and she would have her dream, and the police and the Communists would have their life-prolonging scientist.

Jordan waited only seconds more. Felice, at the green stand marked POLIZIA, was reaching for the telephone receiver which would carry her excited voice directly to the local police station.

There was no time to waste, not even an instant. Jordan wheeled, went down the stone steps even faster than he had come up them, dashed into the square, slowed to a fast walk so as not to draw attention, and came up behind MacDonald. He looped his arm under MacDonald's and gently drew him out of the group.

Putting pressure on the bewildered MacDonald's arm, he slowly began to walk him, then with more haste hurry him, in the opposite direction, away from the square, away from the bridge, away from the informing Felice Huber.

"You were recognized," Jordan said under his breath. "She spotted you and is calling the police. She wants the reward, and we want out of here. The place will be swarming with uniforms in a few minutes. This is going to be close. Keep moving. Let's hit the side streets. We've got to find a place to hide you again. Any place nearby."

▶ ▶ ▶ ▶

During the next fifteen minutes, the local police and the carabinieri had been pouring into the San Marco area from every direction, and throughout that time Jordan, with Professor MacDonald close to him, had been adroitly evading them, weaving into and out of the small streets and back alleys he knew so well. He had been moving them behind the Piazza, behind his office building, toward the Mercerie, with no plan or destination in mind.

All the while he had been racking his brain, taking rapid inventory of his remaining store of Venetian friends, acquaintances, contacts, groping for one more dependable person who might help the professor out of this jam. He needed just one more place to keep the professor in seclusion and to allow himself time to organize some new escape plan. No person came to mind, and he knew that soon, by the laws of chance, they would be seen and the pursuit would be ended.

Once during the flight, he had been frightened by the ominous buzz of a helicopter low overhead. Fearing it might be a police helicopter, he had shoved the professor back against a wall. But as the helicopter passed by, he saw it was not one that belonged to the police but the ridiculous one flying the Cinzano banner.

A short block from the Mercerie, as he realized where he was, an available refuge came to mind. It meant using somebody twice, but the somebody had once been a person of goodwill and might prove cooperative a second time.

Heartened, Jordan led MacDonald across the main shopping street and into a dark alley that opened into the small square called the Campo San Zulian.

As they approached the square, Jordan spoke to the wearying MacDonald. "Professor, remember after we pulled you off the isle of San Lazzaro in the beginning, I told you there was a man who had made it possible. The one whose nephew was the monk taking care of you in the monastery."

"I remember."

"That's where we're going. I can think of no one else. His name is Sembut Nurikhan. He owns a shop in the Campo San Zulian—a glassware shop with an office in the back—and I'm going to ask him to keep you for a day."

"For a day?"

"Yes. I have an idea how to get you out of here tonight or tomorrow night."

The idea had struck him a few minutes ago. At first inspiration, it had seemed a ridiculous idea, but in the intervening minutes it had matured in his head and now seemed feasible. Before he could investigate it, he must safely deposit the professor somewhere.

The Campo San Zulian was like most other squares in Venice, only much smaller, as if miniaturized, with the inevitable old church dominating it on one side. Jordan went into the square first, to scout it. He stood under a sign reading ESTADOS UNIDOS MEXICANOS CONSULADO and took in the activity. There was almost none, a few window-shoppers, no police yet.

He beckoned MacDonald, marched him to the glass shop with its aluminum-trimmed display windows, and brought him out of the hot day into the air-conditioned interior. Their entrance had caused a bell to tinkle, but there was no one in the shop. Then Sembut Nurikhan appeared from his rear cubicle to meet his customers, and his sallow merchant's face cracked into a slight smile as he saw Jordan.

"Tim," he said, "I wondered what happened to you."

"Sembut, I need your help again. Can we talk in your office?"

The proprietor squinted at MacDonald through his gold-rimmed glasses, patted his bow tie, then said, "Come."

It was hardly an office: a cramped room illuminated by two fluorescent lights with a rolltop desk, file cabinet, cot, and two chairs.

"Not very comfortable here," said Nurikhan apologetically, "but there is privacy."

"Sembut, I want to introduce you to Professor Davis MacDonald, the gerontologist who made the great discovery. The man you helped me rescue from San Lazzaro."

"I've been wanting to thank you," said MacDonald, extending his hand.

Nurikhan gingerly shook hands. "I am honored."

"Sembut, I require a place to keep the professor, keep him out of sight, until I can get him out of the city, possibly by tomorrow. If you could let him stay here in the back, let him rest—"

Nurikhan's expression was worried. "I-I don't know. It could mean trouble."

"No one would know. And as I promised you, the professor will help your brother."

"My brother—" the proprietor began to say, when he

heard the doorbell tinkle. He looked off. "Customers. I must attend to the customers."

"Please, Sembut."

Nurikhan sighed heavily. "Very well," he said to Professor MacDonald. "You may stay—for a while."

After the proprietor had left them, MacDonald sat down on the cot. "What can you do by tomorrow?"

"Something, I hope. You'd better lie down and get as much rest as you can. If what I have in mind works, you'll need all your energy. I'll probably be away all afternoon. If I am, I'll send Alison to keep you company. One way or another, I'll see you tonight before he closes the store. Hopefully, you'll be in Paris by tomorrow."

▶ ▶ ▶ ▶

When he arrived at his secretary's office, Jordan found Gloria busily typing, preparing next month's newsletter for the Venice Must Live Committee.

He greeted Gloria, then looked into Marisa's office. It was empty.

"Where's Marisa?"

"She just left for lunch."

"Do you know where?"

"She didn't say. She only said she'd be back by two o'clock."

"Dammit. Well, I'll just have to wait for her."

He went into his own office to see if he could find the information he wanted from Marisa. He went through his personal address book, then through his desk drawers. No luck. Finally, there was nothing he could do but settle down and await Marisa's return. He took out his pipe, packed it, and for more than an hour examined the one possibility for escape he had come upon. After that, he explored other options.

At ten minutes to two, his office door opened and Marisa filled it.

She came to him and kissed him on the lips.

"Gloria says you want to see me."

He studied her briefly. Her eyes were tearful, her face drawn.

"What's the matter?" he wanted to know.

"I wasn't at lunch. I was at the hospital with my mother. She looks terrible. She's in pain. The doctors are finishing their tests today. We will have a report soon."

"I'm sorry."

She pulled herself together, wiped her eyes with the back of her hand, and sat down on the other side of the desk.

"I'm all right," she said. "Incidentally, thank you for not involving Bruno in your scheme to smuggle that courier friend of yours out of the country. He's sore as hell at you for changing your mind, but I'm glad."

"I appreciate all he tried to do, Marisa, and I'll pay him for his time. But at the last minute I couldn't go through with it. I didn't trust his contact."

"Anyway, I'm relieved."

Jordan straightened in his swivel chair and became more businesslike. "Marisa, I was waiting for you because I wanted to get hold of the name of that fellow in town here who owns a helicopter and rents it for advertising and other things. You were the one who arranged for him—I think it was over a year ago—to do that photo survey of the Lido Channel for us. You recall? The crazy guy who once had his helicopter put down in the Piazza San Marco to win a bet."

"Signor Folin," she said. "He's the one. What do you want with him?"

"I've got a notion for a fund-raiser that involves a helicopter. I want to talk it over with him. Do you know his address?"

"He has a desk at American Express. He works part time for them, to pay for his desk space, and he rents out his helicopter the rest of the time."

"Good." Jordan stood up. "Call him up and see if he's

going to be there a little while. Tell him I want to talk to him and I'll be right over."

▶   ▶   ▶   ▶

Signor Folin had bulging eyes, a small mouth that held a cigar in its center, and ashes all over the broad expanse of his chest and stomach.

He was on his feet, beside his desk, pumping Jordan's hand. "Yes, I remember your name," he said. "I did business with you once through your assistant. It was agreeable. I hope we can do business again."

"We can," said Jordan.

"Well, here now, have a seat and tell me what's on your mind."

Jordan glanced around the room. It was filled with clerks and customers, many of them within earshot.

"I'd rather speak to you privately. It's a confidential matter. Can we just step outside and take a short stroll?"

This did not seem unusual to Signor Folin. Obviously, a man who owned a helicopter was ready for anything. "Whatever will please you, Mr. Jordan," he said.

Outside, they strolled slowly, and Jordan lowered his voice as he spoke.

"You still have your helicopter?" asked Jordan.

Folin's porcine face lit up. "I now have two," he said proudly.

"Where do you have them? In Venice?"

"In Venice is impossible. I have my landing pad and hangar between Marghera and Mestre. Only minutes away."

"Was that one of your helicopters flying over the city this morning?"

"But of course. I am the only one in the vicinity with a helicopter business. This morning we were working for our Cinzano account, a handsome account."

"So you had no problem flying over the city from the

mainland, even though there is a ban on incoming traffic?"

"No, this problem does not apply to my business. What harm could I do them?"

"Why, you might fly someone in—or fly someone out."

Folin laughed. "Impossible. Where would I land? In the Grand Canal?"

Jordan eyed him carefully as they walked along, and was silent for a few moments. Well, he decided, sooner or later it had to be said. "For one thing, Signor Folin, you could land in the Piazza San Marco."

Folin looked at Jordan to see if he was joking. "Who would expect me to do a thing like that?"

"Exactly," said Jordan. "No one would expect it. But you could do it."

"Are you serious?"

"Never more so."

"It's—it is unthinkable."

"You thought about it once. I heard you once had your helicopter actually land in the middle of the Piazza."

"Ah, five years ago." Signor Folin chuckled. "That was different. That was to win a bet. It was an amusement. Even so, I was fined—a stiff fine. But it was worth it."

Jordan halted, and Folin halted with him.

"What would it be worth to do it again?" Jordan asked.

Folin had become more serious. "You mean it?"

"Absolutely."

"I could lose my license. Probably not. The mayor is my cousin. But certainly I'd be fined heavily. It depends what you want a helicopter for."

"To take a passenger out of Venice. To Marghera, where a rented car would be waiting."

"That would be against the law, the emergency law, Mr. Jordan."

"Who would know? At two in the morning the Piazza

San Marco is a desert. No one around. Certainly no police. No one would see you land or take the passenger on board. If some late person witnessed it, and reported it, you could claim he was drunk, you took no one on, you had engine trouble, landed where you could, then found you could take off again."

"You make it sound possible."

"I'm sure it's possible," said Jordan.

"Well, I suppose so, and safer if I rented a helicopter from one of my competitors in Padua." Folin threw down his cigar stub and squashed it with his foot. "It would be expensive, Mr. Jordan."

"I can offer you $10,000."

"Not enough, Mr. Jordan. More like $20,000."

Jordan thought about it. Gathering the financial resources that he and Alison had on hand, then writing checks on his New York bank and cashing them at the Danieli and two local banks he did business with, he could raise the sum this afternoon.

"Okay," said Jordan. "You've got a deal."

"Not so fast. Not yet. I must telephone one of my pilots on the mainland. He must agree to this."

"How can you call? I thought all long-distance calls were monitored."

Folin grinned. "My wife is a telephone operator in Venice. She always puts through my calls and no worry about being monitored. She goes to work at six o'clock. You come to see me at seven o'clock this evening, at American Express. I will be there alone."

"Do you think it will work out?" Jordan asked worriedly.

Folin grinned again. "Bring half the sum when you come to see me. Be ready to pay the other half to the pilot when your man gets on board. See you at seven this evening, Mr. Jordan. Good day."

▶ ▶ ▶ ▶

When Jordan returned to the Hotel Danieli suite, Alison was waiting, filled with anxiety.

"I've been sitting next to the phone for hours, expecting to hear from you," she said. "Did it work with Felice Huber? Is Davis on the mainland?"

Jordan shook his head. "No, it didn't work with Felice. And we've been on the run ever since, so there's been no chance to call you."

"Where is Davis? Is he all right?"

"For the moment," said Jordan. "I don't know for how long. There's that $150,000 reward on his head."

Alison was stunned. "A hundred and fifty thousand?"

"I told you about it last night."

"You didn't mention the amount. Why, it's a fortune."

"That's what went wrong this morning. They posted the reward. Felice saw it. She recognized MacDonald. She went for the police. MacDonald and I got out of there in a hurry. He's in a safe place now. And I think I have another means of getting him out of here tonight."

He then proceeded to bring her up to date. MacDonald was hidden in the glassware shop owned by Sembut Nurikhan. Alison remembered him from the San Lazzaro escapade. Jordan went on to tell her his latest inspiration. The idea of dropping a helicopter in the middle of the Piazza San Marco. She listened wide-eyed. He reported on his meeting with Signor Folin.

"You think he'll come through?" Alison asked.

"For $20,000? I think so."

"Can the—the getaway work?"

"I hope so. Now, about the $20,000. Obviously, we can't cash the professor's checks. But let's cash all you have. Leave yourself a few hundred dollars. I'll cash most of mine. Then I'll write some personal checks against my New York account."

"Is there anything else I can do?"

"Just cash those checks of yours downstairs. Then go over to Nurikhan's shop, go to the office in the rear and keep your professor company. Do you know how to get there?"

"I'm not sure I remember."

"It's not far away. I'll draw you a map."

He drew her a map.

"Now I need a shower and a change of clothes." He began to unbutton his shirt. "Then I've got to catch the banks, look in on my office, and meet with Signor Folin at seven o'clock. After that, I'll come straight to Nurikhan's, and we'll dig in there until it is helicopter time— *if* it is helicopter time. See you soon."

▶ ▶ ▶ ▶

By now the route was familiar to Major Boris Kedrov. He strode briskly along the lagoon on the Riva degli Schiavoni, mounted and descended the bridge from which could be seen the Bridge of Sighs, passed the well-guarded Hotel Danieli, climbed and came down one more bridge, then turned into the short street that opened into what the Venetians called Campo San Zaccaria. Here, to the right, was his immediate destination, the unpretentious rust-colored building with the stone-arch entrance and the white plaque beside it reading, COMANDO GRUPPO CARABINIERI.

The building, barracks and headquarters of the local carabinieri, was the one place in this ridiculous carnival city where Major Kedrov felt most at home. Although he frowned on the fact that the carabinieri, who could marry after eight years of service or at the age of twenty-eight, were permitted to live with their wives and children in apartments inside the barracks—distracting, soft, unprofessional—still, Kedrov appreciated the place as a military outpost.

About to enter the headquarters, Kedrov hesitated, held back, and wandered farther into the quiet square, wishing briefly to collect his thoughts. He stopped before the solemn Church of San Zaccaria. He had not bothered to visit it, but had been told it was the relic of a 7th-century convent that ages ago had lodged the loose-living daughters of the wealthiest Venetian families. Venetians, he thought, were not the best allies in the task at hand. They were too easygoing, casual, unaggressive. Perhaps Colonel Cutrone was a step above his colleagues, but even he did not measure up fully. Had this assignment and hunt taken place in Kiev or Odessa or Leningrad, Kedrov's KGB agents would have captured Professor MacDonald in twenty-four hours. There would have been none of the laxity and lack of cooperation that existed here.

He had tried to explain the situation this morning in his daily telephone call to his superior in Moscow. He had tried to explain that these people were a different breed of Communists. They adhered to the party in principle, but there was no proper discipline, no dedication. As a result, their police forces were relatively inefficient. The best of them, the carabinieri, recruited from the poor families of southern Italy, looked upon their work as a job, not a cause. The KGB general in Moscow remained uncomprehending. "*You* are there, Kedrov. You are KGB. *You* must make them understand the importance of this assignment. You must inject yourself more fully into the action. I cannot tell you how vital this has become to the premier and the Politburo. They want MacDonald and his formula in Moscow under the protection of the party. They will not allow his discovery to fall into the hands of the capitalist pigs and be exploited by them. Kedrov, our leaders—they know your name now. They are aware of you. You cannot fail them or me. Once you succeed, there will be ample rewards. A promotion, certainly. A transfer to Moscow. A dacha for vacations with your wife and sons. Kedrov, the premier cannot believe that a fumbling old man can continue to elude you. Find him. Bring him back. I expect good news in your next report."

This exhortation had inspired Major Kedrov to speak

to Colonel Cutrone again. There was one pattern that had appeared and possibly deserved more thorough investigation. Cutrone himself had pointed it out. Three different persons, on different days, had come to the police with information on where MacDonald could be found. The American novelist had revealed to them that the fugitive MacDonald was being hidden in the palazzo of the Contessa De Marchi. When the police stormed the palazzo, MacDonald had not been there. Then the Italian actress Teresa Fantoni had promised them that their quarry would be found in the apartment of a musician named Oreste Memo. The apartment had been surrounded, searched, with no sign of MacDonald. Finally, this very day, a tourist guide, Felice Huber, had actually set eyes on MacDonald before the Bauer Grunwald hotel. Yet by the time the police had arrived and swarmed over the area, MacDonald had vanished.

There was too much smoke for no fire, Major Kedrov concluded. Their informants had not been fanciful publicity-seekers or crazy psychotics. They had been, as far as the evidence revealed, solid citizens. One thing was apparent. MacDonald had accomplices, and possibly a network of sympathetic persons who were taking turns hiding him. The problem was to penetrate this network—once. Toward this end, Major Kedrov had reviewed the transcript of the interrogations of the informants to date. The interrogations, by KGB standards, had been superficial, especially the recent one with Felice Huber, who had been questioned only a few minutes before her interrogators had rushed away to join the chase and permitted her to go off with her group of businessmen to Mestre.

And so, mindful of what Moscow was expecting, it was Major Kedrov who had suggested to Colonel Cutrone a second interrogation of the persons involved, the informants and the suspects. Colonel Cutrone had been insensitive to the implied criticism and had been surprisingly agreeable. He would order the persons involved to appear in his office for another round of questioning at five o'clock in the afternoon.

Now it was five o'clock.

Major Kedrov left the church square, went inside the cool and dark carabinieri headquarters. A guard opened the inner electric gate and directed the Russian to the capitano's office, where the meeting was to be held. Passing through the red plaster corridor, decorated with engravings and photographs of heroic moments in the history of the carabinieri, Kedrov reached the office and entered it.

The small office Colonel Cutrone had borrowed, unexpectedly plain and functional for a Venetian office— no Murano glass anywhere, the walls bare except for a photographic portrait of Cutrone and a photograph of marching carabinieri—seemed filled with people. Actually, by Kedrov's count, there were six persons present. Colonel Cutrone was behind the desk, absorbed in a file of papers, with a uniformed carabinieri guard standing at attention nearby. Seated irregularly before the desk were four whom Kedrov vaguely recognized— a spindly old birch of a woman draped in a floral dress, the contessa; next to her the voluptuous actress, wearing a pout, Fantoni; then the large, effeminate writer in an ice cream–colored suit, Foster; and at the far end the aesthetic, blond musician, Memo.

With a curt nod at the group, Major Kedrov, feeling unmilitary and uncomfortable in his dark suit, proceeded to the desk.

Colonel Cutrone half-rose to welcome Kedrov and indicated a straight-backed chair in the corner behind him. "We're just about ready," he said. "Everyone's here except Felice Huber. She went right out to guide another tour after returning from Mestre. Her office promised to send someone to locate and relieve her. She should be arriving any minute. Should we wait or just go ahead?"

"Go ahead," Kedrov replied.

He settled in the straight-backed chair, tilted it against the wall in a corner of the room, and made ready to watch and listen.

Colonel Cutrone cleared his throat, surveyed the group unsmilingly, and began. "We have summoned you here to discuss again the matter of the fugitive we seek. We have advertised him as a man named Mac-Gregor, a foreign spy. By some means or other, you all know his true identity, Professor Davis MacDonald, a British-American scientist. He has committed a grave crime against an ally of ours, made off with a scientific discovery that rightfully belongs to our ally, and is now in hiding somewhere in this city. As you know, he must be found, and he will be found, and brought to justice. We have sought the cooperation of every inhabitant of Venice, and, indeed, three of you—two now present and the woman who will arrive any moment—have cooperated. We need your cooperation once more. As to the two who have been accused of giving refuge to Mac-Donald and have denied it, we urge you to reconsider whether you have been wholly truthful in your first interrogation. If you now remember something that you had forgotten or overlooked in your first interrogation, we urge you to speak of it, and we guarantee it will not be held against you."

At this point Major Kedrov raised his own voice, addressing the group. "On the other hand, you must know, to withhold information useful to the police would make any one of you an accomplice in the crime. Truth cannot harm you. Subterfuge can send you to jail."

"Yes, thank you, Major," said Colonel Cutrone. He swung back to the group. "Now we will review together your roles in this investigation. I will try, when possible, not to cover all the same ground covered in our first interrogation. But if I repeat myself, please answer again with absolute honesty. I will begin with you, Mr. Cedric

323 ▶ ▶ ▶

Foster. You were the first to come to us with a clue to Professor MacDonald's whereabouts. What gave you the impression that the Contessa De Marchi was harboring the criminal?"

"It was not an impression, it was a fact," said Foster with fervor. "The contessa gave a dinner party in my honor. Miss Fantoni and Mr. Memo were also guests and will confirm what I am about to say. After the dinner, the contessa began to speak of a fascinating man she had recently met—"

"Met where?"

"In Venice. He was a famous scientist, she told us, who was on the verge of discovering a means of prolonging human life. I challenged her story, but she insisted it would soon be true. I remained doubtful, yet wondered about it. The following morning, I confronted the contessa alone and pressed her hard for more facts. At last she confessed that the scientist was not only in Venice but under her very roof."

"Did you ascertain this?" inquired Colonel Cutrone. "Did you actually set eyes on Professor MacDonald?"

"I wanted to. I begged the contessa to let me see MacDonald. She refused to let me see him. Angered, I left her and went to you."

Cutrone bobbed his head and faced Contessa De Marchi.

"Well, Contessa, what do you say to that? Why didn't you let your friend and guest see Professor MacDonald?"

The contessa dismissed the question with an impatient wave of her bony hand. "I've already told you once, twice, ten times. I couldn't let Mr. Foster see Professor MacDonald because there was no Professor MacDonald to see. His presence was a figment of my imagination, just like my story about him the evening before. I made up the story to entertain my guests—"

"Made up the story?"

"There had been some gossip throughout the week—someone—one of my many friends—had heard it—I think from Mayor Accardi's wife, I am not sure—that the fugitive being sought was not a spy but a renowned scientist, a gerontologist, who had discovered a means of doubling the human life-span. That is all I knew about it. So I repeated the gossip at the party. When Mr. Foster doubted my veracity, I tried to strengthen my story, and perhaps titillate him further, by saying I had the fugitive in my residence. I am sorry my gossip caused so much trouble. But it was gossip, and no more. I not only have never seen this MacDonald, but do not know what he looks like, except from your posters."

Major Kedrov had been studying the old lady as she spoke. Was she lying? Had she been a Russian, he would have known. But these thin-blooded, blue-blooded types, new to his experience, were more difficult to read. Of course, he knew, the truth could be learned from this woman if she were interrogated privately and with a certain degree of physical pressure. But Kedrov also knew that the Venetian commandant would never consent to that. To torture the truth out of a fellow Venetian, and an aristocratic one at that—no, Cutrone would abhor and reject the idea.

Well, Kedrov hoped, perhaps one of the others would have more to say.

Colonel Cutrone was speaking to the actress. "Miss Fantoni, if you please, there are several questions." Kedrov noticed that Cutrone's voice had softened, become more deferential.

"I am ready," said Teresa Fantoni.

"You went to the police, who sent you to the mayor," said Cutrone. "You were certain you knew the whereabouts of the fugitive MacDonald. How did you know this?"

"From him," said Teresa Fantoni, pointing to Oreste Memo.

"From Mr. Memo. You are friends?"

"Oh, no, not at all. I met him at the contessa's dinner party. We both were present when the contessa spoke of the fabulous scientist she had met, of his imminent discovery. I was fascinated, of course, and wanted to believe it was true, but could not. The following day Mr. Memo called on me. We had cocktails at the Gritti. He wanted me to appear in a play he was writing. I was not interested. I sent him off. But later that evening he reappeared at my suite. He was quite excited. He told me that he was aware of my interest in the contessa's scientist and the scientist's discovery to preserve youth. He told me he had met the scientist, and if I would star in his play, he would introduce me to the scientist. We discussed this further, and Mr. Memo finally confessed that the scientist was hiding in his apartment. As soon as Mr. Memo left, I did what I had to do, what was right. I went directly to the police."

Colonel Cutrone gave the actress an approving smile and turned his attention to Oreste Memo.

"Well, Mr. Memo, what do you say? Is Miss Fantoni's story correct?"

"Only partially."

"What part would you say is incorrect?"

"That I knew MacDonald. I never knew him. I don't know him. I heard of him only from the contessa's dinner anecdote."

"But did you tell Miss Fantoni you knew him?"

"Yes. She wanted someone to give her youth, so I made believe I could introduce her to that someone."

Colonel Cutrone frowned. "In order to persuade her to do your play?"

"Nothing so crass, Colonel. I simply wanted to make love to her."

"To what?"

"To fuck her." Oreste Memo grinned. "And I did."

Teresa Fantoni was on her feet, wild with rage. "You

lying son-of-a-bitch!" she shouted at Memo. "I'll kill
you, you dirty liar!" She plunged toward Memo, bran-
dishing her handbag, preparing to swing it at him. Cedric Foster leaped to his feet, his great bulk intervening,
keeping the actress from hitting Memo. She struggled
briefly with Foster, cursing, as Cutrone signaled the
guard, who hastened forward and led the actress back to
her chair. She sat seething, glaring at Memo.

Colonel Cutrone, with effort, regained his composure.
"Let us continue with the business at hand. We must get
to the bottom of this. A few more questions . . ."

From his tilted chair, Major Boris Kedrov had watched
the last exchange with disgust. They were all prevaricat-
ing decadents, dishonest parasites, who were making a
sham of the interrogation. And Colonel Cutrone was
treating them like neighbors and friends instead of the
accomplices of a criminal. At this rate, Cutrone would
never get to the bottom of anything. If only this were the
Soviet Union, Kedrov thought, and he were in charge. A
little physical force, and these brittle decadents would
crack wide open.

But this was Venice. Two Venetians, a Roman actress,
an American homosexual, being handled with kid gloves
instead of an iron fist. It was hopeless.

Then Kedrov saw that there was one chair still vacant.
The fifth person, an informant, the woman guide. Maybe
she would have something to tell. Maybe there was still
hope, and he would have news to report to Moscow tomorrow.

▶ ▶ ▶ ▶

Breathlessly, conscious that she was late, Felice
Huber left the Riva degli Schiavoni and turned into the
Campo San Zaccaria.

She was frightened by the summons and dreaded the
interrogation. During her countless guided tours she had

met many of the police, come to know some of them
quite well and was on a friendly basis with all of them.
But she had never met the commandante of the carabinieri, and she was afraid of how she would stand up
before authority. She was vulnerable on two counts. Although she regarded Venice as her second home, she
was still an outsider, a foreigner, a Swiss, and she feared
that she might be treated more uncompromisingly than
a native. More than that, she feared one question. She
prayed it would not be asked.

She had reached the entrance to the carabinieri headquarters, paused briefly to calm herself and then entered. At the electric gate a stony-faced guard wanted to
know her name and business. She gave him both. The
gate opened, and she was admitted. The guard beckoned
her to follow him, and she went up the corridor. He
opened an office door and directed her inside.

She had not expected others in the room and was momentarily disconcerted.

A carabinieri colonel, behind a desk, interrupted his
questioning of someone to take note of her.

"Felice Huber?" he asked.

She nodded.

"I'm Colonel Cutrone. We've been expecting you. Do
have a seat." He indicated the empty chair at the far end.
"I'll be with you in a moment."

Woodenly, she went to the chair, lowered herself into
it, recognizing the person next to her as Oreste Memo, a
musician in the Quadri orchestra with whom she had
several times exchanged banalities.

Not listening to what was going on, Felice Huber
glanced at the others who were present. The old lady,
the Contessa De Marchi, of course, well known to everyone in Venice. The beautiful woman beside her, so familiar, yet the name escaped Felice. As for the big man,
obviously American, he was unknown to her.

She wondered why they were all here.

She heard her own name and stiffened, immediately attentive to Colonel Cutrone behind the desk.

"Miss Huber, you know why you have been called here?"

"About what happened this morning," she said. "About my reporting to the police that I had seen MacGregor, the spy—"

"MacGregor. Ah yes," the colonel interrupted. "For security reasons we gave him that name. Actually, the man is Professor Davis MacDonald, a scientist, a fugitive from the law—but never mind, not important to our interrogation. When we answered your call this morning, we had no time to question you properly. When we tried to locate you later, you were off to Mestre. We'd like to ask you a few more questions now."

"Please."

"As I understand it, you were assigned to guide a group of foreign businessmen to a petrochemical plant in Mestre. They were to assemble in the lobby of the Bauer Grunwald. You had a list of those cleared to accompany you."

"That is right."

"Neither the name MacGregor nor MacDonald was on that list?"

"No."

"Yet when you went around checking off each person, you recognized one as the fugitive MacDonald."

"Yes."

"How did you recognize him?"

"I had just, a minute before, by chance, seen his picture on a wanted poster."

"And you were positive it was MacDonald?"

"Yes, unless he has a double."

"Then you rushed to the emergency phone and called us."

Felice Huber swallowed. "I phoned you immediately. I-I wanted to do my duty."

"And to qualify for the reward, of course. Fair enough. You phoned us. Then you returned to your tour group. What happened next?"

"He was gone. The one you say is MacDonald, he had disappeared. I couldn't see him anywhere."

"Could he have known you recognized him?"

"I-I don't think so. I don't know how."

"Did any of the others in the group see him go?"

"The police asked them. None had been aware of his leaving."

Colonel Cutrone was briefly silent, staring down at his desk pad, tapping a pencil on it. He lifted his head slowly.

"One thing puzzles us, Miss Huber. If we can solve it, we may have the key to everything. We have been told your tour to Mestre was not publicized, your point of assembly at the Bauer Grunwald, the place, the time, were not known. Yet MacDonald knew of the tour, both the hour and the spot where it was to start. He was there at the appointed time, hoping to escape Venice. Someone must have told him, helped him. Indeed, you may have told someone who told him. So I'll give you a moment to think back, Miss Huber, and then I'll want your answer to a critical question. To this question. Who in Venice could have known you were taking a tour to Mestre and arranged to get MacDonald on the tour?"

Who?

It was the one question Felice Huber had dreaded hearing. But now the time bomb was fused, and she had been given a moment to think back.

She had what the colonel wanted, of course. The answer. Timothy Jordan. If she told the truth, spoke his name, his goose was cooked. She had betrayed him before, but that had been different. This morning she had not actually harmed Jordan. She had merely informed on someone he had been trying to smuggle out of the city. She had done that in exchange for financial fortune.

It would not have implicated Jordan in any way, only caused the detention of his friend. Yes, that had been different and somehow justifiable out of self-interest.

But now, to betray Jordan himself, to implicate him personally, this was another matter entirely, and one to be considered.

What if she gave him away? What would happen? They would try to make him lead them to MacDonald. They would question him. Knowing him, she was certain he would never talk, never betray a friend. Since he was not a Venetian, they'd continue to question him, harder, eventually torture him, hurt him terribly. She knew the explosive tempers and angers, the brutality of the Italians under stress. They'd cripple Jordan, perhaps permanently, these sons of Mussolini's black shirts, and they would not get a word of MacDonald's whereabouts from him. And she'd have nothing to show for what she'd done, no financial reward, only a lifetime of guilt. She would ruin the one man—the only man—admit it—who had ever been decent to her in a certain way.

Think back, Felice.

Before she had met Timothy Jordan—met him while guiding him on a tour his second week in Venice—she had engaged in sexual intercourse with a man only one time in her life, and she had hated it, vowed never to participate in the act again. Yet she wanted the company and companionship of men—wanted to be spoken to, taken out, entertained by them—always knowing that they would expect something in return. So her evenings with men had always ended up with her having oral sex with them, and this had gratified her partners. She had gone on a date with Jordan that first time, allowed him to see her back to her apartment, felt sympathy and a rapport with him, and had invited him inside. They had done the usual things, caressing, kissing, and after a while she had told him she did not like intercourse but would make him happy anyway. They had undressed, and she had gone down on him. And then, to her astonishment, he had gone down on her, excited her, and manually brought her to full orgasm, not once but three times. It had been the first time in her life that any man had ever bothered to do so.

She heard her name once more, and the voice was foreign. She was being spoken to by a fierce-looking man, with a Slavic aspect, who was tilted back in a chair in the corner.

"All right, Miss Huber, you have had time to think," he was saying. "Whom did you tell about your guided tour to Mestre?"

All hesitancy was gone. She had her answer, no matter what the consequences.

"I told no one," she said with conviction, "no one on earth. How MacDonald got into the group I do not know. He just materialized, and there he was. That's all I know. I wish I could help you further, but I can't."

Then she spoke softly to Timothy Jordan in her head: Okay, Tim, you don't ever have to forgive me for trying to turn MacDonald over to the police. People will do terrible things for money. But know this someday. I saved you, yourself, from the police. Why? Because, Tim, once you were kind.

▶ ▶ ▶ ▶

The electric lights were going on all over Venice, in the lagoon, in the crooked streets, in the crowded cafés, in the busy restaurants. Evening had come, and just before eight o'clock, Tim Jordan entered the glassware shop. He felt more relaxed than he had the entire day. All his tasks had been attended to, and there was some hope once more. Waving his gratefulness to Sembut Nurikhan, who was saying good-bye to several customers, he continued on into the small back office.

A rumpled Professor MacDonald, who apparently had

just awakened, was seated on the cot, Alison beside him, and they were deep in a discussion. The instant they saw Jordan, their discussion ceased, and both looked at him expectantly.

"Good news," Jordan announced. "Do you know what I'm talking about, Professor?"

"Alison just told me. It doesn't sound possible."

"It is not only possible, it is happening tonight—or let's say, in the early morning. Signor Folin, the man in charge of the chopper, wanted a $10,000 down payment, but I managed to get him to settle for half of that, the $15,000 balance due once you are on the helicopter, Professor, and on your way out of Venice."

"When does this—this effort take place?" MacDonald wanted to know.

"At precisely two o'clock in the morning," said Jordan. "Exactly two hours after midnight tonight. A helicopter—one Folin has rented elsewhere—will come in over the Piazza, drop down fast, and the minute it touches the ground and the door opens, you will make a run for it across the Piazza, climb up the ladder into the cockpit, and the helicopter will lift off. You'll be safely out of here. It's that simple."

Fumbling for his pipe, he now wanted to get off his feet and enjoy a smoke. He turned to take the swivel chair at the proprietor's desk and was surprised to see Sembut Nurikhan in the doorway.

"I accidentally overheard you, Tim," said Nurikhan. "You are actually going to attempt this?"

"Exactly as you heard, Sembut."

"I don't want to intrude on your affairs, Tim—"

"This is everyone's affair."

"Nevertheless, I think such an attempt is foolhardy."

"Only because it sounds so dramatic," replied Jordan. "Otherwise, it is perfectly logical under the circumstances. Besides, Sembut, they've tightened the noose around the professor. He must get away while he can. We have no other choice."

"Well, perhaps . . ." said the proprietor doubtfully.

Jordan went to him, put a hand on his shoulder. "Sembut, it'll work. The element of surprise is on our side. The only problem is seeing that the professor is safe between now and the time he gets to the Piazza." He hesitated. "How long can you keep him here?"

"Normally, I close the shop at nine. But out of consideration for you, I would keep it open until ten o'clock tonight."

"Sembut, we need a hideout until one-thirty in the morning. Can't you keep open until midnight, then let us stay on back here until the time we have to leave? I can close up the shop for you and return the keys tomorrow."

"I'm sorry, Tim, I cannot do it. This shop is my life. I cannot let anyone, even a friend like you, have the keys overnight. As to staying open later, it would not do. It might endanger you. I have a night watchman—all the shopkeepers in the area do—who checks out the place late at night. I have never been open past ten. If he saw that I was, he might become concerned, suspicious, and come inside to investigate. He might see you, would certainly recognize the professor, and all would be lost for you. I'm sorry. I've done as much as I can. You must leave at ten."

"I appreciate everything you've done," said Jordan.

The doorbell sounded, and Nurikhan disappeared into his shop.

"What'll we do, Tim, during the three and a half hours between ten and the time we leave to meet the helicopter?" Alison wanted to know.

"Good question," said Jordan, furrowing his brow. He was lost in thought for long seconds. His face brightened. "I have it," he said. "We'll eat. I know just the place." He reached for the telephone. "I'll make the arrangements now."

▶ ▶ ▶ ▶

At ten o'clock exactly, Sembut Nurikhan saw Dr. Edwards, Professor MacDonald, and Tim Jordan to the front of his shop, opened his door, wished them well, and watched them slip out into the foggy darkened square and make off.

Closing the door, Nurikhan circled through his shop, turning down the lights in the main showroom. This done, he retreated to his office to pack up for the night. He set his attaché case on his desk, lifted the lid, and began to lay two weeks' worth of due bills inside it. These he would examine tonight, at home, while enjoying a late snack.

As an afterthought, he sought today's edition of *Il Gazzettino*. He had not had a chance to glance at the newspaper during working hours. Fortunately, even without the intrusion of Jordan and his friends, it had been an extremely busy and profitable workday. But ritually, he kept abreast of the news, local and world events, and now he would take the newspaper home and read it before going to bed.

He found it folded on the table beside the cot, and bringing it back to his attaché case, he unfolded it to see what had been worthy of the main headline.

What he saw made him stop abruptly, stand stock still.

He stared at the large headline.

130,000,000-LIRE REWARD

His eyes went down to the blown-up photograph of Professor MacDonald beneath it.

He continued slowly to his desk, set his attaché case on the floor, and spread the newspaper page out before him.

He lowered himself into his chair and began to read.

When he had finished, his eyes held on the headline once more. One hundred thirty million lire. His gaze shifted to the telephone on his desk. Then he returned to the headline.

He eased back in his swivel chair, looking absently at the ceiling, trying to think.

▶ ▶ ▶ ▶

Do Forni—Two Ovens—a restaurant little known to tourists, was one of the favorites of well-off native Venetians and acclimated Venetians like Tim Jordan.

After many detours in the blissful fog that had blanketed the city, walking twice as far in order to keep off main thoroughfares, Jordan, Alison, and MacDonald had arrived at the restaurant undetected at twenty minutes after ten in the evening. Jordan had chosen this public place as their temporary limbo because he had been unable to conjure up a single private place in which to take refuge. If it had to be a public place, Do Forni was a better bet than most. It was easily accessible, its entrance off what amounted to a street no more than an alley hidden in the maze of Venice's central San Marco district. Further, Jordan knew the maître d' well, had always been generous to him. For an improvised waiting depot, there could have been worse choices.

Now, in wicker chairs at a wooden table, in a darkened corner of the restaurant, Jordan sat across from Alison, with the professor placed between them at the end of the table so that his back was to the main dining room. Inspecting the room, with its dimly lighted globe fixtures set between high pebbled-glass windows, Jordan congratulated himself on his selection of this place. It was ten-thirty, and the main room had been emptied of most guests. Only two other couples lingered over desserts and coffee at the far side of the room, near the tall serving table over which a brass bucket hung from a hoop.

Jordan had done his preliminary work well. On the telephone, he had requested this particular obscure table. Upon arriving, with MacDonald constantly blowing his nose in his handkerchief to hide his face, Jordan had taken the maître d' aside and inquired how late they would be open tonight. The maître d' had said that they would be closing at one o'clock. Jordan had pressed 15,000 lire into the man's hand and said it would be most useful if they could remain at their table until one-thirty in the morning. The maître d' had been pleased to tell him this was possible and would be permitted.

As MacDonald took his place, Jordan had whispered to him to make constant use of his napkin. When the maître d' came for the order, or whenever the white-jacketed waiter appeared, MacDonald must bring his napkin to his mouth. MacDonald had obeyed, covering the lower half of his face at least four times since they had been seated.

When the menus came, Alison and MacDonald had protested that they were not hungry. Their stomachs were knotted. Eating was not conceivable.

"We're going to be here three hours," Jordan had pointed out. "We've got to order full meals. We don't have to eat them. We only have to push and poke and pretend to eat. But we've got to spend money and be busy. You want me to order for all of us?"

He had ordered a seven-course meal for each of them. And both red and white wines.

As the food was served during the next two hours, it had smelled so good that they all ate, although Mac-Donald ate lightly.

In hushed tones, speaking to one another when no waiter hovered, they had reviewed the steps between the restaurant and the Piazza and the arrival of the helicopter. They had gone over it three times.

After that, Jordan had tried to distract MacDonald by making him discuss his discovery, how he would announce it, whom he would see after that, how the formula would be prepared, and how it would be distributed. There was even discussion, once more, on how C-98 would affect the world, for better, for worse, and the problems it would create and how they would be solved.

The only bad moment came at twelve twenty-five.

Professor MacDonald had been speculating on the probability of the helicopter escape's working out.

"It's a complete secret," Jordan assured him. "It should work out. No one knows about it except Folin and the helicopter pilot."

"And one more," MacDonald said. "Sembut Nurikhan knows about it."

"True," admitted Jordan, "but Sembut's no security risk. He's entirely on our side, as he has been from the beginning. He has to be. His brother is seriously ill. We've promised your formula on a priority basis for his brother. He won't betray us for that reason alone. He wants to keep his brother alive."

MacDonald stared at Jordan a long time. "Tim," he said, "don't you know? His brother is dead."

Jordan's features hardened. "What?"

"The brother died three days ago."

"How do you know?"

"He told me. We were sitting and talking before I took my nap. I wanted him to know how grateful I was that he talked his nephew into helping me get off San Lazzaro and for hiding me today. I said I would not forget our promise. Soon after I got to Paris, and the formula began to be prepared, he would get one of the first shipments to turn over to his brother's doctor. He said to me simply, 'I'm afraid it is too late. My brother passed away three days ago.' "

"My God," breathed Jordan.

"Does that change anything?"

"I don't know," said Jordan. "It could. It might. We have nothing to hold over him. He doesn't need us now. But I think he will protect us out of decency and friendship, as he has done till now."

"Unless," said Alison, "he hears about the $150,000."

"Yes," said Jordan slowly. "That could give him second thoughts. In fact, it's given me a few more right now."

▶ ▶ ▶ ▶

It was a quarter to two in the morning, and Venice was asleep.

They were wending their way, by a circuitous route, toward the bell-tower entrance to the Piazza San Marco. Tim Jordan, acting as guide and lookout, preceded MacDonald and Alison by ten yards. So far there had been no difficulties. The light fog was in their favor. Patches of it, like gossamer curtains, hung over every street. They had encountered no other human beings in fifteen minutes.

As Jordan strode along, his mind was on Sembut Nurikhan. He was worried. He had not expressed his concern again to the others, but Nurikhan's reliability troubled him. The glass-shop owner had been a good friend. He had even been a tested friend, put himself on the line with his call to his nephew on San Lazzaro. But at that time he had had a stake in MacDonald's escape. It had been an opportunity to save his brother's life. Now the brother was gone. Now he might have a stake in MacDonald's capture. If he knew about the $150,000 reward, and if he was tempted by it. Maybe, maybe. There had been no evidence to prove he might be untrustworthy. Still . . .

Jordan stiffened. Up ahead, materializing out of the fog, a person could be seen, a man, head down, shuffling toward them. At first Jordan thought him a beggar, and then as he passed the man he recognized him. It was Gino, one of the news vendors at the daytime stand in the Piazza, and obviously he had been at some bar the entire evening and by now was inebriated and heading for home and sleep.

Jordan watched him go past, half-turned to watch him pass MacDonald and Alison, and then Jordan was struck by a similarity. Gino was almost the same height and build as MacDonald. Not quite, but almost.

A thought came to Jordan, a means of protecting MacDonald against any perfidy on Nurikhan's part.

Coming around, Jordan ordered the other two to wait for him, and he chased after the wobbling news vendor.

"Gino," Jordan called out softly as he caught up with him.

The news vendor halted, considered Jordan with bleary eyes. Then his unshaven features broke into a look of recognition. "Mr. Jordan," he mumbled thickly. "You're out late."

"Gino, how'd you like to make yourself some easy money?"

"Who wouldn't?"

"It may sound crazy, what I'm about to tell you, but believe me, it is true. In ten minutes a helicopter is going to land in the middle of the Piazza San Marco to pick up a passenger, a friend of mine back there."

In his condition, Gino did not appear a bit surprised. A pigeon or a helicopter in the Piazza, one made as much sense as the other.

"Soon as the helicopter lands," said Jordan, "I want you to run over to it and tell the pilot that his passenger is on his way. Think you can do that? Here—" Jordan took out his wallet, removed 15,000 lire, and stuffed it into Gino's hand. "For your trouble," Jordan added.

With the feel of the money, Gino's eyes seemed to clear and become more alert.

"What do I have to do?" he asked.

Jordan carefully repeated his instructions.

"That's all?" said Gino.

"That's all," said Jordan. "The second the helicopter lands, I'll give you a little push, and you run to the mid-

340 ▶ ▶ ▶

dle of the Piazza and tell the helicopter pilot his passenger is coming. How's that?"

"Happy to do it, Mr. Jordan," said Gino, pocketing the bills.

"Okay, come along with us. We're all going to the bell tower to wait for the helicopter. It should be here in seven or eight minutes."

Jordan, with Gino stumbling after him, joined the others, and they continued toward the Piazza.

"Just a precaution," explained Jordan in an undertone. "From a distance, our companion might be mistaken for you, Professor. The moment the helicopter lands, I'm sending him to it first, a sort of decoy. If our friend Nurikhan sold out, the police should come into the open and spring on Gino. If nothing happens, then it'll be safe for you to follow and climb aboard."

They were nearing the Piazza now, and they automatically slowed and proceeded warily.

They were almost there, a dozen feet away, and Jordan gestured to hold them back. He moved quickly ahead, alone, darting behind the first column of the arcade at the opening of the Mercerie.

His gaze swept the Piazza, only thinly obscured by fingers of fog. The Piazza was empty. Desolate. Still. Not a soul in sight.

So far, safe.

From a distance, high up, Jordan could hear the sounds of a helicopter.

He leaned against the murky column, immobile, listening.

The faint rotor sounds were becoming more distinct, louder, yet louder, dinning toward him. He squinted his eyes toward the farthest end of the Piazza, and suddenly from out of a bank of fog above the Napoleonic wing of buildings the small helicopter materialized. It came in over the Piazza, overhead rotor whirling, seemed to hang in midair over the center, and slowly began dropping, lowering.

In seconds, it had landed and stood squatting in the middle of the great square, an amazing, incongruous mechanical apparition.

"Okay, Gino!" Jordan barked over his shoulder. As Gino staggered forward, Jordan reached back, grabbed him, and pushed him into the Piazza. The elderly news vendor, shabby suit coat flying, broke into a weaving, uneven trot, running steadily toward the helicopter, with its door flung open and its ladder hanging alongside.

The lone figure was halfway to the helicopter.

Jordan sucked in a deep breath and held it.

Gino was three-quarters there, and the Piazza remained otherwise empty and silent.

Jordan's excitement grew.

In seconds the helicopter would be freedom's exit.

That instant, all hell broke loose. Jordan's head swerved to his right at the explosion of noise. From both sides of the Napoleonic wing, at the far end, a dozen, two dozen, three dozen uniformed police catapulted out of the camouflage of night fog and into the open, racing toward the helicopter and Gino, running fast, shouting, several of them shooting their pistols into the air.

Jordan recoiled, momentarily watched them in hypnotized fascination.

Then he saw that they weren't heading toward the helicopter at all. The swarm was descending on Gino, certain he was the fugitive MacDonald.

The helicopter pilot, apparently alerted by the tumult and seeing the charge of the police, immediately had his aircraft in motion once more. The chopper was rising, slowly, then faster, eluding the police. It was airborne above the Piazza and beginning to wing away.

And the police were upon Gino, surrounding him, manhandling him.

Jordan had seen enough.

Cursing Nurikhan under his breath, he shoved away from the arcade column, snatched the trembling Mac-

Donald by the arm as he spoke to Alison. "Get back to the hotel," Jordan snapped at her. "We've got to run for it. We've got to get as far away from here as possible."

With that, he and MacDonald plunged into the narrow cave of the Mercerie.

They ran and they ran. Jordan did not know how long they had been running, but when MacDonald was choking for breath, ready to collapse, Jordan stopped and propped MacDonald up.

"I can't go another step," MacDonald groaned. "I'm sorry. I give up."

"Okay," said Jordan. A sign above, half hidden by mist, read, CAMPO SAN LIO. "There's a bridge. We'll go down below it, off this main street. We'll rest down by the canal. Maybe no one will see us."

He had started toward the bridge with MacDonald when he saw a young woman come to the top of the bridge and begin to descend it.

As she passed under a lamp, her sharp-featured painted face, low-buttoned blouse, tight skirt, swinging purse were illuminated, and Jordan recognized her. He had encountered her his first week in Venice, and many times after. Her name was Clara something-or-other. She was a well-known streetwalker, a prostitute familiar to the habitués of the Mercerie and Rialto.

She had just turned off the main street, going toward a building facing the embankment of the canal, when Jordan called out, "Clara."

She halted, startled, trying to see who it was. Supporting MacDonald, Jordan went to her.

"Oh, it's you," she said, mildly disgusted. "One of my no-customers."

"Maybe you've hit the jackpot, Clara. I'd like to be a sort of customer tonight. So would my friend."

"You want some fun? *Marchetta?* Both of you?"

"Both of us. How much?"

"For one hour? All night? What?"

"To tell you the truth, Clara, we want a place for all night."

Clara calculated. "All night. For two. Considering it is already this late, I'll make you a bargain. Let's say 20,000 lire."

"Fair enough," said Jordan.

She winked. "Follow me."

They went down the steps to the canal level, and at the first door of the old apartment building she motioned them inside. There was a dark hallway, and her three-room apartment was the second on the left.

She turned up a lamp in what appeared to be a sitting room, with a bedroom behind it, and a kitchen in an alcove. She locked the door from the inside, put her purse on a mantel, and went up to Jordan. She held out the palm of her hand.

"Pay before play," she said.

"Sure," said Jordan. He counted out 20,000 lire.

After she had deposited the bills in her purse, she came around unbuttoning her blouse, stripping it off. Before Jordan could speak, she had unsnapped her skirt and stepped out of it. Her small breasts were bare, and she was wearing only tight nylon panties.

"All right, gentlemen," she said, "take off your trousers and come to the bathroom. I want to wash you both off first." She started for the bedroom. "What's it going to be, one at a time or both of you together?"

Jordan asserted himself. "Hold it, Clara. Let me explain. . . ."

"What's the matter?"

"We just want a place to stay for the night. A place to rest. That's all. That's what we paid you for."

She could not believe her ears. "No fucking?"

"No nothing," said Jordan. "We just want a place to sleep. You can keep your bed. My friend and I will get some rest right here. When it's morning, we'll leave you."

"I've never had this before," she said, shaking her head. "But everybody's queer in his own way. Well, do what you like. I'm going to sleep."

Once they were alone, Jordan got MacDonald to the sofa and helped him lie down.

"This is better," murmured MacDonald. "What about you?"

"I'll sleep in the armchair."

"That was a close one we had, wasn't it?"

"The closest yet," admitted Jordan, shedding his jacket.

"Tim—"

"Yes?"

"Why don't we give up? There's no place left to go."

Jordan stared down at the old man. "There's one place," he said quietly. "I've been saving it. We're going there in the morning. It's our last hope."

IX

▶ ▶ ▶ ▶ ▶ ▶   ▶

He had not wanted to bring MacDonald here. Throughout the hectic week, it had always been in the back of his mind as a place of last resort. He had constantly resisted this refuge, because while it might be safe from the outside, there were potential dangers inside. For inside was the two-deck apartment in which Marisa, Bruno, and their widowed mother, Ada Girardi, lived.

Since the Girardi apartment, a ten-minute walk behind the Piazza, had been five or six minutes away from the prostitute's quarters, the passage to it presented them with only fleeting exposure. On their way, they had been forced to hide just once, slipping into a tobacco-and-souvenir shop when they saw a pair of policemen strolling toward them. After that, there had been few people to recognize MacDonald and no further obstacles.

Jordan had pushed open a wrought-iron gate leading into a picturesque courtyard, and near the old rain cistern set in an alcove was the entrance to the residential building. They had climbed three stories up the steep turning staircase to the top floor and on the upper landing had arrived at the Girardi apartment.

It was now five minutes after eight in the morning. Marisa did not arrive at work until nine-thirty, so the odds were that she was still at home.

Jordan rang the doorbell.

He could hear footsteps in the corridor and entry hall. The door partially opened. Marisa, in blouse and skirt, running a comb through her long hair, peered out. She was surprised.

"Tim, what are you—" Then she saw MacDonald. "Come in," she said to Jordan.

They were in the entry hall, both men breathing easier. Marisa considered Jordan briefly. "You look like hell. Where have you been all night?"

"It's a long story. Marisa Girardi, let me introduce you to my friend, the one I've told you about, Professor Pearson."

She eyed him speculatively. "How do you do?" she said. "Well, let's not stand here."

She led them down the corridor, past the kitchen and dining room, into the comfortable living room. There were the familiar Bukhara red rug, the antique Tyrolean table with four chairs, the Tuscan sideboard with its pewter plates, the walnut chest beneath the center window covered by white curtains, the oversized divan, and two armchairs. Behind the divan were wooden stairs going up to a mezzanine with doors to the three bedrooms.

"Are you here alone?" Jordan wanted to know.

"Yes. Bruno just left for work. Mamma, as you know, is in the hospital."

"How is she?"

"She has been in pain. But they are giving her heavier sedation. They will finish their tests today. Dr. Scarpa promised a diagnosis no later than tomorrow. I'm worried."

"Let's hope for the best," said Jordan lamely. "Marisa, I'll tell you why we're here. I need a place for the pro-

fessor to stay tonight—well, today, tonight, maybe tomorrow, until I can get him out of Venice. I thought you
might help us."

She was silent a moment. "Of course. There is
Mamma's room. He can stay in her room."

Jordan kissed her on the cheek. "I knew you'd help."

"Did you have breakfast? Would both of you like some
coffee?"

MacDonald spoke up. "To be frank with you, Miss
Girardi, I didn't sleep too well last night. I'd just like to
lie down somewhere for a while."

She started for the stairs to the mezzanine. "Come
with me. I'll show you my mother's room." Over her
shoulder, she said, "Tim, if you're having coffee, I'll
have a cup with you."

Jordan waited until they had gone up to the bedroom,
then went into the kitchen. He found the coffee, filled
two cups, and brought them to the low table before the
divan just as Marisa came down the stairs to join him.
She settled beside him on the divan and stirred her coffee meditatively.

She said, "Of course I want to help you, Tim, but I
don't want to get mixed up in any trouble."

"I promise you, Marisa, no trouble."

She looked at him. "I recognize your professor, Tim. I
recognized him the minute you introduced me. He's no
underground courier working with separatists, as you've
been saying. He's the spy, the one whose face is on a
hundred posters and in the papers. He's MacGregor."

Jordan wondered how much he dared tell her. The
less the better, he decided. "Marisa, please believe
me—I swear to you on all that is holy—he is not a spy.
You're right. He's not an underground courier either.
He's a good, decent man, an important man, a scientist,
who's committed no crime, no crime whatsoever. He's
wanted by the Communists for another reason. He's
wanted by the Soviet Communists, and the local Com-

munists are cooperating in trying to catch him. I'll tell
you more someday. But I can't right now. Will you accept that?"

She smiled. "Of course, Tim."

"Just one more thing. Can you tell Bruno to sleep
somewhere else tonight? It would be awkward if he
turned up. Tell him we want to spend the night here
together."

"Very well. I'll phone Bruno when I get to the office.
He has friends. He'll find a place to stay." She finished
her coffee and came to her feet. "I'm going to the office
early because I need a longer lunch hour. I want to go to
the hospital to see Mamma. Are you coming with me?"

Jordan shook his head. "Not yet. Maybe I'll be in later.
I want to sit here alone and do some thinking."

"Then I'll leave you alone."

She went to the sideboard to get her briefcase, picked
up a manila envelope beside it, began to put it into her
briefcase, then retained it and went back to Jordan.

She was pulling some eight-by-ten-inch photographs
out of the manila envelope. "Perhaps this is something
you should see. I'd better have your approval before I
pass them out. Schuyler Moore wanted photographs of
the Pirelli miniature model in action, and I collected
some. Then he called and asked for photographs of the
actual Lido channel where the inflatable dam is installed. I got Bruno to dig up the latest in his office and
let us have prints. Schuyler Moore is coming by for them
today. Do you want to have a look first?"

Although uninterested, Jordan accepted the half
dozen or more photographs. He peeled through them.
They were mostly aerial shots of the narrow opening of
the Porto di Lido which led from the Venice lagoon into
the Adriatic Sea. Some of the closer shots tried to show
the pumping station for the inflatable dam. He came to
the last picture, which showed a cruise ship passing
from the Adriatic through the channel into the lagoon.

He started to hand them back to Marisa. "Fine, fine," he said. "You can give Moore the lot."

As Marisa took hold of the photographs, something far back in Jordan's brain surfaced and struck him with a thought.

He held on to the pictures, pulled the last photograph free, the one with the ship passing through the channel.

"One second, Marisa. This one. When was it taken?"

"It says on the back. The day before the quarantine was declared on the city. That Greek cruise ship was the last one to enter here before the city was closed down."

"Is the ship still here?"

"I have no idea."

"Let me see the others again."

He took them, went through them, studied the various views of the narrow channel leading out of Venice, the pumping station that had never been used, the vistas of the open sea. He handed them back to Marisa. "Perfect. Schuyler Moore will be pleased to have them."

She went for her briefcase, slid the manila envelope into it, found her purse. Going to the corridor, she stopped beside Jordan, unzipped her purse, and handed him a key.

"Mamma's key, in case you want to go out."

"Thanks, Marisa." He stood up and kissed her. "I will be going out soon."

She hesitated. "I hope you find a way to help your friend," she said.

"I will," he said. "I'm sure I will."

He watched her leave and was relieved when she was gone. He wanted to be alone with his new idea, He wanted to examine it, assess its practicability.

It was amazing, he thought. All the while, all these past days, while on the run, there must have been a half dozen latent escape ideas in his mind. This had been one of them. The murky idea, a mere impression of an idea, had come to full life, stimulated by a photograph.

He began to turn it over in his head, a writer plotting. To the idea he added things remembered, something he had seen, something he had overheard recently, something that had been told to him not long ago.

The idea developed in his head, became a possibility, took on a reality.

He was excited. He visualized it clearly now, the only, the last means of escape.

How had he not thought of it before? But here it was. Of all his ideas, the simplest, the best—and the most dangerous. This was it. There would not be time for another. Going to the telephone to call Alison, he glanced at his watch. There was still a full day ahead of him.

He would need every minute of it.

▶ ▶ ▶ ▶

Alison Edwards, in smoky oversized lavender sunglasses, blue blouse, and jeans, nibbling at a small cucumber sandwich and drinking her coffee, was waiting for him in the second row of Florian's outdoor café, across the Piazza from Quadri's, when he arrived.

As he sat down, and before she could ask, he said quietly, "MacDonald's safe for the moment."

She sagged in relief.

He crossed his legs, lighted his pipe, and said, "It took some doing and some luck. We just ran and ran, no place to go, until we bumped into a prostitute I'd seen around coming home late. We paid her just to put us up."

"Not really?"

"It served."

"Is Davis still there?"

"No. The woman has regular customers she must accommodate. We couldn't stay. This morning I dragged the professor to the last place I could think of . . ."

Considering how he would explain the next, he stalled

briefly by summoning the waiter and ordering tea and a roll.

He decided to be frank. "Remember when we were at the Lido beach and I had a couple of women's swimsuits in my cabana?"

"The one that had too many curves for me." Then she added, "Your Venetian *inamorata*."

"Friend," he corrected her. "She's my assistant in the office. Her name is Marisa Girardi. She lives with her brother, Bruno, the photographer, the one who tried to bribe the captain for us—she lives with him and with her mother in an apartment not too far from here. Well, I turned to her this morning."

"Why hadn't you tried her before?"

"Mostly Bruno. He's too close to the police, covering their hunt. Anyway, Marisa took the professor in, and that's where he is right now. Incidentally, how did you make out last night, after the police swarmed over poor Gino and the professor and I took off? Did you have any trouble?"

"Not much," said Alison. "I ignored the police and just started walking across the edge of the Piazza, in front of the Basilica, a tourist going back to her hotel. A couple of police came over to question me."

"Like what?"

"Who was I? Where was I coming from? Where was I going? I told them, rather indignantly, I'd come to Venice for one day and had been stuck here ever since. I'd just been visiting a friend and was getting back to the Danieli. I asked them what the commotion in the Piazza was all about. They wouldn't tell me. They wanted to know if I'd seen someone running on the Mercerie. I told them I had seen no one running or walking. So they waved me on."

"Good."

"Tim, just one thing bothers me about last night. Do you think the police asked Gino why he was running toward the helicopter? He might have told them who sent him."

Jordan shook his head. "I doubt if he involved me. I had worried about that. But knowing Gino, he probably told them he was drunk, and saw this crazy helicopter land, and ran out to see what was going on. If he had given the police my name, they'd have been after me already. I checked the hotel. No one has been looking for me."

Alison appeared satisfied. "And Davis? Is he safe at Marisa's?"

"If we don't hide him there too long. I arranged for Bruno to sleep somewhere else tonight. But I won't be able to keep him out much longer. And he'd recognize MacDonald in an instant." The tea had been served. Jordan took a bite of the roll and drank the tea. "We've got to move fast."

Alison's anxiety had returned. "What's next, Tim? What's left?"

He smiled, to relieve her concern. "We get the professor out of here—in fact, you and the professor. It's the best idea I've had. I think I'd had it somewhere in my head for days. In the last hour it came together. But it depends on several factors. I'm going to spend the rest of the day looking into them."

"Do you want to tell me about it?"

"Not yet, Alison. I only want to tell you that if it does work out—be ready to leave Venice in the morning with the professor."

"And if it doesn't work out?"

"We're finished." He laid some money on the table. "Now I'd better start moving. I'll walk you to the hotel."

They went back to the hotel in silence, wending their way through groups of tourists being photographed amid clusters of pigeons pecking at food, and in a few minutes he had her back at the Danieli entrance. The two uniformed police guards were outside the glass doors, studying every person entering or leaving.

"Okay, I leave you here," said Jordan.

She was reluctant to go inside. "When will I hear from you, Tim?"

"Tonight, I promise. One way or the other."

He waited for her to go inside, and when she was gone, he resumed walking. He went over the bridge near the entrance and strolled to the edge of the lagoon.

With one hand he shaded his eyes from the fierce sun, and scanned the curve of the lagoon to his left. Then he saw what he wanted to see and had expected to see. About the distant point where he remembered the Istituto di Studi Adriatici was located, sitting high in the water at dockside, was a huge, gleaming white cruise ship. He could not make out the design of its flag, but he was certain that this was the vessel that Dante, his lifeguard friend on the Lido, had spoken about, the ship that could be seen entering the lagoon the day before the emergency. The same vessel he had just seen in a photograph.

All that mattered was that it was still here.

Satisfied, Jordan retraced his steps to the Danieli entrance and went into the cool lobby. No guests were at the concierge's counter. Fabris, the chief concierge, was on the telephone at the end of the counter. He acknowledged Jordan's appearance with a raised hand, then hung up.

"We have not seen much of you lately, Mr. Jordan. Is everything all right?"

"Just busier than ever," said Jordan. "By the way, Fabris, I was taking a walk on the Riva degli Schiavoni and I spotted a cruise ship out there. I thought no ships were allowed into the lagoon during the emergency."

"Ah, the Greek ship—*The Delphic Oracle*. It arrived the day before the emergency, while the port was still open. This was not on its itinerary. It was sailing back to

Piraeus when it needed repairs. So it docked just as the port was shut down."

"Can anyone visit the cruise ship? I've always wondered what one looks like."

"Sorry, no, Mr. Jordan. From the moment of the emergency, the ship has been quarantined. No passengers permitted to leave. No one permitted to visit. They take no chances with the spy. Even the crew is confined, except for the captain and purser."

"Will it be allowed to leave Venice?"

"Absolutely. It was supposed to sail yesterday. But it was held up for one more repair. I believe it now leaves tomorrow."

"You mentioned that the captain and purser can come ashore."

"Oh, yes. In fact, they come by our bar every day for a Bellini or two. The captain left a few minutes ago, but the purser—a very nice fellow, a Mr. Papadopoulos—he still may be in the bar having his refreshment."

"Thanks, Mr. Fabris."

Jordan crossed the main lobby and entered the darkened bar. At this hour of the morning, the bar was unoccupied except for a youthful assistant bartender reading a newspaper and a lone middle-aged man in uniform sunk deep into an armchair, enjoying a Bellini.

Jordan approached him. "Mr. Papadopoulos?"

The craggy-faced purser looked up.

"My friend the chief concierge told me I might find you here. I wanted to speak to you about a matter of business."

The purser seemed more than pleased to have company. "Sit down, do sit down. Will you join me for a drink?"

"You're very kind, but no, thanks." Jordan settled into the armchair beside him. "My name is Timothy Jordan. I'm an American with the Venice Must Live Committee."

"You are an engineer to save Venice from sinking?"

"I used to be. I'm a writer now, actually handling public relations for the Committee. I see your ship is still in port."

"Unhappily for most of the passengers. They're not allowed off. Foolish, but they are not. I guess the police are afraid one of them might return from an excursion with the spy's secrets. The confinement—most of them are very restless by now. Well, it won't be long. We had hoped to sail yesterday, even the day before, but repairs continue. The Venetians are terribly slow."

"When does *The Delphic Oracle* sail?"

"In the morning. Tomorrow morning for sure."

"What time?"

"Ten o'clock."

Jordan did not waste words. "I'd like to put someone—a friend—on your ship."

The purser gave him a long look. "Impossible in port. We would be agreeable, but the authorities would not permit it. It can't be done in port."

"I don't mean in port," said Jordan. "I mean at sea."

Papadopoulos gave him a longer look. "At sea?"

"Surely it's been done before?"

The purser nodded. "Yes. It has been done a number of times. Especially when one of our passengers has missed the sailing."

"This would be a new passenger—two, actually—and even though you'd be on the last leg of the cruise, they'd pay full fare."

The purser was thoughtful. "It would be an inconvenience, slowing the vessel." He shrugged. "Still, why not? It could be done, if we are at sea out of the jurisdiction of Venice. You'd have to find a means of reaching us."

"It would be arranged."

"I see no objections. The rest is up to you."

Jordan felt relieved. "Very well. Then let's get down to business."

▶ ▶ ▶ ▶

It was late morning, but before lunchtime, when Jordan parted the brown swinging doors at Harry's Bar.

He was pleased at what he saw. All but two of the small lacquered circular tables, with their low chairs padded in black leather, were empty. To his left, next to the framed photograph of Ernest Hemingway posing with the elder Giuseppe Cipriani, who had founded Harry's Bar, the cashier sat at the register counting bills while engaged in conversation with the head bartender, the slick-haired, always smiling Alberto, with whom Jordan had enjoyed a cordial relationship since first he had set foot in the restaurant.

Jordan went to the bar.

Alberto and the cashier interrupted their conversation to greet him warmly.

"Alberto," said Jordan, "I'll have a Campari. I want to speak to you privately for a moment."

"Take your place. I will be right over."

Jordan threaded through the room, going to a table as far from the nearest customer as possible, finally sitting down against the back wall of the restaurant under the rectangular oil painting of the Cipriani Hotel.

In a few minutes Alberto came with the Campari, set it down, then leaned forward, palms on the table, head dipped toward Jordan. "Something private?"

"Yes." Jordan kept his voice low. "I don't know if you will remember, Alberto, but a month or two ago, late one night, you and I and a couple of other customers were talking at the bar. You mentioned something about smugglers, that there were a number of smugglers who came in and out of Venice regularly. Were you kidding or did you mean it?"

"But it's true."

"You know this for a fact?"

"One of them, the best of them, he is a close friend of mine."

"What does he smuggle?"

"Goods, imports, to be brought in without duty and sold cheaply. It is profitable."

"How does he get away with it?" Jordan wondered.

Alberto lifted his shoulders. "Who knows? He has tricks of his trade, I suppose. He knows every inch of the lagoon, every shortcut, detour. He has the swiftest private motorboat in the area. And I suppose, it could be, he pays a bribe to some of the patrolmen regularly."

"Are you still in touch with this friend?"

"I see him often. He is much fun to drink with."

"Alberto, I'd like to meet him. Is it possible?"

"Whenever you like, I am sure. Do you wish to speak to him as a writer or for business?"

"There's a job I'd like to have him undertake. I'd like to discuss it with him."

"When?"

"Today. As soon as possible."

Alberto nodded and straightened. "I will telephone him this minute. If he is in, we will soon know."

The bartender went back behind his counter, picked up the telephone receiver, and dialed. Jordan drank his Campari and hoped. He could observe Alberto speaking into the telephone. After an interval, Alberto hung up, came from behind the bar, and joined Jordan again. He appeared pleased.

"The appointment is arranged," said Alberto. "He will meet with you at three o'clock this afternoon."

"What's his name?"

"Rocco. Just Rocco. Do not be put off by him. He is rough in his ways, very straightforward, honest in personal dealings, a kind of honorable pirate. Great physical daring. No fear. Also, I assure you, a man of his word. Be direct with him. Trust him."

"Where do I see this Rocco?"

"Yes, of course. It is a place we call Smuggler's Cove. The first canal after the location of the Biennale. It is the area from which most of the smugglers operate."

"Is there a rendezvous?"

"An exact one. He will be waiting for you on the bridge of the Rio Sant' Elena, just behind the public park. You can take a vaporetto to the Viale Vittorio Veneto. Or you can walk straight there. If you walk, allow perhaps thirty to forty minutes. He will be easy to recognize. He is a big man, muscular, with a scar on his chin. You won't miss him."

▶ ▶ ▶ ▶

In the interval between the time of his conversation at Harry's Bar and the time he was to leave to meet Rocco, he had gone up to his hotel suite, where he found Alison, fully clothed, sound asleep on her bed. Deciding this was a good idea, he had left a wake-up call with the telephone operator and thrown himself on his own bed for a short nap.

At two-ten in the afternoon he had been awakened, and by two-twenty he was on his way out of the Danieli, going on foot to this crucial rendezvous.

He had hiked briskly along the edge of the lagoon, and by now, after twenty minutes and passage over six bridges, he was beside the large white hulk of the Greek luxury cruise ship, *The Delphic Oracle*. At the gangplank were three Venice police guards, armed with rifles. On the first and second decks of the ship, the quarantined passengers could be seen moving about.

Jordan did not loiter. He kept going. There was another bridge to climb, a large, sweeping concrete bridge, and from the top he could see the dense greenery of a park to his left and to his right a dark green statue just above the water that Alberto had told him would be the Monument of the Partisans of the Second World War.

He was almost there.

He accelerated his pace down the last bridge and headed for the more populated section of the park, sparsely wooded, with an outdoor roller-skating rink being used by shouting children. He went into the park, past busts of Giuseppe Verdi and Richard Wagner.

Off to his left was a white canvas sign reading, LA BIENNALE. He proceeded to the end of the park, which curved around to run into a small canal. This was the Rio Sant' Elena, his destination. He saw the stone bridge. A barge carrying cases of soda water was passing beneath the bridge. Jordan raised his eyes, and on the summit of the bridge, leaning on its railing staring down into the water, was a lone muscular man.

Quickening his stride, Jordan made it to the top of the bridge in a matter of seconds.

The man turned his head at Jordan's approach. He had the battered, flattened face of a retired pugilist. The scar on his jaw was a long one. His upper lip curled, revealing two gold teeth.

"Rocco?"

"Yes. You are Jordan?"

"Alberto's friend."

"I am also Alberto's friend," said Rocco. "So I think we can trust each other."

Jordan groped for what to say next, and when he said it he felt foolish. "You—you make your living smuggling in and out of Venice, I'm told."

"It is my job. This past week I have not done anything. I could run the blockade, but it would be a greater risk. There are many more patrol boats. They are more alert. But I would not mind an assignment, if it is a good one. Do you want to bring something into Venice, or take something out?"

"Out."

"What is the cargo?"

"Two human beings. Friends of mine. They must get out of here tomorrow. They—"

Rocco lifted his paw of a hand. "I am not interested in reasons. Where are they to be delivered?"

"To a ship at sea," said Jordan. "There's a Greek cruise ship, *The Delphic Oracle,* in port for repairs."

"I know."

"It sails at ten o'clock tomorrow morning. When it is outside the city's jurisdiction, I would want you to leave and catch up with it. I'm told the ship should have an hour's start to be in safe waters. I'm also told it would still be visible from the Lido. Does that sound right?"

"It is right. Territorial waters begin at twelve miles out."

"Arrangements have been made with the ship's purser. They would expect your passengers and be ready to take them on. The question is—can you run the blockade?"

Rocco seemed to concentrate on the canal below. He turned back. "It is more difficult in daylight. We usually work by night. But it can be done."

Jordan had to be convinced. "How?"

"We would hug the coastline going to the Lido channel. In the open lagoon, traveling normally—so no suspicion—we would head toward the patrol boats. The moment they came up to us, to see my permit, I would cut loose, surprise them, tear away at full speed toward the channel." He smiled pridefully. "The police patrols are no match for my motorboat. I have the fastest craft in Venice. I would outrun them easily. There could be only one obstacle . . ."

Jordan waited, then said, "What's that, Rocco?"

"The police have one large motor launch that is faster than mine, much faster. It belongs to the Squadra Mobile. I could not outrun that one. So if the plan is to work, the police must not know of it."

"There is no way they can know."

"Then I could not be stopped. I could take your friends safely to the ship in the Adriatic."

"It sounds perfect," said Jordan, feeling elated. But he wondered about one thing. "Just to satisfy my curiosity. The police will recognize you. How will you ever get back to Venice?"

Rocco grinned, and his gold teeth shone. "They will not recognize me. I will wear a disguise—false nose, moustache, beard. After I deliver my cargo, I will go on south to Chioggia. I will take a vacation there until the Venice blockade and emergency are ended. Then I will trade in my motorboat for another model and return to Venice."

"Neat," Jordan said with admiration. "All right. Let's get back to the plan. Where would we meet? We couldn't come all the way here."

"You name the place."

"The vaporetto station in front of the Danieli. Right near it. Would that be too conspicuous?"

"Not at that hour."

"What hour?"

"We should leave no later than eleven in the morning to catch the Greek ship in the place of safety."

"Eleven o'clock in the morning," said Jordan. "Then I guess we're set."

"Not quite," said Rocco. "One more detail."

"Yes?"

"The money."

"Okay," said Jordan, "let's talk about it."

▶ ▶ ▶ ▶

He had spent the rest of the afternoon raising the money.

He still had $15,000 left of the $20,000 he had accumulated for the ill-fated helicopter escape, but he had required twice that amount. He had consulted with Alison, gone to the cashier of the Danieli, visited his bank, and by dinnertime he had put together Rocco's price.

Now, early evening, he was nearing Marisa's apartment, feeling at once optimistic about the morning's prospects and tense about the dangers involved.

Almost at the courtyard to Marisa's building, just across the street, he saw a laborer plaster a poster to the wall. He glanced at it, spun toward it again, and stood in shock. Looking at the poster was like looking in the mirror. He saw his own face, his very own face, the face of his passport, staring back at him from the poster.

He read the big black heading over it in Italian, and automatically translated it into English:

FOR ANY CLUE LEADING TO THE ARREST OF THIS MAN, TIMOTHY JORDAN, A REWARD OF $50,000 WILL BE PAID.

He reeled a few steps backward. Now there was not one fugitive but two. Who had told the police he was MacDonald's accomplice? It could have been one of many people, but happening now, it could only have been the news vendor Gino, or Sembut Nurikhan. No matter which.

He gazed at the people passing through the street. It was as if every one of them knew, the whole world knew, that he was wanted by the police. There was no escape.

Yet, there was tomorrow morning.

He regained his balance. Almost stealthily he backed away, then sidled toward the wrought-iron gate of the courtyard. He opened it, and once in the courtyard he raced through it and up the steep stairs, and breathlessly let himself inside.

He sought Marisa, but found only Professor MacDonald, on the sofa with a book.

"Is Marisa here?" he asked.

"She just went out to the hospital again to visit with her mother."

He felt relieved. "Good. I wanted to talk to you alone."

MacDonald kept trying to read his face. "Tim, is it good news or bad?"

"I just had a scare, but never mind. It's good news, Professor. You're leaving in the morning—and so am I. The police just put out the word. They want me too. We're all getting out of here together at eleven in the morning, and it's not a minute too soon."

▶ ▶ ▶ ▶

Morning.

Jordan had awakened to a gray, overcast day. By nine o'clock, dressed for the big adventure, he had gone downstairs expecting to find Marisa and MacDonald, but MacDonald was alone.

"She got a call from her family doctor," MacDonald had explained. "The doctor wanted Marisa and her brother, Bruno, to meet with him as soon as possible in the hospital. I'm sure she's there now."

"I hope there's nothing wrong," Jordan had said, then added, "I hope she gets back before we leave. I wanted to say good-bye to her."

Now, at last, it was ten thirty-five, and in ten minutes they would leave, taking less-frequented back streets, to emerge near the Danieli and meet Alison and board Rocco's motorboat.

"Are you all set?" Jordan asked MacDonald.

"As set as I'll ever be."

"Do you have the formula?"

"All done on one sheet." He patted the breast of his jacket. "In my pocket."

They were alerted by the sound of a key in the front door, heard the door squeak open and then close, listened to the footsteps in the corridor.

Marisa came into the living room.

Jordan said quickly, "I'm glad you're back, Marisa. We're leaving in a few minutes. Now the police want me too, and we've got a chance to get out of the city. I . . ."

He realized that she was oblivious to what he was saying. She had gone robotlike past him and was staring intently at MacDonald. Jordan stepped closer to her and then saw that her eyes were swollen, still brimming, and he knew that she had been crying.

He took her by the shoulder and turned her to him. "What is it, Marisa? Your mother?"

She nodded slowly. "Mamma has stomach cancer. Advanced. She is dying. Dr. Scarpa told Bruno and me. There is no mistake. She is dying."

"Oh, Christ, I'm sorry, darling." He tried to take her in his arms. "I can't tell you how sorry."

She pulled free of him. "You are going?"

"In a few minutes."

"You can't go. Dr. Scarpa told me the truth. He said Mamma was lost but maybe there was one hope. He said he knew about us, you and me, and since I'm so close to you, then perhaps you could help. He said he briefly protected you and Professor MacDonald—yes, I know his name now—and Dr. Scarpa told me all about Professor MacDonald's discovery. He said if the professor's discovery is real, it could save Mamma. 'See Timothy,' he said, 'and maybe he can get MacDonald to save your mother.' I am telling this to you, Tim. I want you to make the professor save Mamma."

"Marisa, believe me, we want to help your mother. As I'd want to help my father if he were still alive. But I'd sacrifice him rather than risk the whole project. Staying here to help your mother would take too much time . . ." He looked helplessly at MacDonald.

"At least a week," said MacDonald, "and I would need the proper facilities—"

"I will get you everything," Marisa cried out.

"The police would get me first. They would send me back to the Soviet Union. I could do nothing for your mother or anyone then. But this way, if we escape, I might be able to get my formula to you in time—"

"There is no time!" Marisa shouted. "You must help *now!*"

Jordan intervened, trying to calm her. "Marisa, listen, we've tried everything to get MacDonald out of here. Everything has failed. This is our last chance. A Greek ship has just left the port. It will be expecting us. I've arranged for a special motorboat to run us out of the city, out to the ship. Then the professor will be free. His discovery will belong to everyone—your mother and everyone. We must do it, Marisa. We simply must."

"No," she begged. "You must save my mother first. You owe this to me. We've been together, Tim, close together for a long time. I have done things for you. Now you must do this one thing for me. I've never asked anything of you. Now I ask this. Please, Tim!"

Momentarily unnerved, he held fast. "Impossible, Marisa. I wish I could, but—"

"You won't do it?" she said.

"I can't."

"All right," she said. She walked quickly to the antique table, yanked open a drawer. "All right," she repeated, and she turned around facing them, "then I'll *make* you do it."

In her right hand she was clasping that ugly Italian revolver, a Beretta. She pointed it at Jordan.

"You are not leaving here," she said hoarsely.

"Marisa, don't be foolish. . . ."

He started slowly toward her.

The gun wavered in her hand.

Gently, he reached out, removed the revolver from her grasp, and pocketed it.

She broke down, bursting into tears, sobbing.

He stared at her a moment, with wrenching sorrow, then leaned forward to kiss her. She tore away, still sobbing.

"We must go, Marisa," he said softly. "I'm sorry."

He beckoned to MacDonald and they started for the door.

He heard her voice.

"I'm sorry too," she called after him.

There was a special quality in her voice. Only later did he realize it was that of love turned to hate.

▶ ▶ ▶ ▶

It was five minutes after eleven in the morning, and the three of them—Alison, MacDonald, Jordan—were securely aboard Rocco's large, powerful walnut-colored motorboat, a sea rocket, and on their way.

Sitting back, as the waters of the lagoon churned around them, Jordan thought it was a miracle to be here at all, to have got this far without detection. The walk from Marisa's apartment to the lagoon pier near the Hotel Danieli had been a heart-stopping experience. The two men had gone swiftly but warily, as if terror lurked at every corner. At least five times they had passed posters—to the mind's eye they loomed as gigantic—showing their faces, offering the rewards on their heads. Every minute had been terrifying until they had reached Alison, suitcase in hand, on a constant lookout for them.

Yards away, a burly stranger, one foot on the side of his motorboat, was beckoning to them. At first Jordan had not recognized him, and then he had remembered that Rocco would be disguised. Jordan realized that the stranger must be Rocco. He was wearing dark sunglasses, an elongated hooked nose probably made of putty, a fake flaring moustache, and an enormous bush of black beard.

"There he is," Jordan had said to MacDonald and Alison.

They had hurried toward him. He had helped them down into the craft, settled MacDonald and Alison in the rear and Jordan right behind him.

"It's really you, Rocco?" Jordan had asked.

Steering the motorboat backward, away from the pier,

swinging it gradually around, he had chuckled. "For this kind of money, it's Rocco, you bet."

And now they were on their way, all chips in the pot.

Rocco's craft slithered along the water, close to the shoreline of Venice, going past the empty berth where *The Delphic Oracle* had stood little more than an hour ago, skimming past the public park Jordan had visited yesterday, then rounding the tip of Venice. For a short time, they rode in a northerly direction toward Murano. Then Rocco gradually began to bend his craft away from the open lagoon, heading southeast, bearing down on the waterway between a small cluster of islands and a larger island.

They had been traveling for twenty minutes without any of them speaking a word.

Now, above the hum of the engine, Rocco pointed ahead, announcing, "There's the entrance to the Porto di Lido."

Jordan could feel the tension growing, behind him and in his own chest.

Noticing a leather case on the floor beside the pilot, Jordan asked, "Are those binoculars?"

"Yes," Rocco answered.

Jordan bent forward for the case, removed the black binoculars, pressed them to his eyes, and began to adjust the focus.What he saw directly in front of him, brought right to him by magnification, was the narrow Lido channel leading into the Adriatic Sea. On the edge of the shore to the left were the pilings that held steel cables attached to the inflatable dam below the water. To the right was the short pier that ran into steps leading up to the electronic pump station.

The binoculars still at his eyes, Jordan squinted straight into the Adriatic. Then he saw it, the funnels, the steam from the funnels, the white sliver of the Greek cruise ship moving slowly on the horizon line.

Suddenly, from either side of the binoculars, two other

boats intruded. They were white-and-blue patrol boats with the word POLIZIA plainly painted on their bows. Each carried four armed guards of the local questura.

Jordan lowered his glasses just as the motorboat beneath him slowed down.

Rocco said loudly, "The police boats are coming toward us to see our permit or turn us away from the channel. I am lowering my speed. The minute they are upon me, in shouting distance, I'll gun the boat and leap between them, straight ahead. The second I do that, all of you hold tight and duck far down. In case they shoot at us. I don't think they'll have time, but protect yourself. We go straight through the channel full speed and burst out into the open sea and make for the liner. They'll never be able to keep up with us. We'll be free."

Up front, on either side of them, Jordan could see the patrol boats bearing down, and Rocco's craft seemed to be floating ever so slowly toward them.

A uniformed guard at the bow of the patrol boat to their left had raised an arm, palm outward, gesturing to them to come to a halt.

Rocco spoke quickly over his shoulder. "Get ready."

He was idling his craft at a crawl into the hole between the patrol boats.

"*Alto là!*" a guard yelled. "Halt! The Porto di Lido is blocked! No one allowed—unless you have a mayor's permit!"

Rocco nodded, nodded again, then hunched over his wheel, accelerated his motorboat in a roar, and plunged between the rocking patrol boats. His streamlined bow lifted high out of the water, his engine screamed, and his craft catapulted ahead into the mouth of the channel.

Dropping to a knee, as he knew MacDonald and Alison had done behind him, Jordan looked over his shoulder as the gap grew between Rocco's speeding craft and the patrol boats caught surprised and flat-footed behind them.

The distance was opening further and further, while the patrol boats tried to maneuver and give futile chase.

Jordan could see land on either side of them as they zoomed into the channel. Grabbing up the binoculars, bracing himself in the shaking boat, he brought the glasses to his eyes and aimed them at the patrol boats. The guards aboard came into focus, and they seemed to be shouting at one another in utter confusion.

The expanse of lagoon was widening between Rocco's craft and their receding pursuers. Freedom was minutes away. Exalted, Jordan was about to lower the binoculars when unexpectedly some kind of streak, something in motion, caught the corner of his field of vision. Jordan moved his head and the glued binoculars sideways for a better view. Puzzled, he began to focus on this distant movement.

Gradually, the thing grew and enlarged.

It was a huge mahogany motor launch with a small cannon protruding in front. It was kicking up water, slicing through the lagoon, coming toward them at a dazzling speed.

"Rocco!" Jordan shouted. "There's another boat, a big one, coming after us!"

He thrust the binoculars at Rocco, who gripped them with his free hand, keeping one hand on the wheel. Rocco turned his head, lifted the binoculars to his eyes. Then he almost threw the glasses at Jordan as he cursed in Italian.

"It's the Squadra Mobile launch, the big police one I warned you about!" Rocco cried out. "It is the fastest vessel in Italy!"

"Can't you outrun it?"

"No chance," Rocco snapped. "Twice as fast as mine. It'll overtake us before we're much into the Adriatic. We haven't got a chance. I warned you, the police must not know. But somebody told them."

Somebody told them.

Jordan's trembling hands had the binoculars up to his eyes again. He tried to focus on the distant onrushing vessel, bring it into sharper view. It expanded in his glasses, and he clearly saw the faces of four men at the prow. Two were police officers unknown to him. One, grim-faced, was Colonel Cutrone, head of the carabinieri. And the other—the other—no mistake about it— was Bruno—Bruno Girardi.

Jordan lowered the binoculars, shattered.

Somebody had told them, Rocco had said. Somebody indeed. I'm sorry, Jordan had said on leaving Marisa. I'm sorry too, Marisa had replied. Now he understood. She was sorry for him, for them, for having to turn them over to the police. No question. After he and MacDonald had left her, she had gone to Bruno, and he had gone to the police—to reveal that MacDonald was in a motorboat heading for the Greek cruise ship—telling this in return for the promise that MacDonald would be forced to treat Mrs. Girardi for cancer before he was shipped to the Soviet Union.

Jordan dropped the binoculars to the bouncing motorboat floor. With his own eyes he could see the Squadra Mobile launch pointing toward them like an avenging devil, eating up the water that separated them, closing in for the kill.

Numbed though he was by Marisa's betrayal, Jordan had no time to dwell on that.

Above him, Rocco was cursing to himself again and saying bitterly, "It's no use, no use, they've got us all. They'll have us in ten minutes."

Rocco's craft was half out of the water, coughing spray on either side as it drove through the Lido channel. They were approaching the width of the channel where the inflatable dam lay resting on the seabed. To his right, Jordan could see the electronic pump station that had been installed but had not once been used.

Some survival impulse, something long buried deep

in a corner of his head, flashed on and told him what to do.

He leaped to his feet, almost fell, held on to the shuddering windshield. "Rocco!" he bellowed. "Turn to your right! Pull up at the pump station! Let me off and wait! I know how to work it. I don't know if it'll work—but it's our only chance!"

Rocco asked no questions. Instinctively, he understood. He slowed his craft, jerked the wheel around, and started his boat toward the pump station.

Reaching the small Pirelli pier, Rocco slid alongside it, bumping it, bringing his boat to a halt.

"Stand by!" shouted Jordan, jumping from the boat to the pier.

"What's happening?" MacDonald cried out.

"Rocco will tell you!" Jordan yelled over his shoulder. He bounded up the pier, turned to the steps of the cement blockhouse that was all windows on top, ran up the steps to the station. Fumbling, he found his key ring, sorted out the red key, stuck it into the door, and opened it.

The electronic equipment, the panel of levers and buttons inside, held no mysteries for him. He had seen it all duplicated on the Voltabarozzo model. He had brought dozens of visiting journalists to this very room.

Jordan glanced toward the Venice lagoon behind the channel. The Squadra Mobile launch was flying past the hapless diminutive patrol boats, zooming nearer and nearer to the channel.

Galvanized, Jordan's fingers darted over the panel, punching keys, buttons, moving levers.

In seconds it was done. The pump had been activated. If it was working, then at the bottom of the channel, only twelve meters beneath the surface, the long, flat inflatable dam was speedily filling with water, filling up, beginning to balloon out, to reach gradually toward the top of the water.

Perspiring, Jordan counted the seconds, the brief minutes, waiting in agonizing suspense.

The mahagony launch with its menacing cannon had reached the mouth of the channel, was screaming into it, swerving toward the pump station and Rocco's motorboat.

Five minutes had passed since Jordan had activated the inflatable dam. Nothing, so far as he could see, was happening. The Squadra Mobile launch, foaming at the prow, was driving toward the stretch of water under which the rubberized dam lay.

It won't work, it won't work, Jordan moaned to himself, temples throbbing. They've got us, they've got MacDonald.

That instant, before his widening eyes, the giant rubber tubing, inflated with water, burst into view across the channel. Like an unbelievable surfacing whale, it rose and expanded, like a solid rock wall, a barrier covering the width of the channel, blocking the channel from the Adriatic.

Seconds later, the Squadra Mobile launch was upon it full speed, trying to swing away, trying to avoid it, trying to avert hitting the giant barrier that blocked it from Rocco's boat.

The police launch smashed into the barrier at full speed before Jordan's eyes, lifted high in the air, breaking in two, splintering, spitting out its occupants, flinging them into the air and into the channel.

Anchored to where he stood, Jordan watched the incredible sight. There was a singing in his head. He had won. They had won.

He wheeled around, ran out of the pump station, scrambled down the stairs, and continued to run toward the pier.

As he reached the boat, MacDonald was on his feet, coming forward to help Jordan into the escape craft.

"Fantastic!" Rocco roared with joy.

Starting to step down, Jordan looked off at the savior water dam.

Then he heard Alison scream, and he saw what she had seen. One member of the smashed police launch had been thrown atop the inflated barrier, was slipping and slithering, trying to maintain his balance. He had steadied himself, this battered man in uniform, and was planting himself on one knee, his gun whipped out of his holster.

It was Colonel Cutrone, and he was pointing his gun toward them.

As MacDonald continued to stand, groping for Jordan's arm to help him into the boat, Jordan yelled at the scientist, "Get down, goddammit, get down!"

There was a series of loud reports as Cutrone's gun fired once, twice, three times.

With the first shot, Jordan dived into the boat, falling against MacDonald. The old man staggered, went backward, collapsing to the floor, with Jordan spread-eagled over him.

Cutrone was firing again as Rocco, crouched low, swung his craft away from the pier and opened up the throttle at full speed.

They were leaving the Lido channel and the beaten police and the quarantined city of Venice behind them— soon very far behind them.

As Jordan pushed himself off MacDonald, he could see Venice growing smaller and the Greek liner on the horizon growing larger, and he felt ecstatic.

They had escaped. They were free.

"Tim!" Alison cried out to him, and he saw that she was pointing at his chest. He looked down at his shirt. It was stained with blood.

Bewildered, Jordan peered at the prone professor, started to lift him, and then he saw the bullet wound in the professor's chest, an ugly wound retching a slow ooze of blood.

He took hold of MacDonald and tried to hold him up. He was limp, immobile, unconscious.

Jordan sat dazed in the reverberating motorboat.

Had they won or lost?

▶ ▶ ▶ ▶

Two hours later, Jordan and Alison stood in a corridor of the main deck of *The Delphic Oracle* as the ship continued sailing south through the Adriatic toward Piraeus, the Greek port for Athens.

Jordan paced, and Alison leaned against the wall, in the corridor outside the ship's sick bay.

For three-quarters of an hour the ship's physician, Dr. Canellos, and a nurse had been inside with MacDonald, and Jordan and Alison had waited apprehensively outside, with no word from the physician.

Jordan and Alison did not speak. They had been standing by in silence and dread.

The door of the sick bay opened and the nurse emerged, not meeting their anxious eyes, hurrying up the corridor, and now Dr. Canellos, a dour, wrinkled Greek, appeared and started toward them, and they came to meet him.

Dr. Canellos looked from one to the other, and then he shook his head sadly. "Dr. Edwards, Mr. Jordan, I must tell you, there is no hope. The wound is a fatal one."

Jordan gripped the physician's arm. "I don't believe you. It can't be. Something must be done. Can't you radio Athens, have them fly the best surgeon in the country out to us by seaplane? Surely the military can—"

"Mr. Jordan," interrupted the physician, "he is dying. I have done what I can, but it is no use. It is only a matter of minutes. Believe me, I feel for you."

Alison broke down and began to weep. Gently, Jordan put an arm around her and drew her close.

Dr. Canellos addressed Jordan once more. "The professor is semiconscious. I was trying to make out what he was saying. He spoke a few words, and I caught a name. Your name is Tim, isn't it? I think he wants to see you. It may be too late, but go inside if you wish. I'll take care of your young lady."

Jordan released Alison, went past the doctor into the ship's sick bay. He went straight through the reception room and then through an open doorway. Professor MacDonald, in a pale green hospital gown, receiving blood intravenously from a bottle hanging above him, lay stretched out on a high hospital bed. His skin was the color of parchment, his features sunken, and his glazed eyes stared up at the ceiling.

There was a chair beside the bed, with MacDonald's jacket thrown over the back of it.

Jordan tiptoed toward the chair, took it, and brought his head close to MacDonald's.

"Professor, can you hear me?"

No answer.

"This is Tim Jordan. . . ."

The professor's head moved, the motion barely perceptible, on the pillow. His eyelids fluttered. He tried to say something. No sound came. His dry lips worked again.

Jordan rose, stood over him, head bent low to catch whatever he might say.

He struggled to articulate something. There was a gurgling, then speech. "Tim—the formula . . ." A lengthy pause, and then, ". . . in my—my coat."

"Yes, I understand."

"Take it."

"I will." Jordan turned away, reached down and searched the pockets of the coat, and then found the folded sheet of paper inside the breast pocket. He unfolded it, to be certain. What he read was undoubtedly the formula for C-98, indecipherable to him. But this was it, the world's treasure. He folded it again and placed it snugly inside the breast pocket of his own jacket.

He returned to the bed, stood over MacDonald.

"I have it, Professor," he said. "What do you want me to do with it?"

"Do . . ."

Jordan waited.

MacDonald's lips worked again. "Do what you think best."

His eyes closed. His head fell sideways. He was still.

Jordan reached down and took the old man's wrist and tried to find a pulse. There was none.

Professor Davis MacDonald, discoverer of the Fountain of Youth, was dead.

X

▶ ▶ ▶ ▶ ▶ ▶ ▶

It was early evening in Paris.

"Pull up here, Pierre," Tim Jordan ordered their driver. "You can park here, can't you?"

"No problem, monsieur," said their chauffeur, drawing his Mercedes up along the curb.

Jordan opened the rear door. "We want to get a little air."

"I will be waiting," said their chauffeur.

Jordan helped Alison out of the car. He glanced around. They were on the Quai de Montebello, across from the café with a red awning, the Restaurant la Bouteille d'Or, on a thoroughfare that ran above the Seine River on the Left Bank.

"I felt like a walk," said Jordan.

"I did too," said Alison.

They strolled slowly in silence.

Jordan could see that the intense grief had finally left Alison's face. In the warm Paris night, she looked calm and reposeful. And beautiful.

It had been a week since Professor MacDonald's death, Jordan remembered, and most of their grief had been spent during the time it had taken the cruise ship to reach Piraeus. Once in bustling Athens, going into and out of the Athens Hilton, they had been too occupied doing what had to be done to continue dwelling on the cruel fate that had befallen MacDonald.

They had telephoned MacDonald's younger sister in London and with difficulty informed her of Mac-Donald's accidental death outside Venice. They had agreed upon a story: MacDonald, in Venice en route to Paris, had signed up for the last part of a cruise on a ship going to Piraeus. He had been intrigued by a collection of antique guns that a private collector on the ship was transporting. Examining one, he had accidentally discharged it and had been killed instantly. They had agreed to ship MacDonald's body by air to his sister, who wanted to have him buried beside his mother in the family plot.

In Athens, also, they had met with the bureau chief of the Associated Press and released to him the news of Professor MacDonald's accidental death. Alison had filled in details of MacDonald's background. The bureau chief had immediately written the story and put it on the wires. It surprised and dismayed Jordan, the following day, to see how little coverage was given to the death. To the press, the world, this was merely one more obscure scientist, well known only among his colleagues, and his passing was worth no more than routine space. But soon, Jordan was pleased to know, the story would be different. Word of MacDonald's thunderous discovery would be released to the world, and his obituary would be enlarged a hundred times over and his name would become a household word and he would have immortality.

The day the notice of MacDonald's death had appeared in print, Jordan had remembered something he had overlooked and was still curious about. Venice. What had happened in Venice after they had fled?

Surely Colonel Cutrone and the mayor would have lifted travel restrictions into and out of the city and lifted the communications blackout. An explanation of sorts would have appeared in the newspapers while he and Alison had been at sea.

Jordan had returned to the Associated Press offices in Athens and requested to see the back file of copies of the *International Herald Tribune*. He had found the story almost immediately, on the front page of the issue published two days after their escape.

There it was, the announcement from Mayor Accardi. The spy had finally been cornered and caught. Venice had become an open city again. Normal traffic had resumed, tourists leaving, tourists entering, commerce once more under way. The spy was in custody. The missing defense plans had been recovered. The carabinieri were interrogating the agent. There would be no further details until the interrogation had been completed. However, several tourists, departing Venice, had spoken of seeing wanted posters—all of them since removed from sight—that had identified the foreign spy as someone called E. MacGregor, who had posed as an American. The United States Department of State, mildly interested to know whether the arrested spy had actually been a United States citizen, had made a routine inquiry.

That was the sum of it. That was all. Jordan had shaken his head over the story. He had always known the Italians were imaginative and adept at fiction.

But there was one more announcement to come.

This morning, at breakfast in Athens, Jordan had found a follow-up news story datelined Venice, brief and conclusive, on page three of the *International Herald Tribune*. The spy who had caused the blockade and quarantine of Venice was dead. He had committed suicide in his cell, hanged himself with his belt. (How convenient, the belt, but what sloppy fiction, thought Jordan.) The spy, who had used the name MacGregor and pretended to be an American, had been identified as Dr. Angelo Perfetti, an Italian inventor from Bologna and a onetime military consultant. He had stolen Italy's secret defense plans, sought a hiding place in Venice, intending to demand ransom for return of the plans, threatening otherwise to sell them to a foreign power. But now, Colonel Cutrone had told a press conference, the city's nightmare was over. Venice was alive and well, and it again belonged to the world.

The smooth Venetians, Jordan thought. All loose ends tied up. And a new language that used victory for defeat.

Only once, in Athens, had Jordan and Alison touched upon the subject of MacDonald's discovery for the prolongation of human life.

Jordan had asked, "Will you be reading a paper on C-98 to the International Gerontology Congress in Paris?"

"No. The congress adjourned two days ago."

"Well, there are other means."

"There are."

No more had been spoken of MacDonald's legacy. Alison had wired for the car and driver she had used before in Paris, and when their Olympic Airways plane had brought them to De Gaulle Airport in three hours, Pierre and his Mercedes had been waiting for them.

On the way to depositing Alison at the Plaza Athénée, Jordan had wanted to delay the moment. He had requested Pierre to take them on a detour along the Seine.

And now they were strolling above the Seine, and Jordan was acutely conscious of one momentous piece of unfinished business.

Professor Davis MacDonald's historic legacy was entirely in their hands.

Jordan was busy lighting his pipe. As they passed a boarded bookstall, Jordan indicated a flight of uneven stone steps leading down to the Seine. "Let's go down there and walk along the river," he said.

Alison nodded.

They descended carefully to a broad cobblestone quay running just above the sparkling green waters of the Seine. They went to the portable rails and stared down into the water. A thousand bright lights danced in the river, reflecting the soaring illuminated spires of the Cathedral of Notre Dame across the way.

Jordan placed a hand on the railing and faced Alison. "There's something we really haven't discussed," he said. He patted the breast pocket of his jacket. "The professor's formula. What do you want to do about it?"

"I don't know. It's up to you. He left it for you, Tim. He told you to do what you thought best."

"It was an odd way for him to put it. As if he didn't know. He had always thought it was right to reveal it to the world. But after Venice, I guess he was no longer sure."

"Nor am I any longer sure," said Alison. Then she added quietly, "Are you?"

He thought about it again. Indeed, he had hardly stopped thinking about it since the day of MacDonald's death.

The potential for good and evil that the formula contained had already been tested upon human beings, in Venice.

Some had reacted sanely, decently. He reviewed the sparse litany of names. The monk Pashal. The Contessa De Marchi. Oreste Memo. They had been good. But two of them only up to a point.

He reviewed his chamber of horrors, the ones who had played Judas, betraying, selling out, hungry for life or money, mostly life—all corruptible, rotten, ready to do anything to their fellow humans for the chance of continued survival for themselves or their close ones. The names came easily to him and—except for the Russians, the Venice police, the mayor—the review of each name, each friend, each acquaintance, was a stab. Don Pietro Vianello. Dr. Giovanni Scarpa. Felice Huber. Cedric Foster. Teresa Fantoni. Sembut Nurikhan. Bruno

Girardi. Marisa. Above all, Marisa, with her final insanity.

Evil, he knew. The formula's potential for evil could transform the world into a population of Mr. Hydes.

Yet, he also knew, there was more. Larger issues to be considered. He reviewed them briefly. The formula offered so much promise of good. The curbing of illness. The postponement of too-early extinction by death. The formula offered Time, the treasure most sought after by humanity. Time for the sweetness of more gentle, balmy spring mornings. Time for the exhilaration of more crisp, leaf-crackling autumn afternoons. Time extended for loved ones and for lovemaking. Time for greater inventions, creations, wisdom. Above all, youth—it offered youth suspended.

But Venice had raised the dark specters also. In Jordan's mind and heart they were real, and they were terrifying. Prolonging human life meant a monstrous expansion of the earth's inhabitants. Stifling overpopulation. Massive food shortages, unemployment, suffering, starvation. In turn, crime, violence, savagery. Dwindling energy. Waste and filth rotting the environment. Constant wars for survival, and quicker senseless wars to balance the perpetually mounting birthrates. Upheavals. Loss of individuality. Elites of the elderly. Boredom, life become a movie that has run too long.

Tonight, he could see tomorrow clearly. He saw the Fountain of Youth, and it was polluted.

He stared at Alison. "You asked me if I was no longer sure of what to do. I am sure. Do you want me to do what I think should be done?"

"Davis wanted you to. So do I. Do what is best."

Jordan dug into his inside jacket pocket, pulled out the folded sheet of paper. Turning his back on Alison, he strode to an opening in the railing and stepped out to the edge of the embankment over the Seine.

He hesitated only a brief moment, and then slowly,

resolutely, he tore the folded paper in two, then tore it again and again, until it was in shreds. With a fling of his arm, he cast the pieces of paper into the river.

For a while he watched the shreds lie on the water, and then he watched them separate and spread and glide away into the darkness.

He walked back to Alison.

He said, "Now I'd better take you to your hotel and look for a room of my own."

She did not move. "You don't need a room of your own. You have one, mine—ours—if you feel as I feel."

He took her in his arms and kissed her—a long, warm passionate kiss.

He had never felt more alive.

Hand in hand they started toward the stone steps and the ascent to Paris.

"What next, Tim?" she asked.

He smiled. "A honeymoon in Paris. Then I'm going to write. Perhaps about this. The truth in fiction." He paused. "Do you think it'll ever happen again in life?"

"Someday."

"Will it ever be good for the human race?"

"I don't know, Tim. Our children will learn. Or their children. Maybe they'll be able to cope with it. Now let's not waste any more time. We don't have 150 years, you know."

Happily, they started up the stairs.

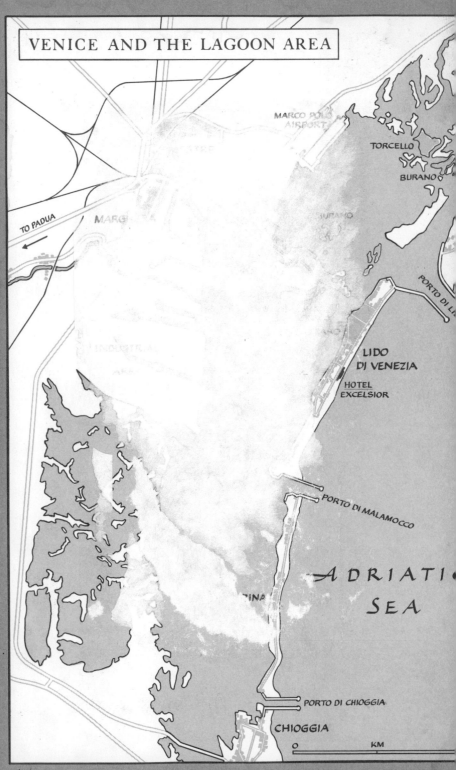

VENICE AND THE LAGOON AREA

MARCO POLO
AIRPORT

TORCELLO

BURANO

TO PADUA

MARG

PORTO DI LI

LIDO
DI VENEZIA

HOTEL
EXCELSIOR

PORTO DI MALAMOCCO

ADRIATI

SEA

PORTO DI CHIOGGIA

CHIOGGIA

0   KM

palacios